QUIET, PLEASE!

BREA BROWN

WAYZGOOSE PRESS

Edited by Maggie Sokolik

Cover design by Keri Knutson at alchemybookcovers.com

(Note: An earlier, slightly modified edition of this novel, with the same title, was originally published in 2012, ISBN 9781983037191)

For all the teachers out there who tolerate other people's children on a daily basis, in order that we should enjoy a learned society. May you have the peace and quiet you deserve on your off-time.

CHAPTER ONE

W hat am I doing here?
        Not literally. I know that. I'm labeling, cataloging, and shelving books, activities that are almost as natural to me as breathing. What's unnatural is everything else about this situation.

I'm in a bright, airy library that's painted in vibrant colors with cheerful murals depicting children who are reading (and looking unnaturally happy about it, in my opinion). But that's not the strangest thing about what's going on. The strangest thing is that I, a professional, highly educated librarian—a librarian for adults, I might add—am in charge of this place. What's most alarming, though, is that in a week, this place will be flooded with kids. "Strange," I can handle. Kids... I don't handle them as well.

I'd better figure it out, though. And quick.

Anyway, I'm up to the challenge. Aside from the fact that I don't have a choice, I can do this. Maybe. I mean, they're only kids, right? It's not like they're going to know that I'm terrified of them. Huh-huh. Or that I'm not at all confident in my ability to do this job. Huh-huh-huh. To them, I'm merely another—gulp—teacher. As long as I look the part and act the part, they won't know that I'm a bundle of nerves inside.

I obviously fooled the school's principal, Renalda Twomey. That, or she made a bad decision after being twenty minutes late for my interview and hardly paying any attention to my answers. I didn't fool her harried secretary, that much I know. I could tell by the wide-eyed, panicked look on her face when Ms. Twomey interrupted me halfway through my answer to her third question—which was technically more about whether I liked her purse than about the job opening—to say that I was hired.

As an explanation for her sudden decision, she added, "I like you, Kendall; you've got spunk! And you're just cute as can be! Those kids are gonna eat you up!" in her heavy North Carolina accent.

I tried to take that as a compliment and block out all mental images of the children picking my bones clean on the first day and leaving them on the floor in front of the shelf that holds the *Berenstain Bears* books.

The secretary, who had introduced herself to me as Sam Kingsley while I waited for Ms. Twomey to arrive, interjected, "Okay, but… Ms. Dickinson, how does your previous experience in"—she consulted my resume—"the Kansas City Public Library system relate to or prepare you for a job in a public school setting?"

Her mention of my former employer immediately made me break into a cold sweat. Vaguely, I answered with a bright smile and wide eyes, "Oh! I dealt with kids all the time at my old job." *And co-workers who behaved like them.*

"Did you work in the children's section?" she persisted, her voice pleasant but her eyes informing me she wasn't going to let me get away with that lame answer.

I gulped and admitted, "No, not specifically. I filled in often, though. And..." Here, I had to fight my natural instinct to be completely and brutally honest about myself. "...I love kids. Love them! They're so cute and... young."

Ms. Twomey saved me then. "Oh, Sam, stop givin' the poor girl the third degree! Whitehall Elementary needs a librarian, and fast." Turning to me, she confided, "Our current one is retirin'. And she was super-experienced, but we need someone younger, I think. That's what I've been sayin', anyway. But all the other applicants are, well, *old*! And I don't want to have to hire another librarian in another coupla years when one of those *old* people retires."

I pretended like it wasn't at all ironic that a person who was not a day younger than sixty would call anyone else who's still active in the workforce "old." Nor did I point out that it's illegal for her to discriminate based on age. Instead, I saw my salvation in this disorganized, seemingly clueless mess of a person and nodded enthusiastically.

Pouring on the Southern accent a little thicker than mine really is, I enthused, "Exactly! And let me tell you, I'm here to stay. Came here to be closer to my parents, so I'm not going anywhere."

Ms. Twomey grinned at Sam as if to say, *"See?"* and directed warmly at me, "Well, anyone with such good family values is a winner in my book. We'll see you back here on the first Monday in August. That's when teachers are supposed to come in to get their rooms ready and stuff."

After that declaration, she rose from behind her desk and grabbed her purse from the floor, where she'd dropped it when she rushed in, profusely apologizing for being late and muttering something about slow service at the hair salon.

"Now, if you'll excuse me, I have to get to a meetin'," she announced.

Sam very obviously rolled her eyes and asked, "How long will you be gone?"

Waving off the question, the principal stayed focused on digging for something in her purse. Coming up with a lipstick, she replied while applying it, "M-dunno. One, two hours?" She replaced the lid on the tube and said, "Don't wait up for me, Mom." Then she smiled naughtily at both of us and swept from the room, leaving behind the cloying smell of Aqua Net and Red Door perfume.

Sam stood and leveled a chagrined look at me. "Sorry about that. If I don't ask at least one legitimate question in these interviews, it doesn't get done."

I smiled brightly at her. I didn't care. I had a job! And I didn't have to go into any detail about why I had to leave my other job. Generously, I said, "Don't sweat it. I kind of noticed she has an… unconventional management style."

Bluntly, Sam corrected, "She's an incompetent buffoon. And she drives me crazy. I'm counting down the days to her retirement."

"When's that?" I inquired, trying not to laugh.

"Probably never. Because God hates me. Come on, let's go back to my desk and get the employment forms you need to fill out. I've got some of them here, but you'll have to go to the district main office to do the rest."

Since that day, Sam's been really nice to me, showing me around the school and introducing me to the other teachers (the ones who are here already). But I'm not letting her get too close. I mean, standoffish isn't in my nature. But I haven't accepted any of her offers to go to lunch or grab drinks after work. Work friends are overrated. I want to have a life outside of work this time around. I have no idea how

I'm going to do that, but I'm sure I can think of something to do with my spare time that doesn't involve hanging out with the same people I see all week at work or playing Skip-Bo with my parents in the evenings.

≈

Fortunately, I have some experience with this reinvention thing. And this time around, it won't even be as difficult as it was nine years ago.

We moved from Colorado to this tiny town before my junior year in high school. The move was a godsend. Suddenly, I was the exotic newcomer from "out west." This preconception made it fairly easy for me to lay the groundwork for going from geek to chic. In Colorado, I couldn't buy friends, but nobody in North Carolina knew that. And if ever I made a misstep in my transformation, all I had to say was, "Oh, well, that's how everyone does it/says it/thinks in Colorado," and it suddenly became a trend. It. Was. Awesome.

But it only lasted for two years. Hardly anyone, including myself, stays in this town after high school graduation. It's basically an outpost for professionals who work in Charlotte but want to live and raise their families in a smaller community. I stuck around a little longer than my classmates, because I went to college at UNC-Charlotte, where my parents are professors. But as soon as I had that university diploma in hand, I tried to find the farthest-flung job openings in libraries across the country. I wanted to be a grownup. I wanted to prove my independence. Biggest mistake of my life.

Since returning from Kansas City with my tail between my legs, I haven't run into any of my former classmates from high school (thank goodness), and I haven't actively sought out anyone, either. Friends weren't my motivation for coming back. What brought me back here was family. My parents, more specifically. I needed to reset with a safety net under me. I moved into my own place with the knowledge that if I couldn't find a job, they'd open their house to me in a heartbeat, just like they did more than twenty-five years ago.

This job has saved me from the ultimate defeat—moving back in with my parents—but I need to remember some old tricks if I want it to be a permanent solution. And I do. I'm sure the terror level will lessen with each passing day. Right?

Anyway, I don't have to change *everything* about myself this time around. No, I merely need to do a bit of research and observation and figure out what this whole "teacher" thing is about. Maybe I'll watch some classic movies about the sort of teachers who inspire, like in *Dangerous Minds*. Yeah... I'll be bad-ass, leather-sportin' Michelle Pfeiffer. Or maybe not. I guess elementary students here in the sticks don't need that sort of direction. Perhaps I should consider channeling "Jess," from *New Girl*. People are constantly telling me that I remind them of Zooey, so why wouldn't I be a teacher like her character on the show? Ooh! Maybe I'll meet a hot, rich, single father who looks like Dermott Mulroney and date him for a while, too. Yes... I like this plan.

During my daydreaming, I've somehow managed to put away all the books that arrived this morning. I collapse the box they came in and carry it behind the counter, where I'll store it until I have a chance to take it out to the recyclables dumpster later. Then I pull out my weekly schedule and study it, as if I don't already have it memorized.

What's most daunting to me is that while the rest of the

teachers each have 25 to 30 students in their rooms each day, 100 to 120 students will come through the library on any given day. I'll have to learn all their names and pretend that I like them. I think the latter part of that challenge is the harder half.

I wish I liked kids. And maybe I will when this is all over, if these kids are nice enough not to make me hate kids even more. Not that I hate them. I don't. That word conveys too strong an emotion about them. I'm almost totally indifferent to them. I don't ooh and aah over babies or the cute, funny things that older children say or do. Most of the time, I don't give any person under the age of 21 any thought at all.

Maybe it's because I don't remember what it feels like to be a kid, so I have no empathy for them. It seems like I've been a grownup forever. As a child, I was precocious, and as I grew up, I was always mature for my age. Being an only adopted child, my parents took me everywhere and included me in everything they did until I was old enough to stay home alone. Since they're academics, I was privy to dinner table conversations that ran the gamut from the weather to the political climate in third world countries. I learned early on how to hold my own in these conversations, but I was lost when it came to playground debates about Barbie versus Brattz. The point is, I met political activist and Holocaust survivor Elie Wiesel at one of my parents' dinner parties when I was eight and had more to say to him than I did to any of my classmates in the lunchroom on a daily basis. That meant I had to actually study pop culture like another school subject to avoid being a complete outcast.

So, I flourished in college. By about the third week of the fall semester my freshman year, when all the lightweights had dropped out and those of us who were serious about learning were left, I knew I was in my element. This was an atmosphere that encouraged intellectual debate and exploration. Sure, there were the fraternities and sororities that seemed more interested in partying, but there were as many of us—if not more—who cared about academics. I was no longer a minority. I didn't have to waste time boning up on reality TV stats.

Naturally, I chose one of the most notoriously nerdy majors: library science. Technology was making it more interesting than ever, and I couldn't think of any other career I'd rather pursue. The idea of being surrounded by books all the time for the rest of my life was thrilling. I'd never run out of knowledge to soak up, and I'd be ensuring that same knowledge was accessible to the masses.

It wasn't until I got my first real grownup post-graduate job in the Kansas City Public Library system that I found someone with like interests who also made me feel that spark of attraction.

But anyway… with less than a week to go before school starts, I'm way too busy to think about him.

CHAPTER TWO

I'm hunched over my schedule, thinking up some mnemonic devices to memorize the sequence of teachers' names in my schedule, when Jane Pleska, fourth grade teacher, union steward (although she's already pointed out sniffily that I'm not eligible to be in the teachers' union), and self-proclaimed cruise director at Whitehall Elementary, bustles into the library and stops at the counter. I straighten my back and give her one of my brightest, friendliest smiles, but I can already tell she and I are *not* going to be buddies.

She slides a piece of paper across the counter towards me and says, "Once a month, we meet before school in the teacher's lounge to discuss any issues, challenges, or wins we're experiencing with our students and to get feedback from the rest of the group. We take turns bringing in breakfast for the group. Something simple and light and, preferably, healthy. *Not* donuts. Here's the sign-up sheet."

Taking a look, I see there are only two slots open: December and May. When I point this out, mainly to verify that I'm interpreting the data correctly, she explains a touch defensively, "Well, I figured I'd leave those two months open for you, since you don't have a *real* classroom and won't be busy with end-of-term grades. You only have to do one, and it's your choice."

I grit my teeth and sign up for December. Trying for levity, I say, "Who's the lucky person who doesn't have a choice at all?"

She wrinkles her nose. "Jamie Chase. It's not my fault that *some* people wait until the eleventh hour to grace us with their presence. Unfortunately, the administration here has fostered the belief that pretty people don't have to play by the same rules as the rest of us."

Wow. I'm not sure where to start with that bitter statement. First of all, I'm slightly offended that I'm grouped in with "the rest of us," and not the "pretty people." Second, this Jamie Chase lady has obviously not toed Ms. Jane Pleska's line in the past and probably suffers dearly for it in more important matters than the monthly meeting breakfast rotation.

The last thing I want to do is get in the middle of a workplace feud, so I nod noncommittally and hand back the signup sheet. "Okay, then! Thanks for including me!"

She doesn't acknowledge my chipper statement at all. Rather, she gasps at the time and laments, "I am *never* going to get my classroom ready in time! I don't know how someone can even *think* about giving themselves less than three weeks, much less only one. Irresponsible, if you ask me." She pushes the list back to me. "Be a dear and keep on the lookout for Jamie. I don't have time to keep going all the way down the kindergarten hall to get a silly signature." With that, she rushes from the library, leaving me in charge of the signup sheet.

Great. The first time I meet this Jamie woman I'm going

to have to deliver the bad news about her getting the least-desirable signup month.

In addition to daring to milk the most of her summer vacation, I wonder what else Jamie Chase has done to incur the Wrath of Pleska. Sounds to me like the biggest beef Jane has with the kindergarten teacher is that she's good-looking. I'm starting to get a clear picture now. Jamie's attractive and young and adored by her students, who see her as a mother figure, considering this is the first time for some of them to be away from their parents all day. She's probably nurturing and sweet and smells like sugar cookies. She never has a blonde hair out of place or lipstick smeared on her teeth. And she doesn't look like a toad, which is something that Jane can't say.

If this is the case, I feel sorry for Jamie. Unfortunately, I know firsthand how damaging co-worker jealousy and office politics can be.

A couple of hours later, I'm eating fast food tacos at the library counter and flipping through some book catalogs, trying to figure out how I'm going to fill the rest of the hours in this week. My predecessor, a Mrs. Dawanza Nicholson, was apparently the most kick-ass elementary school librarian in the history of the profession. It seems she had everything taken care of for *this* school year by the last day of the *previous* school year. There's really nothing for me to do, except add some fun touches to the library, and I don't have the foggiest idea where to even start with that.

I have to think about what the kids would like—an impossible feat, considering how clueless I am about that species of creature—and use the creativity I've allowed to go into extended hibernation in the back corner of my brain. In the process, I should probably also give them some insight into me, to help them get to know me a little better. I'm in way over my head here.

But I seem to have the feeling that if I sit at this counter and look through the meticulously organized lists and materials that Mrs. Nicholson left behind, I'll magically know what to do. Because it seems like no one else at the school knows what she did. She was just sort of *here*. This is a place where they can drop off their students once a week and get an hour of peace. They don't care what goes on here, as long as they're not involved. Fair enough. Plus, I'm supposed to know what I'm doing, so why should I even have to ask them what I'm supposed to be doing?

By the time I see someone walk past the open library doors, glance in on their way past, backtrack, and stop in the doorway, I've worked myself into a near panic attack at this sham of mine that's sure to fail epically on the very first day of school. So when the tan, spectacled stranger grins at me before approaching the desk, I barely have the wherewithal to smile. Plus, I have a mouthful of greasy taco meat.

"You must be the new librarian. Miss Dickinson, is it?" He offers me his hand to shake. "I'm Jamie Chase, one of the kindergarten teachers."

A blob of ground beef plops onto the wax paper in front of me as my mouth drops open before I can swallow everything in it. Classy.

While I crumple the wrapper to try to get rid of the disgusting evidence of my lunch as quickly as possible and hastily wipe my mouth with a coarse brown napkin, he says, "Sorry. This is probably the first minute you've had to yourself in weeks, and I'm bothering you. I'll come back later. Just wanted to introduce myself."

As he's turning away, I feel confident enough to open my mouth to talk without food spraying out. "No! I mean, it's okay. Really. *I'm* sorry." Now I extend my hand and blurt, "I... I thought you were a woman!"

"Huh?" He slowly spins on his heel to face me once more and hesitantly takes my hand, shaking it slowly and smirking at me.

"I mean, because of your name! Nobody told me you were a guy!" I practically shout at him in my desperation to be understood. "And everyone else here is female!" Then I finish lamely, "I'm Kendall. It's nice to meet you, Jamie."

He smiles broadly, revealing white, even teeth, dimples on both cheeks, and laugh lines near his eyes that hint at a healthy, often-exercised sense of humor. "Yeah. You, too. Sorry I haven't been by sooner, but"—he leans in conspiratorially—"I just got in. Literally just landed at the airport and drove straight here."

That sounds incredibly adventuresome, which is completely foreign to me, so I can't help but ask, "Oh? Did you go somewhere exciting?"

Shrugging nonchalantly but with a twinkle in his eyes, he says, "Only India. A quick visit this time."

"Oh. Wow. I've been to *Indiana* before," I joke at my own expense. "Probably not quite the same thing."

He sucks at his teeth contemplatively before agreeing, "Yeah. Not quite. Lots of cows in both places, though."

"Good point."

While he leans a hip against the counter, I toss my lunch trash into the wastebasket at my feet. "Anyway," he continues, "it was the only chance I had to go this year, and I wasn't going to let a little classroom prep stop me. Plus, I brought some stuff back for the students, so I considered my travels somewhat work-related." Now he pushes his glasses further up on his nose and looks around the library for the first time. "Huh. Place looks the same as always."

Considering that I've been stressing about it for the past two weeks, I take his statement as a criticism and reply defensively, "Seems like Mrs. Nicholson had everything in order, so I didn't want to mess with a proven system."

"Proven, but boring. And outdated. The woman was almost as much a relic as the things I used to find on archaeological digs."

I must have a sign on my forehead that reads, *"Trash-talk our colleagues to me."* Maybe I should start charging a fee. Even though Mrs. Nicholson is no longer technically our co-worker, I don't want people to get in this habit with me. All I want is to work my forty hours every week without getting involved in workplace drama and go home with a clear conscience. Is that too much to ask?

I must look offended or hurt (or both), because he quickly qualifies, "No offense. I mean, I'm sure you're trying to figure everything out. Hell, *I'm* still trying to figure everything out, and I've been here five years."

I'm somewhat mollified by his admission and the knowledge I have deep down that this school library isn't as fun or engaging as it could be and that I'm touchy about it because I don't have the first idea how to fix it. But I still don't want to be the equivalent of the workplace bartender, simply because I stand behind a counter and seem to be a captive audience.

"I'm sure she did the best she knew how to do," I defend poor Mrs. Nicholson (and myself, in the process). Then cheerfully and much more confidently than I feel, I say, "Plus, I'll get this place whipped into shape in no time, as soon as I get to know the students and teachers and can figure out where the biggest, most immediate needs are."

Yeah! That was my plan, all along. Right…

Readily, he supplies, "More computer stations for catalog searches." He points to the large, gray computer at a child-sized desk at the end of the counter. "Right now, the kids have to take turns on that Doogie Howser hand-me-down, circa 1985. Or they have to come to you for help. That's inefficient. Not to mention, it doesn't foster a sense of independence or teach them how to find things on their own. *And* it makes for a hectic check-out time."

I nod thoughtfully. "Okay. I'll talk to Ms. Twomey about that."

He snorts. "Forget that. Go straight to Dianna." He nods toward the door that connects the library to the computer lab. "As the school's computer teacher, she has connections with the IT department and can score some spare systems for you. I'd say you need at least three more."

"Really?" I gulp at how unequipped I am in this department but try not to worry too much about it.

"Yeah. Trust me; it'll make your life so much easier." Now he stands up straighter. "Anyway, that's enough of me sticking my nose in your business today. You probably think I'm a real douche, coming in here and telling you how I think it should be done."

I'm horrified when I let slip, "Well, since I have no idea what I'm doing, I welcome any suggestions."

He cocks his head at me, but then he grins as if he thinks I'm joking. "Oh, good. I don't want to be overbearing. But a new regime is always a good time to make improvements."

He's turning to leave when I remember the breakfast signup sheet. "Oh! Hey!"

He stops in his tracks and faces me once more.

I hold up the goldenrod-colored piece of paper, which

he immediately recognizes, based on the dismayed expression on his face. "Aw, man! Really?" he mutters, but he returns to the counter and takes the paper from me. Looking down at it, he says, "Well, what's the point in even asking me, if there's only one effing spot left?"

I wince sympathetically. "There were only two spots left when I got it. I took December, but if you'd rather have that than May, I'll switch with you." I hardly want to start off on the wrong foot with one of my co-workers over a stupid continental breakfast meeting schedule.

Pulling a pen from his pocket and clicking it open, he scrawls his name in the spot for May and grumbles, "Never mind. It doesn't matter. It's typical Jane Pleska shit. The woman hates me and doesn't make it a secret. Every year, she finds new and innovative ways to piss me off. Or get me in trouble. But whatever. Sorry. It's not your fault."

I'm not sure what to say. "Uh, you're forgiven." The prim, childish response is cringe-worthy, but I can't take it back, so I laugh at myself and amend, "Whatever."

His smile turns into a grimace as he keeps a hold on the list. "I'll take this back to Constable Pleska and spare you the encounter with her. Plus, I'm sure she'll be interested to know I've reported for duty so she can note the number of voluntary service days that are no longer voluntary for me, due to my late arrival."

With that, he strides to the library doors and calls over his shoulder, "It was nice to meet you, Kendall. Good luck!"

CHAPTER THREE

A few days ago, I was wondering how I was going to fill my time at work before the first day of school. Now I'm wondering how I'm ever going to be ready on time. I've been working nonstop with Dianna to get three new systems in the library to serve as electronic catalogs. Finding the systems was actually the easy part; Dianna had three surplus machines waiting to go back to IT for recycling into the system at other schools. The snafu came when IT told us we'd have to get three new licenses for the proper software. That's taking a while to go through the requisitions process.

Well, I'm no stranger to bureaucracy and red tape, so I can be patient. I only wish I had thought of this on my own, weeks ago. Then we'd be up and running by the first day of school. As it is, classes start in five days, and right now, it's not looking like the machines will be ready. But that's okay, I think. Nobody's going to notice, because the only things that will be missing are things they never had to begin with.

The bigger issue has to do with aesthetics. What Jamie said to me about the library looking the same—and the disappointed tone in which he said it—has been nagging me. I've decided I *do* want it to be obvious right away that there's a new librarian. I don't want returning students and their parents to come in on Wednesday night for Open House and bypass the library altogether because they think there's nothing new to see here. Not that I want them to come gawk at me and ask me a bunch of questions that I'll be sure to bungle; but it would be nice if they could poke their heads in and tell at a glance that there's something new —and possibly exciting—going on in here.

That's why I'm here on a Saturday night (no big sacrifice, unfortunately), constructing various "centers," built around children's literary themes, throughout the library. There's a *Harry Potter* corner, with posters from the movies, action figures I picked up on sale at Target, and deliberately haphazard stacks of the books; an *Olivia* corner with a cardboard cutout of the precocious pig herself and some dress-up clothes, as well as an exhibition of the picture books; and a display dedicated to Newbery and Caldecott Award winners throughout the years, including the most recent winners. That's all I'm going to have the time (or energy) to do before the term begins, but it's a start. I basically pirated the first three doable ideas I found on the Internet and ran with them.

I'll be damned if I'm going to have some kindergarten teacher imply that my library is lame.

Not that I've seen Jamie or given him much thought since we first met late last week. He's just another co-worker. It doesn't matter that he's "pretty," to quote Jane. I mean, how shallow would that be? I hardly know the guy. Truth is, he *was* sort of heavy-handed, telling me how he thought I should do things. I told him at the time that it was no big deal and that I appreciated his advice (which was decent), but the more I think about it, the more I realize how forward it was for him to be that way. Like he's God's gift to the education system. Swooping in from the far reaches of the globe with his international classroom props. Bah! I don't care what he thinks.

It's what the kids think that matters. And I have to admit, I want them to think I'm cool. At least cooler than Mrs. Nicholson was. I mean, I'd hate for anyone to describe me as "a relic." I haven't crammed this hard about pop culture since high school. I'm hip; I'm down with the lingo (maybe not so much, since I just said, "down with the lingo"); I know all about computers; and I'm familiar with the latest video games (I am now, anyway, since I've been recording every episode of *Attack of the Show* and *X-Play* on my parents' DVR for two weeks straight); I know which tween sensations are supposedly "dating" each other, which ones have their own lines of sickening-sweet fragrances, and what the hottest lunch box style is this year; and I've watched enough tween shows on Nick that I have the characters' names memorized and have even caught myself using some of the slang I've heard on those shows. Thankfully, I've always been alone when these words and phrases have popped out. There's nothing more pathetic than an adult talking like a twelve-year-old, unless it's someone more than twice that age talking to *herself* like a twelve-year-old.

It's getting late, but I want to finish with my *Olivia* cardboard cutout. I'm not a crafty person, but I am techno-savvy, so I came up with an easy way to make my own. I connected my laptop to the projector and cast a huge picture of the character onto one of the library's walls. Then I taped a large sheet of paper onto the wall and traced the picture onto the paper. When that was finished, I took the paper from the wall and colored the picture with markers. Finally, I pasted the paper to a giant piece of fiberboard and, using an Exacto knife and a box cutter, painstakingly cut out the figure. I've been fashioning a stand from the left-over fiberboard while keeping an eye on the clock. I have about twenty minutes left on this project and what will probably amount to about five minutes of cleanup.

Freddie, the school custodian, said he'd be here well into the night finishing the floors in the cafeteria and the main hallway, but I don't trust Freddie to remember what he had for lunch, and I'm worried he'll be done before I am and forget about me. Being alone in a dark, deserted school—even if it is locked—doesn't excite me.

I decide to take a break and check in with the custodian. I put down my box cutter and flex my hand, which is aching from gripping the tool so tightly and for so long. Standing from my crouched position on the library floor, I stretch my arms over my head to release the kinks from my neck and back and lurch-walk from the library into the hallway on one good foot and one that's tingling with pins and needles.

When I get to the intersection that leads to the main hallway, I notice there's a light on in the kindergarten classroom all the way at the end of the hall. I know this is Jamie's room, even though I've never been in it, because I've seen his nameplate on the wall next to the door each day when I enter the building through the side door. I also know it's ridiculous for my guts to jolt at the idea that he's working late on a Saturday night, too.

Men at work are trouble. It doesn't matter how nerdy-chic and cute that one is. Don't even get any ideas, Kendall.

Anyway, it figures he'd have to pull a few all-nighters to get his room ready, considering how late he's left his classroom prep. Maybe I'll stop by on my way out to say hi and see how things are going. It'd only be polite. Right?

By the time I get halfway to the cafegymatorium, I can

hear the whirring of Freddie's floor buffer, so I know he hasn't abandoned me. But since I'm here, I might as well pop into the teachers' lounge and grab a Diet Coke. When I push through the heavy door, I'm surprised to see Jamie sitting on one of the sturdy wooden tables in the middle of the room, his feet in the plastic-and-metal chair in front of him. He has his elbows on his thighs. In his hands is an issue of *National Geographic*.

"Oh, hey," I greet him, suddenly forgetting why I came in here. I stand close to the door, wracking my brain.

He casually looks over at me and back down at the magazine, flipping a few pages and holding the publication sideways to look at the pictures, as if they're pinups. "Hey," he returns dully.

Then he sighs, closes the magazine and tosses it through the air, in my direction. I step quickly to the side but laugh at myself when it hits what must have been his intended target: the trashcan, not me.

The glow from the Coke machine is finally more compelling than the sight of Jamie, and it reminds me why I'm here. I cross to it, feed a dollar bill into the slot, and push the appropriate button. With my back turned to him as I retrieve my can of soda, I ask, "What'd that magazine ever do to you, anyway?"

"Not the magazine," he mumbles. "One of its contributors."

"Someone you met on one of your summertime travels?" I tease, popping the tab and taking my first nose-tickling sip. Now I look his way and feel bad for making the joke. He looks absolutely miserable.

He shakes his head. "Nah. Someone from my other life. Back when I used to do things that were worthy of magazines and documentaries."

Hoping to tease him out of his funk, I urge, "Do tell!"

Chuckling at my salacious tone, he nevertheless keeps his eyes on his folded hands. "Not much to tell. It's a boring, clichéd story. Boy becomes archaeologist, boy goes on expedition, boy meets girl, boy's life implodes, girl goes on with her life without boy."

"Hmmm. I've never heard that one before, and I don't like sad endings."

"It's sad, all right," he affirms. "Whatever, though. I'm feeling sorry for myself, because that's better than actually getting to work on my classroom. I'll do anything to procrastinate." Taking a deep breath, he finally looks up at me and attempts a shaky smile. "What're you doing here? I thought you had everything ready ages ago."

"I had a few brainstorms about how to make the library look more inviting and exciting," I reveal. I take a long drink of my soda and stifle the resulting belch (barely). When I'm sure it's gone and not merely hiding under my diaphragm, ready to jump out and embarrass me as soon as I open my mouth to talk, I continue, "Things are going a lot better than I'd hoped, but I thought I'd better work today, in case I ran into any complications."

"Ah. You're a planner."

He makes it sound like there's something wrong with that, but I don't give him the satisfaction of getting defensive. Instead, I reply sunnily, "Yep. That's me. Plan for the worst; then there are no unpleasant surprises."

"Nice, safe strategy." Again, his tone contradicts the traditionally complimentary meaning of the words. Before I can reply, he nudges his footrest aside and unfolds his tall frame so that his sneakered feet hit the floor with a slap. "Anyway, I guess I should get to work."

"You haven't even started?" I ask incredulously.

He shrugs. "Nah. It's not like it's that hard. Stick a few nametags on the desks and unpack the new stuff I've collected over the summer. Luckily, they didn't move my classroom like they did last year. Now *that* was a mess. But this year, everything's pretty much the same. I have a system that I like and that the kids seem to like, so there's no need to mess with it from year to year. Until I get bored with it, which will probably happen soon."

I nod, admiring his confidence.

"Anyway," he continues, leading the way from the room and turning off the light as we step into the hallway, "they're kindergartners. As long as it looks fun, they don't give a shit about anything else. And the parents believe anything I say, because they're just thankful they're not the ones trapped in a stuffy room with twenty-five smelly little bodies from eight until three every weekday."

I laugh at his vivid description as we make our way down the shiny-floored corridor towards our rooms. "Wow. Do you speak at career fairs?"

He pushes his glasses onto his forehead to rub his eyes and lets the frames drop again onto his nose. "I don't claim to eat, breathe, sleep, and crap teaching, okay? But I'm good at what I do. The proof is in the kids. Most of them leave my class knowing how to sight-read small words and simple sentences, and they can do basic math addition up to ten. Because I make it fun. And stress-free. I get half my lesson plan ideas from Nick Jr. on the weekends. And I make it seem like it's their choice to learn, not a state or federal mandate. You ever tell a kindergartner they *have* to do something?"

I merely shake my head instead of admitting I can't remember ever telling a kindergartner *anything*.

He laughs mirthlessly. "Ninety-nine percent of the time,

it doesn't work. They make rock stars look like conformists. *But* if you act like you don't give a damn if they color that picture or write the letter P over and over again in their writing tablets, they're all over it. The mistake most new teachers make is that they show too much that they care. They make everything seem too important. And that freaks the little guys out."

We've reached the "T" in the hallway that takes us in opposite directions to get to our respective rooms.

More enviously than I wish it to come out, I say, "Sounds like you have a knack for working with kids and like them a lot." I tear off the pull-tab on my soda can, drop it into the empty can, and rattle it distractedly.

"Have you been listening to a word I've said?" he wonders aloud, smoothly relieving me of my noisemaker. "I *work* with kids. And let me tell you, it's *work* to figure out the learning styles of two dozen people who don't even know they *have* learning styles and individualizing their classroom experiences so they can get the most out of every day of learning. So... yes to the first half of what you said and no to the second half. Most days after I leave here, I want to head straight to a bar. Not only can I get a nice, strong drink, but I can be assured there's no one under the age of 21 there."

I suddenly get a vivid picture of the two of us sitting at a bar, getting shit-faced after the first day of school.

"That bad, huh?" I finally manage to ask.

He seems oblivious to my terror. "Yeah, well, I'm in the minority. Everyone else here—and I'm sure you'll fall into the same category, because you seem like the bubbly, enthusiastic type—loves their job and loves their students. For them, it's a calling. For me, it's a job. And the kids are just lucky that I take my job seriously, whether I'm digging around for artifacts in a desert or teaching the alphabet to young minds."

Holding up my Coke can, he offers, "I'll recycle this for you. You going to be here much longer?"

I try to focus on his change in subject, even though my mind is reeling at all the information he's thrown at me. "Uh, no. I have to, uh, finish one more thing. Then I probably won't be back until Wednesday to get last-minute stuff pulled together for Open House."

If he notices I'm suddenly distracted, he doesn't let on. Instead, he walks backwards away from me, rattling my can in his left hand. "Okay. Poke your head in my room when you're ready to leave, and I'll walk you out to your car. The buddy system is one thing that kindergartners totally have the right idea about."

With that, he grins, spins, and jogs to his room.

CHAPTER FOUR

T-minus three hours until Open House, and I'm a jangle of nerves. I think I'm hiding it well, though.

"You should probably think about laying off the caffeine for the rest of the day," Julia Vasquez advises me in front of the soda machine in the teachers' lounge. "You're all twitchy."

I try not to stare at the P.E. teacher's enormous baby bump and stifle the urge to snap at her that she's just jealous I can have caffeine. I'm not the snappy type, so I know it's the caffeine and nerves working together to make me a scary stranger. I'm also disappointed that what I thought was only obvious to me (I'm freaking out!!!) is also obvious to other people.

Graciously, I accept her advice, and I'm about to divulge how nervous I am about tonight when Jamie pushes open the lounge's door. His face lights up when he sees me.

Oh, gosh. That's a nice look. And that's a nice resulting feeling from the look. That settles it: no more caffeine for me.

Men are trouble, girl. Don't forget it!

He crosses the room in a few determined strides. "Hey," he says, practically ignoring Julia and zeroing in on me. "I wanted to apologize for the other night."

I giggle nervously and glance at the gym teacher, who raises her plucked eyebrows at me.

Jamie seems clueless as he continues, "I was in a bad place. That always happens when I return home from a big trip." Now he suddenly seems to care who hears what he says, so he pulls me away from our audience of one and murmurs, "It's hard sometimes to transition from thoughts of what I'd really like to be doing to what I *have* to do."

The seven sodas I've drunk today have completely eroded any filter I may have had (which is pretty useless even in the best of times), so I can't resist the urge to ask him what's been bothering me off and on—when I think of him, which isn't very often, *I swear*—since Saturday night. "So, why is an archaeologist who loves traveling and digging in the dirt and doing, I don't know, archaeological stuff hanging out with kindergartners nine months out of the year?"

He sighs. "It's complicated."

"Obviously."

Esther Wambaugh, the school's music teacher, enters the lounge, humming to herself. She and Julia start the same conversation all the teachers have had with each other this morning: "Are you ready for a new year to start?"

Jamie turns his back to them. "I have to take care of my older brother, and I can't do that if I'm always half a world away." When I wait for him to explain more, he adds, "He was in a car accident a few years ago, and he almost died. He had some brain damage, but my parents were in no condition to take care of him; *he* was actually taking care of them when it happened. Then they both died within six months of each other, so now it's just the two of us. And I can't put him in a home. He's not *that* bad off, so he'd be miserable surrounded by a bunch of vegetables. But he can't live alone, either."

"Wow."

He mistakes my slight offense at his use of the term "vegetables" for admiration. "Not 'wow.' Just, I don't know, life." He rubs the back of his neck. "Anyway, it was wrong of me to vent to you Saturday night. I sounded like a bitter, spoiled jerk. I mean, you barely even know me."

"It's not that big a deal," I downplay it, trying to inch over to the populated area of the lounge. The last thing I need is for people to think Jamie and I are having private, whispered conversations. "You gave me some decent advice, too, so don't sweat it."

"Yeah? Okay, good. Well, I don't want you to think I hate my life or my job... or my students. I don't. Most of the time." Now he grins crookedly and says loudly enough for everyone to hear, "Nobody likes to come back to work after three months off, right? I mean, unless they're lying."

Hearing this, Julia chimes in, "Amen! Once you see all those sunny little faces, though, Jamie, you know you'll be excited again."

Esther begins singing about the kids being the sunshine of Jamie's life.

I've had several encounters with the school's music teacher over the past few weeks, but I'm still not used to the fact that she sings nearly everything she says. It flusters me every time.

Jamie and Julia don't even blink, though.

Jamie replies as Principal Twomey walks in, "Yeah, yeah. I wonder how many criers I'm going to have tomorrow. I'm always glad the first week of school is only two days long."

"I don't have any classes until starting next week, so I can come down to help you out, if you need someone to console the little ones," Julia volunteers readily.

"I wasn't talking about the kids," Jamie jokes.

"My lands, Jamie! You should make up care packages for the parents," Ms. Twomey suggests. "That's what Bonita does. Sample packs of tissues, chamomile tea bags, and a cute poem about free time and quiet houses. Makes the mommies—and some daddies—feel much better about the big day."

"Not my style," he bluntly states. "If I had it my way, the parents would have to say goodbye outside. Only upsets the kids more when their parents hover and refuse to leave."

"You like to act like a tough guy, but I've seen you on the first day, Jamie Chase. You're a big softie," Ms. Twomey accuses.

He takes that as his cue to leave, but he gets the last grumbling word on his way out. "That's a vicious rumor you're spreading, Renalda."

"Oh, Jamie! You're such a hoot!" she flirts to the empty doorway. Then she turns to the three of us who are left in the room. "Well? How're things? Everybody ready to go? Kendall, I poked my head into the library a while ago, and girl! Lookin' good!"

"Thanks!" I beam at her compliment but then ruin it with my customary over-sharing. "None of them are original ideas, and it's not much yet, but I plan to do more as the year goes on and I figure out what the students like."

BREA BROWN

Esther croons from the coffeepot about giving the students what they want.

Ms. Twomey snaps along.

Just when I'm thinking I must be dreaming this surreal situation and that I'll wake up any second, Sam rushes into the room and pulls up sharply when she sees the principal. Her tense shoulders fall several inches. "Oh! There you are! I've been looking for you for half an hour."

"Well, I've been right here!" Ms. Twomey claims defensively. "And a few other places. What's the big emergency, anyway?"

Sam looks close to tears. "Dr. Underhill is here for his walk-through. He's been waiting in the office all this time, while I've been trying to find you."

Ms. Twomey rushes to the door. On her way out, I hear her demand, "Why didn't you page me over the intercom?" to which Sam replies hotly, "I did! And I called your cell phone and texted you!"

Their voices fade as they rush toward the office and the waiting district Superintendent.

Esther's right behind them. "Well, better get to my class if the big man's making his inspection." Then she sings cheerfully as she bustles in the direction of her room about working for the man every night and day.

When she's gone, Julia wastes no time before sidling (more like waddling) up to me. "Soo… What was all that about with you and Jamie? 'Sorry about the other night,'" she coos, imitating his deep voice.

I blush but quickly explain, "He was having a rough time Saturday, and I happened to be here to listen."

"He can cry on my shoulder anytime," she cracks but then immediately regrets it. Horrified at herself, she gasps,

30

"Oh, my gosh! I'm sorry. How unprofessional! I just... It's the hormones. Anyway, I'll see you tonight!"

And she rushes from the lounge, leaving me alone to wonder how unprofessional it makes me that I've been thinking what she said—and then some—almost non-stop for four days. And I can't blame runaway hormones.

CHAPTER FIVE

I'm strangely disappointed that I've had no traffic through the library tonight. I should be relieved, but like a little kid, I want everyone to see the work I've done. Nobody's ventured down this hallway, though. I can hear lots of activity at the other end of the hall, down by Jamie's room. Mostly a lot of women's laughter. But some children's voices, all of which sound excited and intrepid about starting school, not timid and tearful. I realize tomorrow may be a different story, but for now, it sounds like a party down there.

And I'm the wallflower. I thought I was going to have some visitors, but it was only a mother and daughter who had taken a wrong turn on the way to the restrooms. They seemed like they were in a hurry, so I didn't take it personally when they didn't even wish me a good evening before following my directions to their original, intended destination. And those are the only people I've seen.

Therefore, I'm surprised when ten minutes before the end of the Open House, the doors to the library open, and a small blond boy walks with purpose to the counter.

Blinking up at me, he says, "Hi."

"Hi," I reply. "How's it going?"

He shrugs. "Boring. All the moms are asking Mr. Chase a bajillion questions."

My ears perk up, and I forget to be nervous around this strange little person. "Oh? You have Mr. Chase this year?"

With a nod, he answers, "Yep. I like that he's a boy. Maybe we'll talk about *Star Wars* a lot."

I blink down at him, trying to untangle his logic, but before I can even follow his train of thought, he's onto something else.

"So, I like cats, right?"

"I guess you do. If you say so."

"I do. A lot. You got books about cats?"

I try to think of a specific book or character and come up blank, but I'm confident when I say, "Sure. Who's your favorite cat character?"

He looks at me as if he pities me for some reason before saying, "Not cartoon cats. That's for babies. I have a cat book at home that tells about every single cat in the world. What's your favorite cat?"

"Uh…" I grunt inarticulately.

"Mine's the Russian Blue. They have lots of diabetes, but they're super-cute. What's your name, anyway?"

Fortunately, I know this answer. "Kendall—I mean, Miss Dickinson. What's your name?"

"Brody Sawyer. Ken doll? What kind of name is that? Sounds like it's prolly a boy's name."

Stifling a laugh, I say as seriously as possible, "Well, I think it can be a boy's name, too. But I think you're supposed to call me Miss Dickinson, anyway."

He wrinkles his nose. "That takes a lot longer to say."

33

"A little," I concede, "but that's what you have to call me."

"What happens if I don't?"

Uh-oh. I realize I just did what Jamie told me not to do: I told a kindergartner that he *had* to do something. Shit. Quickly, I adjust my strategy, even though it feels counter-productive to say, "Whatever."

"I won't get in trouble?"

"Nope."

"Will you?"

"Maybe." Again, I try to make it sound like I'm not worried.

He contemplates this for a while as he taps his fingers against the wainscoting on the front of the counter. Finally, he says, "I'll call you Miss Dickinson, if that's what the other kids are gonna call you."

"They will."

"Okay. What other good books do you got?"

I'm prevented from answering by the doors bursting open and a short woman with curly black hair rushing towards us. "Brody Daniel Sawyer!"

A tense-looking Jamie arrives seconds later, takes in the scene, and relaxes.

The person I presume to be Mrs. Sawyer gives me a distracted, "Hi," and launches into her son. "What have I told you about wandering off?"

"That it's bad?"

"Yes. It's bad." She rests her hands on his shoulders. "You scared me."

"Sorry," he says sullenly. "I wanted to see if the liberrian had any cat books."

"Oh, Brody." She sighs, does a silent three-count, and

says, "All you had to do was tell me that, and I would have brought you here."

"But you were talking to Mr. Chase forever!"

I meet Jamie's eyes over the two Sawyers' heads. He smiles sheepishly.

Now Mrs. Sawyer straightens and says to me, "I'm Debbie Sawyer, Brody's mom. I hope he wasn't pestering you."

"Kendall Dickinson. And not at all. We were discussing our favorite cats."

She rolls her eyes and laughs affectionately at her son. "Brody…" To me, she says, "He's obsessed with cats."

"They're sort of fascinating," I point out helpfully. Brody brightens at my statement. "I'll show you how to look for books about cats when you have your first library day on Friday. How's that sound?"

"Awesome!"

Debbie takes a firm hold of Brody's hand. "Well, Chief, it's time to go," she announces as she pulls him toward the door. "Say goodbye to Mr. Chase and Miss Dickinson."

"But I didn't get a cookie—"

"We'll grab one on the way out. I think the table's by the front door."

When they're gone, Jamie slumps against the counter and starts laughing. Then he continues until I worry that he's lost his mind. Finally, I shake his shoulder until he looks up at me. His laughing tapers off, and while he's removing his glasses and wiping his eyes, I ask, "What's your deal?"

He deliberately places his glasses on his nose and blinks at me. "That kid's in my class."

"Yeah, I know. So?"

"That. Kid. Is. In. My. Class."

"You're gonna have to give me more than that, Chase. Are you saying that's a bad thing, a good thing, what?"

"It's a difficult thing," he answers. "So much for an easy year."

"I think he's cute."

He levels a killer look at me. "That's probably precisely what's kept him alive to see kindergarten."

I can't help but laugh at his perceived misfortune. "It'll be fine," I reassure him.

He shakes his head at what he must think is my extreme naïveté. "He asked me one question before he deemed my classroom too boring and wandered off to find you. Wanna know what that one question was?"

"'What's your favorite cat?'" I guess.

He closes his eyes and gives me a terse head-shake. "Nope. He asked, 'Do you speak Parseltongue?'"

"What the...?" I wonder in a near-whisper. "What the heck is *that*?"

His eyes pop open. "And you call yourself a librarian?"

"What? I *am* a librarian, thank you very much."

"Then you should know all about Parseltongue."

I glance around, starting to suspect there's a camera on me, and this is all part of an elaborate prank. "What the hell does one have to do with another? I'm not a linguist; I'm a librarian."

I suffer through another marathon laughing session of his, during which he rests his head on the counter and lets loose. Eventually, I get fed up with being the butt of his joke and grab his dark hair (which is surprisingly soft) to tug his head off the counter so he can look at me. "Shut up and tell me what's so funny."

"Oh, shit," he wheezes.

"You're being an ass." But I say it with a smile. His mirth is annoyingly contagious.

"Okay, okay. I'm sorry, but..." He almost breaks down again but manages to rein it in at the last second. He inhales a lungful of sobering library air and announces, "You have to be the only librarian in the country who hasn't read the *Harry Potter* books. I've read the *Harry Potter* books."

Now I'm legitimately embarrassed. I lamely defend myself with, "I've never had time to read them." Honestly, I have no desire to read them. They hold no appeal for me whatsoever. I haven't even seen the movies. I'm holding my own private *Harry Potter* boycott.

"Bullshit," he calls me out playfully. "If you wanted to read them, you'd have found the time."

"Okay, fine. Enough about me. Just explain to me what Parseltongue is and why it's so bad that Brody asked if you knew how to speak it." When he merely continues to stare at me with that dopey grin on his face, I say, "Please," batting my eyelashes at him.

This makes him grin wider. "This is hilarious."

I'm not amused anymore. A glance at the clock confirms the Open House has been over for a while now, so it's safe to retrieve my purse from the locked drawer in my desk and go home. Big day tomorrow, anyway. The last thing I need to worry about is what Jamie Chase thinks about me or my professional skills. Or any skills, for that matter.

"Where are you going?" he asks, suddenly sober. "Are you really pissed off at me? I'm only teasing you."

"I'm not pissed off," I lie with a tight smile. "It's time to go home, though."

"But we're in the middle of a conversation!" he protests.

I contradict, "Not really. You're enjoying your own private joke at my expense. That's not a conversation." I come around the counter and cross to the doors, my fingers resting on the bank of light switches.

He stays where he is but turns to face me. "Okay, I'm sorry. Just… read the *Harry Potter* books; you won't be disappointed. And you kind of need to read them, considering your clientele."

"I'll think about it. Let's go."

When he still doesn't move, I try to force the issue by turning out the lights. Unfortunately, there are so many electronic devices with LEDs that it's not as pitch black as I'd hoped. Plus, the "Exit" sign over my head is like a red spotlight.

"Parseltongue is a language that people in the *Harry Potter* books use to speak to snakes."

"Great."

"Yeah. And I'm dismayed that Brody asked me about it for three reasons: one, he's smart enough to understand what it is; two, he's smart enough to have a fairly deep knowledge of a series of books that's way beyond his grade level; and three, I could tell he was annoyed when I told him that I couldn't speak it." Finally, he pushes off the counter and walks toward me. "This kid is going to be so bored in kindergarten. And bored kid equals pain in my ass."

"Well, it's only fair that you have at least one kid in your class who can dish out your own medicine."

"Hey!"

"He'll be good for you. Now, out!" I shoo him past me and concentrate on not noticing how good he smells as he hovers close to my shoulder while I lock the library doors and pull on them to make sure they're secure.

"You look and act so nice, but you have a real mean streak," he murmurs near my ear.

I shiver, but a series of hard lessons I learned not too

long ago in a city a thousand miles away snaps me out of any trance that he may be capable of putting me under.

Sliding along the wall, I move away from him and start the walk down the surprisingly empty corridor. It's like everyone forgot we were here. That, or it was every woman for herself when the place cleared of students and parents, and it was assumed that no one would linger any longer than they had to.

Either way, the result is the same: Jamie and I are alone.

He keeps pace with me down the hall, but the intense moment outside the library doors has passed.

"Well, good luck tomorrow," he says mildly. "I think you and I have first recess duty together."

I don't say a word.

Stopping to lock his own classroom door, he tells me, "Wait a second. I'll walk you to your car."

"I'm fine!" I insist, not pausing at all. As a matter of fact, I pick up the pace and power through the heavy glass-and-metal door, the hand bar clanking loudly. "See you tomorrow!" There's no way a would-be mugger or rapist could catch me, anyway.

CHAPTER SIX

The screeching is unholy. Somehow, I don't remember this noise from the school playgrounds of my youth. Is this non-stop screeching a new thing? Is this sound the product of children used to playing video games all summer going through screen withdrawals? From the minute this group of students hit the doors that led to their morning recess freedom, it's been unceasing. I'm aurally overwhelmed by it.

Jamie tried to explain to me what I'm keeping a lookout for—kids playing too rough with each other or using the equipment unsafely or venturing too close to the boundaries where the school yard meets the backyards of the houses behind it (I can't even imagine living in such close proximity to this racket nine months out of the year)—but I could hardly concentrate on what he was saying. And now I feel like a small animal that's constantly on the alert for predators. I'm twitchy and irritable and desperately searching for a quiet place to hide. This is going to be the longest twenty minutes of my life.

Jamie, on the other hand, seems completely at ease as

he nonchalantly twirls the whistle attached to the lanyard that should be around his neck but which he apparently prefers to swing dangerously close to my head. Maybe he's deaf to the particular pitch of the playground screams, or....

I try to be inconspicuous as I look at his ear closest to me to see if he's wearing earplugs, but he catches me.

"What?"

"Nothing."

"Is there something on my face?" He swipes at his cheek and neck, suddenly not looking as carefree as before.

"No."

I quickly pin my eyes back to the chaos in front of me.

When he's convinced there's truly nothing crawling on his face, he observes, "You're quiet today," as if he's pointing out a major personality flaw. "Everything going okay so far?"

I've had one class, and it was a group of fifth graders who hardly needed me to be there at all. "It's fine."

"Renalda tells me you used to be some library whiz kid in Kansas City."

"What?" That description makes me laugh, in spite of my taut nerves. "No!"

Without warning, he blows the whistle and points to a kid balancing at the top of the monkey bars. "Darius! Down!" As soon as the child complies, Jamie turns back to me to continue our conversation, but I have my hands clapped over my ears.

"A heads-up next time, maybe?" I request as sweetly as possible.

"Oh, for Pete's sake!"

"I don't like loud noises," I explain, dropping my hands to my sides again after checking the time. My watch must be broken; according to it, we've only been out here five minutes!

He rolls his eyes. "You're in the wrong business, then. Criminey."

As if I needed him to point that out.

Not deterred from our original topic, unfortunately, he says, "Anyway, I'm positive that's what Renalda called you. Now where did she get that idea if it's not true? Did you lie on your resume?"

I know he's teasing, but he's hitting too close to a nerve. Not that I lied on my resume, but... I didn't exactly set the record straight when some people in the school district's human resources department jumped to conclusions about my experience with children based on some vague wording I may have used.

"No, I didn't lie on my resume. I have no idea where she's getting that. I was a perfectly average employee for the Kansas City Public Library."

"Riiiiight. Have you ever been average at anything in your life? BENJAMIN DEXTER, DON'T MAKE ME COME OVER THERE! THAT'S RIGHT... I REMEMBER YOUR NAME! YOU TOUCH HER ONE MORE TIME, AND YOU'LL BE IN MS. TWOMEY'S OFFICE SO FAST I'LL MAKE SURE YOU LEAVE SKID MARKS DOWN THE HALLWAY. WITH YOUR FACE." Without skipping a beat, he says to me, "Yeah. I'm not buying it."

I take two steps away from him so that my ear isn't so close to the whistle or his mouth. "Well, I'm sorry you think I'm so extraordinary, and I'm sorry to disappoint. If I was all that, they wouldn't have let me leave as easily as they did, now would they've?"

He shrugs. "Who says they let you leave without a fight?"

"I do." This subject depresses the hell out of me, and I don't believe in depression, so it's time for an immediate change in conversational scenery. "How are things going with Brody, your new BFF?"

"Like you, he's surprisingly quiet today."

"You make it sound like that's all part of some sinister plan of his."

"Maybe it is."

I laugh at him. "You're so weird."

"I know kids. He's biding his time."

After a big sigh, I ask, "For what? To spring one of his bizarre questions on you? Big whoop."

He tosses the whistle and snatches it from the air. Toss and snatch. Toss and snatch. "I don't know. That's what makes it nerve-wracking. He's a wildcard."

"He's five."

"Anyway, I'd rather talk about you. What'd you do in Kansas City? I mean, it's obvious you didn't work with kids." Subtly, he's closed the distance I've so deliberately put between us, and now he nudges me with his elbow. "You may as well be standing in a super-max prison yard right now, judging by your posture and expression."

Why do I have to be such an open book? Why can't I be mysterious and unreadable? I try to consciously relax my facial muscles, but that would require me to unclench my jaw, which seems locked tight.

"It's nothing to be ashamed of," he reassures me. "It's just... sort of obvious. Did you take this job on a dare, or something?"

"Just trying something new."

He laughs. "Okay."

Impatiently, I look at my watch again and note with despair that we still have at least ten minutes to go. "Listen. It's a boring story, okay? I wanted to move here to be closer to my parents, and the job market's not exactly hopping right now. I took what I could get. I don't think I'm doing *that* horrible so far."

"Yeah. You're still alive after two-and-a-half hours." He rocks on the balls of his feet as he casually surveys the far reaches of the playground, looking for wanderers.

"What is it with you, anyway? You love to pick on me. I've been nothing but nice to you, but I think I'm beginning to see why Jane can't stand you." I roll my eyes at his mock-shocked reaction to my statement.

"Jane can't stand me because I've been teaching for a quarter of the years she has but understand more about it than she ever will."

Ick. Nothing is more of a turn-off for me than that kind of bravado.

"Cocky!"

"It's true! I'm not bragging; I'm stating the facts. She's so busy worrying about following a bunch of rules and making sure that everyone else does that she doesn't see the big picture. She doesn't even like her job."

"Neither do you!"

"Yes, I do. I'd rather be doing something else, but that doesn't mean I don't like what I do. I like it less than archaeology. Who wouldn't?"

I raise my hand playfully. He bats it down.

"Don't touch me!"

"I will if I want to."

"Mr.   Chase!   Miss-Whatever-Your-Name-Is-New-Liberrian!"

44

We stop goofing off as a girl in pigtails—and a medium-sized mob behind her—runs toward us.

Jamie sighs. "What is it, Hannah?"

"A boy named Brody climbed a tree over there"—she points to the far corner of the playground, which butts up against a grove of trees—"and he says he's not comin' down, even when recess is over."

I quickly look away when Jamie tries to give me the "I-told-you-so" look.

"Kids, line up here with Miss Dickinson," he tells the crowd of kindergarten through third graders. He directs to me, "I'm going to go get a cat from a tree." As he jogs in the direction of the gnarly, ancient-looking elm, he waves in my direction the students who are still scattered on the playground. "Line up!" I hear him shout. None of them hesitates to follow his command.

Soon, I'm surrounded by a lot of young humanity.

"You're pretty," one of the younger-looking girls says to me in a dreamy voice.

"Uh… thanks!" I reply brightly. "So are you."

"Ugh! No, she's not!" a boy her age contradicts me, making the other boys around us laugh and snicker. "Girls are so gross!"

"Are you the new library teacher?" a freckly girl of about nine asks.

"Yes. I'm the librarian," I reply while trying to keep one eye on Jamie's progress with Brody. But they're so far away that it's hard to see what's happening. All I can see is Jamie standing at the base of the tree with his hands on his hips as he looks up into the branches. I can't even see Brody at all through the thick leaves. What if he falls down? What if he's so high that none of us can reach him, and we have to call the Fire Department?

"What's up with that weird kid, anyway?" one of the older boys asks disgustedly. "I think I heard him meow when we were lined up to come out here."

Something tells me that I, as the adult, need to say something here. "Uh, let's not call people names, okay?" My heart pounds at having to correct someone in front of the rest of the group, even though I say it with a wide smile and a cheerful head bob.

He glares at me. "What? A kid who meows is weird."

Oh, gosh! *Jamie, hurry up!* I beg him silently. But he's not moving. He puts a hand to his forehead to shade his eyes as the sun comes out from behind a cloud and shoots through the foliage into which he's peering.

"Hey! What's going on?" Bonita Carson, the other kindergarten teacher, has poked her head through the side door leading from the kindergarten hall to the playground. "Isn't it time to bring the kids in? First lunch shift starts in thirty minutes."

"Straight lines, please!" I instruct the students as I lead them to the doors. I keep my tone light, as if I'm leading them on an exciting adventure. To Bonita, I murmur, "Jamie's got a student in the tree."

"Well, how'd he do that?" she asks, smirking. It's comforting to see that she doesn't appear to be worried. "Here. I'll take the kids back to their classrooms," she offers. "You call Sam to come down here and figure this out."

"Sam?"

"Yeah. She'll get him down. Or she'll call his parents to have them come here and do it."

Oh, Lord. I start to sweat at the idea of such a scene. I should have been paying closer attention to what was going on. This is all Jamie's fault!

After the last student files inside with Bonita, I go into

Jamie's room. Picking up the phone on his desk, I dial Sam's extension and listen helplessly to it ring and ring and ring.

"C'mon! Pick up!" I say through gritted teeth. When it goes to her voice mail, I hang up. I guess I could page her, but the thought of talking over the intercom system to the entire school makes me feel queasy.

Now Bonita's back with Jamie's students. "Are you able to stay with these guys until Jamie gets back?"

It's technically my lunch break, so the answer is, Yes, I'm able. But am I willing? Not really.

"Ummm…"

She looks expectantly at me. That's when I realize she wasn't *asking* me.

"I can't get ahold of Sam," I update her on my efforts. "She's probably in the lunchroom already." Or doggedly following Ms. Twomey around to make sure she's where she needs to be today.

Bonita sighs. "Well, this is ridiculous!"

Before we can get too flummoxed, though, Jamie strides through the door. He flicks the light switch on and off twice to get the students to quiet down. "Heads down until lunch," he orders quietly.

"Where's Brody?" I ask him on his way past me to his desk.

At first, I think he's not going to answer me. "Thanks, Bonita," he dismisses his fellow teacher before sitting down. When she's gone, he looks me steadily in the eye and says, "He's still out in the tree."

"What? You left him out there?" I hiss, aware that the students are unusually quiet and are probably trying to listen to us.

He nods tersely. "That's what he wants. He wants to be

left alone. Says he misses his mom and hates school and hates me."

"Okay, but you can't leave him out there in a tree! What if he falls?"

"The next group is out there for recess right now. If he falls, someone will see him." He opens his top middle desk drawer and trades his recess whistle for his school ID, which he loops over his head. "He'll be fine," he says calmly. "If he hasn't come down by the time we need to leave for lunch, I'll call his mother."

I stomp to the classroom door. "Fine. But I'm not going to let him sit out there by himself until that happens," I inform him.

Typical man! Everything comes down to toughness with them. Don't show any sympathy; don't try to get to the bottom of why the kid is up in a tree; just give him a dose of tough love and hope for the best. Idiot!

By the time I get out to the tree, fully aware of every eye on the playground following me, I hate Jamie as much as Brody says he does, so we have plenty in common. As a matter of fact, I may climb up in the tree with him.

CHAPTER SEVEN

N ow that I'm here, I realize I don't have a plan. Not only that, but I have no idea what to say to this kid. I didn't even think to ask Jamie what he'd already tried. No matter. I've done my homework about kids the past few weeks, so if nothing else, I can find something to talk about with him until his mom arrives.

Squinting into the intricately woven branches overhead, I spy a tennis shoe with chewed-up laces dangling about twenty feet above me. How the hell did he get so high?

"Hey, Brody."

A scarily realistic cat's hiss comes from above, followed by, "Go away!"

"It's me—Miss Dickinson."

"I don't care. I want my mom."

"Yeah. Mr. Chase already told me that. I'm here to keep you company until she gets here."

He pauses and says, "She's coming?"

"Probably."

"But she's at work. She'll be real mad when she gets here."

I try not to worry about that. "Where does she work?"

"She fixes people's hair. She's on her feet all day, and when she comes home, she's too tired to play with me," the shoe says sullenly.

"Parents," I commiserate. We're quiet for a few minutes; then I ask, "Did you see *SpongeBob* the other night?"

"They're all reruns," he says.

"Oh. Well, it was the first time I'd seen that episode. It was the one where that squid guy moves to a town that's full of other squids like him, to get away from Sponge-Bob." I lean against the trunk of the tree and pick at the bark.

"SpongeBob's annoying."

"Yeah! That's why Squidyard had to move away."

"It's Squidward, Miss Dickinson," he informs me as if I've made an embarrassing blunder. "Anyway, the only thing I like on *SpongeBob* is that Gary the snail meows like a cat."

"Uh… yeah," I say, although I haven't seen any episodes with this "Gary" character in them. But I don't want him to think I'm even dumber than he already thinks I am. "Anyway, speaking of cats, I checked earlier today to see how many books we have about cats in the library, and there are a lot. I think you'll really like one of them. It's called *The Ultimate Cat Encyclopedia.*"

He sighs. "I have that one at home. Remember? I told you that?"

"Oh. Darn. Well, there were a lot more. We'll have to take a look tomorrow when Mr. Chase brings your class to the library."

"I'm not coming to school tomorrow," he states matter-of-factly.

Valiantly hoping he has something planned with his mom that happens to conflict with the second day of school and that he doesn't mean what I think he means, I ask cheerfully, "Oh? Where are you going tomorrow?"

My fears are confirmed when he says, "Not here. I'll prolly stay home and play with my DS."

DS. Okay. I think that's one of those handheld game things, so I ignore the truancy part of his claim and grasp onto that. "What's your favorite game?"

He thinks about it for a second. "Well… I have this cat game where you get kittens, and you teach them things and feed them and take care of them and stuff."

"Of course," I mutter.

"What?"

"Nothing. Is that the only game you have?"

"No. I also got a *Star Wars* game and a *Harry Potter* game. But I beat all the levels, so they're boring now."

"You like *Harry Potter*?" Now, *why* did I pursue that subject when I've proven so recently that I'm a *Harry Potter* idiot? Because I have no clue what I'm doing, that's why. I'm blindly fumbling through the conversation, hoping Jamie's on the phone with Mrs. Sawyer right now, and she's on her way. I don't care if she's in the middle of coloring someone's hair purple; she needs to get here and save me.

I hear some movement overhead and step away from the tree trunk so I can see what's going on up there. He's moved down a few branches. Now I can see his face, which is red and splotchy.

"I wasn't crying," he immediately tells me when I involuntarily utter a sympathetic sound at his appearance.

"Okay. But it's okay if you were. The first day of school can be scary." Even when you're a grownup.

"I wasn't, though. I have allergies."

I let that one slide. Anyway, I'm distracted by the next thing he tells me.

51

"I don't want to go to Juvie. She doesn't do anything fun."

It's all I can do not to crack up. He might be a smart kid, but he's still so young, and he thinks he knows a lot, but he knows just enough to confuse himself.

Biting down hard on my lip, I nod until I have my giggles under control. Then I say, "I've heard that. You know what, though? The best way to stay away from 'Juvie' is to go to school every day and have fun learning with your friends."

His bottom lip quivers. "I don't have any friends, though."

I remember what one of the students said when they were lined up at the end of recess about Brody being "that weird kid."

"You'll make friends," I say surely.

He shakes his head but moves closer to me.

Now I can reach his foot, so I grasp onto it and gently shake it. "Oh, come on! I'm sure there are lots of other kids here at school who like *Star Wars* and *Harry Potter*."

"And cats?"

"Mmmm… sure!"

"You're just saying that to make me feel better."

"Okay," I admit. "Maybe you like cats a lot more than anyone else, but it's okay to be different about some things. It'd be boring if everyone liked all the same things."

He gazes miserably down at me. "Do you like cats?"

Honestly, I've thought more about cats since meeting Brody last night than I have probably in my whole life, but I know this is an important answer. "Yeah. I do." It's not a lie; I don't *dislike* them. "Now, come down. I'm sure Mr. Chase will be glad to see you at lunch. Aren't you hungry?"

He nods. "But Mr. Chase told me I could eat nuts for

lunch, if I wanted to stay up here. I don't like nuts, though," he reveals. "And I think putting a bunch of nuts in your mouth is gross."

I don't even try to stifle the laughter that statement triggers.

"Elm trees don't have nuts, anyway, so don't worry about it," I inform him. "Come on. Let's go eat lunch in the cafeteria before Mr. Chase has to call your mom and she gets mad at you."

Stubbornly, he shakes his head.

"Brody!"

"I don't want to. Everyone will stare at me and laugh because I cried on the first day of school."

I pretend to be confused. "What? You didn't cry, remember? Allergies."

He half-smiles but then pulls on his mouth with his hand to push the smile away. And he stays put, picking leaves from the branch where he's sitting.

"Well, I'm starving," I tell him. "I'll tell you what. We'll make sure Mr. Chase knows you're down, but you can eat lunch with me in the library. Then I'll take you back to your class when they get back from lunch. Nobody will even notice you were gone."

His face brightens. "Really?"

"Really." I offer him my shaking hand. The adrenaline is coursing through my veins at the thought that I'm going to accomplish what Mr. Teacher Extraordinaire couldn't.

Hesitantly, he takes my hand and eases out of the tree. I act like it's no big deal as we walk toward the building.

As we're halfway across the now-empty playground, he says, "You know, you look normal, but I can tell you're weird like me."

By the end of the day, I'm exhausted. The last thing I want to do is go home to my empty apartment and eat a half-frozen, half-molten microwave meal. So I call my mom as soon as I get out to my car.

"How was your first day of school?" she asks right away.

Her question makes me feel five years old, but I dutifully answer, "Fine."

"Isn't teaching fun?" she gushes.

I pinch the bridge of my nose and think back on the day's events. Instead of disappointing her with a, "no," I merely say, "I'm not really a teacher."

"Oh, yes, you most certainly are!" she protests. "Anything interesting happen today?"

Her enthusiasm is contagious. "I talked a kid out of a tree," I reveal. "That was exciting. Especially because no one else could get him to come down."

"See? And you say you're not good with kids!"

"This kid is different."

"Well, I think you should come to dinner and tell us all about it," she suggests exactly what I hoped she would when I dialed her number.

"Really? That would be great, actually."

"Yeah! Your dad and I are going to put some salmon and scallops on the grill. We have about twice as much as we can eat."

Without hesitation, I say, "I'll be right there. Ten minutes. Gaaaa!" I jump a foot when there's a loud knocking on the window right next to my head.

"Are you okay?" comes a muffled inquiry from Jamie on the other side of the tempered glass.

He winces sheepishly when he sees the cell phone in my right hand.

"Oops. Sorry. I thought... You looked... Never mind!"

"What's going on?" Mom asks, a tiny trace of worry in her tone.

"Nothing," I quickly reassure her. "One of my co-workers was checking to make sure I was okay. I'm sitting out here in the parking lot in my car." I roll down my window and say to him, "I'm fine. Thanks."

He walks around his sporty hatchback, which is parked in the spot right next to mine, and unlocks it. Over the roof of his car, he says, "My bad. Goodnight."

"He sounds cute," Mom observes. "Is he single?"

Before evaluating the wisdom of such a revelation, I answer, "He is. And yes."

"Well, invite him over, then!"

"No, I don't think so."

"Why not? What's his name?"

"Jamie."

"What?" he asks, lifting his head and looking pathetically hopeful.

"Uhh..." Now I feel cornered.

"Ask him!" Mom says so loudly that I'm sure he can hear her.

As a matter of fact, he raises his eyebrows and smiles. "Ask me what?"

So it *is* possible for your parents to keep embarrassing you well into adulthood.

I mumble, "My mom wants to know if you want to come to dinner."

He smirks. "Well, I'll have to ask my parents if it's okay, but..."

Oh, gosh. I want to die.

Mom, who's gleefully listening in, laughs. "Oh, he's funny!"

His smile fades. "Seriously, tell her I said thanks, but I gotta get home to my brother. He tends to get in trouble if I leave him alone for too long."

"Bring him along!" Mom shouts into my ear. "We have plenty!"

"Would you like to talk to him directly?" I ask her, laughing so she doesn't realize how annoyed I am.

I relay her suggestion to him, but he shakes his head. "Nah. Maybe some other time. Johnny hangs out at the civic center on Monday, Wednesday, and Friday nights, so I'm usually free then."

"Great. Okay, then. Some other time." I just want this awkwardness to end.

He waves and gets into his car.

When he's gone, I say, "Thanks, Mom. That wasn't weird at all."

"Oh, lighten up! We're going to have to re-program you now that you're back in North Carolina; I think you got a little uptight in Kansas City."

I slump my shoulders and think about what a major understatement that is.

CHAPTER EIGHT

M y parents' house is one of the warmest places I
know. Even when it's empty—which it often is, as
they both still work part-time and aren't the type of people
to sit still for very long—there's a sense of wellbeing that hits
you in the face like the smell of a baking apple pie the
minute you walk in the door. The house is also a study in
moderation. It's not cluttered, but neither is it neat as a pin.
It's clean but not antiseptic. It has all the modern conveniences, but my parents also like to do some things the old-
fashioned way, so there are a few interesting throwbacks to a
simpler time (if you call using a hand-crank ice cream
maker, "simpler").

It was such a relief to return here from Kansas City to
find the house has the same vibe as always. My parents are
the same people. We're the same family. And I take it for
granted. We have intelligent, deep conversations; we have
silly, inconsequential conversations. We take after-dinner
walks and bike rides. We watch *Jeopardy!* and drink wine and
play dominoes. We stare into the fireplace on winter nights,

even if they rarely get too cold in North Carolina. We reminisce and laugh and tease each other.

Tonight, I've been very careful all through dinner to keep the stories coming fast and furious about the kids at school, hardly giving my parents a chance to get a word in, but now that we're sharing a bottle of wine on the deck in the twilight, I've run out of things to say.

Mom pounces. "So, this Jamie…"

"Mom," I warn her. "Really. Please."

"But Kendall!" She grins over at me and pokes her tongue impishly out of the corner of her mouth. "What's he look like?"

Dad gets up. "That's my cue to leave. I'm going on a bike ride."

"Dad, you just drank two glasses of wine," I point out.

He doesn't seem to see what the problem is with this and merely waves away my concern. "Don't worry, Grandma. I'll wear my helmet. You two don't need my insights on this topic."

When he's gone, Mom looks expectantly at me. "Well?"

I smile in spite of my discomfort. "I already told you, he's cute."

"Details, Kendall! Is he tall, short, thin, stocky, muscular, wiry, dark, fair… what?"

To my great chagrin, I'm excited to talk about him. This is not good. But I feel and act like I'm in high school when I eagerly say, "He's tall, wears these sexy glasses, and has darkish hair. It's really soft, too."

"Oh? How do you know this?" she coos.

I tell her about our conversation last night in the library, alone, after everyone else had gone home.

"Oooh. How romantic!"

I blush. "Mom! Nothing like *that* happened."

"I didn't say it did. But... Well, it's not normal for a pretty, bubbly girl like you to be so alone all the time."

Reflexively, I challenge her assertion. "I'm not alone all the time."

"Your dad and I don't count. You know what I mean. You should have friends and *boyfriends*."

"I've had both those things. They're overrated."

Here's a lesson, ladies: stick to your type. If you normally go for the quiet, shy, nerdy-chic guy, don't let yourself fall in love with an outspoken cocky guy whose muscles have muscles. Guys are not like food. You shouldn't be concerned with "trying new things." On the dating buffet, straying from what your hormones have told you you've liked since you realized you had hormones isn't about broadening your palette; it's a recipe for disaster. Oh, and don't date guys who spell their names with douchey variations, like my ex-boyfriend, Todd. I guess, technically, he can blame his parents for that, but you gotta take into account that most people share douchey DNA with the douchey parents who give them douchey names. But I digress.

Two years. Two long years. That's how long it took for me to wake up and smell the turd. And even then, I had to get a snootful of it in a very public fashion before I would admit that he was, in fact, a turd. By then, it was too late.

And how did I meet such a studmuffin in my line of work, you wonder? When Todd graduated from a ridiculously pretentious private university with a degree in Information Technology (and a minor in weight lifting), the job market was fairly saturated, so he applied for positions in unconventional places... like libraries. We were hired at the same time, attended all the same orientation events, and hit it off. There was chemistry. Or something. I liked that he wasn't my usual type; he liked that I had boobs and a vagina.

At the time, I thought it was great that he was physically attracted to me and didn't see my intelligence as a turnoff. He wasn't intimidated by my brain, like most guys. As a matter of fact, he seemed up to the challenge. Two years later, I was sick to death of his competing with me about who was smarter, but when we first met, it was a relief to be —if not the "dumb" one—the "average" one in the relationship. I liked that he cared more about my tan legs and white teeth than what I scored on the SAT. Turns out, I was in love with the idea of being in love with someone like him.

But he wasn't in love with any part of me, unless you count the part that he could use to get ahead at work. He realized early on that I was likeable and smart and the perfect combination of ambitious and nice. He also figured out a way to use to his advantage my propensity to downplay my intelligence, a habit I'd cultivated thanks to yet another guy in my past. While that's a story for another time, the result of that experience is that I was constantly worried about being labeled a "nerd," so I often exaggerated or downright fabricated my cluelessness about everything from technology to auto mechanics to finances (although, admittedly, I am crap with money management). For years, I was in the closet about having my shit together, afraid that nobody would like me if they perceived me to be a know-it-all.

So when I came up with the idea for a sophisticated computer program that would revolutionize the way the library system catalogued and lent electronic books, I didn't tell anyone… except Todd. I thought of *everything* except the binary code. For that, I needed his help. And he seemed glad to provide it. It meant a few weekends of work for him, as opposed to months and months of conceptualizing and re-thinking and tweaking and perfecting for me, but I had planned to give him equal credit when I unveiled the idea. I felt that was only fair, after all, considering I wouldn't have been able to make my concept a reality without his input.

The night before I planned to present E-Lend to Brad, our boss, Todd left my apartment earlier than usual, claiming he had a headache. I jokingly told him it was just as well, since I needed to get a good night's sleep before my big day. His lingering kiss at my door gave me no clue as to what he was planning to do to me.

Work was already buzzing when I got there the next day at my usual time. One of my best friends, Sara Jo, was waiting for me at my desk and squeezed my arm, saying, "You must be so proud of Todd!"

When I laughed and asked her what he'd been bragging about in the break room this time, she slapped my shoulder gently and said, "Silly! I'm talking about his e-book cataloging program! The one he and Brad are presenting to the Executive Director in a meeting at the Main Branch right now."

I nearly lost my breakfast, until I realized she had to be joking. I didn't know how she even knew the punch line to that particular joke, but I figured Todd had put her up to it, knowing I'd be nervous and the perfect target for his gag.

"Very funny," I said drolly.

She looked offended that I didn't believe her and said, "Didn't your boyfriend even tell you he was developing the program? I mean, it must have taken him ages! How did you not know?"

Annoyed that he'd stolen my thunder a bit by telling Sara Jo about *our* program, I nevertheless smiled proudly and said, "We came up with it together. Actually, it was my idea, but he wrote the code, so—"

She raised her eyebrows at me. "You came up with E-Borrow?" she asked skeptically. I swear, she looked me up and down, too.

That day, I was wearing one of my favorite pinstripe suits with the ruffle-hemmed skirt, a square-necked red blouse, and a brand new pair of red patent leather peep-toe pumps I'd bought specifically for that occasion. In my laptop bag was the thumb drive with the program demo.

I didn't appreciate the incredulous tone she was using, so I said as icily as I could muster, "Actually, it's called E-*Lend*, and yes, I *did* invent it."

"Puh-lease. Shopping online for clothes is about as computer-savvy as you get, Kendall. Stop screwing around."

"I'm not kidding!" I insisted, fumbling in my bag for the flash drive.

Of course, it wasn't there. Because it was in Todd's hot little hands (yes, he had unusually small hands for a guy, and yes, there *is* a correlation) at the main branch of the Kansas City Public Library, where he was passing off my idea for his own.

Anyway, after that, it got ugly, with both Todd and me claiming that the other was a liar. Unfortunately, I didn't have any proof that the program was my idea. My contribution was all intellectual property, after all. Todd provided the tangibles; Todd had the flash drive with the demo; Todd had the only full copy of the program installed on his home computer, which was a lot bigger and more powerful than my three-year-old laptop; and Todd may have been blond and tan, but he wasn't busty, nor did he speak with an intermittent Southern drawl that made everyone downgrade his IQ by a few points every time he opened his mouth.

Most importantly, I didn't have a patent. Because Todd had told me that could wait. Guess what? Todd hadn't waited. He changed the name of the program from E-Lend to E-Borrow, which he then trademarked and patented.

So Todd won. Everything.

Our "friends" sided with him, the computer "genius." In the inquiry into my complaint that he stole my idea, they told everyone who asked that I didn't know how to program my DVR, much less come up with a system as complicated as E-Borrow. Lies. Lies that I had fed them for years. It still hurt, though, that when I came out of the closet, so to speak, they didn't believe me. Or rather, they believed that I was the type of person who would lie about something as sacred as intellectual property.

When the powers that be at work decided in favor of Todd, I knew my days there were over. I couldn't stand to be in the same city with him, much less the same building 40 hours a week. Nor did I want to be around my former friends. But before my two weeks' notice was even over, it became clear that I wouldn't be able to work in a public library in Missouri or the six other states in which the majority of their public libraries gobbled up licenses for E-Borrow (or as I came to think of it, "E-Pirate"). My parents urged me to sue him, but I figured if I couldn't convince a couple of librarians that I was capable of creating the program, then there was no way I was going to risk humiliation in a court of law. Anyway, a lawsuit would mean I'd have to keep seeing him.

And I never want to see him again.

Now Mom shakes her head, her eyes flashing angrily. "See? I knew this would happen. I'm so cotton-pickin' *pissed* at those people."

I always know she means business when she pulls out the

Southern accent she never has any other time except when she's fired up. The woman was born and raised in Colorado and lived there until she was in her forties. There's nothing natively Southern about her. But she really took to the Southern mama persona when we moved here. I was young and desperate to fit in, but even I haven't assumed the accent like she has.

"That they could take someone so happy and full of life," she continues, "and reduce her to someone who's unsure of herself and... and... cynical... it's a cryin' shame!"

"They're not worth your wrath, Ma," I say, trying to talk her down. "It's okay. Really. It's not *that* dire. I mean, I'm fine!" I give her a cheeky smile as proof.

"No, you're not! If you were fine, if you were the same girl you used to be, you'd be going after this Jamie person, because it's obvious you're attracted to him."

Inwardly, I cringe that it's that obvious, but I force myself to laugh lightly. "That's not the only criteria I have for 'going after' a guy. Anyway, *everyone's* attracted to him. You should see how the moms dress to drop off and pick up their kids. The cloud of perfume was so thick this morning that I could smell it all the way down the hall. And not a single pair of sweatpants among them. One woman—hand to heart—was wearing stilettos and a pair of jeans so tight that I'm pretty sure she could only make right turns."

Mom laughs so hard she nearly knocks over her wine-glass. Quickly cupping her hand over it, she leans against it as she gasps, "Oh, my gosh! That's hilarious."

"And the school principal—she's sixty if she's a day, but she's totally in love with him. He walks into a room, and she practically swoons. It drives one of the fourth grade teachers nuts. She hates him."

Narrowing her eyes, Mom defends a person she's never even met with, "Sounds like this fourth grade teacher has a major personality problem, if everyone else likes him."

"She's a cooter," I confirm. Mom, of course, understands exactly what I mean, since we've been using that word for years to describe any spiteful woman. "But Jamie... he's... I don't know how to explain it. He's so... interesting."

"In a good way, though, right?" she checks. "Not 'interesting,' like, 'he's covered in tattoos and is a Wiccan'?"

I roll my eyes. "He's a kindergarten teacher-slash-archaeologist who lives with and takes care of his mentally challenged older brother. You know, he's clean-cut and bookish and outdoorsy. He looks great in a pair of khakis. He has nice forearms."

"What about his eyes?"

"They're nice, too. Brown with little flecks of gold."

"And he has soft hair," she says, remembering my earlier assertion.

"Yes. None of that crunchy, gelled-up nonsense."

"Oooh, I hate that."

"Me too."

We ruminate on nice hair for a while; then I say, "But whatever. I don't want to get involved with someone at work."

"Nonsense!"

"I mean it! It's one of the biggest mistakes I ever made."

She leans over the table, closer to me. "Where else are you going to meet someone, huh? At the grocery store on a Friday night? Get real, Kendall. And your mistake was getting involved with Todd the Bod; it had nothing to do with where you met him."

I snicker but don't participate in the name-calling.

"Plus," she continues, warming to her subject now, "it's obvious Jamie's just as interested in you."

"You're crazy!" I scoff.

"He is! When he turned down our dinner invitation tonight, he made sure to tell you the nights he's potentially free. If he weren't interested, he'd have made up some vague excuse. But he specifically said, 'I can do Mondays, Wednesdays, and Fridays.'"

I pick at a loose thread on my napkin and grumble, "I love how it's '*our* dinner invitation' now. I invited him nowhere."

"Yeah, which is why it's a good thing you have me in your corner."

"To humiliate me?" I joke drily.

"To get you out there! I'm not saying you have to marry the guy. Just explore your feelings." Now her tone becomes more teasing. "You know… he's an archaeologist, right? Take him on an expedition or two."

"Mother!"

"So repressed," she laments.

"I'm not talking about sex with my mom!" The heat from my blush is probably making air conditioners kick on in the surrounding houses.

"Who said anything about sex?" she plays dumb. "I was talking about unearthing some… bones."

I'm glad it's now dark enough that she can't see the color of my face. "You're sick."

"*You* are."

We grin at each other, and she says, "Don't make me arrange a play date between the two of you. Stop being a chickenshit and ask him out."

Nobody else has a mother quite like mine.

CHAPTER NINE

Technically, I'm still mad at Jamie for the way he acted with Brody. That's what I keep trying to remind myself, anyway. I think it was wrong for him to leave the five-year-old out there alone in that tree. For someone who thinks he knows so much about kids, he sure screwed the pooch on that one. Not to mention how badly he misjudged Brody, in general. Being ready for kindergarten (or, as Jamie had suspected was Brody's problem, *too* ready) is about more than cognitive skills. It's about social development, too. And young Mr. Sawyer has a lot to learn in that department.

I also got a glimpse of one of Jamie's most unattractive character traits. Arrogance. Confidence: sexy; cockiness: hate it. The line between the two is fine, I'll admit, but there's a definite difference. I'm glad I saw that side of him, though. That's the kind of thing that usually waits to rear its hideous head until *after* I've decided I like a guy. In this case, Jamie's big mouth has saved me that hassle. *And* all I have to do when my hormones go rogue is remember his smug look when he talked about how great he was compared to Jane. It doesn't matter that it's probably true; only a jerk says it out loud.

So when the jerk drops off his students for their weekly library session today, I give him a curt, dismissive nod before turning my full attention to the kids. I refuse to be another panting member of the Jamie Chase Fan Club. He's just another guy who thinks he's the shit.

He seems to get the hint, because after I let the kids loose to look for books, and I go back to the counter to wait for one of them to need my help, I'm mostly relieved to see that he's gone.

Fortunately, I don't have much time to analyze my complicated feelings, because I notice Brody lingering at one of the catalog computers.

"Hey!" I say to him. "You want to look up some books about cats?"

He nods shyly. "But not cartoon cats."

I smile. "Right. No cartoon cats."

I come around the counter and invite him to sit down at the computer. He takes charge of the mouse like it's another appendage, so all I have to do is point to where he should click. I don't even have to tell him how to type in the word "cat." He, of course, knows how to spell it, and he seems to know his way around a computer keyboard. Actually, I feel sort of superfluous.

However, he still needs me to read some things for him and to help him decide which books to go look for. While I'm writing down the call numbers, I hear a commotion behind us.

"I had it first!" says a little girl with long, gleaming dark hair, her hands clamped on one side of a large, flat book.

"Nuh-uh!" The hands gripping the other side of the

book belong to the blonde pigtailed girl I remember from the playground yesterday as Hannah.

"I'll be right back," I mumble to Brody before walking over to the girls, nervousness building in my belly. "Hey," I say quietly. "Let's not fight over the books. There are plenty to go around."

Neither girl takes her eyes off the other one, but Hannah says, "I want to check out *this* book."

"Too bad!" her rival retorts at a volume that makes me cringe.

"All right, all right!" I raise my voice just enough to be heard as the rest of the class crowds around to see what the scuttlebutt is. "First of all, we all need to lower our voices. The library is a quiet place."

"But Jill-the-Pill took the book *I* wanted!" Hannah cries, giving the book a good yank in an effort to wrest it from Jill's hands.

"Stop it!"

"No!"

Eff this. I take the *My Little Pony* book away from both children, who blink up at me as if they've just realized I'm actually here and not some disembodied voice addressing them from speakers in the ceiling.

Holding the book away from their reach, I say, "Now. No more yelling."

Both girls start to cry. Loudly. And they caterwaul over each other, competing to see who can produce the most tears, snot, and noise.

"You're a mean liberrian!"

"I want the book! I had it first!"

"It's not fair!"

"I'm telling my mommy!"

"I'm telling Mr. Chase."

My mouth is dry, and my heart is pounding from all this drama and confrontation. I try to take a deep breath, but my lungs will only expand to about a quarter of their capacity before they feel like they're going to burst.

"Stop crying," I squeak.

But neither of them hears me. The rest of the kids know a vulnerable situation when they see one and begin feeding off the tension, taking advantage of the growing disorder to settle any grudges they may have with each other, however unrelated they are to what's currently happening. I see poking, and one boy stomps on another boy's foot. Shoving breaks out between another pair of boys; then I see a girl's head jerk backwards suddenly as a boy jumps at the opportunity to pull her hair.

The roaring blood in my ears is mercifully drowning out what I know must be a lot of racket, but I feel powerless to stop it. "Please, quiet down," I meekly request, wishing I had a whistle around my neck.

As if my wish has been heard by a magical teacher-fairy, a piercing whistle cuts through the chaos. Everyone—myself included—freezes and cups their hands over their ears.

I turn to face the source and see Jamie leaning up against the counter, the playground whistle still secured between his teeth but his face blank. When Jill lets loose a tiny sob, he raises an eyebrow at her, opens his mouth, and lets the whistle drop and dangle from his neck.

"I'm sorry, but I didn't authorize this mayhem," he states quietly, looking from face to face. "I actually remember that before we came down here, I specifically instructed you all to be on your best behavior, did I not?"

Despite his use of fifth-grade vocabulary, each and every student nods his or her understanding.

"Okay, then." He turns to me and asks, "What's going on?"

I'm not sure if it's the intense way he's looking at me or my embarrassment at having to be "rescued" from a bunch of five-year-olds or a combination of both, but I find myself tongue-tied and can't seem to explain the situation, much less how I let it get so out of control.

Hannah takes the opportunity to make good on her threat to tattle on me to Jamie, but he cuts her off. "Uh, no! I don't actually want to hear any of *your* stories." When it's obvious he's not going to hear mine, either, he addresses his entire class. "I want to hear *nothing* while everyone picks a book and takes it calmly and quietly to Miss Dickinson at the counter, where she will help you check out. Then you will line up on the wall, by the doors, and wait without making a peep until everyone has their book. Everyone pickin' up what I'm puttin' down?"

Again, twenty-five nods.

"Excellent. Make wise reading choices, because you will *not* be going to afternoon recess; instead, you'll be reading your books at your desks while Mrs. Carson's class gets all the playground equipment to themselves. Now... go."

As if they've simply been playing a serious game of statues, they spring into action, sedately selecting books from the shelves like creepy little robots.

Jamie turns his attention to me. "Sorry about taking over, but you seemed like you could use some help."

Humiliated by my complete lack of control of the situation, I mumble, "Thanks," before averting my flushed face. "I, uh, need to help Brody find his books."

And with that, I hurry to the nonfiction shelves, where Brody's inconveniently already figured out the call number system without my help.

He holds up two books. "I don't know which one to pick," he says, looking rapturously from one to the other. The cover of the book in his left hand features a kitten playing with a ball of yarn and is called, *Before You Choose a Cat: A Guide to Cat Breeds*. The book in his right hand is called, simply, *CATS!* and bears a picture of two sleeping kittens curled up together like a feline yin and yang.

Before I can answer, Jamie butts in behind me. "Dude. You gotta go with the sleeping cats. Look how cute they are!"

"That was going to be my *vote,"* I want to whine, like Hannah and Jill. But in a very adult-like fashion, I swallow my displeasure and agree, "Yeah. You already know all the stuff in that other book, for sure. Get something that's fun and will make you smile."

"Okay!" He returns the more scientific book to the shelf, carefully checking to make sure it's in the right place (which I *really* appreciate), before bouncing toward the checkout counter, where there's already a line waiting for me.

Feeling somewhat recovered from my earlier mortification, I slip behind the counter and set aside the highly coveted *My Little Pony* book. My focus from here on out will be on getting through the rest of the class.

Addressing the first person in line, I say, "Well, hello there! Did you find what you wanted?"

The boy nods shyly.

"Great."

Repeat that process seventeen times, and we come to Brody, who's already looked through his book while waiting in line. "Look!" he says excitedly, plopping the open book onto the counter and pointing to a picture of a velvety grayish-blue cat. "My favorite! A Russian Blue!"

"The kind that has lots of diabetes?" I ask seriously.

I hear a snort in my periphery, but I don't look at its owner, who I suspect is smirking and wondering where the heck that factoid came from. I may not understand frilly little girls who fight over books about pastel ponies, but I get this kid. And some people—people who think they're oh-so-experienced and know everything there is to know about a child's psyche—can stuff it if they think I'm strange because I can identify with such a unique child. Jealous. That's what they are.

Brody glances at his teacher but returns his attention to me. "Yeah! How'd you know that?"

"You told me, remember?"

"Oh. Yeah. Duh."

I scan the bar code on the back cover and slide the book across the counter to him. "There you go. Remember to bring it back next Friday so you can get that other cat book you wanted."

The next two people in line are Jill and Hannah. When Jill slaps her second-choice book on the counter, I see her peek at her first-choice book at my elbow. She glowers at me.

Emboldened by her disrespectful attitude, I say, "You can glare at me all you want, sweetie, but nobody's getting that book today. Maybe next time, if you can learn to obey the rules, and nobody else has checked it out."

She crosses her arms across her chest and actually harumphs at me, which makes me laugh.

"Okay, then." I scan her book and hand it back to her. "I'm sure you'll like the *Hannah Montana* book just as much."

"You're a poop-head," she mutters bravely as she's turning away from me to get in line at the door.

My eyes widen, but I don't say anything. I figure it's best to ignore a brat like that.

Jamie has other ideas. "Excuse me? Little Miss, what did you say to Miss Dickinson?"

I want to tell him to forget it, but I don't want to undermine him in front of one of his students, so I keep quiet and continue checking out books for the students in my line.

When Jill stares him down, he goes around the counter and kneels down to her level. "You don't have to repeat it for me to know what you said, but you *do* have to apologize to Miss Dickinson."

"No!" she refuses.

Jamie points to the library doors and says, "Let's go. You need to pay a visit to Ms. Twomey, I think, and your mom needs to get a phone call."

"I don't care. My mama's gonna beat up that mean liberry teacher."

"March," is the only thing Jamie says in response to that threat. Over his shoulder, he says to me, "I'll be right back."

After he leaves, I despair at what a horrible start I've had with this particular class of kindergartners, so when the last child has his book, and they're all lined up like little angels on the wall and waiting for Jamie to come back, I bend over and rest my weight on my elbows on the counter. "What do you guys think about the decorations in the library? Do you have any favorite books or characters you'd like me to have pictures of?"

I get zero response. One boy actually puts his hand over his mouth and shakes his head.

"Oh! It's okay to talk now. You won't get in trouble with Mr. Chase."

Still nothing.

"Okay… never mind."

Brody comes to my rescue. "I like history stuff," he reveals.

"Like what?" I ask, grasping onto his lifeline.

He bites his lower lip and looks up into his shaggy blond bangs. "Umm, I dunno. Prolly, like, the *Titanic*."

His answer surprises me, but I write it down on a pad of post-it notes I keep handy. The Titanic will make for a nice, visual display, and I'm sure I won't have trouble finding material for it.

"Anyone else?"

Hannah rolls her eyes at me (when did kindergartners get so sassy?), but the girl next to her, whose name I think starts with a "P" (Parker? Priscilla? I've *got* to pay better attention and get these names memorized) says, "I like stuff about outer space. You know, planets and stars and stuff."

"That's another good idea!" I tell her. Then I see Jamie through the transom window next to the library door before he pulls it open, so I say, "Thanks for the suggestions, you two. Maybe the rest of you can think about it and give me some ideas next week?"

The response to that is a lukewarm murmur, but it's better than what I got earlier, so I'll take it.

"Great!" I say, as if my every word has been met with cheers and clapping. "See you guys later, then. Have a great weekend!"

Jamie shoots me a strange look and says to his class, "Okay, let's move. Who wants to march like soldiers?" When their stomping echoes in the hall, he quickly qualifies, "Silent soldiers! On a secret mission! Shhhh!"

When the door closes behind the last student, I slump further so that I'm lying across the counter, similarly to the way Jamie did the night of the Open House when he laughed at my ignorance regarding one of the most beloved children's book series of all time.

I'm exhausted and so relieved that Jamie's class is my last

one of the week that I feel on the verge of tears. As the Formica counter under my torso warms to my body heat, I think, *It's like Jamie and I are chest-to-chest.*

That crazy, uninhibited thought makes me stand ramrod straight and blush. *What the hell?* I wonder at myself. I'm tired. That's all. I'm burnt out from all the stress and the new experiences and… and… it's my mom's fault! She's put ideas into my head about bones! And soft hair and warm eyes.

Oh, gosh. I need a weekend.

CHAPTER TEN

I've made it through the past month of school without crying. I didn't think that would be possible after the first two weeks, when I cried every night before bed and sometimes in the shower each morning. It's not that the job was so terrible after I got used to it and the kids got used to me. Most of them tolerate me now, and a few even seem to like me. No, the cause of the tears isn't any one thing that I can identify, which is what makes it even trickier. It's just... this isn't what I thought I'd be doing with my life. I can't quite seem to let go of the dream I had started to let myself believe when I developed E-Lend. I want to feel that way again, and I can't imagine this life doing it for me. Ever.

But it's gotten better. Like I've said before, I don't believe in depression. I mean, I'm not a moron; I know it exists, and I know it's a serious thing that affects many people, but I don't have any tolerance for it in myself. Until recently, I've been a winner. If I wanted something, I worked for it and got it. It's not that failure was never an option; it was never a *possibility*. And technically, I don't feel that I'm a failure in my current life. But I'm not what I truly want to be, and that's almost the same thing, in my book.

So after the second staff breakfast meeting of the school year, as we're walking to our classes, I start the first personal conversation I've had with Jamie in weeks by saying, "How do you do it?"

He quickly looks over at me, half-smiles and says, "Well, when a boy and a girl really like each other—"

I can't help but laugh through my melancholy. "I'm serious!"

"So am I. Do you want to know how *I* specifically do it, because that's kind of personal and not appropriate work-place conversation." He murmurs the last part conspiratorially and leans in closer to me as we arrive at the hallway's intersection. I make a left with him and walk toward his room.

"I agree. So, what I'm asking is this: how do you do something every day that's—at best—your second choice, career-wise?"

He sighs. "It's not my second choice."

"But you said—"

"I told you, I was in a funk. This job is my first choice among all the jobs available to me at this time in my life."

I jump on that qualifier. "Okay, but you'd rather be digging in a desert somewhere, unearthing dinosaur bones, or whatever, right?"

Stepping aside to let me enter the room before him, he says, "Some days. But other times I'm glad I'm in a climate-controlled building, wearing clean clothes and working predictable eight-hour days, with easy access to indoor plumbing." He crosses the room and sits in the chair behind his desk, leaning back in it with his hands on top of his head. "To be honest, sometimes digs are boring. A lot of dirt, a lot of sifting and brushing and examining things, most of the time for nothing. Tedious as heck."

"And kids aren't tedious?"

He shrugs. "Not if you remember to think like them." When I don't have an answer to that, he asks, "What's this all about, anyway? You've hardly said two words to me since the first week of school, and now you want to talk about my career goals?"

Quickly checking the clock to verify we have a few minutes before the first bell rings, I sit cross-legged on top of his clean, empty desk.

"Make yourself comfortable there," he cracks.

I ignore him and answer his questions. "I'm not asking you about your career goals; I'm asking for advice. How am I going to make it through the next eight months—or eight years—doing something that's not what I really want to do?"

He props his feet on the edge of his desk and taps my knee with the toe of his shoe. "Why would you have to?" is his rejoinder. "It's obvious why I can't do what I originally studied to do, but what's stopping you? You're free as a bird."

"It's not about obligations or limitations in the traditional sense," I acknowledge, picking at a tiny imperfection in the denim weave of my jeans. I donated five dollars to breast cancer awareness for the privilege of wearing them on this Casual Friday.

He (incorrectly) anticipates my next statement when he says, "Even if you wanted to live close to your parents, like you do now, surely you can find a more traditional position at a public library, which is what you'd obviously prefer."

"It's not about my parents or where I live."

"Then what? Every town in the country with a certain population has a library. You could live anywhere."

If the price of his advice is telling him my whole sordid history, it's not worth it.

I hop down from his desk. "Never mind. I thought you'd have a quick tip, like 'I go to the shooting range after work every day and put fifty bullets in a target,' or 'I eat a bag of Cheetos in front of the TV every night.'"

"Those things'll kill you," he jokes, standing in front of me and blocking my way to the door. "Listen. There's no magic cure for apathy. You just have to get over it. Or change your life. I think it's funny that you think I have the answer."

"Forget it." I chuckle and shake my head, as if I agree it's funny, but really, I'm kicking myself. I should have known better than to even come close to confiding in him.

Grinning, he says, "No! I'm sorry I'm making light of something that's obviously weighing on you, but I don't know what you want me to say."

"Nothing. Like I said, forget it." I give him my 100-watt smile.

"I don't want to, though. Wait!" He sidesteps when I try to weave through the squat desks and cuts me off before I can get to the door. "I'll think of something. Give me a second."

I roll my eyes and let my arms drop limply to my sides while I humor him.

He taps his plump (not that I've ever noticed) lower lip and looks up at the ceiling. "Hmm… what do I do to blow off steam? Not stress-eating. Oh! I take long rides on my bike."

Now he has my attention. "You cycle?"

He nods. "A little. Now that the weather's cooler, I'll be

cycling to work a lot more. But even in the summer, I spend a lot of time in the evenings and on the weekends on my bike. Why? You ride?"

I try to act casual, but my heart's thumping at this common interest. My parents introduced me to cycling at a young age, and there were no training wheels allowed... ever. We rode everywhere together; it's something that I've never lost interest in. This town isn't very cycle-friendly, though, so I haven't figured out a good route to get me from my apartment to work without getting killed. Jamie's obviously a lot braver than I am, if he often rides his bike to work. Not to mention, as he just pointed out, it's only recently been cool enough in the mornings.

Trying not to picture all the posters of Lance Armstrong that are still plastered on the walls in my old bedroom at Mom and Dad's, I understate blandly, "I like to ride."

"What kind of bike do you have?"

I suspect this is a test of my cycling mettle, so I can't resist bragging just a bit. "I have a Trek Lane," I pronounce proudly.

He makes a low whistle through his teeth. "Wow. That's a pretty serious bike."

"'Pretty serious'? It cost me an entire paycheck. What do you tool around on, a Schwinn?"

"Hey! Schwinn makes a nice bike—but no. I have a Litespeed."

I will not let on that I'm impressed. "Which model?"

He chuckles at me. "An Ultegra."

Damn. I feel stupid for bragging about my $1500 bike, when he easily spent twice that on his.

"Nice bike," I allow.

The bell rings loudly, making me jump.

"I like it," he says easily. "It was an investment. I take

good care of it."

"Maybe we can go riding sometime," I suggest, but it doesn't come out sounding like the warmest of invitations. "I mean, if you want to."

If I have to tell the truth (and I usually do, because that's how I was raised), I'm lonely. I miss having friends. And I'm not meeting anyone here, because I'm exhausted by the end of the day. It's all I can do to make it home—or to Mom and Dad's—to flop on the couch and stare blankly at the TV for four hours before dragging myself to bed. I'm also not interested in rekindling any of my old friendships from high school. That would be depressing after all these years, like I'd never done anything with my life or gone anywhere else.

The only person who has piqued my interest in the slightest since I've returned to my hometown is Jamie. Unfortunately. I must be a glutton for punishment.

As the students start streaming in and pushing their way past us to get to their desks, he smiles broadly and answers, "Yeah. I *would* like that."

Men are scum, I remind myself now when I find myself staring too intently at his dimples and fighting the urge to look down at his furry forearms, which are peeking fetchingly from his rolled-up shirtsleeves.

Brody sits down at the desk right next to where I'm standing and says, "Miss Dickinson, there's no such thing as Naked Day."

"What?"

Oblivious to my shock at his non sequitur, he attests, "Nope. During Spirit Week, we have Pajama Day, Wacky Hair Day, School Colors Day, Mismatch Day, and Flip-Flops Day, but no Naked Day."

"It's a crying shame," Jamie manages to say with a

completely straight face.

Now that I'm sure Brody wasn't reading my mind when he broached the topic, I try to be equally blasé about it when I tell him, "Well, there are only five days in a school week, so there was no room for Naked Day."

Brody hangs his backpack on the back of his chair and declares, "We should get rid of Mismatch Day and have Naked Day instead."

"Preferably on a Friday," Jamie agrees.

I try not to read too much into that statement and instead, on my way out, I tell Brody, "Maybe you should suggest it to Ms. Twomey. See what she has to say about that."

"Good idea!" he approves. "I'll tell her at lunch today."

I hurry to the library and barely make it inside the doors before laughing out loud.

❧

Brody will have to wait on that brainstorming session with the principal, because she's waiting for me in the library. I almost jump out of my shoes when her voice interrupts my laughter at Brody's latest gem.

"Well, that's a big laugh for such a little thing!"

I push away from the door that I've been using to support myself.

"Ms. Twomey! Uh… good morning."

"How many times do I have to tell you?" she asks as she re-shelves the book she was perusing before I entered and faces me. "Call me Renalda. Nobody calls me Ms. Twomey. Lands! They musta been real formal-like up there in Kansas City."

I merely smile tightly.

"Anyway, I'm here to ask you a favor."

At this announcement, I go behind the checkout counter, where I'm in easy reach of pen and paper to take notes, if necessary. Renalda stands opposite me and fidgets nervously.

"Well, the thing is, the Superintendent of schools, Dr. Underhill, says he wants each school in the district to come up with an 'innovative educational practice,' and... then each idea will be presented to the School Board, who's gonna choose the best one to be put into practice district-wide." She drums her fingers on the counter. "And, uh... well, the thing is... I... I have no idea where to even start."

Dread builds in the pit of my stomach as I realize what she's getting at. "You want *me* to come up with Whitehall's idea?"

She seems relieved that I didn't make her say it. "Yes!"

"Why me?" my terror makes me blurt.

Not meeting my eyes, she answers, "Well, you know, you're young and seem to be fairly techno-savvy, which I can't say for myself on either front. And I've been watchin' you with the kids—"

"You have?" Now I'm horrified. I can only imagine what she's seen in the past six weeks as I've fumbled my way through one awkward interaction after another.

"Of course, I have! That's my job, isn't it?"

Frankly, I don't know how to answer that. I'm not sure what she does all day. I know that Sam operates in a constant state of crisis and always seems to be looking for our boss and that Renalda is rarely present when I go to the office for anything. Sam confided in me once that the principal often takes two hour lunches and returns to the building with a fresh cut and color and that, on more than one occasion, Renalda has let slip that she was with her live-in boyfriend of nearly two decades when she was supposed to be at a meeting at the district offices. And if she's patrolling the hallways or peeking into classrooms, she's one of the stealthiest people in the world, because this is one of the first times I've seen her away from her desk (unless you count frequent visits to the vending machines in the teachers' lounge).

Fortunately, her question's rhetorical, so she continues, "You treat the kids like they're your equals, and I think they respect you for that."

"Thanks, but that doesn't mean I'll be able to come up with some kind of fancy curriculum."

"Oh, it's nothin' *that* complicated," she reassures me. "I think the example Dr. Underhill used from another district was some sort of special fair to get girls more interested in math and science. Or somethin'. I don't remember quite what he said; I'd spilled my coffee in my lap and was kinda distracted durin' his presentation…"

"But…" I don't know how to say the next thing without exposing myself as the fraud I am, so I simply say it and hope it comes off sounding more like humility than what it actually is. "I'm not an educator. I know nothing about learning styles or anything like that."

She waves away my objections and moves toward the door, obviously thinking the conversation is over. "You'll be great. And you can always ask some of your fellow teachers for help and ideas. I'm sure there's a certain kindergarten teacher that'll be more than happy to discuss things with you… possibly over dinner or drinks?" And with a sly look and a cutesy wave of her fingers, she hustles from the library, no doubt late for a manicure or something.

I'm going to have to try valiantly not to break my streak of tear-free days.

CHAPTER ELEVEN

A part of me doesn't want to play into Renalda's transparent matchmaking scheme, but the rest of me doesn't know who else to turn to, so when Jamie drops off his class for their weekly library session, I pull him aside and whisper, "I need to talk to you later. Are you free after school?"

"I guess," he says. "What's up?"

"Too much to explain right now," I insist with a shake of my head. "I'll meet you down in your room after all the kids and parents have cleared out." Which, in his class's case, means about thirty minutes after the final bell. Moms tend to linger longer around him than the other teachers.

He smirks. "Intriguing. Do we need to synchronize watches?"

I wish I didn't like his gooberish sense of humor so much. I wish I could be the cool girl who rolls her eyes at him and walks away without another word. But, alas; I'm the girl who giggles and bats her eyelashes at him like an idiot. I wish I could roll my eyes and walk away from myself.

Guys at work are not for play, I fiercely remind myself.

Using the students as a way out of this uncomfortable situation, I clap my hands, approach the "reading pit," and tell them to gather around for our selection of the day, *Harold and the Purple Crayon*. I could use a magic crayon to draw myself into a whole new life. I don't care what color it is.

❧

Despite waiting an interminable twenty-five minutes after the dismissal bell, I can see through the exit doors closest to Jamie's classroom that he's still out on the sidewalk, talking to one of the moms. Correction: he's standing there with his hands in his pockets while she's talking animatedly with her hands as she tosses her hair and sticks out her chest. And what a chest it is, too! She's obviously best friends with Vicky Secret, who has provided her with the tools to maximize what God gave her.

I sigh and enter his room, where I wander around while I wait for Suzy and the Twins to release Jamie from what I'm sure is a riveting conversation about Little Tommy's off-the-charts reading skills or never-before-seen Play-Doh sculpting vision. (Why do all parents seem to think their kids are geniuses?)

My first stop is an area of the room that immediately makes me smile and forget about the hassle that is dealing with high-maintenance parents. It's a plastic kiddie pool filled with sand and surrounded by professional-grade sieves, screens, shovels, and brushes. A partial—I'm assuming plastic—dinosaur skeleton pokes through one mound of sand. A few feet from there sits a small table with "artifacts" lined up on its surface. On closer inspection, I see an arrowhead, a shark's tooth, some foreign-looking coins, and a plastic teacup. So clever! I bet the kids love this part of the room, which surely comes in handy on days when recess has to be held inside due to uncooperative weather.

And *this* is why I need Jamie's help with the project Renalda has dumped into my lap. He's creative. *Plus*, he has a teaching degree, which has trained him to turn just about anything into a learning opportunity.

I used up my one good idea in life on E-Lend.

Before I can think too much about the unfairness of that, I move over to where Jamie's written a series of the students' Haikus on a giant whiteboard. I seek out Brody's name, knowing his take on the ancient form of poetry has to be interesting, if not downright hilarious, and I'm not disappointed. His is called, "Sick" and reads:

Stomach hurts real bad.

Medicine tastes like earwax.

TV is boring.

I'm chuckling at this blunt summary when Jamie rushes into the room.

"Oh, good. You're still here," he observes.

"I am," I reply, following the conversational trend of stating the obvious. I point to Brody's Haiku. "Classic Brody Sawyer there. You'd better keep that for when he's famous someday."

He rolls his eyes, but I can tell he's proud of the work when he says, "He's the only one who got it. And at least his subject matter was a little deeper than what his favorite color is."

"Haiku's pretty advanced for kindergartners, though, right?"

"It's more of an exercise in counting syllables," he replies as he places chairs on top of desks so that Freddie can come in later and mop the floors. "Anyway, I like to set the bar high."

Automatically, I pitch in. Gives me something to focus on other than the muscles in his forearms, which are displayed quite nicely below his pushed-back shirtsleeves. Is it weird that I have a thing for guys' forearms? I mean, biceps are one thing. Then there's the obvious butt obsession. Even an admiration of guys' legs is pretty standard. But forearms? I think that's not normal.

He interrupts my in-depth self-analysis with, "So, what's up? Did you figure out the secret to contentment while eating your rectangular pizza at lunch today? I find those tiny pepperoni cubes to be quite inspirational, personally."

I laugh. "No. I have much bigger problems, now, than how I'm going to get through my work days," I inform him.

He grasps the legs of the chair on the desk in front of him. "What could possibly have happened in less than eight hours?" he wonders.

I place the last chair in my row on top of its desk. "It actually took less than five minutes from when I talked to you this morning." I tell him about the conversation with Renalda, minus her parting shot about dinner and drinks with him. He listens impassively until I say, "I need your help."

Then he laughs. "Oh you do, do you?"

"Please, don't make me beg," I say, already halfway to pleading.

He shakes his head and wends his way to the blackboard, which he starts erasing in long, aggressive strokes. "I have so many questions that I don't know where to start," he says. "First of all, why did she come to you?"

"Jealous?"

"No! Just wondering." He drops the eraser onto the chalk tray with a poof of dust and turns to face me.

Well, I can't very well tell him, can I? I can if I'm a moron. "I think she's trying to fix us up."

The dismay on his face is not what I expected. "Really? Oh, shit. What is the deal with that woman? I was never so relieved to see a co-worker get knocked up and married as I was when it happened to Julia. At least it killed Renalda's dreams of a wedding in the main hallway."

"Oh."

"No offense. And not that I'm expecting you to go to the same lengths."

"Thanks."

"You know what I mean, though. You get two single people of the same age working together with a bunch of other older people, and it's automatically assumed they should hook up. It's tiring, that's all," he explains as he pushes away from the blackboard.

"Totally," I agree easily, managing a convincing snicker at the expense of the matchmakers. "Anyway, my point is that I think she would have come to you first—you were probably her first choice, actually—but you would have taken the assignment and run with it all by yourself, whereas she knew I was going to have to ask for help, and you would be my obvious go-to guy."

He raises his eyebrows. "Why would she jump to that conclusion? It's not like we're best friends."

"It's like you said," I explain. "Same basic age, both single… Wishful thinking on her part? Anyway, that's not important. The thing is, she's right." When he looks sharply at me, I quickly clarify, "I need help with this. And who else am I going to ask? Jane? Esther-The-Broken-Record Wambaugh? Not only don't I like them very much, but I don't think they have an original idea between them. Julia's about to go on maternity leave, and I don't know anybody else more than to say 'hey' to them in the hallway."

"That's a sad story, but…" He busies himself packing papers into one of the compartments of his laptop bag.

"Jamie." My firm tone gets his attention. His hands freeze, but he refuses to look at me. "I don't want this responsibility."

"I don't want it either!"

"I'm not asking you to take it on alone. C'mon—it'll be fun!"

We both laugh at how lame and false that sounds as soon as it leaves my mouth.

When we've recovered, I say more seriously, "It would mean a lot to me. I have no idea what I'm doing, and I'm going to humiliate myself if left to my own devices."

"That's not my problem!" The way he says it, though, tells me he's decided to have mercy on me. He shakes his head as if he can't believe he's about to agree to help me. Then he points at me and says, "I'm holding you to your promise that it's going to be fun."

"I was lying, though."

"Too bad. You better find a way to make it happen."

I'll have to rediscover my "fun" gene, but I guess it's the least I can do.

CHAPTER TWELVE

This is slightly uncomfortable, but I'm okay with it. I'm willing to put up with some "uneasy" if it means I don't have to come up with Whitehall's contribution to this district-wide competition all by myself. *That* would be much more untenable. Getting together at Jamie's house to brainstorm ideas on a Monday night is worth it. Even if I did get lost three times on my way here and had to finally call my dad for directions to the correct Peacock Court, which was several blocks south of the Peacock Court where I currently was. Why can't this town have a normal grid street system like every other rational city in the country? Because North Carolinians thrive on being original, that's why.

Anyway, now I'm here, parking my car on the curb in front of a tidy bungalow that does *not* feature a couch on its front porch, surprisingly enough. For some reason, I had it in my head that Jamie and his brother still lived like frat boys, despite the fact that their college days are years (or in Johnny's case, decades) behind them. But this place is nice. The paint looks fresh, the landscaping is well-maintained...

if I didn't know better, I'd say a woman lived here. I'm such a sexist!

Eventually, I muster the courage to exit my car and make my way up the stone-paved walk that leads to the porch steps. Then I try not to fidget too much while I wait for someone to answer my knock.

Was it too timid, though? What if they didn't hear it? Maybe I should ring the bell. I hate doorbells. They seem so intrusive and impatient. Which I'm not. But maybe I should ring the doorbell in this case. Or what if they heard me knock, but they're just taking a while to get to the door? If I ring the bell, I'll seem too eager. But if they didn't hear me, I could be standing out here a while. Or, worse, if someone comes to look out the front window to see if I've arrived, I'll be standing here on the porch, looking like a weirdo. I'd rather seem like an overeager dork than like a creepy person who lingers on porches without effectively announcing her arrival.

I ring the bell, but my finger hasn't even stopped pressing the lit-up button before the door swings open.

Damn! I knew it! Fuck, shit, balls!

"Hi!" I smile sweetly at the stranger on the other side of the screen who looks vaguely like Jamie, in a grayer, chubbier way.

He blinks once and again before saying, "Hello. Are you here to pick me up?"

"What? Oh. No. I don't think so."

Huh? I *know* so. Why am I confusing both of us with that bizarre answer?

After a swift mental kick to my own ass, I declare confidently, "I'm Kendall. I'm here to see Jamie."

He opens the door for me. "I'm Johnny. Jamie's in the bathroom, but I'm not supposed to tell you that. I'm supposed to say"—he gazes up at the ceiling as if he's reading from a cue card there—"'Jamie will be right out. Please have a seat and make yourself comfortable.'"

I bite my lip so I won't laugh. "Oh. Okay. Thanks."

I drop my tote bag by a coat tree next to the front door and sit on the loveseat. Despite the other seating choices available in the room, Johnny takes up residence on the cushion right next to me. It's a little close for comfort, but I pretend it doesn't bother me. It bothers me more that I have no idea what to say to this guy. Thankfully, he's not shy.

"I'm going to play Bingo tonight. I think Frank is picking me up, like always. You knock sort of like Frank."

"Oh. Sorry."

"That's all right. I just noticed it. Frank and me are buddies."

"That's nice. Are you good at bingo?"

I didn't think it could be possible, but it appears that I'm worse at interacting with people with mental disabilities than I am with children.

He nods but doesn't verbally address my inane question at all. "You're nice. Jamie's other girlfriend isn't nice. She tells Jamie to put me in a home with people who drool. I want her to fall in a hole in the ground."

I don't know what to say to that other than, "Well, I'm not Jamie's girlfriend."

Again, he seems to ignore what I've said and continues his train of thought. "She's prettier than you are, but lots of times pretty girls aren't very nice."

Hmmm… I try to follow the logic. Is he saying I'm ugly? He said I was nice. Then he said pretty girls *aren't* nice. Therefore, I think that means he thinks I'm *not* pretty. Okay. Hurts the ego, but I've been insulted in harsher ways. He's actually being fairly diplomatic about it.

The only thing I can think to say next is, "Jamie has a girlfriend?"

Johnny shrugs. "Sometimes."

It's a puzzling answer, but I'm beginning to resign myself to the fact that I'm not meant to understand what's going on in this conversation.

"Okay."

"I hate her."

"I gathered that with the whole thing about how you want her to fall into a hole in the ground." When he doesn't reply but merely stares off into space, I say uncertainly, "Anyway…"

I look down at my hands in my lap, and that's when I see it. *It.* His… well, there's no way to put it more politely than to say that he has a very obvious, very large erection. I'm not sure what's causing this (and I'm not sure I want to know), but there it is.

There. It. Is.

"Oh, gosh!"

Instinctually, I jump from the couch and skitter across the room. It's not that I'm afraid of it or that I feel threatened, since he's sitting there perfectly calmly, looking away from me, appearing as if he could be contemplating something as innocuous as the color of the evening sky outside the window. Rather, I'm caught off-guard and startled by the randomness of the whole thing. I guess talking about mean girls falling into holes in the ground does it for him. Or that mean girl, in particular. Again, I don't want to know why this is happening. I merely want it to stop happening. I can't stop looking at it.

Jamie picks that exact moment to enter the room. I barely glance up at him before my eyes (over which I apparently have no control right now) move right back to the tent in Johnny's lap. I turn completely away, basically putting my nose against the wall like a naughty child in time-out, but it's not quickly enough.

Jamie follows my line of sight and curses under his breath. But he's remarkably patient and calm when he says, "Hey. Dude. You're a little excited there."

I half-turn to see what Johnny's reaction to this information is. Surely, he knows!

He snaps out of his trance and looks down at his lap before saying on a sigh, "Yeah."

Jamie widens his eyes and tilts his head. "Well, that's not appropriate when we have a guest. Why don't you go wait for Frank on the front porch? Some fresh air might do you some good."

Obligingly, Johnny stands and walks to the front door. "Okay. Good idea." At the door, he turns as he's stepping onto the porch. "It was nice to meet you, Kendall. I hope you guys have fun tonight."

"Uh, thanks. Yeah. You, too, Johnny. See you around." I'm sweating and blushing and have a strong urge to laugh or cry, although I'm not sure which one.

As soon as the front door is closed, Jamie turns to me with his hand on the back of his neck. He looks as if he feels about the same way I do when he says, "Sorry about that. He's... well, you know. I already told you that he's... not quite... like us."

Uh, yeah! He seemed to have left out the part about the spontaneous woodies in his original telling, though. Or did I space that out? No. I would have remembered that.

As if he's reading my mind, he adds, "That's one of the odder, more embarrassing side effects of his particular type of brain injury. It doesn't mean anything."

"Good! I mean, *not* good! I mean, I know what you

mean... I think." A giggle slips out, so I slap my hand over my mouth. Tersely, I tell myself, *You are an adult. Boners aren't funny. They're biological. Especially when someone has one that's not even related to anything sexual... as far as we know.* But my scolding conscience's use of the word "boner" doesn't help matters at all.

A giant bubble of laughter pops from my chest. Through my watering eyes, I can see Jamie barely holding onto his own amusement at the situation. When he lets go, I feel like it's okay to stop resisting, but I still don't want Johnny, sitting patiently on the front porch swing and waiting for his ride on the other side of the living room wall, to hear me, so I snort and wheeze painfully as I try to laugh as quietly as possible.

Jamie reassures me, "It's okay. He has no idea we're laughing at him. It wouldn't even occur to him that we are "

"How do you know?" I ask when I can breathe, since I'm still not convinced.

"I've lived with the guy for years. He could be sitting right there on the couch, still, and it would be totally beyond him why we're laughing. That part of his brain is just broken, I guess."

I wipe the tears from my face and take a deep breath. "I am *so* sorry that I'm laughing."

"Don't be! I'm glad you're not freaked out."

"Oh, I was," I admit. "I was totally freaking out when I first noticed."

Rubbing one of the earpiece on his glasses, he reassures me, "He wouldn't hurt you—"

"No, no, no! I didn't think that at all." Now I blush anew. "No. I was surprised, that's all."

He looks relieved. "Like I said, it's involuntary... I mean, it usually is for any guy, but, well, you know what I mean." He breathes in so deeply that I think he might pop a lung before saying, "Okay, then. That was a nice ice breaker, but... Moving on!"

He'll get no arguments from me. The more we talk about this, the more chance there is of my saying something mortifying.

But neither one of us seems to have a clue what to say next.

Finally, he regains his usual relaxed demeanor and suggests, "Let's sit on the back porch. It's nice out there tonight."

After I retrieve my tote bag, he leads me to a western-facing all-weather room that's still glowing orange as the sun continues to sink toward the horizon on this perfect fall evening. There's a patio table and chairs in one corner of the room, but he takes a seat on what looks like a wrought iron park bench with a padded seat and puts his feet up on an upholstered cube ottoman. From the small table next to him, he grabs a legal pad and pen.

I sit a few feet down the bench from him and pull my writing materials from my bag. The matching ottoman in front of me becomes my desk, where I place my pad and pen. "I have a couple of ideas already, but I don't think they're very good," I announce.

Suddenly, he pops up. "Oh! Before we start, do you want anything to drink? I got distracted earlier by... well, you know... and I forgot to ask."

I'd like to get to work on this so I can stop worrying about it, but I don't want to seem anti-social or ungrateful. "Water would be great," I accept.

He goes into the house, but I can hear him through the open kitchen window that looks out onto the sunroom. "Well, just so you know, I'm drinking something stronger than water. I'm thinking"—I hear glass bottles clinking —"gin."

"No, thanks," I cheerfully decline, doodling aimlessly on my notepad. I'm no teetotaler, but liquor does crazy things to me in a hurry. Or at least it used to. I haven't had anything stronger than wine in a long time.

He pokes his head through the window and looks down at me. "Oh, come on! Don't make me drink alone. I'll make you something mixed and sweet and fruity. More sugar than alcohol."

I pretend to consider it, just to be a good sport, but then say, "Nah. I'd better not."

"It's only one drink," he promises. "It'll get the creative juices flowing."

It seems like this argument is wasting a lot of time, so I cave. "Fine! Just... light on the liquor, okay? I have to drive home." *And* I want to get to work on this sometime tonight.

He grins. "Great! I'll be right there." His head disappears back through the window, but he continues to talk to me while he clanks around in there. He tells me a mildly funny story about Brody, but I one-up him with something I overheard him saying to another kid in the lunch line —"There were a lot of dead cats in Egypt, back when there were mummies." He counters with Brody's take on homeless people—"I'm not cool with them"—and returns to the porch with our drinks.

He hands me my very orange cocktail and clinks against it his large glass of what appears to be straight gin. Then he downs half of his drink. I take a cautious, experimental sip and determine he's followed my instructions to make my drink weak... and delicious! I don't even ask him what's in it, because it tastes like candy in a cocktail glass, so it doesn't matter what it is. I gulp the rest of it down and set the empty glass on the floor at my feet.

I instantly feel warm and happy. "Okay! Thanks! That was excellent."

He settles back in his seat and takes another large drink before setting his glass aside. "Right. Now that we're sufficiently refreshed, let's hear your ideas."

"Yours first," I say, unwilling to stick my neck out only to have him suggest something awesome that makes me look lame.

He doesn't argue. "Well, I only have one so far. I thought maybe we can do a modern variation on the pen pal theme and use Skype to connect to a class overseas once a month. We could have students exchange cultural information and learn about each other by asking questions through video calls."

It's a good idea, but I don't think it's any better than mine, so I counter, "I was thinking we could do something closer to home that teaches the kids about being eco-friendly. Like adopting a stream or planting a garden to grow our own healthy foods."

He writes down the idea. "Before we go any further—"

"No more drinking." My teeth already feel disturbingly numb.

"No. I was wondering if Renalda had given you any more information about the scope of this assignment or if there was a budget involved or… I don't know. Anything! Is this supposed to be something that a whole school can do or each individual class or… or… I mean, is it a lesson plan or more like a school-wide practice?"

I tap my left front tooth with a fingernail. I hope it looks contemplative, not simple, but my objective is to see how hard I have to hit it to feel anything. "Super-hard" is the answer, considering I can't seem to get there. Finally, I give up and answer him, "Dunno. She didn't say. She was kind of vague."

"Typical Renalda," he mutters. "Well, I'm going to write these questions down so that the next time we see her, we can ask her. Because, really, that makes a difference. If we don't have to worry about what this idea costs, we can come up with some b.a. concepts. But if it has to be done on a budget—which I suspect it does—then our possibilities are a lot narrower."

While he scrawls down some reminders about what to ask our boss to help clarify our assignment, I stare at his forearms. Again, with the forearms! I know. I have a problem. But he has such nice ones! Furry enough to be manly, but not overly hairy. Muscled and still tan from the summer...

"Hello?" he says, waving his hand in my line of sight.

"Oh! Sorry!" I laugh at myself and hope he has no idea what I was thinking about. How could he? Who fantasizes about forearms?

"Other ideas?" he prompts.

Sheepishly, I admit, "No, that's all I have right now. Everything I think of seems either lame or impossible... Even those ideas—the stream cleanup or garden thing—I don't think they're plausible. They both require a big commitment from parents and students, and I don't know if we'll get the participation we need to make them work."

He wrinkles his nose. "Yeah. I didn't want to say anything, because we're brainstorming, and there's no such thing as a bad idea when you're brainstorming, but it's my experience that it's very difficult to get parents to do anything that infringes on their personal time."

"It's not difficult for *you*," I say, laughing at his baffled expression. To illustrate my point, I stick out my chest and coo, "'Oh, Mr. Chase! You're so funny! Plant a garden? Sure! You can plant your seeds with me anytime!'"

He screws his mouth to the side to avoid smiling. "You're hilarious," he says drily.

Even though I can hardly talk because I'm laughing so hard at my own joke, I continue, "'What? Spend my free time picking trash out of a stream? Will you be there in a Speedo?'" I toss my hair and bat my eyelids, pretending to chew gum. "'Oh, Mr. Chase!'"

"They do *not* act like that around me!"

Back to myself, I insist, "Basically, yeah, they do. Who wears Prada to pick up their kindergartner from school? Why would anyone apply a fresh coat of lipstick in the parking lot before walking to the school doors? They all have the hots for you, and it's embarrassingly obvious." I tap my pen against my teeth. Still numb. "Damn! I am derrunk!" I blurt. "You didn't go easy on the alcohol, like you promised!"

Now he grins and insists, "Yes, I did! I barely put any in there at all." He leans over, picks up my empty glass, and sniffs it. "Smells like sugar and... sugar!"

"Well, it doesn't matter. I'm still drunk. And it's your fault. Now I'm not going to have any good ideas!"

He shrugs. "Who cares? Let's say any idea that comes to mind. It's better than nothing, which is basically what we have now."

Stumped, I shake my head, so he carelessly tosses out, "Harnessing physical power—picture a kid in a giant hamster wheel—to save the district money on utilities."

I laugh. "Good one! Uh... Wait, wait..." His thought makes me think of something else, but it takes a while for my mouth to catch up to my brain. "Implant tracking devices on the kids so they never get lost!"

"Why would we want to do that?" he jokes. Then he says, "Hmmm... I know! Make the kids wear color-coded nametags—green, yellow, and red—to identify how difficult their parents are. That way, you know whether it's worth it to even bother trying to make the kid learn, if he doesn't want to."

Not for the first time I'm glad I don't have to deal with parents like the "real" teachers do. I wince sympathetically and scoot to the edge of my seat as I get inspired by one of my own childhood memories. "Oh! Here's one that may actually work. It's not an original idea, but when I was in elementary school—"

"You make it sound like it was so long ago. We're not that old!"

Ignoring him, I continue, "When I was in elementary school, we had this school supplies shop that ran twenty minutes every day before school started. It was in a corner of the library, actually. Students ran it, and kids could buy stuff like fun pencils and novelty erasers and stickers... and all the proceeds went to the PTA, or something. I don't remember. But it was really popular! There was always a line."

"Kids don't care about shit like that anymore. They're sophisticated and jaded and cynical. They all carry iPods and cell phones."

I stick my tongue out at him. "Fine. What's your next bright idea, if you're so smart?"

His eyes twinkle. "Live models for sex ed."

I narrow my eyes at him and say mock-disgustedly, "Nice. And parents trust you with their children?"

He downs the rest of his drink and states unapologetically, "Not at the elementary level, of course. That would be wrong."

We laugh at that understatement, but then I declare, "Well, if I didn't have to see those students every day, and it was a guaranteed lay—for instructional purposes, of course —I'd be tempted." As soon as it's out, I can't believe I've said it.

Neither can he, apparently. "You *are* drunk." When I don't deny it, he declares, "Well, if you're in, I'm in."

The next thing happens so fast that I'm only aware of what's going on in strange, disjointed flashes, like my internal camera is set to ultra-zoom. His eyes darken. He licks his lips, which then shine moistly. His jaw tenses; then his face is getting closer to me. But it's not because he's moving; I am. I'm scooting along the bench, hoping it looks more graceful than it feels (but not really believing that's true and not caring). Still, he's still.

Just as I'm starting to wonder if I'm about to make a huge ass of myself, he lurches toward me, grabs my face, and catches my lower lip in his teeth before pulling me onto his lap and kissing me with the perfect combination of tenderness and force. I'm too relieved (not to mention too drunk) to reconsider the wisdom of this; plus, this feels way too good to stop. He's good at this. *Really* good at this. And I can tell when he readjusts his position under me and subtly rubs his crotch against mine that he's *really* good at lots of things.

But then… as suddenly as everything started, it stops. It's like someone hit switches on both of our backs, shutting down our libidos. Panting, we stare at each other for what feels like an hour. Then we say at the same time, "I'm sorry."

I have to admit, it's not quite the simultaneous event I was hoping for a few seconds ago.

I wipe my mouth. "Did I mention that I'm a little drunk?" I say by way of explanation.

He nods sluggishly, his eyelids heavy. "Yeah. You're a real lightweight."

Somehow he makes something of which I've always been ashamed sound like a cute quirk.

Then, like a flash, I realize what stopped me from letting my body do what it wanted to do. One word: girlfriend.

"Do you have a girlfriend?" I ask, painfully aware that it sounds like I'm applying for the job. I clarify, "Johnny said that you do." I leave off the strange and confusing, "sometimes" from the original quote.

He shifts, subtly but effectively sending the message that he'd like me to dismount him. I do. I tuck my hair behind my ears and wait for an answer that seems like it's never going to come. The longer the silence stretches, the surer I am that the answer is, "Yes," and something inside me hardens so that it won't hurt so much when he says it. Finally, I look over at him to try to force him to say something.

Looking the picture of sexual frustration, he chuckles humorlessly and bites at his lower lip. "No."

"But Johnny—"

"Johnny doesn't understand the difference between oatmeal and grits, much less something as complex as my relationship with Marena," he snaps, standing and gathering our empty glasses.

Marena? It sounds like the name of an expensive drug for impotence.

When he goes into the house, I pack my bag. Marena.

Marena! I can't compete with a Marena, especially one who's already been deemed prettier than me.

Bag on my shoulder, I nearly collide with him when I enter the house as he returns to the porch.

He doesn't ask why I'm leaving, but I explain anyway, "I'm gonna head home."

I don't ask, but he explains anyway, "I wouldn't have kissed you if I already had a girlfriend. I don't do that."

"Okay."

"Is this going to be weird now?" he asks.

"No!" I lie sunnily. "Not at all! Do you feel weird?"

I can tell he's lying, too, when he says, "Nah. It was just one of those flukey things."

"Yeah! Flukey. Silly. Now you know to listen to me when I say I shouldn't drink. Heh heh."

He bends at the knees to look into my eyes. "Speaking of, are you okay to drive? I mean, you *seem* sober now, but—"

"Oh! Absolutely! As a judge! Don't worry about me!" I edge past him and find the shortest path through the dining room and living room to the front door. "See you!" And that's when I almost puke through the screen door onto the front porch. It has nothing to do with the alcohol, either. Swallowing it down, I start over and make myself finish the awful phrase that encapsulates the reality of this nightmare. "See you... at work tomorrow!"

CHAPTER THIRTEEN

I t's okay, though. It's okay.

That's what I tell myself when I wake up this morning. I repeat it in the shower and at the breakfast table, where I stare at a bowl of fruit that I know I'm not going to be able to eat. I say it over and over again while I drive to work. And I tell myself I'm using a different door than I usually do to enter the building *not* because I'm avoiding Jamie's room, but because I need to stop by the office to chat with Renalda about what got me into this mess-that's-not-really-a-mess, because it's okay.

Totally okay.

When I walk through the door, Sam looks up from where she's manning the phones as they ring with the daily absence call-ins. Over the noise of the ringing, she says, "Hey. What's up?"

"Nothing. Everything's good. Or 'okay,' actually, is a better way to describe it. Just okay. I mean, is anything ever completely 'good' without some drawbacks? No. But everything's okay, as usual. Nothing out of the ordinary." I exhale loudly. "Renalda in?" I lean around her open office door to see for myself. The messy room is unoccupied. "Damn. I need to talk to her."

"You need a valium," Sam mutters before picking up the phone and saying pleasantly, "Whitehall Elementary, Sam speaking.... Hi, Mrs. Sawyer.... Oh, no! That's too bad! Well, tell him we said we hope he feels better...." She laughs. "Oh, how precious! He is so funny! Let me know if you want Mr. Chase to send home his schoolwork while he's out.... Yeah, at least it'll be something to keep him from getting bored while he recovers, poor thing! All right. I'll let Mr. Chase know. Bye!"

"What's wrong with Brody?" I immediately ask when she hangs up.

She makes a note in the attendance book and says, "According to him, he has the 'chicken pots.'"

I laugh with her about that for a second until the information sinks in.

My smile fades. "Oh, no!" I lament. "Poor guy!"

"I know. I remember when I had the chickenpox. Horrible." She shivers at the memory.

"Never got 'em."

"Really? Lucky. Kids don't get it very much anymore, thanks to the vaccine. But it's not one of the state-mandated shots, so some parents don't make their kids get it. I guess Brody's mom is one of those parents."

I quickly check my mailbox and flip through the usual memos from Jane. "Or he got a strain that the vaccine doesn't protect against."

The phone rings again, but she doesn't make a move to answer it. "I don't know enough about that kind of stuff. All I know is he's got the pox. She says he has 'em bad, too."

Tossing the junk mail into the trashcan next to Sam's desk, I say, "If Jamie sends any schoolwork up here for Mrs.

Sawyer to pick up, let me know. I'll send a few special books home for him to read." My mention of Jamie sets my stomach to fluttering again.

Sam doesn't seem to notice my squirminess. "Good idea."

"Oh, and, uh, if Renalda comes in, can you please tell her I need to talk to her when she gets a chance?"

"*If* she comes in, yes." She picks up the phone. "Whitehall Elementary, Sam speaking…. Uh-oh! Good grief, you're the second one I've had today! Sounds like it's going around…. Nope, first time I've seen anything like it in the ten years I've been working here." She mouths at me, *"More chicken pots,"* which makes me laugh as the first bell rings.

I join the flow of children making their way toward the tiled tributaries that flow from the main hallway to the classrooms. The further away from the office we get, the taller I feel as the fourth and fifth graders trickle away, leaving their younger counterparts to drip in their more random, haphazard patterns to the gentle, warm tide pools that are the kindergarten rooms.

When I get to the "T," I can't help turning my head to look in the direction of Jamie's class as I make a right to go to the library. Thankfully, he's not in the hall, so we don't have to suffer through a meaningful gaze worthy of some sappy made-for-TV movie, courtesy of my pathetically indulgent and irresistible urge to see if I can look him in the eye after last night.

It was just a kiss, anyway. It's not like we had sex, pressed up against the steamy windows of the sun porch. Not that the idea didn't cross my mind. But the mere existence of a Marena out there somewhere quickly killed that dream. Not that I dream about it. Well, only that once. But I think that's more because I ate pistachio ice cream before bed while watching *True Blood*, which is basically primetime porn. But whatever.

The point is, nothing *really* happened last night. If *Reader's Digest* were to condense it, it would go something like this: "Got lost. Got directions. Met Johnny. Met Not-so-Little Johnny. Drank a fruity drink. Brainstormed. Got a little silly. Ground my naughty bits up against a co-worker's naughty bits and stuck my tongue down his throat. Went home." The end. Big damn deal.

I can hardly let an evening like that distract me from my real problems, which are, well, *real*.

Anyway, it's Tuesday. I never see Jamie on Tuesdays. So, like I've been saying all morning, it's okay.

"Hey! What are you doing here?" I say and smile through gritted teeth while blinking rapidly.

Jamie looks at the counter, the ceiling, the walls, the floor, his shoes, his hands, and finally me while answering, "Sam said you wanted to add some books to the stuff I'm sending home with Brody's mom."

I aim for sounding upbeat and carefree but miss when I declare too brightly, "Actually, I told her to let me know, and I'd bring the books up myself, but—"

He gestures to the folder I now notice he set on the counter between us when he first appeared before me like a very cute but bad penny. "Well, I'm on my way up there right now, so it made sense for me to stop by to get the books."

"But I don't have them ready yet."

The final bell of the day only rang ten minutes ago. I'm surprised he was able to shake his groupies so quickly.

"Do you have a list? I'll help you," Serenity personified offers.

"That would be great!" Robo-Kendall replies. (She's a lifesaver in ridiculous times like these.) I copy down three of the six call numbers from the slip of paper on which I've already listed them and hand the scrap to him. "There. They should all be close to each other."

"And if not, I understand how the Dewey decimal system works, so I'm sure I'll be able to find them, but I'll call for help if I need it," he reassures me as he walks away.

I ignore his sarcasm and go to the first shelf I need, which is three rows away from him.

After about thirty seconds, he calls out, "What's the deal with all the tsunami books?"

"He likes tsunamis," I answer stupidly. "One of his many obsessions."

"That kid! He's either going to be the next Stephen Hawking or a serial killer."

I wrinkle my brow as I pull a cat book and move to the next row over. "Neither one of those is a very attractive future. Sort of grim, don't you think?"

"Okay, then, Bill Gates. Is that better? But I stick by the serial killer possibility."

"Nope. Your theory's crap. He loves animals, especially cats. Don't serial killers torture animals when they're Brody's age?" I add a book about electricity to my stack and slide down the row a few paces. There, I locate the final selection, a picture book based on the movie, *Titanic*. "Hello?" I say into the silence that meets my question.

"Where are you?" is the response I get.

Flipping through the *Titanic* book, I distractedly give the uninformative answer, "Over here. This book is actually pretty cool. I loved Leo and Kate in this movie. Still do."

After following my voice to my location, he stops next to me and holds up one of the tsunami books. "A kid who enjoys reading about death and destruction is a serial-killer-in-the-making."

I glance up and back down at a photo of Leonardo DiCaprio in a tux. "He's inquisitive. So shut up." I close the film book with a thump and add it and the two others to the pile in Jamie's hands.

He looks up from the stack and smiles at me. "I know. He's the oddest kid I've ever met. And that's saying a lot."

"Think how boring this year would be without him, though," I point out.

Shaking his head once, he says, "There are other things that would keep it from being boring." Then he lets the books drop from his hands and pushes me gently against the shelf behind me. He leans down and presses his lips against mine.

I pull my head away slightly and look down the aisle toward the more open area of the library. But I can't see more than a small cross-section of the check-out counter, much less something as important as the door. Nobody but Jamie ever comes in here after school hours. It's paranoid to be worried that someone will today, right now.

When Jamie continues his pursuit of my mouth, I decide not to play coy. I've been thinking about this all day, so it's stupid to pretend I don't want him when he's right here, offering himself to me.

He's just... so much taller than me. Fueled by lust, I keep my lips locked onto his as I push *him* across the row and against the shelves and climb him like a beautiful tree with yummy fruit at the top. He puts his hands on my waist and lifts me enough so I can wrap my legs around his waist.

"Oh, yes, Miss Dickinson," he whispers with a wicked

smirk. "Tell me a poem about hanging out with a worm and a snake in your room."

Impressed, I smile against his lips, "You know Emily Dickinson?"

"That poem, at least. Kids love it. Grosses them out."

"Snakes and worms don't scare me."

"What about sexually repressed poets?"

"They're a little scarier," I declare.

"Why?"

Coming back to my senses in a hurry, I stare at the golden flecks in his dark eyes. "Because we're all just a few bad men away from becoming that woman," I explain, straightening my legs and standing on my own two feet. I right his crooked glasses.

"But I'm not a bad man," he claims, reaching for me.

I let him pull me to him again. When he kisses the top of my head, I think, *Unfortunately, there's no way for me to know that.*

CHAPTER FOURTEEN

I don't feel so good. I mean, it's not the worst I've ever felt in my whole life, but that was when I had strep throat and mono at the same time, so that would be hard to beat. I'd say this is the second-worst, easily. I'm not sure how difficult it is to get a substitute for me on short notice, but they're going to have to deal. Because I feel horrible, and I probably shouldn't be around other people.

When I call Sam to tell her I won't be in today, she jokes, "I hope it's not chicken pots. It's crazy how many kids are out with it right now! But most of them are mild cases, since they've been getting the vaccine since they were babies."

I stare at a bright red, itchy dot on my inner thigh. "What if it *is* chickenpox?" I ask, trying to keep the panic from creeping into my voice.

She laughs. "It's not! Or if it is, you'll get a mild case, like the kids, thanks to your vaccine."

"What vaccine?"

"The one you got when you were hired."

"I didn't get a vaccine when I was hired!"

She pauses and laughs nervously. "Cut the crap."

As adamantly as I can without crying, I say, "I'm *not* kidding, okay? Nobody told me I had to get anything more than a flu shot. I sure as hell didn't get a chickenpox vaccine. Nobody told me to!"

Sam curses not-so-under her breath. "Renalda was supposed to tell you!"

"Oh, my gosh! What? My wellbeing was left up to her?"

"Okay, calm down. It's okay."

"This is *not* okay! I have itchy red bumps popping up on my stomach and legs and boobs... and"—I examine a particularly irritating spot inside my panty line—"you don't even want to know where else. Not okay."

"You need to get to the doctor," she advises as I hear her other lines ringing.

"Sam... I'm going to kill Renalda."

"Go to the doctor first. Feel better soon! I'll call you later to check up on you, but right now I have to go."

"Sam!"

"Bye!"

Motherscratcher!

I don't even have a doctor in this effing town, unless you count the pediatrician my mom insisted on taking me to see, even when I was in high school. Actually, that's infuriatingly appropriate and ironic. But I refuse to call her. Instead, I do the next-most childish thing and call my mommy.

"What's wrong?" she immediately asks when she picks up.

"I have chickenpox," I bluntly announce.

She laughs.

"It's not funny!"

"No, it's not. I'm sorry. It's just... this is not the sort of news women your age usually call their moms with."

This is not a good time for her to remark on my socially

115

stunted life, no matter how good-natured she's being. "Mother…"

"I know, I know! I'm sorry. Well, you need to get to the doctor."

"So I've been told. Problem is, I don't have one closer than a thousand miles away, and I don't think I can drive sixteen hours right now."

As if we're discussing a referral to a good hair stylist, she cheerfully offers, "I'll give you the number to my doctor. She's wonderful! Hang on a second." I listen to her tap around in her phone; then she says, "Are you ready for the number?"

Twenty minutes later, I have an appointment for later in the day, I've dabbed anti-itch lotion on every bump I can see (and a few that I couldn't), and I'm lying on top of the covers on my bed, spread-eagle in my underwear, when my phone rings on the pillow next to me. Seeing the school's number, I put the call on speakerphone so I can talk to Sam without holding the phone to my ear.

I'm surprised and chagrined when it's Jamie. "This is a joke, right?" he asks, a grin in his voice.

"Why does everyone think this is so fucking funny?" I snap.

"You have to admit, it kind of is."

"Says the guy who probably gave it to me when he stuck his tongue down my throat in the library after being around a bunch of germy kids all day."

The angrier I get, the more he laughs. "You're so crabby!" he finally asserts between snickers.

"I feel like shit! Have you ever had chickenpox?"

"Of course not. I'm a fine specimen of healthy living. Plus, Renalda remembered to tell *me* to get the vaccine."

"Screw you."

"Oh! Wow." He sobers somewhat. "Actually, I got the vaccine way before I started working here. Had to for travel purposes. If it had been up to Renalda, we'd probably be in the same boat."

"It's a miserable boat."

Completely serious now (which makes me feel better), he says, "I really am sorry you feel so terrible. You're going to the doctor, right? Chickenpox can be dangerous in adults, I've heard."

Deep breath. "Yes. I've heard that, too."

"I'm annoying you."

"A little," I confess. I don't want to hurt his feelings, but I'm struggling with Maslow's hierarchy of needs right now, and I can't focus on anything past basic survival. His feelings are coming in low on the list of priorities, which only has two other items on it right now: breathing and scratching my private parts.

"Okay. Well, call me if you need anything. Or want to talk or—"

"Okay, thanks. Bye."

I can't take another second of the conversation. I'll apologize later for hanging up on him, but right now I have to lie here and think about… nothing. It's taking every bit of concentration I have not to rake my fingernails from my toes to my scalp in a series of overlapping bloody scratches and doing that until it's time to drag myself from my bed to go to the doctor.

Logically, I know it's irrational to be irritated with him. I know that he and I are exposed to the same germy kids (I'm actually exposed to *more*, if I want to get all technical about it, which I don't, because that takes too much energy), but the student who had the first known case of this disgusting disease in this whole breakout came from *his* classroom. So, I blame him. After Renalda. And myself.

Because I'm *really* angry at myself. I mean, I know my medical history. I know I've never had chickenpox. When I first heard that Brody had it, I should have made the connection and brought it to light that I'd never been vaccinated. Why did I need someone else to tell me that when you work with walking petri dishes, you need to protect yourself from any and all communicable diseases? Dirty little kids. I should have taken the initiative and worn a body condom to work every day.

I don't know if it's because of the fever or the energy it's taking to remain still, but I fall into exhausted sleep with that image dancing behind my eyelids.

Home from the doctor. Don't remember much about getting there, being there, or getting home from there, so I probably should have had someone take me, but I'm all about being independent. More than I am about being alive, apparently. It all worked out okay, though. I even somehow made it as far as the couch before I decided I couldn't move any further. So here I am, draped facedown over one of the sofa's arms, which is pressed against my waist in such a way that if I wiggle my hips just a bit, it acts as a perfect scratching post. The doctor told me not to scratch the lesions, but what does she know?

Ouch, ouch, ouch. Okay, maybe she knows something about it. Scratching eventually hurts a lot.

Anyway, I'm going to rest here for a while until I get the energy to…

A soft knocking on my door wakes me up.

"What? Who's there? Ow! My neck!"

When I hear a key scraping into the lock and the dead-
bolt clicking, I know it has to be one of my parents. Or I've
been lying here for days, and the landlord's gotten a
complaint about the smell. According to my neck muscles,
this could be the case. It feels like I'm in the early stages of
rigor mortis.

Sure enough, I can tell by the jasmine-scented body
spray that Mom has arrived. She gasps when she sees my
position on the couch, so I muffle, "Mffokayff."

"Oh, Honey! What's happened?" She hurries around
the sofa and stares down at me for a second before dropping
an armful of canvas shopping bags at her feet and kneeling
in front of me. "Are you okay?"

I lift my head enough so that my face is no longer in the
puddle of drool on the cushion and say, "Not really."

"Let's get you more comfortable. I'm sorry it's taken me
so long to get here, but I had a lecture that I couldn't miss.
Then I wanted to pick up some supplies before heading over
here. And I'm so glad I did!" While she bubbles away, she
gingerly rearranges my limbs so that I'm eventually in a
sitting position.

"You didn't even take your jacket off!" she admonishes
me.

"I don't care," I whimper pathetically. "I hurt."

"Have you taken the medicine the doctor gave you? You
need to get that first dose in you as soon as possible." She
spies the white pharmacy bag on the floor, where I dropped
it upon arriving home. "Oh. There it is. Let's just"—she
rips it open and pulls out the bottle of pills, shaking two

into her hand—"take two of these." Then she digs in one of her canvas bags and pulls out a huge bottle of water. "Here. Take them with this. Then you need to drink this whole thing within the next hour or so. Gotta stay hydrated."

My head lolls heavily on my neck as I toss back the pills, and she has to help me hoist the bottle.

"Oh, dear. I think you're already dehydrated a bit. You're so lethargic!"

"I'm sick, Mom," I point out unnecessarily, dribbling water down the front of my jacket.

She unzips the outerwear and pulls it from my arms. "Come on, now. You need to get in bed."

The slightest friction of clothing against my skin has reawakened the itchies, so I begin to scratch. It starts with my shoulder, but then I feel a spot on my neck and another one on my face. And another one on my face. And another one on my face.

"My face!"

She nods sympathetically. "Yes. It's a bit of a mess. All rashy."

"What? It wasn't like that earlier!"

"Honey, that's what happens when you have chickenpox. You're going to have spots all over. Don't fight it."

"But—"

In her most soothing voice, she cuts me off, "Now, I know what'll make you feel better."

"A time machine?"

She ignores me as she leads me by the hand into the bathroom. When she flicks on the light, she mutters, "Oh! It's a bit of a mess in here." Louder, she continues, "Never mind about that, though. I'm going to run a nice oatmeal bath for you. Then we're going to cover all your spots with calamine lotion, and you're going to take an antihistamine, and you'll be right as rain."

"Oatmeal bath? No! I don't want to take an oatmeal bath!"

"Trust me, it'll feel good."

"It'll be all lumpy and sticky and get in my hair," I protest weakly. Unfortunately, I know that if she's intent on doing this, I have no chance of resisting.

She laughs at me. "Oh, Sweetie! It's ground up into a fine powder. You'll see. Get undressed, and I'll run the bath."

It's official: I'm six years old again.

Before I can say anything else, I catch a glimpse of myself in the mirror. Squeaking, I bring my hands up to my face and stare at the monstrosity reflected back at me. It's about fifty times worse that I thought it was. Not only are there a hundred nasty blisters on my face, but my head seems to have swollen to about twice its normal size. "Gaaaa!"

Mom looks over her shoulder at me. "Oh. Yeah. You probably shouldn't look in the mirror, sweetie."

"Too late!"

"This'll all be a memory in two weeks."

"*Two weeks?*"

"Yes. Didn't the doctor tell you that? You'll be feeling better a lot sooner than that, though. It'll just take a while for the blisters to heal and disappear."

I don't want to admit to her that I don't remember what the doctor said, because everything after eight o'clock this morning is all a haze in my memory, so I simply say, "This is a nightmare."

"Oh, now! Where's my sunny girl? Once you feel better, you'll be laughing at this. It's one of life's silly adventures!"

My head is pounding. My neck feels like someone's sticking an ice pick into it when I try to turn my head to the left or look at anything higher than my eye line, which is pathetically low, given my petite stature. I have red, now-oozing sores all over my body, including my face, which is starting to resemble "Sloth" in the movie, *Goonies*. I itch all over, but when I scratch, it hurts. This is *not* a silly adventure.

She knows it, too. As I'm lying submerged with only my head sticking out of the strangely soothing, silky, oatmeal-filled water, I hear her talking to Dad on her cell phone out in the living room. "Oh, Ted... She looks terrible! No! I've been trying to keep her spirits up, but she feels awful and looks worse.... I don't know.... She won't be contagious after a few days, but I wouldn't want to go to work looking like that if I were her.... I know.... That's a good idea; I'll tell her that.... Okay, well I have to go before she gets out of the bath. I'm going to dope her up with antihistamines so she can sleep through most of the weekend, and by Monday she'll at least be feeling better.... Okay. Love you, too. Bye!"

I'm actually relieved to hear that she knows how bad it is. I was starting to think she was reality-challenged with all her talk about "silly adventures" and everything being "right as rain." I mean, who even says that, especially when speaking to an adult? It's sweet that she's trying to make me feel better, even though she's freaking out on the inside as much as I am.

When I emerge from the bathroom, wrapped in a fluffy robe she purchased especially for me today, I make an effort to be more patient, less cranky, and altogether calmer. Without argument, I take the antihistamines she offers (her plan to have me sleep through the next three days of my life sounds pretty damn good to me), submit to the calamine-lotion painting session, and go straight to bed.

Chickenpox aside, it feels good to be taken care of again.

CHAPTER FIFTEEN

W hen I wake up hours (days? weeks?) later to the sound of Mom talking to someone down the hall in the living room, I assume it's my dad, stopping by to check on us. I figure he's bringing Mom some food and keeping her company for a couple of hours before heading home to grade papers or—more likely—smoke some weed out in his "woodshed" (as if we don't all know what he's actually doing out there).

But then I hear her say, "It was so nice of you to stop by, but she'd die if you saw her like this," followed by a slightly evil giggle and, "No, Jamie! Don't. She'd never forgive me."

His voice carries down the hall when he pleads, "Oh, come on! Just a peek. I'll be really quiet, I promise. She won't even know I was here. And I'll *never* tell her."

I nearly pull an eardrum straining to hear what Mom says next: "Well, you did bring her such pretty flowers…"

She wouldn't!

She couldn't!

She daren't!

I hear the slow footsteps approaching my door and the

knob turning, but then I'm too busy diving under the covers to listen to anything else. I tightly grip the edges of the duvet, hoping I have the strength to keep it from being pulled back.

"Gosh! Isn't she hot under there?" Mom whispers. "I don't know how she can sleep with her head covered up like that."

Someone tugs gently at the corner of the bedspread, but I keep the covers clamped down.

"She's really dug in," he hisses.

Another attempt at a gawk at me yields the same result.

"It's like she's holding the covers down," Mom brilliantly observes.

"Go away," I sing sweetly to hide the fury under the surface.

"Oh, shit, she's awake!" Jamie mumbles, and I hear the two of them scramble to leave the room, bumping into each other and the door. "Get well soon!" he calls before the door closes with a bang.

I roll my eyes and throw back the stifling covers only to see both of them standing inside the closed door. Mom looks sheepish; Jamie looks gleeful at first but then nothing short of horrified.

"Mom!" I quickly retreat to my quilted cave, but the damage is done. "You two suck!"

They're both trying not to laugh as they talk over one another.

"It's not that bad."

"He wanted to make sure you were okay."

"I'm sure the swelling will go down soon."

"He brought you flowers!"

I squeeze my eyes shut and shout, "Why are you still here?"

That quiets both of them.

Apprehensively, Mom asks, "Which one of us are you talking to? Do you want to be alone with Jamie?"

Now I can't help but laugh at the absurdity of the situation. But my answer is still, "No! And I'm talking to both of you! Stop treating me like a sideshow freak!"

By the sound of his voice, Jamie's grin is still going strong when he says, "You look incredible. Come on; pull the covers back one more time so I can get a better look."

"No!"

"Please? Don't be so vain. This is for educational purposes."

"I hate you so much right now."

He's not even trying not to laugh now.

"Mom! Get him out of here!" I can't believe she would let someone she just met into my bedroom—my *sickroom*—to point and laugh at me.

That demand gets no answer at first, but then Jamie says, "Uh, yeah. She's gone."

"Nice."

"I think so." The edge of my bed sags as his weight settles on it. "You have to admit—"

"I admit nothing except that you're a big fat asshole who delights in kicking people when they're down," I interrupt sulkily.

"Now, now." He grabs my foot through the duvet. "Don't be so testy. I'm doing no such thing."

I snort.

"I came by here tonight to bring you some flowers and try to cheer you up."

"Epic fail."

"I'm getting the impression that's the case, yes."

Tears sting my eyes, but I know they're going to hurt like

hell if they actually track down my cheeks over these damn sores, so I blink them away. "What made you think that having you see me like this would cheer me up?"

"Honestly," he replies, "I had no idea you'd look like this. I thought you'd be a cute little polka-dotted thing, but"—he pauses before breaking the news to me—"you have slits in your face where your eyes used to be."

"I know!" Now I do break down. "I'm hideous!"

"Awww." I feel him patting around on top of the covers in random places before he asks, "Where are you under there? Come here. I want to give you a hug."

"I'm contagious and gross and and... oozy!" But I scoot my body closer to where I can feel the mattress dipping. When my butt makes contact with his hip, he leans over and rests his body on top of mine, the bedspread acting as a barrier between us. It's not hospital-grade protection, but at least none of my open wounds is touching him.

"It's going to be okay."

"I wish everyone would stop telling me that."

"Okay. This fucking sucks. Is that better?"

"Yes. Thank you."

"You're welcome." He's quiet for a while before sitting up again. "I brought you something from the students, too. A card. They all signed it. It's with your flowers."

"How big is this card?" I wonder.

He laughs. "Oh, it's only from my class. Sorry. Didn't mean to make it sound like the whole school cared about you. That would make this suck a lot less, and we don't want that."

Grudgingly, I tell him, "It was nice of you to come over here tonight. Before you came in to make fun of me, anyway."

"Just doing my part to ensure maximum suckage."

My shoulders shake with the laughter I'm trying to conceal from him.

"Are you laughing or crying?"

"Crying," I lie.

"Oh. Good. Mission accomplished, then." The mattress rises to its normal height as he stands. His voice is further away, near the door, when he says, "Well, gotta get home to Johnny."

"Tell him I said, 'hi.'"

It's getting unbearably hot under here.

"Nah. That'd get him all excited. Wouldn't want anyone to lose an eye. It's been a rough enough day."

I don't even try to hide that I'm laughing this time. Monday night seems like so long ago, but it's only been four days. Four days ago, I had a normal face with real eye sockets. Four days ago, Johnny could have poked my eye out. Now, there's no way anything's getting through to these peepers.

"Get some rest," he tells my shaking bed.

"Okay. And thanks for the card and the flowers. And for cheering me up."

"Bah!"

"But please don't visit me again while I'm like this."

He sighs. "Fine, fine. Vanity, thy name is Kendall."

"Yep, that's me. I'll see you in a week or two."

"But however will I survive?"

"Figure it out. Goodbye."

"Bye!"

I hear the door close softly and peek cautiously over the edge of the blankets before committing to my full exposure this time. He's truly gone.

I already miss him.

When I told him not to visit me, I didn't mean that he had to completely break all communication with me. An already interminable week has seemed even longer, since I haven't heard a word from him other than one text on Tuesday night. (*"Hope you're feeling better. We've let the kids take over the library, and it's not pretty."*) I texted back a big smiley face and my assurances that I should be back to work by the following Monday, for sure. That was met with a silence that has stretched for days.

I don't know how to interpret that.

What happened to the guy who dropped everything—literally—to make out with me between the six- and seven-hundreds of the Dewey Decimal classifications? What happened? I'll tell you what happened: he saw my *Mask* face, that's what happened. He'll never look at my lips the same way again, knowing what's been oozing around them for the past week-and-a-half. I saw his expression when he got a load of me. It's burned in my brain, even though it couldn't have taken longer than two seconds for it all to happen.

Damn, damn, damn.

Well, it's back to reality today, scabs and all. I've already been away from work too long for vanity's sake. I could have come back as soon as I was no longer contagious and didn't feel sick anymore, but I was still too hideous for public consumption. So I took some precious personal days to give my face time to return to some semblance of its former self. I've been diligent to the point of obsession about my personal hygiene and my skin care regimen during this healing process, but there are some stubborn hangers-on that had to come to work with me this morning. I'm not risking any scarring by pulling them off prematurely. As long as nobody stares, I'll be okay.

Except I forgot that the least of my worries is that I look like someone who's had an "ugly" curse placed on her. Still hanging over my head is Renalda's assignment, which she was happy to point out when I passed her in the hallway after the first bell this morning. I almost called back, "Yeah, and I'm feeling much better, thanks for asking," but I merely grinned and lied, "All over it! I just have a few questions for you when you have a minute," as I backpedaled through the throng of students. She said something about "meetin's all day" before disappearing into the office.

It didn't take long for me to move on to other problems, though. I thought Jamie was kidding about the library being a mess. That was an understatement. It was a disaster area. When I got to the library this morning and flipped on the lights, I actually gasped at the sight in front of me. Apparently, they don't call substitute teachers to fill in for the librarian, even if she's gone for six days. Nope, they simply let the teachers handle their own library time with their students. I'm sure no one has shelved a single book (correctly) the entire time I've been gone.

There were stacks of books everywhere. My cardboard cutout of Olivia had fallen (or more likely, had been pushed) flat onto the floor, bent up and floppy-eared. Scrap pieces of paper with call numbers scrawled on them lay scattered on the counter, floor, and next to the catalog computers. It took me all day to get things back in order. I think Olivia's headed for the cardboard recycling dumpster, if I can't find a way to reinforce her creased parts.

And I kind of feel like she looks. The day would have been trying for my normal body, but I still tire easily, so I'm exhausted and emotional by the time the last bell rings. My rational, logical side tells me it's a bad idea to seek out Jamie in this state of mind, but I figure as long as I keep everything light and breezy, it'll be fine.

I give it a good forty minutes before I make the walk down the hall to his room and knock jovially on the door as I poke my head around the doorframe. When he looks up from the papers he's grading, I say, "I know I look like a leper, but that doesn't mean you have to treat me like one." It doesn't come out as casually as I'd aimed, but it still gets a big smile from him.

"Oh, hey! How'd the first day back go?" he asks as he sets down his pen. "I had a feeling it'd be a busy day for you, so I've been staying out of your way."

"Likely story," I tease some more.

"Really!" he insists, leaning forward to rest his elbows on his desk.

I don't want to spend our first conversation in days complaining, especially considering how cranky I was the last time he saw me, so I simply say, "It was a long day, but I think tomorrow will be back to almost normal, so—"

"Knock, knock," comes a throaty voice from the doorway.

Jamie jumps up like he's been caught doing something wrong and says, "Hi!" He glances at the clock. "I wasn't expecting you this early."

I turn to face the newcomer, a stunning, tall, athletically curvy brunette with amazing... everything! Her blue eyes are what grab my attention first, though. They're like turquoise pools in her tan face. But they have some competition for attention when she parts her beautiful, full lips and grins, revealing an unbelievably white set of straight, perfect teeth.

Not even acknowledging my presence, she addresses

Jamie's statement. "I know. I can wait outside if you're not ready," she tells him, pointing over her shoulder with her thumb.

Thinking (hoping, praying) this is the mother of a new student who's here for a "meet-the-teacher" conference, I smile welcomingly and say, "Hi! I'm Kendall Dickinson, the school librarian."

Her lips remain in the same smiling position, but the sparkle completely leaves her eyes as she turns her attention to me for the first time. "Uh, hi. Nice to meet you. I'm—"

Jamie crashes onto the scene, grasping my shoulders and steering me to a spot far enough away from his visitor that I can't shake her hand. "Yeah. Kendall, this is Marena."

"Marena," I repeat stupidly, as I try to place the familiar name.

He removes his hands from me and stands awkwardly to the side, equidistant to both of us. "Yep. Marena. She and I worked together on some expeditions in New Zealand, Ireland, and… and…" He defers to her. "I'm blanking on the third place, for some reason."

Smoothly, she supplies, "Tunisia. I don't know how you could forget Tunisia!" The way she says it leaves no doubt that the dig wasn't the only thing dirty going on there.

Screw me! Marena! The fancy impotence drug! Indeed!

"Oh, shit!" I blurt, bringing her piercing gaze back to me. "I mean," I try to cover, "I just remembered something… that I need to do… right this very second."

Jamie inquisitively cocks his head at me, so I say, "You know… that thing. In the library…" Inexplicably, the words, *with Colonel Mustard and the wrench,* pop into my head and make me giggle, even though I know this is no laughing matter and that I'm in deep shit.

Marena is a goddess. Aphrodite's and Athena's best

features combined would produce someone who looks downright dowdy next to her. Johnny should have been clearer when he said she was prettier than me. He should have said, "She's prettier than you and every other woman you've ever come in contact with, and that includes that time you saw Angelina Jolie with Brad Pitt shopping on the Plaza in Kansas City." As a matter of fact, Marena could be Lara Croft's sister. But poor Lara would be the ugly duckling of that sibling duo.

I become uncomfortably aware they're both looking at me. For someone who's supposed to be somewhere else, doing *something* else, I'm oddly hesitant to leave.

Marena squints down at me and points to my face. "You have something..." she begins but then trails off when I bring my hand up quickly to my face and cover the spot with my palm.

Blushing, I mutter, "I'm getting over something."

"Yeah, Kendall recently had a wicked case of chicken-pox, if you can believe that," Jamie volunteers excitedly. "Her face was all..." he puffs his cheeks out and pulls at the corners of his eyes to demonstrate. "It was one of the craziest things I've ever seen."

She wrinkles her delicate nose and laughs. "Ugh! You actually saw her like that? Weren't you worried about catching something?"

He exhales and lets go of his eyes. "Nah. I mean, I've gotten the shot, so..."

"Still. They always say there's a chance you can catch a mild case."

My hand still up against my scabby cheek, I sing-song, "Well, he obviously didn't!"

"You've always been so brave." She gazes at him affectionately. "Or stupid. I could never figure out which one."

They laugh like a couple who has quite the colorful history. Buh-arrrf!

"Okay. It was nice to meet you, Marena," I continue my streak of lies. "I hope you have a nice visit."

I'm about to tell Jamie goodbye when she volunteers, "Oh, I've been here for a week. Getting ready to ship back out, actually. Jamie was nice enough to let me crash at his place while I got some much-needed R&R and tried to coax him back into the business." She reaches out and rubs his upper arm with the backs of her fingers. "But I'm already restless. I don't know how you people live in this place! It's so sleepy!"

She's right; this town *is* sleepy. But that's precisely why people like it. It's relatively quiet and feels like a safe place to raise a family, but it also has all the conveniences and amenities of a mid-sized town. It's the best of both worlds. However, I refuse to rise to the bait as the local yokel who defends her hometown to the worldly adventurer. It's not like I'm going to change her mind, anyway.

"Yeah, well... safe travels, I guess."

I guess is right. I'd really like to tell her not to let the city limit sign smack her on her perfect ass on her way to the airport.

"Thanks, Kenna." Having dismissed me, she turns to Jamie, "Are you ready to go, then? I'd like to stock up on a few things at the store and turn in early tonight. You promised me you'd take me to that vegan place we keep passing everywhere we go."

I don't correct her about my name or wait to hear what he says. As I speed-walk to the library (getting my purse, locking up, and getting the hell away from them is the only thing I *need* to do right now), I try not to panic.

So, she dropped into town to visit an old friend—who

happens to be someone that used to be way more than a friend—while she was between jobs, or whatever. Big deal. And Jamie's been too preoccupied with her to give me the time of day ever since she breezed into town. A little bigger deal, but still not anything I have a right to be upset about. I mean, we kissed on his back porch and made out for two seconds in the library. We're hardly seriously involved with each other. I've had deeper relationships with my pillow (unfortunately). So, now's not the time to get all possessive and scary and insecure.

After locking the library doors, I force myself to stand still for five seconds and take three deep, cleansing, sanity-reviving breaths. When I pass by his room again on my way to the exit, it's dark, but as soon as I step out into the dusky parking lot, I see them getting into Jamie's car.

My heart thumping against my sternum, I walk as quickly as I can to my own car without it looking like I'm rushing. Then I follow those taillights.

CHAPTER SIXTEEN

I wish I could say this is the craziest thing I've ever done, but unfortunately, Jamie's not the first guy I've stalked. Granted, I was in high school the other time I did anything like this. And it was on our senior trip, where I basically followed my crush around an amusement park for an entire day. Not really the same thing. I think I've taken this to a whole new level of creepiness now.

It's not too late to back out, though. I don't have to follow them into this Wal-Mart. But I'm gonna.

I want to watch the two of them for a while to see how they act together when they think no one's watching. I'd merely like an idea of what's been going on with them the past week, while I've been home alone, examining the pock marks on my face, watching my flowers wither and die, and wondering why Jamie hasn't called me. Is this an international booty call? Are they friends with benefits (hence, the "sometimes" girlfriend classification by Johnny), or is this more serious?

Jamie was clearly uncomfortable. He didn't know how to act or what to say. And he kept fidgeting with the earpieces on his glasses. I've noticed he does that when he's nervous and doesn't know what else to do with his hands. And the dynamic between them was odd. One minute, they seemed very intimate but then the next minute seemed fraught with tension and resentful things left unsaid. Or was I just imagining all of that?

Now, as they're walking through the huge sliding doors of the superstore, they seem more at ease. She's laughing at something he's said, but I don't want to chance getting close enough to hear. I only hope they're not laughing about me.

Inside the store, I'm dismayed by the bright fluorescent lights and wide-open spaces. Having never tried to spy on someone in a Wal-Mart, I've never noticed how poorly suited the layout is to such an activity. But I think I can make it work if I peek around corners and can find some merchandise to disguise myself. Like these massive sunglasses right here on this display. For additional cover, I snag a large nightshirt from a rack. I figure I can hold it up and hide behind it as I pretend to look at it if I notice them looking my way.

After pausing at the jewelry counter (I note with satisfaction that Jamie stares off into space and doesn't even glance down into the case before moving away and saying something that gets Marena to follow him), they move more purposefully toward the health and beauty section. Jamie grabs a hand basket from a rack when Marena starts to load him down with products. Tossing the boxes and bottles and tubes in his arms into the basket, he dutifully follows her as she wanders up and down the aisles. She sniffs shampoos and lotions and hair care products and even dabs something that looks like hair wax into his hair, pulling it into goofy-looking spikes that he almost immediately finger-combs away while laughing and telling her to "cut it out."

Then they seem to be having a real conversation. As in, real serious. I want to get closer so I can hear, and I figure I may be able to do so in the adjacent aisle without being seen, so I dash across the center aisle and take cover on the other side of the metal shelf where they're standing. Yes. Perfect! I can hear them just fine.

"…about time for you to get on with your own life, now that things are more settled?" she's asking in a seductive voice. "Come on! How fun would it be to be back out there again? Don't you wish you were stocking up on your own travel supplies right now?"

"Yeah, let me call Expeditions-R-Us and have them hook me up with an assignment."

"We have room for a few more people on the team going to Iceland."

"I don't think that would be a good idea. And anyway, what am I supposed to do, quit my job in the middle of a school year?"

"Yeah! Who cares?"

"I do. And even if I didn't care about my job or my students, I still have to think about Johnny."

"Oh, God!"

"What? I *do*. You're not going to change my mind about what's best for him. He has a job here, too, you know. And he loves it."

"He's a grunt at a bakery, Jamie. I'm sure you can find him something to do to keep him busy anywhere in the world."

"He hates traveling. As you already know too well. He only goes with me on my trips in the summer because I bribe him the rest of the year with porn magazines and candy. But he'd be miserable if we were always on the move."

"When are you going to worry about your own happiness?"

Their voices are starting to move away from me, so I walk parallel to them down my aisle. "I'm effing happy, okay, Marena?"

"You sound like it."

"I am! Just because I'm not doing something that *you* approve of doesn't mean it's not worthwhile."

"Fine, fine. Geez. I don't want to waste my last night here fighting. I just thought... you know, I'd ask one more time."

They're on the move again, so I don't hear Jamie's response. Damn. I take a few more steps, which brings me nearly to the end of the aisle, when the two of them come around the corner and almost run right into me.

Fuuuuuuuuuuu...!

I raise the nightshirt, but it looks completely unnatural.

"Oh, gosh! Excuse us," Jamie apologizes reflexively, pulling on Marena's elbow to remove her from my path.

I mutter, "It's okay," while keeping my shaded eyes pinned to my feet, praying that they're too involved in their conversation to give me a second look. It seems to have worked, too, and I've even slipped into the next aisle, but before I can catch my breath as I hang onto the shelf in front of me, I see Jamie's head pop into my peripheral vision.

He walks closer. "Kendall?"

Like an idiot, I look over at him, instead of turning and walking away, as I would if the name meant nothing to me.

"I thought that was you. What are you doing?"

The jig up, I push the sunglasses onto the top of my head, but self-preservation prevents me from telling the truth. I hold up the humongous nightshirt on its hanger,

139

noticing with dismay as I do that it proclaims, "Big is Beautiful," in glitter across the front. Gulping audibly, I answer, "Shopping?"

Marena joins us, looking unpleasantly surprised to see me again so soon.

Jamie points to the sunglasses. "What's the deal with those?"

I pat them as if they're my best friends and claim, "Oh, you know… Small town and everything… Sometimes it's easier if I can get in and out of the store without students or my parents' friends stopping me to talk."

"We'll leave you alone, then," Marena readily offers, flashing a sarcastic-looking smile. Until now, I had no idea one could smile sarcastically, but she's just demonstrated it wonderfully.

"Thanks," I reply equally sarcastically.

"Wait!" Jamie protests, looking like he's trying to figure out the answer to a riddle. "I thought you were working late."

Ah, shit. Yeah. That old story.

I wave it away, though, and reply, "It didn't take me as long as I thought, so I decided to swing by here and pick up a few things I need."

"Something for those sores?" Marena asks mock-sympathetically.

Pretending I don't think she's the biggest bitch in the world for continuing to point out my healing chickenpox, I snag the closest thing on the shelf next to me and say, "No, actually… this." I hold up the box as evidence.

Both of them widen their eyes, but while she laughs out loud, Jamie hides his smile by turning his head, raising his arms like he's stretching, and covering his mouth as if he's politely hiding a yawn.

"Good luck with that!" she barely manages to sputter.

From behind his hand, Jamie says while nudging her, "Hey. Come on, now."

I know before reading the box that it's going to be embarrassing, but I had no idea it could be *this* bad. Tampons, I could handle. Even something like anti-diarrhea medicine wouldn't be the end of the world, but when I look more closely and see that I've grabbed a four-pack of glycerin suppositories, I immediately turn maroon and feel my eyes well up. I'm too thrown to even put them back on the shelf and claim I grabbed the wrong thing. The whole situation is hopeless. I've told more lies in the past hour than I have all year, and it's tiring and depressing.

Bravely, I tuck the box into the crook of my arm with the nightshirt and lift my chin proudly. I will rise above...

Marena pretends to be chastened by Jamie. "Oh, I'm so sorry. How could I be so naïve?" She blinks innocently at me. "You know, I find good diet and exercise are just as effective at maintaining a healthy weight, without all the mess."

I sigh and try on a sarcastic smile of my own. "Thanks for the tip."

"No problem." She looks into the basket in Jamie's hands and says, "Oh, darn. I forgot to pick up some sunscreen." Looking into his face, she sweetly asks, "Do you mind running back a couple of rows and picking some up for me?"

He looks uncertainly at me, but he's too nice to say no, so he transfers the basket to Marena's hands and goes without complaint.

"SPF 8, please! You know what brand I like!" she calls toward his back. He raises a hand to let her know he's heard and disappears around a corner.

As soon as he's out of earshot, she grabs the supposito- ries from me and tosses them on the shelf. "You use those about as much as I eat meat," she declares. "Now, what's going on? Sister to sister. You can tell me. Did you follow us here? Because I have to say, that's a pretty pathetic move."

I laugh nervously but don't deny anything. Instead, I say, "I'm not your sister, Marena." I make sure I pronounce her name so it sounds like a dirty dock.

"It's Mar-AY-na," she snootily corrects me. "And, just so you know, Jamie's told me all about you two."

"He has?" I get a flash of me climbing him in the library and break into a sweaty blush.

"Yeah. You guys seem like good friends. And obviously something a *little* bit more, right?"

I nod mutely, still trying to get over the fact that he's talked about me to her.

"I know, he's cute and flirty, but that's just his personal- ity. It doesn't mean anything. A guy like him has to have something to do to keep himself entertained in a town like this. In this case, it's you. For now." She pats my arm sympa- thetically. "But he's not going to be able to stay here much longer, no matter what he tells himself is the right thing to do. And eventually, he'll come back to me, like he always does."

Remembering the conversation I "overheard," I narrow my eyes at her. "I don't believe you," I say, even though it tips my hand and makes it obvious that I care more than I want her to know.

"That's your prerogative," she allows. "I'm only trying to save you some trouble. He's an easy guy to fall for, so I don't blame you. And someone like you, who hasn't seen a lot of the world, could easily mistake a fun flirtation for something more serious. I get that. But I'd feel so guilty if you're hurt sometime down the line when he and I get back together, which is sort of inevitable. Don't say I didn't warn you."

Jamie returns, jogging with a bottle of sunscreen in his hands. He drops it in her basket and looks from me to her and back again.

He smiles innocently and asks, "What'd I miss?"

CHAPTER SEVENTEEN

I'm with Johnny. I want Marena to fall into a hole in the ground. Then I'd take huge shovels-full of dirt and toss them on top of her. This is what I contemplate as I try not to openly stare at Jamie while he somehow manages to make eating string cheese look sexy.

I was in the otherwise-empty teachers' lounge eating an apple and drinking a Diet Coke when he came in, waved casually to me, and headed straight for the vending machine. I tensely watched as he contemplated his choices for a long time before he decided not to buy anything but, instead, retrieved the string cheese he keeps in the staff refrigerator. Shame's kept me from saying anything to him. After last night, he either thinks I'm a frequent user of suppositories or—worse—Marena the Maneater told him that I was pretending to buy suppositories while I was actually stalking them. I'd rather be thought of as a bulimic who wears tacky nightshirts and trolls Wal-Mart incognito in my spare time.

Plus, now that I know what Marena looks like, I realize how ridiculous it is for me to think I'm anywhere close to being in his league. What she said to me must be true: he's bored and using me as a diversion from the burden of responsibility he carries around a town in which he's stuck indefinitely, against his wishes.

He finishes his cheese and tosses the wrapper in the trash. Then turning to me, he says, "I'm sorry about Marena."

This is a most unexpected and confusing apology. I gaze down at the brown soda that's collected in the lip of the aluminum can. Finally, I say lightly, "It's not your fault she's beautiful and smart and—"

"She's a bitch," he interrupts my list, which was going to be rather long and effusive.

Ha! He doesn't even know the half of it. I hope.

I don't refute his statement or try to excuse her behavior or the effect it had on me, but considering what I was doing when they ran into me—literally—I think it's best to downplay the whole thing. "It's not a big deal."

But he won't let it go. "She was rude and cruel to you last night. Don't think I didn't notice."

"Yeah, well, at least now I know what you've been so busy *doing* lately."

He nods. "She's kind of high-maintenance—Wait. What? No! We didn't—"

Still preferring to look at my soda can rather than him, I put up a hand. "Uh, please. You don't have to tell me anything. And I saw her, so I completely understand."

"Your opinion of me is depressing as hell."

"It's not an opinion or a judgment. But I'm a realist."

He crosses to the table where I'm sitting and flattens his palms on the surface. Bracing his weight on his straight arms, he leans toward me and says, "Let me get this straight: you think I'm the type of guy who walks around kissing and making out with and… and… *screwing* anyone who's ready and willing and available?"

"Well, maybe not *anyone*. I mean, there are only so many hours in a day and so many days in a week."

"So, I make out with you on a Tuesday in the library, but when you're out of commission for a week, and my ex-girlfriend—"

"Stunning, smart, gorgeous, worldly, *sometimes* ex-girlfriend."

"—blows into town without even giving me so much as a minute's notice, then I take it as a sign and toss her into bed, because after all, a guy has urges, and it's not my fault you didn't have the common sense to get every vaccine under the sun when you started working with a couple hundred germ machines on a daily basis? Is that how you think I operate?"

"It's not my fault I got sick!"

"That's not the point, and you know it." He pushes away from the table and stands with his arms crossed over his chest. "That's what you're taking away from what I just said? Really?"

"Well, you never called me!" I hate how lame I sound, but I have to defend myself somehow.

He tosses his hands in the air. "When I left your place, you said you didn't want to be bothered while you were recovering. I told your mom to call me if you needed anything, but I didn't want to be some kind of overbearing weirdo who can't take a hint. Plus, I texted you!"

"Once."

"Yeah, and got a dismissive response."

"What?"

Before he can explain, the door to the lounge swings open. He turns his back on me and walks over to the windows, where he pretends to enjoy the view of the parking lot. I make a show of going back to eating my apple and surfing the Internet on my phone.

Renalda gets halfway to the vending machine before stopping in her tracks and staring first at me before focusing her attention on Jamie. "Uh-huh!" She wiggles her eyebrows. "The tension in here is mighty thick."

I wish she weren't my boss. That way, I could tell her to shut up, get her snack, and go away so I can ask Jamie what the hell he's talking about, calling my reply text "dismissive."

Then I remember that Jamie and I need to talk to her, and that's actually why I've been hanging out in the lounge as much as possible, considering she's in here more than in her own office. Without acknowledging her declaration, I say, "Hey, we were discussing some ideas for that… whatever… that Dr. Underhill told you about."

"Oh, yeah! Operation Educate?"

"Is that what it's called?" I ask incredulously. Before I can filter, I add, "That's a terrible name."

Jamie coughs.

"Well, it *is*," I insist. "Anyway, good to know. Uh, it's just that I —we—were wondering a few things, like…"

Jamie turns around and takes control. "What kind of budget are we talking about here?"

"Budget?" She looks completely befuddled by his question.

"Yeah. Money. Funds. Do we have any available to us to implement whatever idea we come up with?" he asks impatiently.

She finishes her journey to the vending machine, inserts a dollar, and makes a choice without hesitating. "Oh. That. Umm… It probably has to be a self-funded idea."

"Told you," he mutters to me.

I ignore him and ask, "What does that mean, 'self-funded'?"

Taking her time, she retrieves her candy bar, unwraps it, and takes a bite before saying with her mouth full, "Free or run by volunteers or self-supportin'." Bits of peanut and chocolate spray from her mouth.

"Oh." I'm as disappointed by that concept as I am disgusted by her horrible manners.

"Project Educate. Does that mean this idea has to be more of a curricular idea, or can it be a school-wide practice? Give us some parameters here," Jamie requests.

She swallows. "*Operation* Educate can be whatever you want it to be. As long as it's a good idea. I want Whitehall to win, ya know?"

"Is there a prize involved?" I ask, desperate for more information.

Looking at me as if she thinks I'm crazy or stupid or both, she says, "Duh! I told you! The winnin' school gets a brand new library, and I'm not just talkin' about redecoratin' and gettin' rid of that nasty mural we have now. This makeover includes fancy new computers with a whole new online e-book lendin' program that's supposed to be the number one program in libraries across the country! That's why I asked you to come up with the idea, silly!" Taking in my open-mouthed stare and another bite of candy bar, she claims around her the food, "I'm sure I told you this!"

I shake my head, suddenly getting a flashback to how I felt a week ago: weak, chilled, sweaty, and faint. "W-what's the name of the program?" I make myself ask, even though I already know the answer.

She wrinkles her nose at me. "I don't know! E-Borrower, or somethin' like that. You heard of it?" When I nod limply, she says, "Of course, you have. I'm sure you know all about this stuff, since you worked in a big-city library for all those years. Anyway, this is somethin' worth gettin' excited about! I can't believe you don't remember me tellin' you about this. It's a prize worth workin' for, don't you think?"

Again, I nod, but I can't speak right now.

Jamie steps in. "That *is* an awesome reward, but if we're going to win, we need more information."

"I told you everything I know, Jamie!" she defends herself. "Call Dr. Underhill directly if you need more than that, because that's all he gave us!"

He gives me a look as if to say it's worth a shot to call the Superintendent for more guidelines. I blink blankly.

"Okay, then," he says to Renalda, who's making her way toward the door. "Thanks."

Before exiting, she turns back to us and asks, "Were y'all really talkin' about Operation Educate when I came in? Cuz it didn't look like you were talkin' about something so... normal."

Neither of us answers her, so she shrugs. "All right, then. I guess I gotta believe you." She leaves and heads down the hall in the opposite direction from her office.

A few seconds pass, and I mentally shake myself. I scoot back from the table and cross the room, where I drop my apple core in the trash and my Diet Coke can in the recycle bin.

"What's the matter with you?" Jamie asks. "Why aren't you more stoked about this? If we win... that would be great, wouldn't it?"

The bell signifying the end of our lunch shift saves me from having to give a detailed answer. Heading out the door without waiting for him, I say dimly, "Yeah. See you later."

Feeling sorry for myself is my favorite activity today. It's about the only thing I'm up for, anyway, besides going to Mom and Dad's and making them feed me and entertain me and keep my mind off things for a couple of hours. The work day couldn't have dragged any more than it did. For one thing, I was particularly anxious to get out of there without having to talk to Jamie again. He came by fairly soon after the dismissal bell, but I actually dove under my desk and hid so he'd think I was in the bathroom, or something. He waited for a few minutes, but then he eventually left, and he never came back.

There's absolutely no topic he'd want to discuss with me right now that I'm interested in discussing. I don't want to talk about Marena or my comparative awkwardness (as proven last night in a very public place) or suppositories or Operation Educate or E-Borrow or the library makeover in general or insulting him or kissing him or falling in love with him or anything!

What I really want to do is hang out with Lance Armstrong.

The first place I go at my parents' house, before I even announce that I've arrived, is my old bedroom. It was only my room for two years, after we moved here from Colorado, but I spent a lot of time here, staring at my Lance posters and reinventing myself every time a new fad surfaced.

Nobody at my new school cared what grades the new girl made as long as she had the right hairstyle and wore the right clothes and talked about the right TV shows, music, and celebrities and knew the names of all the MTV vee-jays. I was a decent mimic, too, so I did an okay job of convincing everyone I was just like them, accent included. It was great. My nerdy history stayed behind at my old school, thousands of miles away.

And I thought this town was going to serve yet again as my "reset" button. But my adult history doesn't care how many miles it has to travel to follow me. It has a longer attention span than its teenaged counterpart. It's tenacious and pervasive and persistent. And new hairstyles and clothes and subscriptions to every celebrity and entertainment magazine on newsstands aren't going to chase it away.

What would Lance "Live Strong" Armstrong do? Well, I doubt he'd run to his mommy and daddy's house and hug a fun-fur pillow to his chest while feeling sorry for himself. Lance would probably tell me to suck it up. He's battled and beaten cancer, not to mention how many times he's won the toughest cycling race in the world. He doesn't let the Marenas and Todds of the world dictate to him what he can and can't do. He doesn't compare himself to people who may be stronger or prettier or smarter or funnier or better in bed. He's not a victim.

He's Lance Fucking Armstrong.

And you know what? I'm Kendall Fucking Dickinson.

I created E-Lend. I created it to change the way people use libraries as the publishing and literary worlds undergo some of the biggest changes in their histories since the advent of the printing press. I created it to keep libraries relevant and current and cutting edge. I created it to keep books and reading in people's lives as they become more and more addicted to staring at screens and less and less interested in turning paper pages or visiting dim, musty buildings. It doesn't matter who's getting rich from it (well, it matters a little, if I'm honest, but still), because I didn't create it with the goal of becoming rich. Just because I'm not getting the credit for creating it doesn't change the fact that I *did* create it, damn it, and that it's doing exactly what I intended it to do.

And if I can pull myself out of this ridiculous funk that I've been fighting unsuccessfully for months and channel the person who created something as mighty as E-Lend, the other schools in the district don't have a prayer at winning that library makeover.

CHAPTER EIGHTEEN

"How do they go from being *that* to the mouthy little creatures we deal with every day?" Jamie murmurs so only I can hear as we keep our distance from the rest of the group crowding around Julia's sweet, sleeping newborn son in the school office at the end of the day.

I wince as Jane's voice hits a register somewhere near car-alarm level while she coos down into the poor kid's face. I bet he's pretending to be asleep in the hopes that everyone will leave him alone. Esther comes up on the scene and immediately starts singing, "Baby, Baby," by Amy Grant.

Waving to Julia when she catches my eye, I mouth, *"Later!"* and lunge for the door. I can't take another second of this estrogen-saturated tableau. Jamie immediately follows, tossing a "Congratulations!" over his shoulder at the beaming gym teacher.

In the month since Marena left town, Jamie and I have been professional and friendly with each other, but neither of us has spoken a word about the argument Renalda interrupted, nor has either of us broached the topic of our being anything more than friends.

We haven't discussed Operation Educate, either, so I still don't have a single viable idea for it.

Oh, but my face is back to normal, so there is that. Thank goodness I'm shallow enough for that to make a big difference in my attitude; otherwise, I'd be feeling really down.

"You walk fast for a little person," Jamie remarks as he catches up to me outside the gymnasium.

"Uh… thanks?" I laugh. "Just because you're a giant doesn't mean I'm a 'little person.'"

"You're below average height for a woman, face it."

"Okay, by like, two inches."

"Two inches is a lot."

"That's what she said."

When he's finished laughing, he says, "I needed that."

"Rough week?"

"Yeah. The kids are always crazy around Halloween. Beforehand, they're excited. Afterwards, they're on a sustained sugar high for a good two weeks. Not my favorite time of year."

"Wow," I tease. "I never would have pegged you as someone so allergic to fun."

"I like fun!" he objects. "But dealing with hyper five- and six-year-olds isn't fun."

"They always seem hyper and loud to me; I haven't noticed a difference that I've connected to Halloween. Speaking of, Brody told me he dressed up as a—wait for it—cat for Halloween. Shocking."

We laugh about that together, and I'm surprised when he continues with me toward the library when we get to our hallway. We haven't been alone in the library since… well, for a while. I've been trying very hard not to think about the last time we were.

When we get inside, he pulls up a chair next to my desk and stretches his legs out in front of himself, resting his hands on top of his head. "You know what he told me the other day?"

"I wouldn't even dream of guessing," I reply as I tidy up and check some things off my to-do list.

"Completely out of nowhere, he said, 'You probably shouldn't take a cat on a plane; it might spray on everything.'"

After cracking up, I say, "Yep. That sounds exactly like something he'd think about. Where does he come up with this stuff?"

Jamie shakes his head. "I don't know. He also asked me last week how to spell 'naked girl,' during one of our writing exercises. I told him he should ask his mom that and keep all the clothes on any girls in his school stories."

It takes me a long time to get my breath back after that one. My prolonged laughter gets Jamie chuckling, too. Finally, he says, "Ahh… anyway. That's the latest Brodester Report. Never a dull moment."

We sit without saying anything for a while, but I can tell Jamie wants to say something else. When his right hand sneaks up behind his ear and starts fiddling with his glasses, I say, "What's up?"

"What?"

"Is there something you want to talk about or something?" I nudge uncertainly.

"No. Am I bothering you?"

I smile. "Not at all. But you seem poised to say something."

"Oh. Well…" He seems to think about it for a second, then admits, "I was thinking about something, but… I dunno." He fidgets, bending his legs and sitting in a more upright position. "I'm worried you'll think it's a dumb idea."

I perk up a bit. "Is it an idea for Operation Educate? Because I'm all ears. That stupid contest has me stumped!"

"Uh, no. Sorry." He looks sincerely regretful that he can't help me, but then he doesn't say anything else.

"O...kay."

After a couple more minutes, I think he's going to remain mum, so I shut down my computer and grab my purse from my desk drawer. When I stand to leave, though, he blurts, "I think we should go out on a date."

This is probably the last thing I thought he was going to say, so it catches me completely off-guard. I open my mouth and close it a couple of times before managing to say, "Now?"

He laughs nervously. "No! I don't mean an afterthought cup of coffee at the end of a shit-tastic week in a dumpy café, where all we talk about is work. I mean a real, proper date. A Saturday night date. With dinner at a nice restaurant with cloth napkins and multiple eating utensils."

"Go on." I like this idea very much, probably much more than anything he would have told me regarding Operation Educate.

Standing and facing me, he says, "It's just... I've been thinking about things. And how I can't blame you for thinking the worst of me when *she* was here, because... Well, I really did think you wanted me to leave you alone, but I can see how you'd misinterpret my silence, since... " He takes a deep breath. "You don't know me. At all. And I don't know you. I mean, I know what you taste like and that you make these cute little noises when I kiss you, but I have no idea about the type of music you listen to or when you had your first kiss or where you went to college. That's just backwards."

I pinken at his blunt word choices, but I nod and work hard not to look away from him.

"So... what do you say? Are you willing to sit down at a dinner table with me and talk about everything *but* work? No Brody, no Operation Educate, no stupid Renalda stories... just us?"

It's absolutely ridiculous how happy his proposition makes me. I almost say no on the principle that I shouldn't need a man—however cute and funny and smart he may be—to ask me on a date to make me feel so good.

But of course, I don't. I say, "Yes!" and when I sound too much like the eager lonely girl who sits at home every weekend fantasizing about one of her co-workers, I tone it down with, "I mean, that sounds great. I'd like to eat a meal with someone other than my parents."

Now, why did I say that? I lament silently. He probably thinks I'm such a loser. Maybe he's reconsidering his invitation right this second.

But he simply grins and says, "I take it, then, that you're free tomorrow night? Or would your parents be too disappointed if you cancelled on them on such short notice?"

"I think they'll get over it," I bravely predict.

&.

"I hope you don't mind, but I thought we'd go somewhere out-of-the-way but cool. Very classy."

We're in the car, but it's not his car. One of his best friends works at a BMW dealership and gave him a loaner for the night, "just for fun." And it *is* fun. I've been playing with all the toys and gadgets and switches and knobs since we got on the road. I think Jamie's having even more fun, though, making the car do what it does best: drive really fast.

"Why would I mind?"

He laughs and makes a face at himself. "I don't know."

"I'm not picky. I just don't like—"

"Loud noises," he says at the same time I do.

"Are you making fun of me?" I press a button that makes the radio and GPS console flip into a hidey hole. "Whoa… sweet!"

"Don't break anything. Remember, teacher's salary."

"Yeah, yeah. I know you only spend money on exotic trips."

"You should try it sometime. It's great to get away from here for a while and visit someplace completely different." His face lights up. "When you don't even know the language, you're at the mercy of the locals, learning as you go, surviving on your wits…"

"Sounds terrifying." I'm picturing a tribe of scary people with face paint and animal horns and teeth sticking through their noses and ears.

"No! It's awesome. As long as you're respectful and not the typical obnoxious tourist, people in other countries tend to be kind of tender towards you. They're protective."

"'Tender'?"

He glances over at me. "Yeah. What's wrong with that?"

I turn my head to look out the window and hide my smile. "Nothing. Anyway, I'm not adventurous enough for that. I like being around people who speak the same language I do. I like knowing what goes into the food I eat, even if it's mostly chemicals, and that—unless there's some-thing wrong with the food—it's not going to make me sick. I don't like wondering if I'm inadvertently offending someone with a hand gesture or facial expression that's totally innocuous and innocent to me but means something like... I don't know... 'my brother screwed your mom seven ways 'til Sunday last night, and she liked it.'"

"Boring."

"Yep!" I agree cheerfully. "That's me. I think there are plenty of exciting things to do and see in English-speaking countries with all the modern conveniences that I like."

He laughs. "Well, at least you know what you like, even though you've never experienced anything else to know that you don't like it."

"I don't need to experience being held hostage in a Middle Eastern country to know that I won't like it." I say it playfully so he knows I'm not taking anything we're saying too seriously. I don't want him to think I'm making a political statement about how the United States is better than any other country in the world. First of all, I'm not sure I believe that. And second of all, I make it a rule never to discuss politics... with anyone. I don't think my parents even know who I voted for in the last Presidential election.

A few miles of highway pass without either of us saying anything. Then Jamie makes a turn off the main road, and it's like we've entered an era sixty years in the past.

"This town is frozen in the sixties," I marvel, gazing out at the old-fashioned storefronts and streetscapes, complete with faux sodium gas lights.

"I love this place," he says with a grin. "I stumbled on it one day when I was out for a bike ride."

"You rode your bike all the way out here?"

"Yeah. I do stuff like that all the time. Especially if I'm in a bad mood, or whatever. I'll get on my bike, point myself in a direction, and ride and ride and ride until I feel like I can't pedal another inch." He stops at the light at the intersection of streets marked "Main" and "Washington." "Anyway, one of those days, I found myself here in Hartford. And I thought it was the sweetest place I'd ever been."

"Ever? In all the world?"

He nods. "Yep."

The light turns green, so he inches forward. I notice a speed limit sign we pass that says, "20 MPH." And slow children play in this town, too.

"Everything seems so much simpler here," he reflects. "I know it's an illusion, that these people live in the same world we do—they've only chosen to make things *look* different—but I think there's a lot to be said for matching your lifestyle to your surroundings. I'll have to bring you back here sometime during the day. In the summer, even. People in this town cut their grass with those old-fashioned grass clippers on the little metal wheels. No motors, no gas. It's really cool."

As we make our way down Main Street, I get the strangest feeling, like I'm riding through a set on the TV show, *Mad Men.* Before I can say anything about it, though, Jamie angle parks in front of a charming bistro adorned with fairy lights and announces, "Here we are."

CHAPTER NINETEEN

At our tiny, out-of-the-way table, I finger the stem on my wineglass; Jamie rubs the corner of his napkin between his thumb and forefinger.

Then he says, "Okay, I'll start," which makes me smile. I'm glad he's not going to try to pretend this isn't awkward.

"I grew up in a tiny town about thirty miles from Charlotte. Johnny was an only child for seventeen years before I came along (I was obviously a big surprise), so my parents were a lot older than my friends' parents. And Johnny was clearly their favorite." When I tilt my head sympathetically, he states, "Oh, I didn't care. I was an independent kid. I was glad they lavished all their attention on Johnny; gave me the opportunity to do what I wanted to do without their interference. Anyway, I'm not sure who was happier when I went to college. I was thrilled to be getting away from this area; my parents were excited to get on with their retirement, eighteen years later than they'd originally planned. I went to NYU, and at the first opportunity, I joined an archaeological field team between my junior and senior years. After that, it was like college was my part-time job. I went to class when I felt like it and spent the rest of my time researching my next trip."

"You caught the bug."

"Big time."

"When did you have time to get a teaching degree, if you were always traveling?" I wonder, pulling at a piece of bread from the basket the server left when he brought us our drinks.

Holding up a finger, he replies, "Ah, yes. Well, my academic advisor somehow managed to convince me to minor in something 'useful,' considering how unsteady the work can be in my primary field of study. So I took some elementary education courses and got my teaching certificate. Came in handy, too, because I was unable to find any expeditions to join immediately following graduation. I taught third grade in Charlotte for a year while frantically searching for 'real' jobs. Then someone I'd worked with in New Zealand"—his sudden returned interest in his napkin tells me this "someone" must have been tall, leggy, and brunette—"put in a good word for me and got me on board a study in Ireland. It wasn't a dig—it was classifying artifacts that had already been recovered and cataloging them for display in a Dublin museum—but it was better than teaching multiplication tables to third graders."

"And you were in Ireland for how long?"

"A year or so, off and on," he answers. "Then I found a place on a team that spent two years in South America— Brazil and Argentina—before meeting back up with the same folks from Ireland in Tunisia. It was there that I got the news about Johnny's car accident."

"Oh."

Yes, the memorable Tunisia. So Johnny's misfortune

interrupted the tent-rockin' good time in Tunisia. Way to take one for the team, Johnny.

Instead of saying any of those insensitive things, I merely declare, "That must have been hard. I mean, er, difficult."

He finishes his wine and pours himself some more. Seeing that my glass is almost empty, he tops mine off and says, "Yeah. Well, it's not a typical year when you lose your career, your brother (for all intents and purposes), and both of your parents. I couldn't tell you much about what happened for many of those months. I sort of just existed, doing what needed to be done but not thinking much about it. When things settled down, I started looking for teaching positions in the area. I got the job at Whitehall, bought the house we live in now, and that's where we've been ever since."

Sincerely, I tell him, "Well, I'm impressed."

He chuckles. "Impressed at how depressing that is?"

"No!" I laugh and nudge his foot with mine under the table. "I'm serious. Nobody would have blamed you if you'd settled your parents' affairs, found a nice residential care center for Johnny to live in, and high-tailed it back to your real life."

"*I* would have blamed myself."

"Exactly! You chose the tougher option, because you knew it was the right thing to do. That was brave."

"I guess. Some people don't seem to think so. And it's not like it's some selfless act. I stay here because I couldn't live with the guilt, otherwise."

Since I know who "some people" are, and I despise her, I say vehemently, "That doesn't diminish the fact that you *do* stay. And *some people* obviously don't know the first thing about family if they don't understand that." When he keeps

163

his eyes down, I tap the back of his hand and repeat, "I'm impressed."

Now he looks up. "That means a lot. Thanks."

Segueing before things get too serious, I say, "Well, I haven't had quite as exciting a life as you so far." He snorts, but I continue. "I haven't! But there are a few things about me that are unconventional."

"More than a few, I'm sure," he interjects.

"I'm an only child, which isn't that exotic, but... I'm adopted."

His mouth drops open, which makes me laugh. "Really?"

"Really."

"But... That picture on your desk... I mean, you look so much like your mom!"

I nod. "Yep. Everyone always says that, which Mom and I get a real kick out of. I guess it's a matter of people seeing similarities where they think they should be."

"Hmm, interesting. Have you and your parents always lived in North Carolina?"

Shaking my head, I answer, "Nope. We lived in Colorado until I was a junior in high school. Then Mom and Dad were both offered teaching positions at UNC-Charlotte, so we relocated here."

"Was the move traumatic?"

"No! I was so glad!"

When he seems surprised by my answer, I explain, "I was thankful for the fresh start. I was kind of a nerd at my school in Colorado. Well, not 'kind of;' *really* a nerd."

"Come off it!"

To prove it, I reveal, "True story: my first kiss only happened when it did because one of the most popular kids in the school was trying to settle a debate with one of his friends about whether or not I was a lesbian. I kept to myself, wore baggy unisex clothes, and for a couple of horrible months had a super-short haircut that my mom thought looked cute on the model in the magazine but on me looked like... well, *not* cute at all."

Grinning, Jamie says, "Sorry. I can't picture this at all."

"I know, I'm so chic now," I joke self-deprecatingly.

"You're the best-dressed person at work. Besides me."

"No offense, but that's not saying much. Anyway," I continue, "when we moved to North Carolina, I decided all that was going to change. I reinvented myself—"

"Wait, wait, wait! Go back to the first kiss story. So... the guy just walked up to you and laid one on you, and that was supposed to prove you weren't a lesbian?"

I'm starting to regret bringing this up. Typical of me to over-share first and think about it later. "Not exactly. It was, uh... a little more complicated than that."

He waits expectantly when I pause, so I recite as quickly as possible, "He befriended me and asked me to tutor him, and when we were at the library one day after school, he told me it would be quieter and more private in the microfiche room, which no one ever used, and so we went back there, and I knew what was going to happen, and I *wanted* it to happen, so when he kissed me, I kissed him back, because I thought, you know, that he was sincerely into me, even though I had no idea why he would be. And when it was over, he stepped back and laughed and said, 'Ha! I told Nathan you weren't a lesbian. A freak, but not a dyke.'"

Jamie's lack of response to my story is unsettling, so I sum it up with, "It's a variation on a story that's happened to a million girls, so it's no big deal, but it was a major factor in the decision I made to be a completely different person when I got the chance with a whole new set of classmates."

He shakes his head. "Wow. Kids are so cruel."

"Whatever," I shrug it off. "I *was* a nerd."

"So? What was it hurting? Why couldn't they leave you alone?"

"Who knows? They were bored, I guess. I wasn't as mad at him as I was at myself for thinking he'd be interested in me at all. I mean, the guy was Mr. All-American. I was an idiot for falling for it."

"All-American douche." He laughs sadly. "That's a horrible first kiss story."

"Isn't it?" I agree lightly. "Oh, well. It was a long time ago."

"Not that I think you should tell me about it right now, but I hope the story of when you lost your virginity is happier than that one," he says.

I pretend to think about it for a second before revealing, "Yeah. Slightly."

That unconvincing affirmation makes him laugh. "Another time, then."

"Only if you think you can handle it."

"I'm getting more and more scared of it by the second, actually," he claims. "But maybe someday I'll be brave enough to—"

The server interrupts by arriving with our food and setting our plates in front of us. Jamie orders another bottle of wine and pours the last two glasses of the first bottle. Lifting his glass, he holds it poised for a toast, so I lift mine, too.

"To do-overs," he proposes.

Clinking my glass against his, I affirm, "Hear, hear!"

We're both feeling loose and warm by the time dinner's over, so as Jamie helps me into my jacket, he says, "Let's go for a walk."

"Okay. I'd love to see more of this town," I agree.

"I think there might even be some shops still open. We can duck into a few of them if you want," he offers.

"We'll see." I guess he thinks that since I'm a girl, shopping would be high on my list of things to do on a date, but I'd rather continue our conversation, which hasn't slowed down at all over dinner.

I've found out: his first kiss happened when he was in fifth grade, behind the slide on the school playground, with an older girl (a sixth grader) named Kimi; he ate a stink bug on a dare when he was in high school and wound up in the emergency room when he couldn't stop vomiting afterwards; before he discovered archaeology, he was convinced he wanted to be a professional competitive cyclist; and he and his friends still occasionally wrestle in the middle of the living room floor, like they did when they were kids ("but only when Johnny's not around, because it freaks him out").

I've told him: I went to UNC, because I got a full scholarship there *and* free books and room and board, since my parents were on the faculty; I usually listen to contemporary music, but I have a soft spot for seventies and eighties soft rock, because that's what my parents always used to listen to in the car, and it makes me feel nostalgic; when I was ten, my parents were able to convince me that three different hamsters were the same pet after the first two died; and my senior year in high school, I broke my leg dancing in my bedroom on rollerblades, but I told everyone at school that I broke it when I jumped into the shallow end of the pool at a frat party on the UNC campus.

As we walk down the sidewalk, past a side-by-side barber

shop and beauty salon, he says, "So, what I'm hearing is that you're practical, sentimental, gullible, and clumsy, and you can be dishonest when it suits your needs?"

"Yes. And what I know from what you've told me is that you're a noble, gross, immature cougar magnet." To soften my assessment, I slip my hand into his and squeeze.

He squeezes back. "That's, unfortunately, fairly accurate. Your traits are all endearing, but everything I've told you about me just makes me sound ridiculous."

"You might want to save the stink bug story for the second or third date… or never tell it to another soul. Ever," I advise. "A noble cougar magnet isn't the worst thing to be, though."

"Brings to mind someone like Mr. Darcy. At least the noble part does."

"You could do a lot worse than Mr. Darcy. Although I have a hard time picturing him wrestling on the floor at Pemberley with Mr. Bingley."

We both laugh at that image; then Jamie says, "You know what's even funnier than that?"

"That you know exactly what I'm talking about when I mention Mr. Darcy, Pemberley, and Mr. Bingley?"

"Uh, that, too. But I was going to say that you're the only person I've ever told most of that stuff to." He lets go of my hand and puts his arm around my waist as we continue down the sidewalk, stopping now and then to peer into shop windows that hold mannequins, furniture, books, and toys, depending on the type of store. Most of the stores are dark, but a few—like the bookstore—are still open for a couple of hours.

"Oh," I answer, surprised at both his revelation and the jump in my tummy when his hand comes to rest on my hip.

"I could have done without the stink bug story, but I'm glad you told me the rest."

"I hope I don't regret it," he kids, looking down into my face.

"You can trust me."

The real question is, can I trust *him*?

CHAPTER TWENTY

I'm uncovering and arranging the scones, fruit, cream, and assorted plates and plastic cutlery when Jane clears her throat and says, "All right, everyone, let's get settled and start the meeting." She claps her hands once as an exclamation point, and not for the first time I feel like one of her students. I try hard not to look at Jamie, but it's useless, so when I glance at him, and he quietly "Ribbits," before flicking out his tongue like he's catching a fly, I immediately and loudly laugh, drawing the attention of most of the teachers attending this month's breakfast staff meeting.

"What was that, Jamie?" Jane challenges haughtily.

As he loads his plate, he replies unapologetically, "I'd rather not share with the rest of the class."

"Okay, then," she lets him off the hook. "We have a lot to discuss today, so I'm going to start while you all get your food. Thank you, Kendall, for providing this morning's breakfast."

I nod graciously.

The food line moves down the long table in the teacher's lounge, and people take their seats in the folding chairs set up along the perimeter of the room. I remain standing behind the table, making sure everyone gets what they need and pouring orange juice into plastic cups for people who have their hands full with their plates. Jamie, the last person in line, takes the chair closest to the table and me after he has his food.

"The toy drive is well underway," Jane begins. "Thanks for sending notes home with your students so that we can make this a great holiday for kids in the area who are less fortunate. The last day for donations is December 15, so you may want to make one more push in the next week or two to make sure parents aren't forgetting.

"Next item: the holiday assembly. For more about that, here's Esther."

Esther sets her fork on her plate and her plate on her chair. She sings about the most wonderful time of the year while swaying to the front of the room. "All right, girls and boy, each of the grades is going to be singing one holiday song for the assembly, which is open for parents, guardians, grandparents, etcetera. That's all taken care of, but I still need two volunteers to help out. Don't be shy, now!"

Nobody says anything, but I see a few eye rolls. It seems like an eternity passes, but eventually Jamie stabs viciously at his fruit and sighs. "Fine! I'll do it… again."

Esther claps her hands gleefully. "I knew I could count on you, Jamie. Thank you! Now, who else? All I need is one more teacher-elf, people!"

Even after she starts singing, "Volunteers of America," nobody raises a hand or makes a peep. This doesn't seem to discourage Esther in the least. She keeps belting out the same line over and over again. Now that everyone's made it through the food line, I busy myself with covering everything and wiping off the dirty serving spoons, which I then place in a plastic bag so I can carry them home to wash them. I've almost succeeded in blocking out Esther's warbling as I think about Christmas shopping with Jamie after work. Then I hear my name.

"Kendall will do it."

My head snaps up.

Keeping his eyes on the fruit on his plate, Jamie casually repeats, "Kendall will help out. Right?"

"Well... I... uh..." I stutter. "I'm... uh... not sure what it entails, so..."

"It's nothing much," Esther assures me. "Mostly helping me get the students lined up and—"

"You have to wear a set of pointy elf ears and a pointy elf hat, and there's usually some sort of skit involved," Jamie interrupts. Then he pops a strawberry into his mouth and grins at me.

"Oh. Then... no."

"She'll do it," he tells Esther confidently. "She owes me one."

Everyone else is simply watching this triangular conversation, probably thankful they're off the hot seat.

Esther quickly accepts that answer without giving me a chance to speak for myself. "Great! Okay, then. That's all I have. Back to you, Jane!"

Jane retakes her position at the front of the room, but I'm still focused on Jamie, who's studiously ignoring me.

"Jamie!" I hiss at his profile.

He raises an eyebrow but keeps his attention on the two blueberries rattling around on his plate.

"Why did you do that?" I whisper fiercely while Jane goes on about building safety and the rules (that no one follows) about keeping all the exterior doors locked after hours.

He lifts one shoulder and murmurs back, "It'll be fun. And I couldn't listen to her sing that effing song for one more second."

"Gee, thanks. And what's up with the whole 'she owes—'"

"Excuse me!" Jane interrupts. "You're being very disruptive back there!" she directs at Jamie and me. "Can your conversation wait?"

I mumble a swift apology, but Jamie gazes belligerently at her. "I suppose," he answers. "But what you're talking about isn't very interesting, so…"

A few people snicker, but most have the same response I have, which is to stare open-mouthed at him and quickly look up at Jane to see her reaction. She juts out her lower teeth like a bulldog and stares him down.

When he doesn't blink or look away, she asks, "What would you rather talk about, Jamie? How about the district's and the teachers' union's policies about workplace relationships? Maybe you and Kendall would pay better attention to that topic, considering…"

He casually rubs at a scuff on his shoe and replies, "Well, we're not hiding anything, and there's nothing that precludes us from dating each other, so I don't know how that would be a more interesting topic. Now, *bullying*…" He resumes intense eye contact with her. "The district's pretty clear about that. Granted, it usually applies to students, but I'm sure there's a harassment policy that would apply to teachers who are hell-bent on asserting what little authority they have, to the detriment of other staff members."

Instead of addressing that thinly veiled threat, she makes a big show of looking at the clock over her shoulder and says, "We're running out of time, anyway. Unless someone has a *legitimate* issue they'd like to discuss in the last five minutes."

Jamie's answer is to get up, cross the room, toss his plate and cutlery in the recycling bins, and leave the lounge, allowing the heavy metal door to slam behind him.

As soon as the meeting grinds to an awkward close, I finish gathering my stuff as quickly as possible and hustle down the hall. I go to Jamie's room first, but it's empty, so I turn around right away and head for the library. Just as I'm hitting the doors, the first bell rings.

"Sonofa…" I mutter, pushing against the wood and glass.

Jamie's waiting for me inside my office. Taking a deep breath, I join him and close the door behind me.

"What the hell?" I ask him, tossing the bag noisily into my desk drawer.

"Everyone knew already, anyway," is his inadequate answer.

I laugh. "Uh, that's not what I'm talking about."

"The holiday assembly will be fine. You'll make a much cuter elf than I will."

"Not talking about that, either, although I'm plenty annoyed at you for that stunt. I'm talking about your temper tantrum with Jane," I clarify so he can't play dumb all day.

"It wasn't a temper tantrum. She's a bitch. I did what I've wanted to do for five years and called her out on it." He goes to the door and puts his hand on the doorknob. "I gotta get to my room."

"Wait," I implore. I go to him and rest my hand on his cheek, hyper-aware that my office walls are glass and that anyone who walks into the library can see what we're doing. "Why do you let her get to you?"

He turns his head and kisses my palm. "I dunno. I hate

how she thinks she owns this place and everybody who works here. And I hate how she uses every possible opportunity to put me in my place. And now she's going to pick on you, too? I don't think so."

I chuckle at his protectiveness. "I think you might want to rethink your strategy with her. She's not the type to let something go when she gets a little push-back. Just the opposite, actually."

He opens the door and steps out into the library, away from me. "Well, then, I guess we'll see who can push harder. Because I'm done letting her push me around. And we can take it all the way up to Dr. Underhill, if necessary."

Not waiting for my response (I don't have one, anyway), he turns and says, "See ya," as he exits the library.

☙

Tinsel, garland, lights, and wreaths adorn the quaint storefronts of Hartford, which is sparkling with Christmas spirit. Carolers traverse the main street, singing all the classics in the style of Bing and Frank and Rosemary and Dean. The only thing missing from the scene is snow, and some shops have even provided that detail with the fake version of it in their windows.

Anytime we spend more than five minutes in a shop, I roast in my wool coat, scarf, and knit hat, but it wouldn't feel like Christmas if I were dressed in anything less. Since this is North Carolina, though, I'm conspicuously overdressed for the weather, which is pleasantly cool but nowhere close to cold. Jamie's wearing a more appropriate peacoat, but even he's spent more time carrying it than wearing it. He's working up quite a sweat, anyway, making fun of my getup.

In a store meant to resemble an old five and dime, I

break the first rule of our fledgling relationship by asking, "Do you think it would be wrong for me to get Brody a Christmas present?"

"Yes," he answers succinctly. "After this store, do you want to stop into the coffee shop across the way? I'm dying for a macchiato."

I'm not deterred. "I know we're not supposed to talk about work when we're not at work, but—"

"Really?" he groans.

I laugh. "Sorry, but I really need to know your opinion."

"Then ask me at school on Monday," he retorts.

"But we're here right now, doing some Christmas shopping, and look!" I hold up the hand-crocheted winter hat with ear flaps. It's made to look like a cat. "It's perfect. He'd love it."

"He'd get his ass kicked. And anyway, no, it's not ethical for you to buy one student a gift." He snatches the hat from my grip and places it back on the rack with the other animal-shaped hats.

I follow him in the direction of the precious macchiato waiting for him across the street, clutching at his hand as I catch up to him. "But here's the thing. You know how we've been wondering what the deal is with his parents? How he only ever talks about his mom, and we never see his dad at school events?"

Looking both ways first, he tugs me lightly across the street at a jog. When we reach the curb on the other side, he says, "I feel a sob story coming on."

"Why do you always have to act like such a hard-ass when it comes to your students?" I ask, exasperated.

"I don't like to get emotionally attached. And you should probably take my lead on that." He holds the door to the shop open for me.

I duck under his arm and roll my eyes. "I have these kids for more than one year, though." It's the first time I've hinted at staying at this job after the school year's over, but I rush on before he can do more than raise an eyebrow at me. "Anyway, I found out the other day that Brody's dad *died* when Brody was a baby. 'Pancake cancer,' is what Brody called it."

Jamie stops studying the chalkboard and makes a face at me. "'Pancake cancer?' What the…?"

"I'm assuming he meant 'pancreatic,'" I explain, trying not to laugh, because it's not funny, even if it *is* sort of funny. Brody tends to put me in that strange no-man's land of protocol a lot.

He screws up his mouth to keep from laughing but eventually gives up and chuckles. "That's a good one. Anyway… you found out Brody's dad died, probably when he was too young to even be attached to him and have memories of him, so now you want to buy him a cat hat for Christmas? Like that's going to make it all better?"

"No!" I reply defensively. "I don't think it's going to make it better. And that's not the whole reason I want to buy him the hat. I just… I don't know. He's my favorite."

That admission elicits, "Tsk-tsk. That's not allowed."

"Well, it's not saying much, still, considering I can't stand most of the other kids."

"Now who's a hard-ass?" He goes back to squinting at the menu.

"They're brats! They sass back all the time, no matter what I say to them, and it's obvious they think they're the center of the universe." Since we're next in line, I try to concentrate on my options. "Oooh, peppermint mocha cappuccino! That's what I want."

"Okay." He digs his wallet from his back pocket and

steps up to the counter, where he orders for us. As we stand off to the side to wait, he says, "Well, you can't blame them for being that way. Their parents have instilled that in them from birth."

"I don't have to work with their parents all day, though."

"And consider yourself blessed that you don't. Now, can we *please* stop talking about work? It's been officially the weekend for"—he looks at the clock on his phone—"two hours. You're in serious violation of statute 06.231.45."

"Fine." I sigh. "You answered my question. I already knew the answer, anyway. I'm sure Jane would be all up my ass if I bought a student a Christmas present."

"I'm going to sit at a different table from you if you mention that name again."

"Sorry."

"Grr."

I could punch myself for bringing up Jane, especially after what happened earlier today. I was pleasantly surprised when Jamie was in a good mood and seemed to have forgotten all about the breakfast meeting by the time we met in the library after school. And now I've threatened our fun outing by sticking my foot in my mouth.

When we sit down at an old-fashioned high-top table for two, he looks across the table at me and smiles. "You look like someone told you for the first time that there's no Santa Claus, Easter Bunny, or Tooth Fairy."

I try to laugh at myself. "Well, I feel like a jerk for mentioning You-Know-Who. I'm such an idiot sometimes."

He wraps his hands around his coffee mug and rolls his eyes. "Good God."

"Seriously! Why don't I mention your dead parents and go for the real mood-kill?" I close my eyes. "Sorry. Again."

Since I have my eyes shut, I don't see his expression, but

his tone is calm and quiet when he says, "I don't mind talking about them. I don't get the chance very often."

I open one eye and see that he's casually sipping his coffee and looking right at me.

"Really?"

"Yeah. I mean, Johnny never talks about them, and they never come up in the conversations we have: 'Hey, pass the remote.' 'Can we watch *SpongeBob*?' It's not really deep, meaningful, reminiscent discourse." He half-smiles. "What do you want to know?"

What a loaded question! Ever since our first date, I've been dying to ask him more about them. I have *so* many questions. And now that I have my chance, I can't decide what I want to know the most. I feel like I have to pick one question only, because I don't want it to seem like an inquisition. But if I choose wisely, his answer may cover some of the other questions I have.

After mulling it over for a bit, I go with, "What happened? I mean, the way you described it, they were ready to ride off into their retirement sunset as soon as you had your high school diploma, but then just a few years later, they were both so bad off that Johnny had to take care of them."

He nods and pushes at a spike of whipped cream with his pinkie. "Yeah, well, I'm sure I'll catch hell about that the next time I see them," he jokes.

"Seriously, though," I urge.

He smiles sadly. "My mom was always what we called, 'flighty.' She'd forget stuff or do strange things like put the milk in the microwave. We chalked it up to her being distracted, one of those people who was always in her own little world. But halfway through my sophomore year in college, she was diagnosed with early onset dementia."

"Oh, geez."

"Yeah. It sucked."

"How old was she?"

He closes one eye to do the math. "Er... 64-ish."

"Wow." This topic isn't elevating the mood, but it's fascinating, so I selfishly prod, "Then she passed away?"

"Nope. At this point, she and dad were still independent. Her good days greatly outnumbered the bad, and Dad could keep up with her disorientation okay. I went off on my travels without much worry. Dad and Johnny had things under control. But then... Dad started to get run down. I noticed it while I was home on a break, but he took it as a criticism and got all pissy with me, told me he could handle things and that I should mind my own business in Bora Bora, or wherever I was headed next."

"Gosh!"

He waves away my shock. "Ah, you had to know my dad. He was rough around the edges, but that's how he masked emotion and sentimentality, which were frowned upon by his generation."

Actually, that sounds familiar, I think but don't say. After all, Jamie's probably ten times more emotionally evolved than his dad, but still... as he said earlier about Whitehall's students, it's hard to fight what you've been taught since infancy.

He continues, "Anyway, I chose to believe what I wanted to believe and did exactly what he suggested, only in Argentina, not Bora Bora. A year or so passed, and Johnny started mentioning to me during our infrequent phone calls that he was worried about Dad but couldn't get him to go to a doctor, not even for a routine physical." Ruefully, he shakes his head. "I told him to leave the cranky bastard alone and let him rot, if that's what he wanted." Quickly, he adds, "I was only kidding; I didn't mean it."

"Of course you didn't."

"I still feel like a jerk for saying it, considering... Well, he finally couldn't ignore the pain, so he went to the ER, thinking he had appendicitis or a kidney stone, but... it was cancer. Everywhere. Stage 10, or whatever number they give it—times two—when you should technically already be dead." I widen my eyes but don't interrupt. "He was gone three weeks later."

"But I thought both your parents were alive when Johnny had his accident." The timeline's getting all confused in my head. Maybe some more peppermint mocha cappuccino will help. Ah, damn. It's gone.

When he sees me tilt my cup and look regretfully into it, he offers, "Would you like me to get a refill for you?"

I shake my head and push my cup away. "No, I want to hear the rest of the story."

"All right. Well, they *were* still alive. Both of them. But Dad was in the hospital full-time, and Johnny had a career and a fiancée—Tiffany—and a life, so Mom had to go to a retirement home, where she could get the round-the-clock supervision she needed." He rubs his chin. "I was about a month away from the end of my stint in Tunisia, but I wasn't happy there. Plus, I was worried about what was going on over here, so I decided to bail early to come back to the States and give Johnny a break from his constant trips to the hospital and to the nursing home, but before I could get everything in order... I got the call from Tiffany's parents."

"Oh, no."

"Oh, yes. She was gone; Johnny was—at that time—comatose; my dad was disappearing in front of everyone's eyes, although no one had told me how bad it was; and my mom… well, she didn't know who she was, much less who anyone else was, so she might as well have been dead. It was a pretty depressing situation to return home to."

Suddenly, he drains the cold dregs of his coffee, sets the cup down, and looks around. "It's getting busy in here; let's go walk."

"Okay."

The wind has picked up, and the temperature's dropped dramatically. Compared to the steamy coffee shop, it's particularly chilly outside, so when the first gust of wind hits us, I narrow my eyes and wrap my scarf more tightly around my neck, tucking it down into my coat to keep it secured. Jamie shoves his hands into his coat pockets but holds his elbow out away from his body so I can thread my arm through and slip my own hand into his pocket.

When we've covered a quarter of a block of the darkening sidewalk, he says, "Anyway, Dad died before Johnny even woke up, and Johnny was still in the hospital when Mom slipped away for real six months later. It was like she knew there was nothing good left to live for."

Quietly, I ask, "Do you honestly feel that way?"

He watches his feet as we walk. "I did. I mean, her favorite son would never be the same again (not that she even remembered he was her favorite); her husband was gone (again, not that she knew who he was); and all that was left was beleaguered me—a stranger to her, as well—and a string of identical days. There was nothing physically wrong with her, as far as anyone could tell; she just let go."

I rest my head against his shoulder.

His voice measurably brightens. "It was a rough year or two, but things have decidedly started to look up. I'm getting the feeling your mom would adopt me."

"Definitely," I agree, looking up at him. "She thinks you're the cat's pajamas."

"The bee's knees?"

"And arms and legs and head."

"I've never been so glad to be an insect."

We've made it back to the car, which is parked at a meter that's about to expire. He rests his lower back against the door and pulls me up against his chest. I briefly kiss his chilly lips, tasting the sweet, milky coffee and whipped cream still on his breath. When I pull back, he leans forward for more, which I'm happy to give.

"Come home with me tonight," he offers quietly after another kiss that leaves both of us smiling.

I want to. I really do. Really, really, really. But I feel my smile slide from my lips. "What about Johnny?" I hide my hesitancy behind logistics.

He smirks. "What about him? We gave up the bunk beds years ago. Even have separate rooms now."

I laugh nervously at his joke. "I know, but still."

The image of accommodating, he suggests, "I can call Frank and see if he'll stay over with Johnny. Then I can stay at your place."

Oh, boy. How do I tactfully break it to him that the invitation isn't on the table?

My eyes must say everything (and maybe not as tactfully as I'd have liked), because he takes a step back. "Oh. Okay. Never mind." He looks past my shoulder. "Oops. Meter's up. Better get moving. Unless you want to shop some more... I can add some more time to the meter."

"Jamie..."

"Hmm?" He looks over his shoulder at me as he rounds the back of the car to get around to the driver's side.

He pops the lock and gets into the car, so I follow suit and try to explain, "It's just—"

"Nope. No explanation necessary. I was being presumptuous. And horny." He pulls the seatbelt across his chest. After buckling it, he glances at me and smiles. "Really. Let's change the subject."

I realize there's nothing I can say to make him feel better. Plus, I don't know if I can articulate the reasons for my reticence without sounding like the protagonist in a poorly written young adult novel about the virtues of abstinence. I don't even believe in most of those virtues, so it would ring hollow. I only know I'm not ready to go *there* yet… with anyone.

Considering we have at least a thirty-minute drive ahead of us, I feel a responsibility to at least try to make light of the tension. "Would you believe me if I told you there's a large Guatemalan family staying with me at the moment?"

"No." He reverses from the parking spot.

"Damn." I bite my lip. "Ummm… I'm saving myself for a vampire?"

Hanging a right, he points the car toward the main highway and presses the gas. "You and every other woman, it seems."

"See? It's not your fault. You're just not undead enough. Sorry."

Finally, this gets a laugh. Then he gives me his best smoldering, tortured look.

"You look constipated."

"Screw you."

"I told you, not tonight!"

CHAPTER TWENTY-ONE

D id I sleep at all last night? It sure doesn't feel like it. Judging by all the kinks and aches in my joints and muscles this morning, I spent half the night twisted into the shape of a pretzel.

Now, as I listen to the morning deejays poll the listening audience about what they'd bring to work if there were such a thing as adult show-and-tell, I remember a private show-and-tell from the middle of the night and groan.

I'm no stranger to sex dreams. I have them all the time, and they don't always mean anything (at least I hope they don't, considering one time I had one about my high school geometry teacher, who was a troll with hairy knuckles). Other times, like last night, they do mean something.

Last night, I had the most vivid dream of my life. It didn't feature a celebrity (those are usually pretty good, though) or someone from my past in some surreal setting that would clue me in right away that this wasn't reality. In this dream, I was with Jamie. And we were at his house, in his bedroom, which I've never seen. It was dim in the room, but I could still see everything. Everything. He turned on some loud music, "So Johnny won't hear us," which made me feel a lot better. Then he did things to me that made me feel *a lot* better than I've ever felt before. And I stopped thinking and allowed myself to feel his tongue and his fingers and his…

Well, before I knew it, I needed the loud music to drown out my moaning. Then I was so confused. Because the more intensely I felt what was happening to me, the more I seemed to be pulled away from the feeling. That's when I realized with crushing disappointment that I was dreaming. I woke up with my hands clamped over my breasts and the sheets tangled between my legs. Still jammed into my ears were my earbuds, through which Adele was belting out a lusty tune. I yanked them out and listened for several minutes to my beating heart and ragged breathing. As the spasms subsided, I delicately cupped a hand over myself while I fought the urge to cry. Interestingly enough, it didn't take long for me to fall back asleep.

It wasn't the first (or second or third or seventh) sex dream I've had about Jamie. But all the others were Polaroid snapshots compared to this one. This one was in 3D with stereo surround sound.

Now that I'm fully awake, there are certain parts of the dream that are slowly coming back to me, parts that should have alerted me to the un-reality of it. For example, his bed was glow-in-the-dark. And made entirely out of a material that looked like Fruity Pebbles but felt like velvet. Plus, there was a picture on the wall that was weird, but familiar. What was it? I rub my eyes as the image tickles the edges of my brain but doesn't quite reveal itself to me. Then it hits me: it was the same framed print that Todd had on his bedroom wall, a black and white photo of a computer motherboard. I hated that picture! But it seemed like I was always staring at it, especially during sex. Great. Now I associate sex with that stupid picture and vice versa.

Irritated, I slap my alarm clock silent and shuffle to the bathroom, where I pee while the shower warms up. By the time I step under the stream a few minutes later, I've consoled myself with the fact that at least I didn't have a spontaneous orgasm in the middle of the night due to a sex dream featuring Todd. As a matter of fact, I've never had a sex dream about Todd, which is telling.

Dumb Todd. I have him on the brain, thanks to the knowledge that he's going to be making even more money off my idea through the very school system for which I work, once the E-Borrow software is installed at whichever school wins the Operation Educate contest. It's just as well that I can't think of a decent idea for the contest, considering I'd have to be reminded of his betrayal every time a student checked out an e-book.

Come to think of it, the whole idea of having the software at an elementary school is stupid. How are the kids going to read these e-books? It's not like they're carrying around tablets or Kindles or NOOKs. Some of the older kids have smartphones or iPods (which is ridiculous, in my opinion, but no one's asking), but they sure as heck would never imagine using them to read anything longer than a ten-character text. What I'd need to make the software relevant is a bunch of tablets on which the students can read the e-books.

I drop the bottle of conditioner, barely noticing when it lands on my instep and shoots an obscene-looking blob of goop into the air and onto the shower curtain.

Oh. My. Gosh.

That's it!

I'm waiting in the hall outside Jamie's classroom when he stumbles through the side door, wearing his cycling gear, pushing his bike, juggling his laptop bag, holding his keys in his teeth, and cursing under his breath. The first time I saw him in his helmet, spandex (although he swears it's not spandex), and special cycling shoes, I nearly wet my pants from laughing so hard at him (behind his back, of course; we didn't know each other very well at the time). Now, I'm used to it and can even admire how well he fills it all out, even if it does seem a little (okay, a lot) over-the-top that he insists on wearing such specialized clothing nearly every time he gets on a bike. And today, I barely even take note of it.

"I have the idea," I blurt, making him look up sharply at me.

His keys drop from his mouth onto the floor. "Oh, shit. You scared me. What are you doing out here?" He props his bike against the wall next to me. When he reaches down to retrieve his keys, I'm almost too psyched about telling him the idea to notice his tight butt and the defined muscles in his legs.

"I know what we need to propose for Operation Educate. I thought about it this morning in the shower."

"Okay…" He unclips the chin strap to his helmet, which he removes and jams onto the tiny bike seat. His hair's matted down from the headgear, but he doesn't do anything about it as he unlocks his classroom and wheels his bike to its spot behind his desk. His shoes click on the asbestos-tiled floor.

"Do you want to hear it?" I ask, even though I'm going to tell him no matter what his answer is.

"Can I hear more about the shower?"

"No."

"Can I change my clothes and get a cup of coffee first?"

"No."

He tousles his hair and puts his hands on his hips. "Damn. This must be some idea."

On second thought, his garb is distracting, especially the parts below his waist, so I relent, "Fine. Get dressed. But hurry."

He ducks into the "emergency" bathroom in the classroom, where he keeps a couple of pairs of pants and some dress shirts hanging on the hook on the door.

"I can hear you, if you want to talk to me through the door," he offers.

I take him up on it. "Okay. Uh..." I fast-forward in my head through the parts of my morning that he doesn't need to know about and decide that it'd be best to simply tell him the idea, not what led up to it. "We should start a district-wide e-book lending program. Each school library will have a certain number of tablet readers for in-school use. These tablets can be used to read books or do other educational activities, such as math and spelling, or even writing."

When I stop, he says, "Go on."

"That's it!"

"That's it?"

"Yeah. It's a simple idea."

"Except for the part about who's going to buy these devices and pay to maintain them and replace them, when they inevitably get broken," he mentions. I hear a zipper.

Not discouraged, I tell him, "The IT department will be in charge of maintaining them, like any other computer. And kids will use them under strict supervision, so there shouldn't be a great deal of breakage."

"Okay, how do we buy them? Renalda said the idea had to be—what did she call it?—'self-funded.'"

Now I grin, proud that I've even thought of this detail. "We'll have the tablets donated. Either by the manufacturer or a local retailer or... we could ask a prominent local philanthropist to chip in."

The bathroom door swings open. Jamie emerges in his school clothes, minus socks and shoes, which he extracts from one of his desk drawers. As he pulls on the dark socks, he asks, "How many prominent local philanthropists do you know?"

"None," I grant. "But so what? We don't have to have all the details ironed out; we only have to provide the idea, remember? I'm sure the big-wigs in the district, Dr. Underhill included, know exactly who to go to when they want something they can't pay for."

He nods. "True. But..."

"What? This is a perfect idea!" I insist. "It combines technology with learning with the kind of fun gadgets and toys that kids—and parents—love. And it's a *library* idea, incorporating part of the prize into it. What good is some fancy e-book lending program like E-Borrow"—I somehow manage not to gag when I say the name—"if the kids have nothing to download the books to?"

"Most people in this district have PCs or laptops at home," he points out.

"Most, but not all. That's another thing: this idea levels the playing field and narrows the gap between the haves and have-nots."

He doesn't say anything while he finishes tying his shoes. Then he slides his desk drawer shut and looks up at me, a slow smile spreading across his face. "Congratulations."

"Really? Do you think this is it?"

"If you can write it up as convincingly as you just told it to me, I think so. That last part sealed the deal, in my book."

When he stands, I rush across the room before thinking about it and hop into his arms. He laughs at my exuberance as he returns my hug.

"I just... it just *came* to me."

"In the shower," he reminds me.

"Yes."

I let go of his neck and land lightly on my feet. Grinning up into his face, I reveal, "I feel incredible."

"You should. That's an awesome idea. And it's all yours."

That acknowledgment almost causes me to levitate. "You're right."

"I know." He pecks my lips on his way past me. "Now, I'm dying for a cup of coffee. Let's hurry before the first bell." When I catch up to him in the hallway, he says, "Okay, big thinker. Your next challenge is upon you."

"Huh?" I reply distractedly, still reveling in the glory of my success and the relief of not having the assignment hanging over my head for the first time in weeks.

"Yep," he answers seriously. "But this one's a real brain-buster." After a dramatic pause, during which I say nothing, he asks ominously, "What's going to be our holiday assembly act?"

CHAPTER TWENTY-TWO

I never realized before how high up the stage is in the school's cafegymatorium. Standing on it now, I feel like a giant. *So this is what it's like to be Jamie,* I think hysterically. The music starts, and Jamie moves, but I'm seemingly stuck to this one wooden plank of floor.

"Uh, that was your cue," he informs me, in case I didn't know.

"Yeah, I know," I snap.

"You're not moving."

I shoot him a fake dirty look and laugh at myself. "Stop pointing out the obvious! You're making me more nervous!"

He stops the music and motions to the empty basketball court below us. "What the hell is there to be nervous about? Nobody's here. You made sure of that."

"Hey!" I shake one leg, then the other, in an attempt to loosen up and partly to prove to myself that I'm not glued to the floor. "Don't be cranky at me because I wanted to practice a few times without the possibility of anyone coming in here and seeing us."

"On a Saturday night, when we could be doing something... else."

"You can kick my parents' butts at Apples to Apples some other time. The assembly is Thursday!" Saying it out loud gives me heart palpitations.

Exasperated, he cries, "It's an elementary school holiday assembly, for Pete's sake, not Broadway."

"It may as well be Broadway. If you had thought to ask me before so kindly volunteering me for this, I'd have told you that I get terrible stage fright."

He's utterly unsympathetic. "All the greats do. Now, let's go. We have this down. Three minutes of humiliation, and it'll all be over."

"That's what she said," I mutter without thinking.

When he laughs, I drop my sulk and join him.

"Okay, okay," I finally declare, closing my eyes and taking a deep breath. "Ready."

He starts the music and gets into his place, in front of the cardboard fireplace, next to the pathetic-looking artificial Christmas tree and under the dangling mistletoe. During the intro music, he shifts a large bag onto his shoulder and mimics stroking the Santa beard he'll be wearing as part of his costume.

As arranged, I sashay over to him carrying a plate of fake cookies and an empty plastic cup. I insisted on making this a dress rehearsal (for me), so I'm in costume—a typical 60's housewife's shirtdress, apron, and heels—to make sure I can do all the dance moves without falling on my face. Arriving in front of "Santa" as the Ronettes sing the opening lines to "I Saw Mommy Kissing Santa Claus," I set my props on a small table next to the Christmas tree and peck his cheek, and we start our routine. There's some circling, eyebrow jiggling, and even some ass tweaking. Then

I tickle him "underneath his beard so snowy white," and we look around as if we're suddenly afraid of being caught.

The instrumental break begins. That's our cue to do our stupid little choreographed dance.

As we sway and slide, I ask anxiously, "Are you sure this isn't inappropriate?"

He twirls me and pulls me against him, my back to his chest. "Of course it's inappropriate, but it'll be funny."

"I don't know; I don't want to get in trouble. What if one of the parents—or Jane—raises a stink?" I let my head fall back as he dips me and tugs me upright again.

"If you're worried, we can always go with Plan B, 'Nuttin' for Christmas.' It won't be as funny, but it's still a cute idea. And we can stay in our elf costumes for that one."

I hate those elf costumes. I bite my lip and repeat, "I don't know."

"This *is* fun."

I do a silly trot on my tiptoes in a circle around him. "Yeah, but it's not worth getting fired. Maybe I shouldn't pinch your butt at the beginning."

"That's the funniest part. C'mon. I'll be wearing a Santa suit, so it's not like you're going to really be pinching anything. I think the parents will get a kick out of it. The kids will, too."

When I'm in front of him again, he puts his hands around my waist and lifts me gently off the floor, carrying me a few steps before setting me down again, underneath the mistletoe where we began. As the music reaches its finale, we freeze with our eyes closed, noses touching, and I kick my foot up behind me in time with the last note.

We open our eyes at the same time and grin. "It's good," he reassures me. "Trust me."

There's that phrase again.

"If you think so…"

"I do."

Turning away from the intense look in his eyes, I walk to the back of the stage and peer around a curtain. "Now, where are we going to make our costume change?" I wonder. "There's so much junk back here that there will hardly be enough room to line up the students who will be waiting to take the stage."

Jamie walks past me and trots down a set of stairs in a narrow passageway next to the stage. Under the stairs is a door, which he opens to reveal a closet that's currently stuffed with janitorial supplies, including a cart, a trashcan, a bucket, and a mildewed mop. When he removes the large items, he pulls on the string hanging from the small square of ceiling to turn on the bare bulb and waves me into the close space. After I'm in, he follows, closing the door behind him. We can barely turn to face each other, much less move our limbs to remove clothing or don costumes quickly without nudging and hitting each other.

"Hmm," he murmurs, inches from my face. "It's cozy."

"There's no way this will work," I state, squirming against him.

"No. Probably not. I guess we can run to the restrooms across the hall while the fifth graders are singing their songs. I think they're doing two."

I blink the dust from my eyes and twitch my nose against the lingering moldy mop smell. "How long does it take for you to get into that Santa suit?"

"A minute, tops. How about your dress?"

"The same, except I'll need someone to zip me."

"So we'll meet back out in the hallway, I'll zip you"—he wiggles his eyebrows suggestively—"then we'll slip through the way-back backstage door."

"Sounds like a plan," I approve.

He stares at my mouth for a second. Meeting my eyes again, he smiles crookedly. "Do you think this is where Freddie brings his girlfriends?" he asks, referring to Whitehall's perpetually stoned janitor.

"I think the only girl Freddie loves is named Mary Jane," I reply drily.

"I think he's missing out on a golden opportunity." All it takes is for him to lean forward an inch for our mouths to be touching. Then I contribute a centimeter so that our mouths and bodies are pressed more firmly against each other. Without breaking contact, I bat the light's pull-cord so that it's not hitting us in the side of the face. The metal end tings as it makes contact with and catches on one of the brackets on a shelf overhead.

Soon, my back's against the cool, painted cinderblock wall. I rest my arms on his shoulders and link my fingers together against the back of his neck. His fingers get to work unzipping my dress. I shrug my arms from the sleeves and let the costume fall to the floor around my feet. He pops open the bra clasp between my breasts.

"Ahhh," I sigh into his mouth when the undergarment falls away and his palms graze my nipples.

His breath quickens. I unbutton and unzip his jeans. He takes one hand off my breasts to nudge his pants past his wiggling hips. Then he uses both hands to do away with my panties, nearly tearing them in the process. I don't mind. He also doesn't seem to mind that his shoes and the cramped quarters prevent him from stepping completely free of his pants. Nor do we mind that neither one of us happens to be carrying around a condom. The only thing I mind is that he's stopped kissing me.

I open my eyes to see him staring blatantly down at me.

"What's wrong?" I ask, almost unable to keep from giggling at my husky voice.

"Absolutely nothing," he answers just as thickly, lunging for me again.

I nip at his lips as he lifts me onto himself. He bounces me experimentally a couple of times and sighs contentedly before burying his face in the space between my neck and shoulder. Pressing me against the wall once more, he thrusts deliberately and firmly.

"Oh, God," he whispers rapturously, raising goosebumps on my neck and chest with the breath that feathers against them.

I tighten my legs around his waist and pull gently on the back of his hair so he'll look at me.

"Hi," I say softly when he finally manages to focus on my face.

"Hello," he replies craning his neck so his lips can reach mine.

I lower my head and fall into a kiss that eventually leaves both of us gulping for air in the dusty closet. We barely have our breath back when he quietly advises, "Hold on," grips me around the waist, and moves me up and down while I wiggle against him. This frantic, less-than-graceful maneuvering effectively hits all the right spots, and within a few minutes, we're spent, slick with sweat, and grasping onto each other to remain upright.

I straighten my legs, surprised and relieved when I'm able support my own weight.

Jamie's legs are done. He falls to his knees, wraps his arms around my lower back, and rests his forehead against my belly. "Fuck me," he mutters between heaving breaths.

"I just did," I pant back.

Oh, gosh.

I just did.

I just… did.

I had sex in a janitor's closet at work. With a co-worker. Who happens to also be my boyfriend. For now. Oh, gosh! What the hell did I just do?

CHAPTER TWENTY-THREE

"*S*tupid people for $1000, Alex.*"*

"*The answer is: The stupidest person on the planet.*"

"*Who is Kendall Dickinson?*"

"*Correct!*"

I'm watching *Jeopardy!* with my parents as I try to avoid Jamie at all costs (hanging out, watching a *Jeopardy!* rerun with one's parents is an expensive price, too).

Okay, maybe I'm not being fair to myself. Perhaps I'm insane, not stupid. You know, insanity can be hereditary. And since I don't know much about my family health history, there could be some rampant crazy in my birth parents' gene pools. In that case, it wouldn't be my fault that I insist on doing the same stupid things over and over and expect a different result. It would also account for the fact that I can't stop thinking about Saturday night in the closet and wishing I could go back to the minute right before I realized what an idiotic thing it was to do.

I think I covered my panic well as we pulled ourselves back together. It probably seemed like I was having trouble breathing because it was hot and close in the closet, and we had exerted ourselves quite a bit. There was no way for him to know I was screaming at myself. And when I asked him to open the door so we'd have more room to get dressed, he probably didn't notice how my voice was all pinched and squeaky. Or if he did, he likely attributed it to the aforementioned conditions. And if he thought it was odd that I wanted to go straight home—alone—when we left the school, he didn't call me on it.

I mean, I kissed him in the parking lot by our cars, and it was a sincerely naughty kiss, much to my chagrin, because despite it all, I still ached for him. But as soon as it ended, and he stepped away from me, I remembered that I wasn't supposed to want that.

It's like as long as he's touching me, I don't have any worries. But the minute there's no skin-to-skin contact, the spell is broken. I've done nothing but worry since driving away from him last night. I'm hoping that I can come up with an awesome solution to my lust-induced idiocy before I have to face him tomorrow. I have to play it cool. I can't be all giddy and giggly and fawning. That's how it started with Todd. But it didn't take long before I was just this brainless thing on his arm. After two years of that, I started to believe it. And everyone we knew believed it, too. Then I was left with nothing.

No, it's best to nip this in the bud before it gets any more serious than it already is.

Jamie's call at 9 a.m. gave me some insight into what a crack addict must feel like on her first day at rehab. I wanted so badly to answer his call, but I knew I wouldn't be able to act like everything was normal, so I let it roll over to voicemail. However, as soon as my phone chimed to let me know he was finished leaving his message, I dialed into my mailbox with shaking fingers.

"Good morning. Uh… I thought you'd be awake by now. I hope I didn't wake you up. Anyway… just wanted to let you know that Johnny and I are going to that crazy flea market you like. He wants to do some Christmas shopping. I should probably be worried. But I was wondering if you wanted to tag along or… if you needed anything while we're out. We can swing by and get you. Or drop off anything you need. Or whatever. Oh, my gosh. If I was smart, I'd so hang up right now and delete this message, because I sound absolutely, effing pathetic, but I know you kind of get off on stuff like that, so I'll let you keep this message so you can laugh your ass off when you listen to it. Just… whatever. Call me when you get this. Bye."

Reflexively, I almost did. I almost told myself, *To Hell with worrying about making a fool of myself over yet another guy,* because this is a guy who allows me to see him make a fool of himself on a regular basis, and a guy like that can't be a guy like Todd. But I know that logic is wacko, so I forced myself to set the phone aside while I finished getting ready to go to Mom and Dad's for brunch.

The next time I heard from Jamie was when he sent me a photo of a Lance Armstrong lunchbox with the accompanying text: *"I just saved you from getting this from Johnny for Christmas. Agggghhh! Can't promise any more heroics like that, though. ?"*

My thumbs twitched, but I did not send a reply.

Another call (sent straight to voicemail) at around noon: *"Me again. You probably mentioned that you have plans today, and I'm being a pest by calling you in the middle of them. Honestly, I'm having trouble concentrating today. But… anyway… that's a creepy detail that I'm sure you'd rather not know. Like the stink bug story. Oh, well. Too late. Maybe we can get together tonight? Let me know. Bye."*

I had escaped to the bathroom to listen to the message. When it was over, I closed my eyes and took a deep breath. That done, I studied myself in the mirror, wondering if I looked like a woman who'd been screwed senseless under some stairs in an elementary school janitor's closet less than twenty-four hours earlier. The person staring back at me just looked sad. I'd say the average woman who has an experience like mine doesn't look sad. Probably because she's looking forward to many more experiences like that one, whereas all I have to look forward to is eventual heartbreak.

But I don't believe in depression, remember? So I checked my teeth for spinach from Dad's quiche and kept my lips pulled back from my teeth in an expression approximating a smile. Or close enough.

The next text came during a cut-throat game of dominoes. I waited through two whole rounds before making a big show of reading it out of obligation. *"Miss you,"* was all it said. I rolled my eyes, smiled, and muttered, "Clingy," before taking my next turn.

Now, after the fifth chime that makes me jump, fumble for my phone, and anxiously read what's on the display (*"At batting cages with Johnny. C U 2mrrw?"*), Dad asks, "What's going on with you over there? You waiting for a call from your agent, or something?"

"No!" I respond too seriously to his jokey question.

"Okay, then," he mutters under his breath.

I make myself vertical for the first time in hours. An imprint of my body stares up at me from the microsuede couch. "I should probably get going. It's a school night."

Mom tries to sound casual, but the worry's all over her face when she asks, "Is everything okay with you and Jamie? I was surprised he wasn't with you today."

"He had plans with Johnny. Plus, we don't *always* have to be together." I try to use laughter as a punctuation mark to that sentence, but it only ends up making me cough. My laugh box is broken.

She gives me a sideways look as I mope toward the front door. "All right..."

I blow them both distracted kisses and make my escape.

"BOO!" That, combined with the loud slap of palms on the counter, combined with my raw nerves, combined with lack of sleep, make me pee in my panties a little. Well, enough that I'm glad I'm wearing black pants.

I plaster a smile on my face before turning from switching on the catalog computers.

He doesn't even give me time to say anything fake, though. Cheerfully, he asks, "Where were you yesterday? You fell off the grid! Johnny and I were all over the place. Did you get my stupid messages and texts?"

I put my hands in front of my face and pretend I'm overwhelmed by his questions. I don't have to act too much. Working hard to keep any defensiveness from my tone, I say, "I was at Mom and Dad's. They say hi. Left my phone at home, though. Didn't even realize it until I tried to call you on my way home from their house." Wow, this lying thing is easy! He's soaking it up, too. "Anyway, by the time I got home and checked my messages, the battery was dying, so... It was just as well, because I was tired."

He nods. "Yeah, I figured it was something like that. I knew you wouldn't let me get away with being such a goober if you were within arm's reach of your phone."

I laugh weakly and play with my hair.

That's when he pulls back his head and squints his left eye at me. "Are you okay?"

"Yes!" I say a mite too emphatically before toning it

down with, "I'm fine. You?" *Yeah, that's it; go on the offensive. Good non-plan. Way to improvise.*

Unfortunately, he's too smart to fall for it. "I'm not the one who's acting strange."

"I'm not!"

He looks skeptical, but instead of pushing me, he proposes, "Coffee?" pointing with his thumb over his shoulder at the door.

Play it cool, Kendall. "Nah. I mean, no thanks. I'm going to straighten up here before the first bell."

Confusion clouding his features as he looks around the immaculate library, he accepts, "Okay. I guess I'll, uh, see you at lunch, then?"

I give him what I suppose is my usual chipper response. "Sure! Absolutely! Lunch."

"Alrighty, then."

"See ya!" I straighten the already-straight stack of scratch paper next to the computer beside me. As soon as he clears the library's threshold, I sag into the child-sized chair, my knees knocking together in a clumsy A-frame, and put a shaking hand to my forehead.

This is going to be a lot harder than I thought.

I'm a smidge smarter than I've given myself credit for, because at lunch, I get the brilliant brainstorm to sit in the noisy cafeteria with all the students, instead of the quiet teachers' lounge, where conversation would be much too easy, or—worse—the library, where private conversation would be inevitable.

At first, I think my plan has worked even better than I'd

hoped, because several minutes pass before Jamie finds me at the otherwise-empty teachers' table (nobody actually chooses to eat in here). He tosses his paper bag next to my sectioned tray of something that's supposed to be Salisbury steak, mashed potatoes, and peas. Oh, and chocolate pudding. Straddling the bench, he sits down, but instead of throwing his other leg over and sitting square to the table, he remains facing my profile.

"I've been waiting for you in the teachers' lounge," he shouts, leaning closer to my ear so I can hear him.

I poke at the congealed gravy on my "steak" and pretend like I'm too busy inspecting it to look at him. "I forgot my lunch at home!" I yell.

He nudges my shoulder with his finger. "Why didn't you tell me or come get me?"

The noise level's too high to compete with, so I merely shrug. It's actually uncomfortably loud in here. I have to resist the urge to plug my fingers in my ears and squeeze my eyes shut.

Finally, after staring at my profile for what feels like forever, he scoots even closer to me and says straight into my ear, "What the hell is going on?"

I twist sharply to look at him, "What? Nothing!"

He grits his teeth. "Bullshit."

"Jamie!" I glance around us, irrationally paranoid that someone's going to hear him.

"I can't even hear myself think in here, so no one else is going to hear what I'm saying," he insists.

"Well… they may read your lips," I counter lamely.

"Kendall…" He stops and takes a deep breath. "Did I freak you out yesterday? Did I call you too much or send you too many texts? It's just…"

When I try to interrupt him, he puts his hand on my

shoulder and continues, only a little louder, "...I didn't want you to think I wasn't thinking about you after—"

"I get it!"

"No, really. Let me explain."

"Not here!"

"WOULD YOU SHUT UP AND LET ME TALK?" he booms, his deep voice trampling over the kids' racket.

A hush falls over the cafeteria as 150 pairs of eyes land on us. After what feels like an eternity, Brody says clearly and mildly, "Mr. Chase is P.O.'ed."

"Forget it," Jamie mutters, grabbing his unopened lunch sack from the table and storming out.

"Yep. Told ya," Brody tells everyone willing to listen. "He is *mad*."

"Thank you, Brody," I say in an effort to get him to be quiet.

"You're welcome, Miss Dickinson. But I think he's prolly mad at *you*."

When I pretend like my biggest worry is how I'm going to eat all my chocolate pudding, the students eventually get bored with watching me and go back to their vociferous lunchtime chatter. As soon as I'm not the center of attention anymore, I slink to the trash and dump my tray's entire contents before sliding it onto the metal shelf with the other dirty trays and slipping from the cafeteria.

I'm half-expecting him to be waiting for me in the library or in my office, but my relief at not finding him in either of those places is short-lived. I know the time for "the conversation" has arrived, and it makes no difference whether it happens now or in three hours or three days or three weeks.

CHAPTER TWENTY-FOUR

O r not. Apparently, when Jamie said, "Forget it," he meant it. Because he hasn't talked to me since his outburst on Monday.

I've stayed busy, though, writing the proposal for my Operation Educate idea. I'm not going to lie; I want to win. So I'm on about the seventh draft of the proposal, and I'm thinking about going back to my first version, which was more no-nonsense and straightforward. But it was boring. Hence, the other versions, which are slightly peppier. What I need is a second opinion. From my only friend.

But when I get down to his room, it's dark and locked up, even though it's not even 4:00 yet. From across the hall, Bonita sees me stop outside his door and stare at it. She calls out, "He left right after the last bell. Said something about not feeling well."

"Oh."

What I really want to know is, since when does Jamie feel the need to explain anything to another teacher? The fact that he gave Bonita a reason for leaving early tells me that he was lying.

"I hope he's not coming down with something right before Christmas Break. That happened to me last year, and it was horrible!" she shares.

"Yeah," I say distractedly. Then I shake my head clear and smile faintly at her. "Well, thanks, Bonita. Maybe I should call him to make sure he's okay."

That's what a normal girlfriend would do. Ha! What is "normal," anyway? I probably wouldn't know it if it screwed me in a janitor's closet.

When I pull into his driveway, I immediately see him through the open door of the detached garage situated slightly behind his house. He's standing next to a mostly disassembled bicycle that's flipped upside down on blocks. He looks up when he hears the crunch of my tires, but he returns to his tinkering before I even alight from the car.

As I approach the garage, I say lightly, "The only thing that looks sick here is that poor bike. What are you doing?"

"Trying to figure out how this thing works," he answers curtly.

I don't point out that he could accomplish that by going on Wikipedia and save himself the trouble and mess and risk of major expense when he can't get it back together correctly. Something tells me he's not in the mood for any advice from me, though.

I glance over my shoulder at the house. "Is Johnny home?"

"Nope."

"Bingo with Frank?"

"Yep. It's Wednesday."

"Right… Bonita said you left because you were sick."

He grunts as he twists off a bolt with a wrench. "Yeah, well, it's none of her business, but I'm a firm believer in 'cover thine own ass.' Wanted to make sure someone had a story to tell Jane or Renalda if they wandered past my room."

"Or me. When I wandered past your room. Actually, your room was my destination."

He says nothing to encourage further disclosure, but he knows me well enough to recognize when encouragement isn't necessary.

"Yeah. I, uh, wanted to run my Operation Educate proposal by you." I hold out three sheets of paper, folded lengthwise. "I have a couple of versions, but I'm not sure which one to submit."

Studiously avoiding eye contact, he examines the bolt he's removed and places it in a pile with a bunch of other bolts on the work bench behind him. "It's your proposal. Submit whichever one you like."

"I don't know which one I like."

"That sounds like a 'you' problem."

Gulping, I pull the papers closer to my chest. "Oh. Okay. I just thought—"

"What? You thought that you were ready to talk to me now that you need something from me?" He turns and looks fleetingly at me for a reaction before working to remove the next bolt.

I don't know what's sadder, his attitude toward me or his destruction of that beautiful bike. I decide the bike is the bigger travesty. At least his attitude toward me is somewhat justified.

Folding the proposals into fourths, I tuck them into my coat pocket and quietly say, "I was waiting for you to come to me. I thought you didn't want to talk to me."

Still utterly calm, he asks, "Now, why would *I* come to *you* after you made it obvious that *you* didn't want to talk to *me*? *You* were the one screening your calls—don't deny it— and eating your lunch in the noisiest place on the planet, despite your raging phonophobia, and slamming the door in my face every time I tried to start a conversation. What kind of masochist would I have to be to keep coming back for more of that?"

"I'm sorry. I—"

But he's on a roll now, becoming more animated, obviously saying everything he's been thinking for the past two days. "I mean, I know I've set a precedent in this relationship—is it okay for me to call it that, or is that going to freak you out?—where I have to initiate *everything*, at extreme risk to my pride in some cases, and have to be okay with watching you withdraw afterwards and wonder if it was something I did, said, didn't do, or didn't say, or if it has nothing to do with me at all, and it's all down to you or… whatever!" He tosses the wrench onto the concrete floor with a clang. "I'm tired! Tired of playing whatever game this is. I don't even know the fucking rules, other than Rule Number One, which is to never try to get close to you." He jabs at his temple with his index finger. "That's messed up, Kendall!"

"I know."

When I don't say anything other than that, he widens his eyes disbelievingly and tosses his hands up. "That's it? *You know?*"

I shrug, not sure what else he wants me to tell him. "You're right," I finally settle on, but I don't get any more specific than that.

He snorts. "Oh. Great. Well, I feel so much better now, knowing that I'm right about not knowing anything. That's sooo helpful." After retrieving the wrench, he goes back to destroying his bike.

Hmmm... Must tread lightly here. The last thing I want to do is reveal that I have trouble trusting him based on my relationship with Todd. First of all, he'll be—rightly— offended to be suspected of being anything like someone like Todd. Secondly, he'll spend a bunch of time trying to convince me that he's nothing like someone like Todd, which, of course, he'd say. I mean, who owns up to being like that?

So, I offer a safe piece of information: "It's not about anything you've done or said or not done or not said."

"Perfect."

I move close enough that I can wrap my hand around the tube that connects the seat to the rest of the bike frame. "Maybe it's easier if we're just friends."

For the first time in the whole exchange, he stares straight into my eyes. He scoffs at that suggestion, the outside corners of his eyes tilting downward like the corners of his mouth. "Maybe you should have thought about that before screwing me Saturday night. You should have told me to stop."

"I wasn't thinking," I admit. "And I didn't want you to stop."

"Because you weren't thinking."

"Partly?"

He shakes his head. "Unbelievable."

"It sounds bad, but that's not what I mean."

"I'm afraid to ask what you *do* mean." Having said that, he stalks off toward the house.

After a millisecond's hesitation, I follow him and nearly get a face full of "ouch" when the screen door to the sunroom bounces back from his slamming of it. I find him at the kitchen sink, washing bike chain grease from his hands.

Before I can try to explain myself, he asks, "Do you have feelings for me, or not?"

"Of course, I do!" I'm starting to get pissed off that he thinks so little of me that I have to defend *everything*.

"Then I honestly don't see what the problem is or why you'd have to think about anything or why any thinking would lead to the 'we-should-just-be-friends' conclusion." Wiping his hands on a dishtowel, he turns to face me.

"It's complicated."

"Frankly, I find that hard to believe."

If he thinks that statement's going to prompt me to tell him all about it, he's sorely mistaken. I stubbornly stare him down.

"Well, I can't help you make it less complicated if you don't tell me how it is."

"Maybe I don't want or need your help. Did you ever think of that?"

It's obviously something that's never occurred to him, because he suddenly looks like he's hit a rock in the road. Like a veteran cyclist, though, he quickly regains his balance. "Fine. But I'm not interested in your proposal."

Initially, I think he's talking about the Operation Educate proposal, and I'm thrown by the quick change in subject, but I say, "I'll figure it out. I just thought you wouldn't mind giving it a onceover before I hand it in to Renalda."

In a long-suffering tone, he informs me, "Not *that* proposal. I mean the other one, the one about just being friends."

"Oh." I feel like I've been punched in the gut. It never crossed my mind that we wouldn't always be friends. "But you're still friends with Marena!" It's out before I can think better of it.

Precisely folding the dishtowel and draping it over the edge of the sink, he replies, "Well, that's a lot different."

"How?" I want to know the new way that I'm different from or inferior to Marena. I was sure I'd already thought of them all.

"First of all, I'm not friends with Marena; I don't like her. And"—I see the pulse in his neck when he pauses, swallows, and says—"I was never in love with her, so... Big difference."

When I stand there with my mouth hanging open, he adds, "Anyway, if you don't feel the same way, then you're right to tell me. I wish you'd said something sooner, but this clearly isn't about what I want."

My eyes well up with tears and my chin wobbles. "This has nothing to do with how I feel about you, okay?" It's just as well that he bites his lip and looks down at his shoes, since I'm very conscious of what an ugly crier I am, but there's no stopping it now. "This is about a promise I made to myself after learning a very hard lesson. So this is not about what I want, either. It's what's for the best. For me. And if you think that's selfish, then too bad!"

As he slips past me to exit the galley kitchen, he pauses and pats my shoulder. "I think you spend a lot of time thinking about how you feel and not very much time thinking about how you make others feel. You can label it however you want. Good night."

A few seconds later, I hear a door shut softly in the other end of the house.

CHAPTER TWENTY-FIVE

Well, this is beyond awkward. Like something out of a nightmare, actually. Only I'd prefer to be in the nightmare where I'm about to go onstage in front of the whole school without any clothes on, instead of wearing this manifestation of sex. More specifically, this dress is the embodiment of sex with *Jamie*, who's standing as far away from me as he can, kitted out in his Santa getup, in the wings of the tiny backstage area.

We have not been happy elves during this assembly. And a few seconds ago, when we met in the hallway, as planned, for him to zip my dress, he almost didn't wait for me to lift my hair out of the way before pulling up so hard on the zipper that it raised the whole dress almost past my butt. I caught the bottom hem in time, but before I could protest, he was striding for the backstage door.

I don't know what he's so mad about. After all, I'm the one who's been told in no uncertain terms that I'm a selfish user.

I wanted to stay friends. I tried to make it as painless as possible. I mean, what else does he want from me? He's the one making this difficult. I was completely content to go back to the way we were before our first date. We were good as friends. Maybe not as good as more-than-friends, but good enough. And we were our own people back then, not one entity. When we weren't a couple, we were both intelligent people. But what if people start seeing me as the window dressing and Jamie as the brains of the operation?

That's what happened with Todd. Like Jamie, he was gorgeous and good at getting people to like him and to think that he was good at everything he did. So, at work, he was Todd the God, and I was Todd the God's girlfriend who shelved books. But "Aren't they the cutest couple?" That was supposed to be my consolation for never getting any credit for my hard work and intelligence. And I taught people to treat me that way.

Not this time. I can't do that again. I need to be respected at work in my own right. And I'm afraid I'll never get that as Jamie's girlfriend. It'll always be, "Oh, yes. Jamie's a very talented teacher; he has the greatest ideas! And so good with kids! Did you know he's dating the school librarian? They make a really cute couple." Period. Nobody will care how inspired my library displays are or how creative I am about getting kids to like reading and try new books. Nobody will see anything past my sunny personality and how well it complements Jamie's intellectualism.

Screw *that* in a janitor's closet.

Three minutes. Three minutes. I keep repeating this to myself as the fifth graders wrap up their wobbly rendition of "Silent Night."

Then Esther enthuses into the microphone, "For our final performance, our very own librarian, Miss Dickinson, and the charming Mr. Chase will delight us with 'I Saw

Mommy Kissing Santa Claus.' Let's give them a warm welcome to the stage."

Jamie steps out ahead of me and strides across the stage to the accompaniment of much giggling from the students and throaty laughter from the adult females. My emergence receives half of a wolf whistle when one of the dads is brave —or stupid—enough to attempt it with his wife sitting right next to him and realizes how foolhardy the idea is halfway through it. I smile nervously and gratefully in the direction of the whistle before standing on my mark. Jamie nods at Esther, who starts the music.

Everything goes according to plan until the butt-tweak, which I decide not to do at the last minute. It seemed inappropriate in practice, when we were alone, but now—especially in light of recent events—it feels wrong on too many levels. Unfortunately, Jamie's still anticipating it, so he fake-flinches anyway, and it looks dumb. Plus, his overcompensation moves him out of my reach, so when I try to twirl his hair, I stumble in my high heels and have to grab his arm for balance. But the Santa suit is so baggy that I don't grab anything more solid than his velour sleeve, and he has to catch me with his other hand to keep me from falling on my face. By this point, our timing is all off, and we're rushing to catch up to the song so we can go into the dance sequence on time.

We make it—barely. But I'm seriously flustered that it's going so badly.

"Hey. Relax. Smile," he mutters in my ear when he gathers me to his chest after the twirl. We're not mic'ed, so there's no chance of anyone hearing us.

I try to follow his instructions, but it's hard to smile when you're about to cry. I merely nod. Step, step, step, dip. After he pulls me up from the dip, he reaches behind me and gives my bottom an impromptu goose, which makes me yelp and grin at the resulting reaction from the audience, which is surprised laughter.

"That's better," he encourages, smiling through the ridiculous beard.

While I circle him on tiptoes, I say, "You look so dumb in that beard."

"You look hot," he replies, grasping my waist and lifting me. "It's a good thing this suit is baggy."

I can't help but laugh at the idea that he has a boner somewhere in there.

Under the mistletoe once more, we finish the song, eyes closed, noses touching, and my foot kicked up. At first, I can't bear to open my eyes to see what I imagine—based on the silence—must be the audience's horrified expressions. But then they start applauding and cheering... loudly. If I weren't so relieved, I'd be bothered by the volume of the response, which hurts my ears. I open my eyes but keep my nose pressed to Jamie's, almost afraid to move. His eyes twinkle down at me.

"Told you it needed a butt-pinch. They loved it."

I simply smile broadly. Just as I'm about to back away from him to face the audience, he pecks my lips, but before I can even register what he's done, he turns and shouts to his class, seated on the floor right at the base of the stage, "Huh? How'd you like that?"

They respond by jumping to their feet and clapping even harder. A couple of them rush the front of the stage and slap at the floor with their hands. Brody gazes up and announces to his classmates, "Miss Dickinson wears red panties, like Christmas!" as he stares straight up my dress.

I step back a few feet, too amused by his observation to blush.

Then Esther's taking control of the assembly once more, and Jamie and I give one final wave before walking backstage. I hear her say, "Well! I'd say that's one of the more *lively* performances we've had from our faculty participants. Very cute. Anyway—that's all we've got, folks. See you after the holidays!" She sends them off with a vibrato-heavy demand to have a holly, jolly Christmas. While she sings, I stand just off-stage, listening to the parents meeting up with their kids.

"You sang so great! Of course, I could hear you!"

"I saw you standing on the back row, like always, you tall thing!"

"You were definitely the best reindeer."

Next to me, Jamie takes off his beard and Santa hat and runs his fingers through his hair. He pulls his glasses from his pocket and slides them onto his nose.

"You okay?" he asks when I don't move for several seconds.

Staring into the middle distance, I nod spacily. "Yeah."

"I, uh, got a little carried away at the end."

"It's okay," I quickly reassure him, focusing my eyes on his face.

He smirks. "Oh, I wasn't apologizing."

I smile indulgently at him. "Then you're not forgiven."

After a conceding nod, he says, "Fair enough."

Suddenly, I blurt, "What did you tell Marena about me, back when she was here visiting?"

When he looks blankly at me, I clarify, "She told me that you'd told her 'all about' me. What did she mean? What did you tell her?"

He appears to be sincerely thrown by my question. Finally, he says, "I didn't tell her anything. I mean…"

Staring at a spot slightly over my shoulder, he seems to think harder about it, but I pat his arm.

"Never mind. It's just something that's been bothering me ever since she said it. I should have known she was lying. Merry Christmas, Jamie."

Neither of us moves, though.

Realization dawns on his face. "Wait. I think I know what she was talking about. She was fishing for information about women in my life, and I… well, I've made up women before to get her off my case, so she didn't believe me—you were in your self-imposed chickenpox quarantine—and it was too soon to call you my girlfriend…."

He blushes and fiddles with his glasses. "Anyway, where was I going with this? Oh. Yeah. I kept telling her more and more about you to get her to believe that you were real." Now he laughs at the memory. "I told her how much we had in common; how we both liked cycling and *didn't* particularly like kids and how we were the recycling Nazis here at the school… I think I even told her about Operation Educate—although we didn't know that's what it was called at the time. I told her way too much. But once I started, I couldn't stop talking about you. I still think she was shocked when she met you and found out you were a real person. She probably thought it was impossible that there was… *is*… a woman out there so much like me."

"Mr. Chase! You up there?" comes a shout from one of his students down in the gym.

He shrugs. "Anyway. I guess I'd better get back to them. Have a merry Christmas."

"Yeah, you too."

I watch him descend the stairs and emerge through the archway at the bottom, where his adoring public awaits.

When I exit the bathroom after changing clothes, I nearly run straight into Renalda.

She seems out of breath. "Oh, Kendall!"

"Renalda…"

"What a sweet little dance routine you and Jamie did! That song makes me think of Christmases from when I was a little girl. Memories!" She blinks rapidly. "And I got your proposal on my desk. So professional! You didn't have to go to all that trouble to make it look so nice!"

"It wasn't any trouble," I reassure her. "So? What do you think of the idea?"

Waving her hands in front of her chest, she answers, "Oh, I haven't read it yet. It's been a busy coupla days, you know, leading up to the break, what with the end of the quarter and all… And I haven't even started my Christmas shoppin' yet!" She laughs nervously. "But I'll try to give it a look before I deliver it to Dr. Underhill."

She makes it sound like she's doing me a major favor.

"Okay."

"I'm sure it's fine. Better than fine; great! You don't need me to tell you that." She's edging away from me. Frankly, I'm surprised she's still in the building.

"Happy holidays," I eventually tell her, getting the feeling that she's waiting for me to give her permission to leave.

She looks relieved. "Oh, you too, Kendall! I hope you get to do plentya smoochin' under the mistletoe with Jamie."

My already-strained smile freezes. "Yeah," I manage to say. "Well, gotta get this dress back to the costume shop before it closes." I wave and turn, letting the painful smile fall from my face.

In my office, as I'm struggling to maintain my composure with my back pressed up against the closed door, I notice a large gift bag sitting in the center of my desk. With much trepidation, I cross the room and open the small card that's peeking from the nest of tissue paper inside the bag.

In childish handwriting are the words, *"Merry Christmas, Kendall! Love, Johnny."* In different, more familiar handwriting is the message, *"Some things are destined for each other. Johnny insists that's the case with you and this gift. Live strong."*

I pull out the tissue paper and peer down into the bag. Staring up at me from the front of a plastic lunchbox is Lance Armstrong.

CHAPTER TWENTY-SIX

I've made it to New Year's Eve, but I can't stand it a minute longer. I can't let Jamie continue to think I'm a selfish, insensitive user-bitch. Well, maybe he'll still think that after I explain myself, but I'm going to at least try to explain myself. Even if it makes me sound crazy. If nothing else, it'll make it easier for him to accept why we can't be more than friends. Who wants to date a crazy person? Maybe he'll be relieved to be rid of me.

Not that I think he's been spending his Christmas Break pining over me. Hopefully, he's spent at least part of it reassembling his bike.

In the event that that's the case, I ride my bike from my apartment to his house. It's a sunny fifty-degree day, perfect for a three-mile ride through mostly empty streets. If he's not busy with Johnny, maybe he'll take a ride with me. Exercise and fresh air may serve as a nice diversion.

His car's in the driveway, parked in front of the closed garage door. I glide to a stop at the base of the porch steps and lean my bike against the porch rail but don't remove my helmet. At the front door, I take a deep breath and assertively use the doorbell. Every other time I've been here, Johnny's answered the door, so Jamie's appearance surprises me when the door swings open. He's scruffy and sleepy-looking.

"Hey," I say stupidly.

He blinks into the bright sunlight, which contrasts greatly with the dimness of the living room behind him and glints off the lighter hairs in his stubble. "Hey. What're you doing here?"

I'm relieved that it doesn't sound uninviting; rather, he sounds befuddled.

I fib, "I was riding around, since it's such a nice morning, and I thought I'd stop by." From my jacket pocket I produce a card. "I have a thank-you note for Johnny for my Christmas present."

He takes the card and steps aside from the door. "Well, come in, I guess. Johnny's still at work."

"Oh. I didn't even think of that," I reply, reflexively accepting his invitation to enter the house, even though my intention was to stay on the porch. It's only after I'm inside that I regret it.

Now what?

"Did you get your bike fixed?" I immediately ask, remaining standing and within reach of the door as he tosses Johnny's card on the cluttered coffee table and sits down on the couch.

"Sort of." He casually takes a sip of coffee from a steaming mug and reveals, "I had a few extra parts, so I'm not comfortable riding it until I figure out if that's a big deal."

"So, no bike ride today?"

He raises an eyebrow at me, "Is that what you had in mind?"

His tone makes it sound like he thinks that's a dumb, random idea, so I shrug. "I guess not."

"Why are you really here?" he asks bluntly, setting down his mug and rubbing his chin with a rasp.

I sit on the arm of the loveseat. "Well… to be honest, I wanted to talk to you."

Lifting his cell phone from the table, he makes a show of checking to make sure it's on and charged, so I say, "In person."

"Mmm."

In my head, it was a lot easier, but I can't even remember what I wanted to say now that I'm here.

"I don't want things to be uncomfortable for the rest of the school year," I begin.

He looks unmoved by this statement.

I go on, "I mean, nobody even knows yet that we've… we're not a couple anymore."

"They'll figure it out soon enough," he states dully.

"Yeah, but I don't want them to figure it out by noticing that things are ugly between us. That's just going to be awkward for everyone. And they'll think they have to choose sides—"

His bitter laughter stops me midsentence. "I don't give a damn what they think, Kendall. And this isn't high school. I'm going to go to work every day and do my job. I suggest you do the same thing. You might be surprised that nobody gives a shit."

I blink at him. "Well, I know from experience that they will. Even if they only care enough to be secretly glad that we're not together anymore."

He stares at me for a few seconds, during which I have no idea what's going through his head. Then he says, "It would be hard enough to take this conversation seriously, but it's downright impossible with you wearing that helmet."

Self-consciously, I unclip the chin strap and lift the helmet from my head. I set the headgear on the back of the loveseat. "Better?" I ask. "Am I more credible now?"

He rubs his eyes. "Not really."

"See? This is what I'm talking about," I snap. "You're going to treat me like this, and everyone's going to start speculating about what happened, and——"

"Let me get this straight. You're basically asking me not to be mean to you at work? You're making sure I'm going to play nice-nice and not make any scenes and not turn everyone against you?"

I glare at him for oversimplifying it and making me sound like an infant. "No."

"That's what it sounds like to me. You're looking out for yourself. You don't care if it's awkward for anyone else, as long as *you're* not uncomfortable."

"Oh, here we go!"

"Where? Where are we going?"

"I'm selfish. Self-centered. Egotistical. Uncaring."

"Well, I won't tell anyone if you don't," he says with a smirk.

I take a deep breath. This is not at all how I wanted this conversation to go. I'm doing nothing but reinforcing what he assumed two weeks ago when we broke up.

I push down the hurt and decide it's soul-baring time.

"I'm going to tell you something very personal," I begin awkwardly.

He wrinkles his nose. "If it's supposed to make me feel sorry for you, save your breath."

"Why are you making this so difficult?" I ask, exasperated.

He looks like an unshaven child when he crosses his arms over his chest and mutters, "For some reason, I don't feel like making anything easy for you."

"It's nice to see that you got over being in love with me so quickly," I snipe. "Because you sure don't treat someone you love like this."

"Don't even presume to know how I feel, okay? Just tell me your 'very personal' story and let me get back to sitting here with my hand down my pants. I have some football to watch."

Snatching my bike helmet from the back of the loveseat, I stand. "Never mind. You obviously want to think whatever you want about me." I jam the helmet onto my head and secure it with a loud, plastic snap of the chinstrap.

"And you obviously want me to think you're deep and complicated, to justify your insensitive behavior."

"You're a dickhead."

"Ta-da! What a revelation!" he cries sarcastically.

"Yeah, I should have figured it out earlier, considering that's my type."

Mock-sympathetically, in a baby voice, he declares, "Poor Kendall." Then in his normal voice, he adds, "It's astounding that you've turned this around to make yourself the victim."

"I haven't! If you'd listen to me for one second, you'd know that I hate myself, okay?! And I hate that I've put us in this position." When he doesn't reply, I say, "But whatever. I understand that it's easier to think the worst of me and be angry at me."

His eyes suddenly soften, but I don't want his sympathy anymore. I don't deserve it. And it's not going to change anything.

I go to the door and pull it open. "It's just that… you

wanted an explanation weeks ago, but I was too chickenshit to give you one."

I push the thumb latch on the storm door to open it, but his voice stops me.

"I want you. Period. I don't want to understand why I can't have you. Or why it's better for me to accept that I can't. All that is bullshit." He says it quietly but vehemently.

Matching his volume, I insist, "It's not bullshit, Jamie. It's not."

"What are you so afraid of?" he asks.

I bite my lip and blink away tears while I stare at my hand, still on the door latch. "Disappearing," I whisper. "Because I'm not good enough or bright enough or *enough* to be a person in my own right."

He slowly rises from the couch and walks over to me. Gently, he removes my helmet, pulls my hand away from the door, and takes me in his arms. He smells like toast and coffee. At first I'm tense, but his hug feels so good that I relax into it after a few seconds.

"What the hell have I said or done to make you think that's gonna happen?" he wonders miserably.

I shake my head against his chest. "Nothing. You're just *you*. You're smart and funny and everyone likes you and respects you."

"That's not true."

"Yes, it is. For the most part. And that's great. That's why I like you, too."

"So far, this is all good," he points out. "And you're all the same things. What the hell am I missing? What is the problem?"

I sniffle. "To everyone else, I'm just cute. And we're cute together. And without me, you're still all those good things; but they think I'm nothing without you." I push away from him, frustrated that I can't make him understand.

His jaw tightens. "So... I—*we*—have to suffer because of other people's perceptions of you? Or what you perceive those perceptions to be? Kendall, that's crazy."

"I know! You think I don't know that?"

Rubbing his temples, he says, "Come here."

"No. I can't. We can't."

He drops his arms. "You think no one at work respects you? Why do all the kids love you? Why did Renalda come to you for the Operation Educate idea? Why does everyone ask you to serve on every committee under the sun?"

"Because they're kids and don't know any better. Because she was trying to set us up. Because I'm a pushover and don't know how to say 'no' to anyone."

"Is that what happened between us that night? You just don't know how to say no?" Before I can give him an answer, he continues, "Why do you hate yourself? Because you had sex with me? What's the point in hating yourself for something you can't go back and change? Would you even want to change it, if you could?"

He looks so tortured when he asks me that I can't bring myself to lie, even if it would strengthen my argument. "No," I admit. "But it should have never gotten to that point. I *knew* better."

He pushes away from the wall. "I think you should go," he mutters.

"Jamie, that's not what I meant!"

Shaking his head, he says through tight lips, "No. It's fine. I get it. If you feel so strongly about everything, then I respect that. Even though I think it sucks. And I'd like to go on record as objecting very strongly to your theory."

Handing over my helmet he asks, "You know what you need, Kendall?"

"Therapy?" I joke weakly.

He pretends to consider that for a second and says, "Might not be a bad idea, but I was thinking about something more like a sibling. If you had a brother or sister, you'd be used to always being compared to someone else. Sometimes you come out on top; other times, not."

"Are you volunteering for the job?"

"I don't want to be your brother."

"Fair enough." I open the door and step onto the porch. "Well, Happy New Year. I guess I'll see you at work the day after tomorrow."

"That you will," he confirms wearily. "Then 80 days until Spring Break."

Despite a near-crushing sadness in my chest, I'm still laughing at his Spring Break countdown two streets away. Life would be so much easier if I didn't love everything about him so damn much.

CHAPTER TWENTY-SEVEN

"Good morning." Jamie platonically pats my shoulder on the way past me to the coffee machine in the crowded teachers' lounge.

Taken aback by the physical contact—however glancing and un-romantic—I stutter, "G-hello."

Pouring his coffee, he asks, "How was your Christmas Break?"

Other conversations around us screech to a halt.

"Uh, fine. I guess. Kind of boring. But the weather was nice."

He moves away from the coffeemaker, rests his lower back against the counter, and blows into the hot liquid. "Yeah, it was. Unfortunately, Johnny and I didn't get out of the house much. We were lazy bachelors."

"I rode my bike a lot," I reveal.

Sam chuckles nervously. "Uh, did I miss something? I figured you two would be inseparable for two weeks."

Jamie turns his attention from me to her, staring her down, making it obvious that he doesn't appreciate her intrusion into our "private" conversation. Just when the silence is starting to get uncomfortable, he simply says, "Nope," pushes away from the counter, and exits the lounge.

I quickly scurry after him, not wanting to be the one left explaining. In the hallway, I keep a respectful distance from him as he strides ahead of me. *The better to watch his butt in those gray pants.* I mean… er…

Hearing my stupid clickety-clackety shoes, he half-turns to look over his shoulder at me but continues without pausing. And as far as I know, he doesn't look at me again for the rest of the week.

❧

Nobody's been ballsy enough all week to come right out and ask about Jamie and me… until now. I'm shocked we've made it all the way to Friday.

"What's this I hear about you and Jamie breakin' up?" Renalda asks. Loudly. With Jamie's class mingling in the library behind us.

I shrug and try to smile. "Oh, you know. Sometimes things just don't work out." My upbeat tone of voice makes it sound like we're talking about something as innocuous as a rainy day ruining picnic plans.

She looks crushed. "Well! Who decided *this* wasn't going to work out?"

Squirming, I hedge, "I don't know. It was mutual, I guess."

"Ha! No such thing. Someone always likes someone else more in a relationship. I just can't figure out which one that was with you and Jamie. You both seemed smitten." She pats her frosted hair. "Was there somethin' wrong in the boudoir?"

Considering I've never been in Jamie's "boo-dwore"

BREA BROWN

(and vice versa, at least for *that* purpose), I don't feel bad at all saying, "No." Brightly, I add, "Renalda, I don't think this is a good time to be talking about this. And it's private, anyway."

She waves away my concerns. "You two are like my kids!"

"Not really—"

"And I want you to be happy. You're the perfect couple! So cute!"

I can feel my jaw set.

"What?" Renalda wonders. "What's wrong with bein' cute?"

I try to recover. "Nothing. It's just… whatever. Never mind." Her repeated use of the word "cute" spurs me to say unapologetically, "I'm not comfortable talking about this," but I still say it with a smile to soften the rebuke.

She doesn't seem at all ashamed by her intrusion. "Okay. Fine. Be that way. I understand you're probably still hurtin'. The more I think about it, the more I see Jamie as the heart-breaker."

That fishing expedition is going to yield her nothing. I don't feel the need to set the record straight. If anything, I'm glad to let people think that.

"I think I may hop down to his room while his class is down here with you. Make sure he's okay. Happy workers are good workers, and all that. I'd hate for this to affect either of your work performances."

"That's not going to happen," I reassure her. "We're intelligent, mature professionals."

She says nothing to that statement but makes her determined way to the library doors. "Well, TGIF! Have a good weekend."

232

I stare after her for several seconds, but movement in my peripheral vision distracts me from wondering what she's saying to Jamie (and how he's handling her questions). Brody's at the checkout counter, expectantly blinking up at me.

After closing my gaping mouth, I smile warmly at him. "Hey, Brode. Whatya know?"

"Good," he answers incongruously. "I know Mr. Chase's first name."

"Okay."

"Yeah. So what did Miss Twomey mean when she said that you and Jamie had 'brokeded up'? Does she mean you were boyfriend and girlfriend, like Sam and Freddie, but that you're not boyfriend and girlfriend anymore?"

"Sam and Freddie?" This is new information. I had no idea the school secretary and the janitor had a thing going. He doesn't seem like her type at all!

As I'm frantically searching through my memory for any instances of Sam and Freddie even being in the same room or talking to each other, Brody says, "Yeah, like on *iCarly*! Sam and Freddie are boyfriend and girlfriend."

"Oh! *iCarly*..."

"Yeah! But if Sam and Freddie brokeded up, they wouldn't be boyfriend and girlfriend anymore." Now I can practically see smoke coming from his ears as he works this out. "Miss Twomey just said that you brokeded up with 'Jamie.' That's Mr. Chase, right? You were boyfriend and girlfriend with Mr. Chase?"

I open and close my mouth as I work up a response. I finally settle on, "Brody, I don't think you should worry about it."

He tilts his head. "Oh, I'm not worried, Miss Dickinson. I was jus' wonderin'."

"Wonder away. Now, did you pick out a book to check out this week?"

"Yes," he answers but doesn't move to put the book on the counter. "But did you and Mr. Chase break up?"

A sigh escapes me when I say, "I'd rather not talk about it right now."

Nodding knowingly, he replies, "Yep. That's what my mom says when I guess something right, but she doesn't want me to know it. Like about Santa Claus. I figured out that he's not real, cuz I found my presents under her bed. But when I asked her about it, she said, 'Not now, Brody.' So I asked her later. And she told me I was right. Do you want me to ask you about you and Mr. Chase later?"

I reach my hand out for the book he's selected. "No. I don't want you to ask me later, either. Now, let's check out that book."

§

The phone rings on my desk. I pick it up, but before I can even say "Hello?" Sam asks in a rush, "Is it true?"

Thinking she's referring to my breakup with Jamie, I pinch the bridge of my nose and answer dully, "Yes."

"Oh, my gosh! Renalda's freaking out!"

Annoyed, I snap, "If she'd spend as much time on her real job as she does on matchmaking around here, she might actually be a decent principal. I don't even understand how this affects her, much less why she'd be freaking out about it."

Sam replies a touch defensively, "Well, now we're going to have to hire a new kindergarten teacher." Then she tones down her response with, "I mean, it's still not something to cause a normal person to freak out, but... we're talking about Renalda."

The blood leaves my face and drops to the same place as my stomach, which feels like somewhere around my knees. "What are you talking about?" I practically whisper, looking over my shoulder to make sure my office door is closed, even though I've been alone since the final bell rang more than an hour ago.

She pauses. "What are *you* talking about?"

"I was answering your question, which has nothing to do with Renalda needing to hire a new kindergarten teacher. Please tell me Bonita's retiring," I beg before I can stop myself.

"Bonita's *not* retiring."

"What do you know?"

"Hang on; I'll be right there." And she hangs up, presumably to come tell me in person the worst news I've heard in a while.

CHAPTER TWENTY-EIGHT

I need more information, but I definitely have enough already to get a good panic started.

According to Sam, a distraught Renalda burst into the office what must have been minutes after leaving the library and announced to her that Jamie's not returning to White-hall next fall, and that "it's all Kendall Dickinson's fault, no matter what he says." Then she went on a rant about the hiring process and how she's going to have to get the district to post the job right away so she'll have a decent applicant pool by this summer.

When I have no verbal response to Sam's story, she waits for a few minutes and says impatiently, "Well? What the eff happened with you two? Before Christmas, you were literally kissing under the mistletoe, and now not only are you caput, but he's quitting? And you look like you're about to throw up at the news."

That's when I tell her everything. *Everything.* Yeah. Not the smartest thing I've ever done, but—unfortunately—not even close to the stupidest thing. After the part of the story in the janitor's closet, she fans herself with her hand and says, "I had no idea that closet was even there!"

We sit without speaking for a while, but eventually Sam says while picking at a hangnail, "I just don't understand why you're so freaked out by this thing with Jamie. I mean... he's sort of... awesome. Not my type," she quickly adds, "but you guys have great chemistry and complement each other well."

I bite my tongue to keep from saying, *"You mean he's the smart one, and I'm the fashionable one?"* Instead, I take a deep breath and tell her what I've never had the guts to tell Jamie. I tell her all about Todd and E-Lend/E-Borrow and about how terrified I am of making the same mistakes in a job that I've grown to (sort of) enjoy.

When I finish, she asks, "How much of this does Jamie know?"

I roughly estimate, "Forty percent?"

"Good grief," she mumbles, obviously disgusted with me.

"It's not like it's relevant!" I defend myself. "Who cares *why* I feel this way? That doesn't change anything."

"How do you know?" she challenges. "It might mean a lot to him that you trusted him enough to tell him, if nothing else."

"He knows that trust isn't the issue."

"Does he?"

"Yes!"

"What else do you think he knows? Do you think he knows you love him?"

Uncomfortable with such sentimental talk, I fidget, look away, and mumble, "I dunno. Prolly."

"Did you ever say it to him?" she presses.

To my astonishment, I find myself admitting, "No. But

he *has* to know! I told him that breaking up with him had nothing to do with how I feel about him (in other words, 'in love' with him). Surely, he can read between the lines."

Sam laughs. "Oh, shit. He's a *man*, Kendall. Are you sure this isn't your first boyfriend?"

Somewhat embarrassed, I reply, "Okay, so I've been dense, but that's not exactly a news flash. And again, it's a moot point. It's probably better if he doesn't know, actually. It'll make it easier for him to move on."

She stands and says doubtfully, "I don't know…"

"I don't, either, but it sounds good. So that's where I'm leaving it… for now."

"Alrighty then." Glancing at the clock, she said, "Well, on that note, I'm outta here for another week."

I tell her to enjoy her weekend.

It's past 5:00, but I can't make myself move from my chair. I spend ten minutes with my head down on my desk, trying to think of ways Renalda could have gotten it wrong or how something could have gotten lost in translation when she told Sam about it. When that doesn't work, I sit up and open a blank email to Jamie, but I can't make myself ask him to fill me in through such an impersonal medium.

Now I keep going over and over what Sam told me, what I told her, and how she responded. Maybe she's right. Maybe Jamie does need to know that I love him. Part of me still thinks, though, at this point, what *is* the point?

As I'm torturing myself with all of these thoughts, my work email chimes to let me know I have a new message. This is highly unusual, given that it's a Friday and it's close to 6 p.m. I'm even more surprised when I see who sent the message. It's a forward from Renalda with the subject line: *Operation Educate*.

Even though I'm technically off-the-clock, curiosity gets

the better of me. My heartbeat picks up; my mouth dries out; my fingers shake against the keyboard. I double-click the message.

WE DID IT!!! See mssg blw frm Dr. Underhill re: Whthlls OE idea!! Gd jb, grl! Tlk on Mon! R.T.
Sent from my Mobile Device

Below her nearly indecipherable message is the original text from Dr. Underhill's email.

Renalda,

The Operation Educate selection committee has unanimously decided to implement district-wide Whitehall Elementary School's proposal. We feel your proposed program will make an outstanding addition to the already-stellar standard of cutting-edge education that Fulton County Schools provides to each and every one of its students, regardless of household income.

The official Operation Educate announcement will be made the day before Spring Break in a special ceremony in the Whitehall Elementary library. By that time, we hope to have secured a donor for the electronic tablet devices so that the program will be available for implementation at all district schools in the upcoming school year.

Congratulations to Whitehall on this accomplishment!

Sincerely,

Dwayne Underhill
Superintendent of Fulton County Schools
Leeville, North Carolina

Yes!Yes!Yes!Yes!Yes!Yes!Yes!
YES!
I hit "print" and dance to the printer/copi-er/fax/scanner in the library proper. "I won! Cha-cha-cha!"

I sing as I shake my butt and wait for the paper to shoot out. When it does, I hold it up, re-read Dr. Underhill's message, and kiss the page.

I now have the perfect excuse to talk to Jamie tonight.

Well. This excuse is flimsier than I originally thought. I feel silly going to Jamie's house to talk to him in person about something that I could have just as easily forwarded to him in an email. I'm feeling particularly insecure after hearing his wary tone when I called ahead to make sure it was okay for me to stop by (I figure I only get so many drop-ins before he stops answering the door). He didn't say much, but what he did say was decidedly hesitant.

When I get to his house, he doesn't even answer the door but shouts, "Come in!" from somewhere inside.

I say "somewhere," because when I let myself in, he's nowhere to be seen.

"Helloo?" I say quietly and uncertainly into the seemingly empty house.

"I'll, uh, be out in a sec!" I hear to my right, down the hallway that leads to the bedrooms.

"No rush!" I assure him as I look around.

It's a lot tidier than it was the last time I was here only a few days ago. As a matter of fact… I look closer. There's absolutely no clutter. None of the usual stuff lying around. No junk mail on the coffee table, no stray shoes abandoned next to the couch, no baskets of clean laundry waiting to be folded, no empty drinking glasses or coffee mugs scattered on end tables. Even the framed family photos are gone.

"What's up?" Jamie asks as he enters the room behind me.

I spin around. "Hey. The place looks nice."

"Yeah, that's what happens when I kick Johnny out of the house for the night," he jokes, finger-combing his wet hair. "Actually, uh, I'm staging the house. One room at a time. I figure by the time I get through the whole place, it'll either be sold, or I'll have to start all over again."

"Sold?" I squeak. Then I clear my throat so I can ask more assertively, "Where are you going to live?"

He shrugs and says with exaggerated nonchalance, "Not here. Haven't decided yet."

"Oh."

"So."

"So."

"You wanted to tell me something?" he prods, looking undeniably expectant.

What a loaded question! The question is, of the things I want or need to tell him, which one am I brave enough to say?

I start with the easiest one (I never claimed to be courageous). Holding up the printed-out email from Renalda, I make a trumpeting noise with my mouth. "Guess who liked my tablet idea? A lot."

His furrowed brow relaxes. "For real? They've already decided?"

I shrug and say cockily, "They knew brilliance as soon as they saw it." More seriously, I add, "Or nobody else submitted an idea, so it won by default. Either way…"

He pumps his fist. "Yes!"

"That's exactly what I said," I tell him, smiling. "Only about thirty times in a row. And really loudly. And I did a little dance and sang something that ended in 'cha-cha-cha.'"

His eyebrows shoot up. "That would have been inter- esting to see."

"I'm sure it was. Anyway…" I hand over the email and wait while he reads through it.

By the time he's finished, he's grinning almost as broadly as I am. He opens his arms, and without even thinking twice, I step into them. Grabbing me firmly, he pulls me a few inches off the floor and kisses my hair.

"Congratulations."

"Mfank you," I muffle into his warm, fragrant, smooth neck.

Still holding tightly, he says, "I know how much this must mean to you."

I simply nod. I don't want to let go. Apparently, he doesn't want to, either. We stay like that for a few more wonderful seconds before he loosens his grip on me by degrees so I'm standing on my own feet again.

I stay close, staring at the buttons on his Henley thermal shirt. Then I chance a peek up at his face. He hesitates for a split second, but when I stretch onto my tiptoes, he needs no further encouragement.

Slipping his hand through my hair, he cradles the back of my head and lowers his mouth to mine. I eagerly kiss him back. Screw playing it safe. I'm high on adrenaline and euphoria.

I wind my fingers into his still-damp hair and whisper against his lips, "I'm sorry."

"'Sokay," he replies distractedly. The email printout flut- ters to the floor.

"I've been an idiot," I insist. I know I should shut up and eat his face off, but I feel like he needs to know this is about more than being overexcited about Operation Educate, which is nothing compared to this.

He shakes his head and chases my mouth down. "'Sokay," he repeats. "Shhh."

I pull my head back. "Really. Hear me out."

"No talking!" he whines. "Talking leads to fighting."

"Not this time," I promise, keeping hold of his shoulders. "I want you to know that this has been the longest three weeks of my life."

"Yeah, for me, too. Now, shhhh."

I can't help but laugh at his persistence as he backs me up to the couch and forces me to sit on it before trying to push me onto my back on the cushions. I remain valiantly vertical.

When he's unable to nip at my lips, he goes for the neck nuzzle, but I soldier on. "I've been comparing you to a very bad man and taking my insecurities out on you, and that's not fair."

"Life's not fair. I'm used to that lesson," he says between kisses on my throat.

"And I've let fear get in the way of my feelings for you. I've made it a higher priority than *your* feelings."

"Oh, shit. You've gotta stop talking," he pleads, running his hands up the inside of my sweater.

"Okay," I grant. "Just one more thing." My eyes roll back in my skull as he strokes my breasts through the thin cotton of my bra.

"No more things."

"I love you."

He freezes. Slowly he lifts his head. He takes one of his hands out of my shirt so he can straighten his glasses while he looks down at me. His brown eyes soften affectionately and somewhat remorsefully. "Oh. I love you, too. I'm sorry I keep telling you to shut up."

I shrug and smile. "It's okay. Now, no more talking."

CHAPTER TWENTY-NINE

A loud clunk wakes me up in a pitch-black, unfamiliar room. After a few disorienting seconds in which I can only ascertain that I'm naked, I'm slightly chilly, and there's a warm person pressed up against me, I remember the toe-curling events of the previous few hours and snuggle further under the covers with a tiny shiver. My movement encourages a very sexy forearm to snake over my hip and pull me more tightly against the body behind me. When lips make contact with my shoulder blade, *everything* in my body reawakens.

I turn over so we're face to face in Jamie's bed (which I was relieved to see does *not* glow in the dark, nor does it look like it's covered in velvety Fruity Pebbles). He grins sleepily at me.

"Are you awake?" he checks, despite looking straight into my open eyes.

"Nope," I reply.

"Then you won't care if I…" He lowers his mouth to my breast.

I moan quietly, hyper-aware that Johnny's bedroom is

right next door. So this is what parents have to do to keep their sex lives a secret. Not that I'm a very vocal lover, anyway, which Jamie so helpfully pointed out earlier when he observed, "You're even quiet when you come. That's a deep commitment you have to the art of silence."

Hours ago, when Johnny returned from playing Bingo, Jamie slipped into the hallway to talk to his brother for a few minutes. I heard him say, "Kendall's here, so..." to which Johnny responded, "Yeah. I saw her car. Is she having a sleepover?"

Jamie answered in the affirmative.

Johnny asked, "Will you still get donuts in the morning for breakfast? I like to eat donuts on Saturday."

"You'll still get your Saturday donuts," Jamie assured him. "But maybe later than usual? Deal?"

I didn't hear Johnny's response, but since Jamie returned to the bedroom shortly thereafter, I'm assuming they struck a compromise.

Now the mere thought of donuts makes my stomach growl.

Jamie lifts his head. "Hungry?"

"A little," I admit, "but not enough to stop doing this."

That receives no argument. He rolls me onto my back and nudges my knees apart with one of his knees. Looking down the lengths of our bodies, he watches as he enters me. I rub my palms on his chest and around his ribs to his back.

In perfect time with his first thrust, the bedroom door crashes open.

"We're out of toilet paper, Jamie," Johnny announces frankly, holding up the empty cardboard tube for us to see in the light spilling from the hallway.

Jamie rolls off me and pulls the covers over my nakedness faster than I can do anything more than think, *What's happening? Because I know* this *isn't happening!*

"Fuck me, Johnny! Ever heard of knocking?" he snaps.

"I have to knock to tell you we're out of toilet paper?" Johnny asks, clearly confused by this new rule.

"Yes. When my bedroom door is closed, you have to knock. Period. I don't care what the hell you have to tell me."

Untroubled by the situation, he simply says, "Okay," turns, and leaves the room.

Seconds later, there's a knock on the door.

Jamie presses his hand over his eyes and yells, "I know we're out of toilet paper! You don't have to knock now."

The door swings open a few inches. Through the crack, Johnny says, "But you said I had to knock."

At this point, I'm laughing hysterically into the pillow. What else can I do? I'm sure Johnny didn't see anything. It's too dark in here to see more than a few inches in front of one's nose. And it's obvious he either has no idea what we were doing or doesn't care.

Jamie starts to laugh, too. "I'll get more toilet paper in the morning. Good night!"

"Okay. I don't need any right now, anyway. Good night, Jamie. Good night, Kendall."

After a tiny snort, I manage a faint "Good night!" in the direction of the closing door.

The latch has barely clicked into place before Jamie jumps from the bed, lunges across the room, and pushes the lock in the center of the doorknob. I'm suddenly very sorry it's so dark in here.

The next time I wake up, it's considerably lighter in the room. It also seems somehow lighter in the bed. Experimentally, I straighten my leg and push my foot slightly behind me to see what I come in contact with, but all I feel are cool sheets. I flop onto my back and turn my head to see an empty pillow with a head divot in it. And a note.

Please, don't leave. Ran out to get t.p. Figured you'd need that. —J

What a host, I think with a giggle. Then I wonder, *Who runs out of toilet paper?*

Oh, well. Guys. I'm sure there are a lot of things that go on in this house that would blow my mind and make a toilet paper shortage look pedestrian.

I'm not going to think about that. I'm going to think about last night. And I'm not going to freak out about it, even though we never got around to discussing a very important subject: Jamie's resignation and subsequent decision to sell his house. I wonder if it would be egotistical of me to think he may reconsider those two choices in light of what happened last night.

Or maybe those decisions had nothing to do with me in the first place.

Or maybe my breaking up with him freed him to do something he's wanted to do for a long time: get the heck out of this town.

But wait! my thundering heart objects. *What about Johnny?*

Yes. Exactly. I was hardly the one keeping him here. I'm a very recent addition to his life. Johnny is a long-term commitment. Unless he's decided that Johnny's going to have to suck it up and go with him. But Johnny hates traveling and usually makes it miserable. Jamie's told me very illustrative stories about trips gone awry thanks to his older brother. There was an especially funny one involving a monkey, an apple, and a backpack…. But anyway!

My stomach cramps with the next thought: he's not taking Johnny with him, wherever that happens to be.

I hear the back door open and close, followed by muffled male voices from the kitchen.

Oh, gosh. Why didn't I get through all the talking points last night before sniffing his neck? That was my undoing. That, and the sight of his frickin' gorgeous forearms poking from his pushed-up shirt sleeves. I swing my legs over the side of the bed and search the floor for my discarded clothes. Where the hell are they? I don't remember twirling them around my head and flinging them to points unknown, but they're nowhere to be seen.

"Shit!" I mutter, contemplating grabbing any of the other articles of clothing littering the floor. Apparently, Jamie hasn't gotten around to staging this room for the sale.

Just as I'm draping a large men's dress shirt around my shoulders and doing up the buttons, the bedroom door cracks open, and Jamie slides in.

To my back, he asks, "Whatcha doin'?"

"Nowhere!" I defensively and incomprehensively answer, keeping my back to him.

"Looking for these?" he asks. I hear him slide open a closet door. A glance over my shoulder reveals he's holding my neatly folded clothes from yesterday, panties and bra on top.

"Did you hide my clothes?" I demand, my current worries pushing me into an unreasonably outraged state as I stand and pull at the bottom of the dress shirt to cover my naughtiest bits.

Still holding the clothes like they're on a platter, he pulls them away from my reach when I try to grab them. "I was worried you'd try to do a runner before I could get the toilet paper and donuts home."

"That's a seriously creepy thing to do," I accuse. "Like serial-killer creepy. Like you're holding me hostage, or something."

Balancing the pile of clothing on his hand above his head, which is way out of my reach, he steps toward me. Something crunches under his foot. Without taking his eyes off me, he says dully, "Damn. My spare glasses."

My lips twitch, but I don't give into the laugh bubbling up from my chest.

Up against me, he cups his free hand over me, under the long shirt. "You're free to go, as soon as you eat a donut."

"Do you have any custard-filled ones?" I ask innocently, my eyelids fluttering despite my best efforts to not react to what he's doing.

His pupils dilate, but otherwise there's no change in his face. "Nope. Only cream-filled. And jelly-filled."

"Give me my stuff."

"I don't think so. Not yet."

Gently, he pushes me down onto the bed and lets my clothing fall in a heap on the floor behind him.

"Jamie, I'm hungry," I declare weakly.

"So am I," he concurs, roughly pulling his sweatshirt over his head. "So breakfast is going to have to wait."

CHAPTER THIRTY

Powdered sugar and jelly conspire against me to foil all my attempts to eat breakfast gracefully. I can feel the confectioner's sugar collecting on my lips and in the corners of my mouth; meanwhile, a huge blob of raspberry jam has squirted out the backside of the donut, through my fingers, and onto the paper plate on the table in front of me. How very attractive.

So far, Johnny's provided the soundtrack to this meal, hardly needing a word from either Jamie or me. Every once in a while, Jamie nudges me under the table with his foot, and we share a private smile, but for the most part, we're enjoying an easy silence that I've never had with a boyfriend.

I'm just thinking about how confused everyone at work is going to be regarding the two of us when that nagging little voice in my head stops me short. *Are we back together? Or are we simply screwing each other?*

I mean, we still have some issues to resolve, not the least of which are Jamie's future plans and whether they include me, the lowly elementary school librarian from Small Town,

North Carolina. And I still haven't figured out how I'm going to avoid being dismissed as a stylish accessory in his wardrobe, not unlike one of his snappy ties or argyle sweater vests (I do love those silly sweater vests, though).

On second thought, maybe Operation Educate has worked out that problem for me. Surely now people will see that there's some substance to me. And I never noticed that the students "loved" me until Jamie pointed it out, but since then I've paid more attention to the response I get from the students. I've had some interesting and meaningful conversations with some of the kids recently on topics that run the gamut from popular culture to social issues to religion and philosophy. ("Where do cats go when they die?" I squirmed out of that one, though, and referred Brody to his mom for the answer. That's a little above my pay grade.)

Johnny's voice breaks through my ruminations. "What do you think, Kendall?"

I look to Jamie for help, any clue about what Johnny's been talking about for the past ten minutes. He nods, winks, and mouths, "Awesome," so I repeat the word as enthusiastically as possible.

"Awesome," Johnny agrees. But he chooses this of all moments to stop talking altogether, so I have no idea what we both think is "awesome." All I know is that Jamie's fighting hard not to laugh.

I kick him under the table, but that doesn't erase his grin. If anything, it gives him an outlet for his laughter. "Ow!" he cries on a chuckle.

Johnny ignores us. He polishes off his donut and gets up to put his plate in the trash and empty milk glass in the dishwasher. "Well, I'm gonna spend some time in the bathroom," he announces bluntly.

"You're well-equipped now, so go for it," Jamie encourages. "I even put a roll on the holder for you."

"Thanks, bro!"

"Don't mention it."

As soon as he's gone, I demand, "What did I just say was 'awesome'?"

"You done?" he asks in return, gesturing to my messy plate. When I nod, he stands to clear the table but makes a wiping motion around his mouth. "You've got a little…" Then he leans down and kisses my lips. "Never mind. I got it."

"Oh, thanks." I lick my lips to make sure there's nothing still there. After all, he's proven he can't be trusted not to lead me into embarrassing situations. "But stop trying to distract me. What was Johnny talking about just now?"

After tossing our plates in the appropriate recycling bin, he dusts the powdered sugar from his hands and refills our coffee cups. On his way back after putting the coffeepot on the burner, he answers casually, "He was expressing his desire to someday see Celine Dion in concert. And he asked if you'd like to go with him." He breaks down now at my horrified reaction.

I narrow my eyes at him. "I so hate you."

"No, you don't!" he manages to wheeze between giggles. When he's recovered for the most part, he says, "Anyway, that'll teach you to zone out during a conversation with him. Dangerous."

"I can't believe you!" I lick the sticky jelly residue from my fingers and pretend to be pissed off.

"Well, I'm sure as hell not going with him, and he's been talking about it for years. I wish I could blame his brain injury, but he liked her before the accident. Thought she was hot." He fake-shivers. "I saw an opportunity to get out of it and grabbed it. I think she's still out in Vegas. I can hook you up with travel arrangements and show tickets for when I'm away this summer."

That statement grabs my attention and sobers me up immediately. "Oh. This summer?"

"The sooner the better. You guys will have so much fun!" He reaches across the table and covers my hand when he sees I'm no longer pretending to be upset. "Hey. You know I'm kidding, right?"

Hope rises in my chest. "About going away this summer?"

He sniffs, looking down at the tabletop. "Um, no. Probably not."

I pull my hand away from his. "Oh. What about Johnny?"

Half-smiling, he answers, "He'll be hanging out with you and Celine."

When I shoot him a dirty look, he amends, "No, actually... he's going to go live on his own for a while."

"On his own? But I thought—"

Jamie leans forward eagerly. "Yeah. I know. But I found this place—"

"A home?!" I try not to sound judgmental but fail miserably.

His face falls. "Well, no. Not in the traditional sense. It's an assisted living community."

"A home."

"No! That's just it. He'll have his own apartment and a job on-site, and he'll be around other people like him. Not people on machines and confined to wheelchairs and beds." Using his hands, he tries to illustrate for me, placing "buildings" on the table in various places. "It's like a micro-city with its own bank and movie theater and and bakery—that's where he'd work, since he has experience with that. And medical and emergency staff are on-hand round the clock. They do wellbeing checks on the hour, and there are these sophisticated alarm systems that alert them to trouble between checks."

Now he jumps up from his chair and goes to a drawer in the kitchen. He pulls from it a pamphlet for this "community," Phoenix Ridge, and thrusts it at me.

"See? I've even been there to visit, and it's cool."

I flip through the glossy trifold flyer, trying to picture his brother in this setting. "And has Johnny gone to visit? I mean, what if he hates it?"

"He won't. Look!" He points to a picture of a group of people I assume are the residents, sitting at tables, playing games. "They play a different game every evening. Tuesday night is Bingo night."

I gulp. "Oh. It sounds nice." Bravely, I smile and will myself to swallow my tears. A nice, unselfish person would be happy for him. And Johnny.

Thankfully, he's too excited about Phoenix Ridge to notice my distress. "Yeah, it is. And he'll have his life, and I'll have mine, but I won't have to feel guilty or wonder if he's okay." He slides the pamphlet in front of himself and stares wistfully at it. "It's perfect!"

Someone who truly loves him—as I do—wouldn't care so much about her own stake in this. She'd only care that he's found a solution to a problem that's been preventing him from being happy for years. She'd smile and congratulate him and not worry about the jelly donut that feels like a rock in her stomach.

Then she'd ask, "So, where are you going to go this summer?" as if it's the most fascinating, happy topic in the world, and she'd brace herself to "ooh" and "aah," no matter what his answer is.

"Maybe Iceland. I might be able to get on that team that Marena was talking about. I have to get my foot in the door somewhere, and I'm not too proud to do it by taking someone up on a favor they've already promised me." He taps his index finger against the table and rubs the earpiece of his glasses as he stares into space while considering it.

Yeah. I'm sure Marena already has a spot ready for him in her tent. I bet she's a screamer. She seems like the self-indulgent type who'd want everyone in a four-mile radius to know when she's having an orgasm. Marena!

I'm going to puke. Literally. And Johnny's tearing up the house's only bathroom, so…

I quickly rise, spin, and run into the adjoining kitchen, holding onto the edge of the counter while I lean over the stainless steel sink.

Jamie looks up sharply. "Are you okay?"

"I'm fine!" I lie. "Just… Gosh! That donut isn't sitting right with me." I try to nervous-laugh it away, but uttering the word, "donut," brings on a full-force retch.

"Oh, shit." He joins me at the sink, holding back my hair while I relinquish every last bite I've eaten for the past sixteen hours that hasn't already gone down a different chute.

Between stomach spasms, I apologize, and he keeps telling me to stop apologizing.

When it's been several seconds with no action, I turn on the tap and rinse out my mouth the best I can.

"I'm so sorry I made you eat that donut," he laments as he grasps my upper arms in an effort to lend me some support.

I gag again, but there's nothing left to throw up. "Stop saying that word."

"What, 'donut'? Oh! Sorry! Shit. I hope there wasn't something wrong with those."

"I'm sure they're fine. I'm… maybe it was too much sugar on an empty stomach. I ate kind of fast." I start spewing as many excuses as I can come up with, besides what I know to be the real reason. "I'm sort of tired, too. And there's been so much excitement."

He steers me from the kitchen to the couch, where he presses me down onto the cushions. "It's not normal to start puking for no reason."

"Oh, it happens all the time," I lie some more.

"Then you need to go see a doctor. Lie down. I'll be right back."

Oh, geez. Now I'm an invalid with some possibly undiagnosed disease, because I'm too proud to simply come out and tell him that I'm upset at the prospect of him going away. With Marena.

He strides down the hallway and bangs on the bathroom door. "John. Out. I need to get in there."

"But I'm not done! Wait your turn!"

"Hurry. And make sure when you're done that you spray the air freshener." Muttering, he returns to me with a blanket. "Good Lord! That'll get anyone's gag reflex going."

"I'm really okay. I promise," I try to sit up.

"Kendall, so help me God, do not make me restrain you. I haven't seen someone barf that much since college." I feel extremely guilty when I notice that his hands are shaking as he presses the blanket around me. "Johnny!" he bellows. Then with gritted teeth, he grumbles under his breath, "How long does it take one man to take a shit?"

"There's no rush," I reassure him. "I'm done, I think."

"That's what they all say."

"No, really."

"Well, I want to get you some mouthwash and—"

I clamp my hand over my mouth, suddenly terrified that my barf breath is offending him.

"No! Not that you need it. I'm just saying, you probably want it."

I nod, but my eyes still well up. This is a nightmare.

"Oh, shit. I'm sorry." He looks miserably down at me. "I'm the worst nurse ever. Ask Johnny. That poor guy had to recover from a traumatic brain injury with my help. I mean, I couldn't teach a fish to swim, much less a grown man how to re-learn to walk."

"But you're a teacher!" I cry, laughing with my hand still covering my mouth.

He pulls it away. "Yeah, but I'm not a physical therapist or a nurse. I have zero patience. And I always say the wrong thing. I think I'm being encouraging, but it sounds down-right insulting or like I'm being a bully."

The sound of the bathroom door opening gets Jamie off the couch again. "Finally!" he says with relief. "Were you making a diamond in there? Shit! Literally."

Johnny stands in the hallway, his arms hanging limply at his sides. "I had to go."

From inside the bathroom, I hear Jamie digging around in cabinets. "Yeah. Obviously. Aggghh! You didn't spray the air freshener like I asked!" The sound of Jamie doing it himself goes on for what seems like forever. "God bless America."

Johnny picks up singing about the land that he loves, then cuts off to say, "Hey, Kendall. Celine Dion sang that song one time on TV. It was beautiful. Maybe she sings it at her concert, too, and we'll get to hear it."

"Bahahahahaha!" I crack up, suddenly feeling a lot better in spite of everything.

CHAPTER THIRTY-ONE

I barely managed to prevent Jamie from taking me to Urgent Care, especially after I almost threw up while rinsing out my mouth with the mouthwash he gave me (who still uses the original Listerine? Jamie, that's who). But he finally took me home and rode my bike back to his house after I promised I'd call him if I puked after my next meal. I knew it was a safe promise. As long as we're not talking about him changing everything by quitting his current job to travel the world, I'll be okay. As long as I don't think about him and Marena in a softly lit tent in Iceland, keeping each other warm, I should be able to hold down food.

The crazy thing is, he's acting like I already know he quit his job at Whitehall, but he still hasn't mentioned it directly. And how else would I know, if not from him? Sam told me as soon as Renalda told her, which was right after Jamie told *her*. But there's no way for him to know that. And I haven't said anything that would lead him to believe I know. For all he knows I know, he's selling his house because Johnny's moving out, and Johnny's new home means he'll be able to join an expedition this summer during his free time, before school starts again.

Therefore, I can only deduce that he thinks he's keeping this information from me.

But why?

And next dilemma: do I let him know that I know?

I stare at the banana and hothouse berries I've been trying to make myself eat for so long that the banana slices are browning. Eating's not going to happen today with all this swirling around in my head. Plus, as long as I don't eat, I can honestly report to Jamie when he calls later that no other food has made me sick today.

Eerily enough, my cell phone rings as I'm dumping the fruit down the garbage disposal, but the caller ID reveals that it's Mom, not Jamie.

"Honey, Jamie told me you were sick, and I was so glad to hear it."

"What?"

"Oh, that didn't come out at all the way I meant it," she says, laughing. "What I mean is, I'm glad Jamie was there to witness your being sick."

"How can that make you glad?" I wonder. "It was humiliating."

Again, she laughs. "Well, I don't mean it that way, either. You were with Jamie. And I'm happy that you two were together. I'm not at all glad you're sick, though. What's the matter?"

I sigh. "There's nothing physically wrong with me," I reveal. "I'm just upset." Then the dam breaks. Painfully. I've been holding in the tears for so long (even when I technically didn't need to hold them in anymore, since I've been home, alone) that they still don't realize it's okay for them to spill. They squeak like faulty brakes.

"Oh, dear. From the sound of things when I talked to Jamie, things seemed okay, other than that he was worried about you blowing chunks all over his kitchen," she tacks on descriptively.

"Mom!"

"Those were his words, not mine," she defends herself.

This accusation almost immediately stops my crying. I sniffle and say snottily, "I did *not*… do what he said I did. I very daintily heaved into his kitchen sink."

Skeptically, she says, "Uh, I've seen you throw up, sweetie, and there isn't anything dainty about it. It's always mystified me how someone so small could create such a big, scary noise while vomiting."

"Can we *please* talk about what really matters here and stop trying to come up with a thousand different ways to describe how I empty the contents of my stomach?"

"Yes, of course. Now, why are you upset to the point of heaving?"

I give her the PG, condensed version of what happened last night and this morning, summing it up with: "So I still haven't heard directly from him that he's quit his job, and there's no reason for him to think I'd have heard such fresh news from anyone else. He's purposely *not* telling me."

"Well, it sounds like you've had a rather"—she clears her throat—"busy time since you got back together—"

"*Are* we back together, Mom?" I inquire, anguished. "I don't know that we are."

"Honey, a man doesn't hold your hair while you're… 'daintily heaving…' unless he's obligated by the bounds of a monogamous relationship."

"Is that a fact?" I sardonically press her.

"Nearly. Plus, after he took you home, he called me to let

me know you were under the weather and asked that I check up on you later."

I'm starting to think that people assume my small stature means that I'm helpless or childlike or both. It seems I've had to point out this fact: "I'm a freakin' grown-up!" a few too many times lately.

"I know that. And he knows that. But you tend to be independent to your own detriment sometimes." She pauses. "Now tell me more about this Marena. I don't like the sound of her."

I press my cool fingertips into my hot, swollen eye sockets. "Oh, she's a first-class cooter, for sure," I state. "Problem is, there's no competing with this woman. She's every man's wet dream. She's physically perfect——"

"I find *that* hard to believe."

"Mom, if you saw this woman, you'd understand. I've never been in the presence of such an outwardly beautiful person as her. It was... awe-inspiring. And I'm a straight female with every reason to find fault with her. But I couldn't. I can only imagine what men think when they're around her."

"Sorry. I can't believe she's any prettier than you," Mom insists.

Ah, spoken like a true mother. "Well, believe it. Because the word, 'pretty,' is a joke when used to describe her. That's like calling Antarctica, 'chilly.'"

Impatient with my adamancy, she sighs. "All right. I get it. She's a knockout. Big deal. Does she have brains like you?"

"Hmmm, let's see. Considering she's a flipping archaeologist who's traveled the world and seen and done everything——"

"Including Jamie," she mutters helpfully.

"Yes. Thanks for pointing that out. But anyway, she has brains enough for both of us and some left over for poor people who can't afford them," I gloomily state.

Cattily, Mom snaps, "Well, good for her. She should donate it to science someday, then. What about her personality? I know she's not nearly as darling as my Sunshine."

"She's a bitch," I confirm. "But guys seem to like that. Or at least expect it. I think they see it as a more-than-fair trade-off. 'Perfect body; smart and worldly; bitch. No problem. She's worth the trouble.'"

"Jamie obviously doesn't like it."

"How do you know?" I challenge. I never told Mom about the time I followed them to the store. I've never told anyone. (Oh, except Sam. Yeah. Why did I tell her so much? How am I going to face her at work? Oh, well. One problem at a time.)

She explains to me as if I'm slow, "Because he's been there, done that, and he's moved on to better things."

"Or more convenient things."

"Stop it! Were you raised to be so down on yourself?"

"I was raised to be a realist. It's hard to be with someone who's always half a world away. But when someone's right down the hall from you five days a week and only three miles away on the weekends, it's a lot easier."

"Kendall Louise Dickinson!"

Her use of my despised middle name sets my teeth on edge.

"Now you listen here, Little Miss." Oh, crap. She's got her North Carolina on. "If he wanted to make it work with *Indiana Jones* Barbie, he would have found a way. The fact that he hasn't is telling. Plus, there's nothing easy about you lately, so please! He's got his work cut out for him, no doubt about it, no matter how quote-unquote *convenient* you seem to think you are. And you're going to blow it with all your nonsense and overanalyzing and second-guessing and mistrusting. You're right: he's going to sell his house, leave his brother in the hands of professionals, and fly far away from here—unless you give him a reason to stay. So far, you're doing a piss-poor job. All you're giving him is a pain in his cute little ass."

"Mother!"

"Don't 'Mother' me!"

Frustrated that she doesn't understand where I'm coming from, I say, "Forget Marena. Even without her constantly lurking in the background, don't you think it's disturbing that I'm making the exact same mistakes I made in Kansas City? Don't you see that?"

She tones down the tough love. "Oh, Sweetie. The only mistake you're repeating is that you're not trusting your intuition. You knew Todd was an idiot and a jerk; you know Jamie's worth his weight—and then some—in gold. Period. Everything else is just you trying to talk yourself out of falling in love with the guy who's perfect for you. And I'm going to have to look at your mopey, heartbroken face for months when you finally succeed in chasing him off this continent."

"Geez…"

"Well, someone needs to talk some sense into you!"

I sniff and tug at my sweatshirt sleeve while picturing Jamie on a plane, flying away from me and toward Marena. Her sexy voice taunts me, *He always ends up coming back to me.* Well, that's not going to happen this time, Marena. He said it himself: he never loved her; he doesn't *like* her. And she's delusional if she thinks she's ever going to see him naked again.

"Mom?"

"What?"

"Thanks."

Her characteristic smile is back in her voice, and the Southern accent is gone. "Oh. You're welcome. But Sweetie?"

"Yes?"

"Let's not mention to anyone that I said Jamie has a cute little ass. That might make things awkward in the future."

I wake up on Monday with a resolve to be like the old me, only new and improved. That may sound like an oxymoron, but it makes sense to me. I'm going to be happy-go-lucky, and I'm going to see the best in people, but I'm not going to let people make the mistake of underestimating me. And I'm sure as hell not going to be looking for trouble around every corner.

"Oomph!" I run smack-dab into Sam on my way to the teachers' lounge for my first cup of coffee and my first glimpse of Jamie since Saturday (I hope he's wearing one of those sweater vests I like).

"Oh, hey!" I greet her warmly as she tugs on my arm and pulls me into the empty music classroom. I'm *not* going to worry about all the personal and potentially embarrassing things she knows about me thanks to my motor-mouth Friday afternoon. Nope. She's my new best bud. I can tell her anything, and she'll keep it confidential. I can tell by looking into her cornflower blue eyes. Which look slightly worried right now, but I'm sure that's Renalda-related, as usual.

Before she can explain why she's dragging me around, I

say, "Hey! We should totally go out for drinks after work some night this week."

She completely ignores my invitation. "Listen, I have a confession to make, something I want you to hear from me. I've been worried all weekend about you finding out from someone else."

I laugh at her dramatic tone. "Okay. Lay it on me."

She bites her lower lip and sounds truly tormented when she says, "Oh, gosh. You're in such a good mood. You probably got laid a lot this weekend."

"Sam!" I blush but then smile wickedly. "Well, it's not my fault you guessed…"

"Never mind! I mean, *keep* that in mind when I tell you what I'm going to tell you," she instructs cryptically.

"What?"

"I sort of… called Jamie right after I talked to you on Friday afternoon."

My grin freezes. "Sort of?" I seek clarification, hoping that she somehow thinks that means "never."

She winces. "I did."

"Okay."

"Okay?" She relaxes, looking as if she can't believe her luck at my response.

"Yeah. Okay. You called him and… what? Wished him a happy weekend? Told him he forgot something in the office?" I suggest wildly and stupidly optimistically.

Shaking her head with her eyes closed, she admits, "No. I told him what you told me."

"No, you didn't."

"I did."

"No. What part?" When she looks even guiltier than before, I clutch my stomach. "Not *everything*."

She steps back from me a few feet. "Everything."

I swallow audibly. Still, I'm in denial. "Now, when you say, 'everything…'"

"All of it."

"E-Lend?"

She nods.

"Todd?"

"Yep."

"Oh, fu-unky chicken."

"Now, hear me out," she says, going into damage-control mode.

"Sam—"

"No, listen. It's a good thing."

"You had no right!"

"But it all worked out, right? I mean, Jamie's whistling in the teacher's lounge; you looked happier than I've ever seen you until about three minutes ago."

"He knows everything."

"Yes! And what's so bad about that? Nothing."

"He knew before I went over to his house, before I even called him. He knew all weekend and didn't say a word to me about it."

"Maybe you should sit down. You look pale," she observes, pointing to the desk-chair combo next to me.

I drop into it and stare at a creepy poster of Ludwig Van Beethoven hanging from the cork strip above the chalkboard.

"He knows I know."

"Knows you know what?"

"That he quit."

"But that's the thing! There's no way he can quit, knowing everything he knows now! That's why I called him."

My eyes widen. I move them from Ludwig to Sam, but

I've been staring at him so intently without blinking that for a few seconds his image is superimposed on her features.

"That's why you did this? So you wouldn't have to hire a new kindergarten teacher?"

Sheepishly, she replies, "Yes. But I also believe in true love! And you guys are such a cute——"

"Don't. Say. It."

"But——"

"Your life should be flashing before your eyes right now, Samantha. Because if you say that last word, I will kill you," I say deadly seriously.

She laughs nervously. "Okay, okay. But I had the best of intentions when I called him. And don't be mad at him; I told him not to tell you I told him. But the more I thought about it this weekend, the more I realized that you deserved to know what I had done."

Yeah, and now I know that other than the news about Operation Educate, there never was anything for me to tell him that he didn't already know. Even those three words that I thought were so momentous were old news to him.

"I want to be alone," I tell Sam now.

She's happy to oblige me, but on her way out the door, she flings a final, "I'm sorry, Kendall. I really meant well."

So much for thinking the best of people. People suck.

CHAPTER THIRTY-TWO

W*here were you this morning before the bell? I'll meet you in the library for lunch. —J*

I stare at the email while I wait for my next class to arrive. Lunch is still two hours away, but I'm not ready to talk to Jamie now, and I don't think I will be by then, either. I'd like to be strong enough to wait for him to decide when he wants to tell me things, but... I mean, it's good in theory, but how am I going to stand knowing that he knows all those things about Todd and me and E-Lend/E-Borrow, and not say anything about it, because I'm not supposed to know he knows? Not that I'm under any obligation to keep it a secret (and if Sam thinks I am after the stunt she pulled, then she's crazy), but what's the protocol in this situation? I wouldn't know.

Option A: Play dumb, tell him everything that Sam already told him—as if I don't know he already knows—and hope he returns the favor by telling me everything Sam told me, as if I don't already know. Then we'll be even.

Option B: Throw Sam under the bus and see what his reaction is.

Personally, I'm leaning toward Option B. Unfortunately, he can claim to be as much of a victim as I am, because he didn't ask Sam to tell him anything. Plus, he could come back on me and ask why I didn't tell him all of that myself. *And* he can call me on knowing all weekend that he quit his job but never asking him about it.

On second thought, Option B doesn't work well in my favor. Too bad, too. Because I'd really like to throw Sam under a bus.

Actually, I'd rather go with Option C: Say nothing and hope this magically goes away. I don't want to have some exhausting heart-to-heart only to have him say, "I felt sorry for you this weekend after what Sam told me."

Nobody likes to be pity-screwed.

But a pity screw is a one-time thing, right? It's not an overnight marathon that continues into the next day. Unless he wasn't sure how to get rid of me. Luckily, the donut did that for him.

NO! This is ridiculous! I'm doing it again. I'm looking for trouble where there is none.

As my group of third graders arrives for their library hour, I reply to his email, *See you then,* and hit "send."

Coming around the checkout counter, I greet the students with, "Hey, guys! Who's ready for another chapter of *Harry Potter and the Sorcerer's Stone?*" I know exactly what I'm going to do. I just have no idea what the results are going to be.

Unfortunately, I'm distracted from my mission of honesty when Jamie enters my office at lunch, closes the door, checks over his shoulder to make sure no one's around to see us through the office windows, and makes a beeline for my lips. After a long, lazy kiss, he pulls back just enough to say, "I've wanted to do that all morning. How are you feeling?"

I sit down at my desk, worried that my jelly-knees aren't going to hold me much longer. "Better, but don't you think that's something you should have asked before kissing me like that?"

"Wouldn't have made a difference," he states.

"Oh."

"Yeah." He backs away, takes the seat on the other side of the desk, and opens his lunch.

I open my Lance Armstrong lunchbox and take out my cup of applesauce and peanut butter and jelly sandwich.

"Grownup lunch you have there," he teases as he opens the baggie containing his turkey sandwich and takes a bite.

Defiantly, I remove the final component to my lunch, a fruit punch juice pouch, and set it on the desk between us. He nearly chokes when he sees it. I merely smile at his reaction and watch to make sure he doesn't need the Heimlich.

When he stops coughing and laughing, he asks, "Seriously, did you steal one of the students' lunches this morning? Is that where you were before the first bell?"

And there's my cue.

I coyly sip from the narrow straw sticking into the side of my drink to buy myself some time. After swallowing, I open my mouth to tell him the unvarnished truth (what's the point in making him sit through a bunch of stories he's already heard once?) only to be interrupted by my office door swinging open. Renalda's arm is attached to the doorknob.

"Hey, you two! This looks cozy!" she gushes. "I heard a wonderful rumor that you were back together, but I had to come see for myself. Why you got the door closed? A little lunchtime hanky-panky planned?"

Jamie doesn't even look away from his sandwich when he answers, "Yep. You caught us." He takes a huge bite and chews while it appears he's looking for the perfect place to take his next bite.

She giggles. "Oh, Jamie! You're such a hoot! Actually, I need to bend Kendall's ear about this Operation Educate ceremony. Did you hear that we won?" she asks him solicitously.

He merely nods, swallows, and bites again.

I look from him to her, wondering what the deal is with the cold vibe he's throwing her way. Before the uncomfortable silence drags any more, I step in. "What's up?" I ask her, turning away from my food to give her my full attention.

"Well!" she begins, her voice wobbling with excitement. "I just heard from Dr. Underhill, and let me tell you! They have somethin' real excitin' planned for the ceremony." She clasps her hands in front of her chest.

"Already? Wow. They're all over this."

"That's because it's such a great idea!" she coos. "And they need to get movin' if they're gonna have everything planned out for the announcement. They've even rustled up a donor for the tablets (some old fart who lives way out in the county), but... guess who's gonna be presentin' the award to Whitehall?" She practically does the pee-pee dance in my doorway.

While I'm trying to think of someone who would elicit such glee from a sixty-year-old educator, Jamie purrs, "Wayne Newton?"

She stops dancing and puts her hands on her hips. "Jamie Chase! Now, that would be somethin', wouldn't it?

But no. Not quite. Although this person is just as dreamy, from what I've seen in the picture Dr. Underhill sent me. Keep guessin'!"

"Some kind of country singer?" I toss out, so I can say I guessed before giving up.

"No!"

"Just tell us already," Jamie grumbles, tossing the last bite of sandwich into his mouth and brushing crumbs from his fingertips.

She seems disappointed that we're not playing along better but admits, "You'd probably never guess in a million years, anyway, so—Todd Marshall. You know, the guy who invented that fancy e-book program we're gettin' as part of the library makeover!"

"No, I don't know him!" I blurt reflexively and defensively.

Renalda looks sharply at me. "I didn't say you did. It was a rhetorical statement, honey."

I haven't even had a chance to eat a single bite of my lunch, but that doesn't mean I'm not going to throw up. Breakfast is waiting in the wings to revolt in three… two…

No! I will *not* puke in front of Jamie again. Ever.

I gulp down the nausea and keep swallowing rapidly until I'm fairly confident I won't lose it as long as I don't open my mouth.

Across the desk, Jamie mutters, "Uh-oh. I know that look."

I shake my head at him and croak, "Nope. I'm fine."

"What in the devil is wrong with you, child?" Renalda wonders.

"Nothing. I'm fine. Just… so excited about that ceremony."

Clueless as ever, she believes me. "I know! Isn't it great?

He's like some big-time millionaire—very busy, you know—but he's comin' to Whitehall to see us and congratulate us on winnin'. He seems like a real nice guy."

"I doubt it," Jamie asserts. He plucks my juice pouch from the desk and drains it in two gulps.

"Oh, now, Jamie! There's no need for you to be jealous! He'll only be here for a few minutes, anyway; then you'll go back to bein' the cutest thing in the building." When her statement doesn't get a reaction, she says, "Well, anyway, I had to come share the news. I'll let you two lovebirds get back to your lunches. By the way, it's so good to see you two have patched things up!"

"Goodbye, Renalda," Jamie dismisses her curtly.

"Okay. Bye now."

She pulls the door closed and leaves us in stifling silence.

I poke my plastic spoon in and out of my applesauce cup while I try to think of a disease that I can possibly come down with on precisely the day of that award presentation. Because there's no way in Hell I'm going to eat that huge portion of irony with Todd manning the fork.

I've worked my way through the alphabet to "m" for "mumps," when Jamie asks stonily, "Do you still have feelings for this guy? Is that why you're attempting to hide—very badly, I might add—that you're not freaking out right now?"

My head snaps up. "No!"

If he's surprised that I'm not surprised that he knows I know Todd, he doesn't show it. Apparently, we're going to skip over those details.

From the look on his face, he obviously doesn't believe my denial, so I expound on it. "Unless you mean hatred, loathing, disgust, and shame. Then, yes, I still have a *lot* of feelings for him."

Placated, he backs up by confessing in an oh-by-the-way tone, "I know about you and Todd."

"I know."

"I know you know."

"What?"

He rolls his eyes. "Sam told me she told you about telling me."

"Oh, for..." I'm too exasperated and exhausted by this whole thing to even finish my sentence. Slumping in my chair, I let my arms hang loosely at my sides.

He gathers his trash, stuffs it into his lunch sack, and crushes it into a ball before lobbing it at my trashcan. It dinks off the edge and comes to rest a few inches from my feet.

"Anyway, now that that's out of the way," he continues, "I'm sure you're upset at me for not telling you I knew when you came over Friday."

"Not really," I reply, relieved to realize it's true. "I mean, I was at first, but I'm actually glad you know and that I didn't have to tell you the whole pathetic story. It's not something I like to talk about. I was… It was a moment of weakness with Sam. I was upset after she told me you aren't going to be teaching here next year."

He leans forward, bracing his elbows on his knees and looking down at the floor between his feet. "I can't come back here."

My heart sinks. "So, it's true?"

He nods.

"Even now?"

Looking up at me, he asks, "What do you mean?"

Though I feel ridiculous having to spell it out for him, I bravely answer, "I dunno. I thought… maybe… that part of the reason you were leaving was because we had broken up, but now that we're not..."

His mouth drops open. "That has nothing to do with it." Ouch.

The hurt must be written all over my face, because he quickly adds, "That's not what I mean. This place is killing me."

"But you said—"

"I lied, all right?" He unfolds himself and paces in front of me.

"Which time?" I can't keep the bitter tone from my voice.

"All the times I said that I liked this job just fine and that it was good enough and that I'm happy cleaning up puke and scrubbing crayon from desktops and grading papers and reading aloud stories about Clifford. I effing hate that stupid, big red dog!"

Shocked, I pull my head back. "How can you hate Clifford?"

"I just do, okay? I hate him, and I hate PTA meetings, and I hate dealing with sycophantic parents and psycho parents and Jane Pleska and Renalda Twomey. And if I have to do it for another year, I might lose what's left of my mind." He stops, presses his hands against his cheeks, closes his eyes, and takes a deep breath. "I'd already decided to quit before we broke up."

"Really?" I whisper, feeling my heart break.

Oblivious, he answers emphatically, "Hell, yes! I found out about Phoenix Ridge around Thanksgiving and figured that if I sold the house, I could afford for Johnny to live there while I do what I want for a while."

I refuse to ask where I fit into this plan. I can't get a word in, anyway.

Eyes still closed, he rants, "I'm sick of trying to make up for the fact that I didn't come home sooner when my dad was sick and Mom was gone, for all intents and purposes. Being miserable for the rest of my life isn't going to bring them or Tiff back or make Johnny normal again. Phoenix Ridge is going to be good for Johnny. He needs to feel independent again, even if it's just an illusion. If nothing else, he won't have me resenting him every day for holding me back."

"Wow."

His eyes pop open at that word. I think he may have forgotten I was here.

"You think that's harsh?" he challenges.

"Uh, yeah. I do."

"Try feeling that way. It sucks. And Johnny deserves better than that."

When I say nothing, he blushes. "You probably think I'm a real asshole, but I'm being honest with myself for the first time in five years. And *I* think I'm a real asshole, too. But it's your fault."

Outraged, I nearly shout, "*My* fault? What's that supposed to mean?"

He holds out his hands and wiggles his fingers, as if inviting me to grasp them. I don't move, so he steps forward and grabs my hands, pulling me from my chair. I try to twist away from his grip, but he holds tight.

"I want my own life. With you."

"Do *not* pin this on me!" I say, finally managing to wrest my hands from his.

Hurt and confusion fill his eyes. "I'm not *pinning* anything on you. I'm only saying that I've realized I've been living half a life for five years, thinking that's all I deserve, when it's untrue. And unnecessary. I didn't have any motivation to change anything before, though."

There's a knock on my door; Bonita's arrived with her class. I'm stunned when I see the time on the clock. "Oh, shit! Your class is probably in your room, waiting for you," I tell him, sweeping my untouched lunch into the trashcan and opening the door to the other kindergarten teacher.

"Hey! Sorry. Lost track of time."

"Everything okay?" she asks cheerfully.

Mindful of the twenty-five curious faces behind her, I grin and say, "Of course! Mr. Chase and I were just finishing lunch. Hey, guys!" I greet the students.

Bonita quietly informs Jamie, "Your classroom's a little out-of-control down there."

He sighs and looks at me. "See? This is what I mean."

I laugh nervously, glancing at Bonita to get her reaction to his obvious funk. "We'll talk after school," I tell him.

Edging past us, he replies too loudly, "Yeah. I've got a stupid, big red dog to read about."

"Clifford!" one of Bonita's students astutely recognizes from his description.

I smile shakily in response to Bonita's questioning look but turn my full attention to the students. "All right, guys! Let's see what Olivia's up to. Who likes winter sports?"

CHAPTER THIRTY-THREE

I knew Jamie was too good to be true. Should have known that lurking under that sexy exterior was what always seems to be lurking under sexy exteriors: self-centered innards. And to think he had the nerve to insinuate that *I* was the selfish one when I broke up with him the first time! *He's* selfish. Not just for what he said about Johnny, either. He's selfish for making me break up with him *twice*. And for leading me—and everyone else—to believe that he's some-thing he's not. He and Marena will make a beautiful couple when they reunite in Iceland.

Harrumph!

Then to try to blame me, like I'm the one who brought out his selfish side, a side that had been lying dormant until I moved to town. As if, Jamie Chase! When I say I'd like people to give me a little credit sometimes, this is *not* what I have in mind.

"It's your fault... I want my own life. With you."

Was that supposed to turn me into a puddle? Was I supposed to say, *"Oh, in that case, it's okay for you to be a selfish jerk. I'm so flattered! Let's run away together and forget that anyone else exists in the world but you and me. How fast can you pack?"* Is that how I was supposed to react?

Actually, the last part of that still sounds pretty good. I think that's what pisses me off the most, followed closely by having to endure dinner tonight with that selfish jerk and my parents.

&

Mom and Dad's house looks as welcoming and cozy as ever with light pouring from its windows, both of their cars parked in the driveway, and the inside front door thrown open, expectantly waiting for our arrival. There's even a trickle of smoke wafting from the chimney.

It's a shame that such a potentially pleasant evening has to go to waste.

When I park my car behind my mom's car, underneath the basketball goal, Jamie says the first thing to be uttered since we left the school parking lot ten minutes earlier (other than, "Red light!" when I almost ran one in my distracted, annoyed state).

"I'm sensing you're not thrilled to be around me tonight," he ventures quietly.

Without glancing his way, I say, "Well, we're here now, so I guess it doesn't matter, does it?"

He laughs. "It would take you fifteen minutes to drive me home and get back here. It might be worth it to you."

I remove my seatbelt and pull the keys from the ignition. "Not really. My mom would never forgive me. So let's get this over with."

I exit the car without waiting for his next smart-ass response.

He catches up to me as I'm walking through the front

door, so we walk up the stairs to the open-plan living/dining/kitchen area together like the happy couple we aren't.

"Hiiiiii!" Mom's enthusiastic greeting slides like a note on a trombone when she sees our faces. Jamie looks like a puppy who's been scolded for eating a pair of shoes. And I can only imagine what I look like (probably the pair of shoes). Thrown, she asks, "Can I take your coats?" even though neither of us is wearing one.

Dad glances up from slicing the roast beef. "Whoa. Rough day at the office?" he jokes.

"Yes," I answer honestly and shortly, going to the counter and pulling up a barstool, so I can snatch hot pieces of the meat straight from the knife.

Jamie side-hugs Mom, who, in response to his thanks for the dinner invitation, says, "Oh, don't mention it! I know you're home alone on Monday nights. How is Johnny, anyway?"

"You mean the millstone around his neck?" I feel like asking. Instead, I keep shoveling beef into my mouth. I'm starving.

"Save some for the rest of us, will ya?" Dad implores, pulling the plate from my reach.

Jamie tells Mom that Johnny's doing well and uses the opening to extol the praises of Phoenix-effing-Ridge, the key to his freedom, although that's not how he couches it to her, of course. In this portrayal, he's the dutiful caretaker brother, and Johnny's best interests are the only motivation for the change in living arrangements. Can't have his biggest fan thinking any less of him, after all.

"I haven't eaten since breakfast," I explain to Dad so he doesn't think I'm gorging myself for the heck of it.

"Then five more minutes won't kill you. Setting the table should keep you busy enough during that time."

I sigh like a teenager but go around the counter to collect the plates, glasses, cutlery, and napkins we'll need.

Finished discussing Johnny, Mom asks Jamie, as if I'm not basically in the same room with them, "What's the deal with Storm Cloud over there?"

Matter-of-factly, he answers, "Oh, I pissed her off. I think."

"What'd you do now?" she wonders. "Wait! Let me guess." She taps her finger to her cheek while I make a big show of ignoring both of them. "I know! You threw an aluminum can in the trash rather than the recycling bin?"

Earnestly, he assures her, "I'd *never* do that."

Dad jumps in. "Now, now. She had a bad day. Let's leave her alone."

Mom unexpectedly agrees with him. "You're right, Ted. Anyway, it's unwise to poke an angry hornets' nest."

"I'm sure she'll tell you all about it later," Jamie adds, not sounding at all concerned.

She nods. "And I'm sure she'll get over whatever it is."

Sick of being talked about in such a patronizing manner as if I'm not here, I calmly set the pile of plates on the table, with the cutlery and napkins stacked on top, and quietly leave the room. I take the stairs two at a time up to the hallway that leads to my room, the door to which I close without a sound. I will not give them the satisfaction of a noisy display of temper. *They* may act like children, but I work with kids all day and refuse to act like one when I'm off the clock.

Screw them. I throw back the covers and climb into bed.

When did I get the reputation for being prickly and petty, anyway? To hear Jamie and Mom tell it, they have to walk on eggshells around me all the time. That's not me! I'm peppy and perky and prone to giggling at the slightest provocation.

Aren't I?

I try to objectively view my behavior over the last few weeks and realize with a sinking heart that my self-image is sorely skewed. Wanting to be one way and actually exhibiting that behavior and attitude are very different things, especially in this case.

But it's like a conspiracy! Every time I think life is going to allow me to reset to the person I've been for years, my personality time machine goes back a few too many years and takes me to the way I was in Colorado, where I had no friends and was the serious, nerdy, self-conscious target of cruel, popular boys. Maybe the past fourteen years have been one long struggle against my true nature. Maybe it's time to stop fighting it.

I've decided to stop fighting sleep when I hear a knock on my bedroom door. I sigh, sit up, and say, "Come in," as I prop myself up against the headboard.

A contrite-looking soon-to-be ex-kindergarten teacher (and -boyfriend) pokes his head around the door as if he's using it as a body shield. "Ummm… your mom says you're being rude."

"So what?"

He considers that for a second. "I don't know. I told her I'd come up here to get you." For the first time, he looks at the room around me. "Holy Lance Armstrong shrine," he breathes, stepping the rest of the way in. "I had no idea you were so insane."

I laugh in spite of myself. "Shut up. I was a teenager when I put all this stuff up."

"But this is still where you go when you're upset." He

points to the largest poster. "Do you ever sit there and pour your heart out to Lance?"

"No," I lie, tucking my hair behind my ears and playing with the edge of the bedspread.

He walks over to it and says in a lisp, "Oh, Lance! My boyfriend is such a shit. He teases me mercilessly. And my mom likes him more than she likes me."

"She does not!"

He turns around to face me. Seriously, he says, "I know. But I think you think that sometimes."

"You think you know everything."

"I know you're royally pissed off at me for being honest with you today."

"Nope. Wrong again. I'm pissed off that you blame *me* for your self-centered thoughts and actions."

He puts his hands in his pockets and rocks on his feet. "I don't, you know. Not really. But I do give you credit for helping me realize that a little selfishness is sometimes necessary."

"I want no part of that."

Smiling, he widens his eyes. "Too bad! You're not allowed to be pissed off at me because I'm not perfect, and I have faults."

Indignantly, I retort, "Putting the toilet paper on the holder backwards is a fault. Resenting your mentally challenged brother for quote-unquote, 'holding you back' is... is..."

"Honest. Self-aware," he finishes for me. "And I told you I wasn't proud of feeling that way. If I were—now, *that* would be shameful."

"It's still shameful," I insist bullishly.

He perches his "cute little ass" on the edge of my bed with his back to me. Staring at the Lance Armstrong poster that he was only moments before confiding in, he says quietly, "I thought… I don't know. I felt safe telling you that. Considering everything Sam told me about you without your knowledge or permission, I felt it was only fair to share with you something that I'm not proud of."

"I have nothing to be ashamed of. I did nothing wrong." I've said it to myself so many times over the past year that it comes out sounding like I'm reading a script.

Twisting slightly and looking at me over his shoulder, he asks, "Then why didn't you tell me yourself? Why is it your most closely guarded secret?"

"Just because I was in the right doesn't mean I don't feel stupid."

"Well, maybe I should make you feel bad for how you feel."

"It's hardly the same! I was the victim." I hate how that last sentence tastes. It's the first time I've said it out loud, no matter how many times I've thought it or felt it.

"I was a victim of circumstance," he points out stubbornly.

To scoff at that would be insensitive, but I can barely stop myself in time. It's like he senses my disbelief without my voicing it, though.

"Hey, I can't help the way I feel, okay? All I can control is the way I react to those feelings. And I don't think anyone would be able to find fault with the level of commitment I've shown to Johnny for the past five years. It's not like I've ever let on to him that I feel put out, either. I'm not cruel to him; I always have his best interests at heart."

"Even Phoenix Ridge?" I challenge, starting to feel ridiculous that I'm lying in bed like a Southern Belle with the vapors. To remedy this, I swing my feet over the side of the mattress, rise, and smooth the covers the best I can with Jamie sitting on them.

He takes the hint and stands, too, when I yank a few times on the bedspread under him. "Especially Phoenix Ridge. I told you, he needs to be more autonomous. He *can* be more autonomous but not while living with me. I can't give him the level of safety and security they have there without being right there next to him all the time. That's no way to live."

"For you, either."

"I'm not allowed to benefit from it, too? Is that what you're saying? If it works out for me, too, then it's selfish? Does it make it seem less selfish if I tell you that it's incredibly expensive and that I *have* to sell the house to make it happen? And even then, I couldn't afford it on my teacher's salary after the first few years." He rubs the back of his neck. "This is an investment on his future. And, okay, mine too. Excuse the hell out of me for trying to improve our lives."

That hadn't occurred to me. "Oh."

"Yeah." Rounding the foot of the bed, he joins me on my side and grabs my limp hand. "Mom and Dad left us some money, but it wasn't much, and it's almost gone, thanks to Johnny's medical bills. Even if I sell the house quickly—which isn't at all a given, considering the current market—I'm going to have to figure out what I want to be when I grow up, and it had better be something lucrative."

Since I have no idea what someone with his educational and professional qualifications makes or even what sorts of jobs are available to him—other than jobs on field teams with sexy, smart co-workers—I don't know if this news is good news or bad news in the context of our relationship, such as it is right now. I feel ridiculous asking, too. So I don't. It may be none of my business, when all is said and done.

I stare down at our hands. He rubs mine with his thumb.

"What can I do to convince you not to dump my ass tonight?" he eventually asks.

He laughs sadly when my head snaps up, and the look on my face is an amalgamation of panic and guilt.

"It's obvious," he explains before I can ask how he knows what I've been considering since his lunchtime meltdown. "Doesn't take an archaeologist to unearth the clues."

That joke leads me to observe, "You're full of chuckles for someone who thinks he's about to be dumped."

"Is my assessment accurate, though?"

I turn away from him and go to my bedroom window, which looks down on the driveway. I stare at a blob of bird poop on the roof of my car. "Maybe," I answer.

Coming up behind me, he grasps my upper arms and rests his chin on top of my head. "Well, maybe I'll dump you first. I mean, I'm not going to passively allow you to keep ditching me whenever the mood strikes you."

His threat is uttered in such a bored tone of voice that it's obviously an empty one. I don't even object to his trivialization of my reasons for breaking up with him, because I can tell he's not being serious. I lean my back against his chest and sigh. Bending down further to put his lips next to my ear, he murmurs, "I'm sorry, but I really don't like Clifford."

Whirling, I slap him on the chest. "Jamie!"

He grins. "He's a doofus who's always screwing things up. If he were a real dog, he'd have been put to sleep a long time ago."

"Sounds a little bit like someone I know," I grumble, unable to keep from smiling.

He bites his lower lip. "Well, if that's a dealbreaker, so be it. I think you'd better sleep on it before you make such a big decision, though. Because this is it. A man's pride can only take so much." With a brisk pat on my head (am *I* Clifford?), he says, "Now, let's go eat. Your parents are waiting for us."

CHAPTER THIRTY-FOUR

I slept on it.

And under it. And with it.

I am weak.

And I don't care. I'm sick of caring. It's tiring and depressing (I'm beginning to believe more in that concept for myself, now) and turns me into a raging bitch.

Plus, I believe there's such a thing as caring too much, especially when it comes to putting stock in the wrong things. I hate to admit it, but Jamie was right; I was disappointed that he's not perfectly noble, like I'd imagined him to be. I know he can't help how he feels; I know he's made a lot of compromises; and I know he's not Mr. Darcy. When he said those things about Johnny and his parents, I had to say goodbye to that fantasy once and for all. I mean, I always knew it deep down, but there was no denying it after what he said. And that pissed me off.

I also know he loves Johnny and would do anything for him. It's cruel of me to even question that based on a moment of weakness in which he conveyed one of his most shameful thoughts. The more I think about it, it wasn't even that shameful. I was shocked when he first said it, because it was so *un*-Jamie. He's rarely even hinted at the idea that he wants his own life away from Johnny. I guess it goes without saying, but it was unexpected to hear him voice it so explicitly.

So I've tried to reconcile my ideal of Jamie with the real thing and cut him some slack when he doesn't quite measure up to the unreasonable expectations I've placed on him.

It's just like buying my first serious bike. I waited a long time to find the right one; then I patiently saved up the money to buy it; then I ordered it, but almost as soon as I hit the button to confirm my order, I had major buyer's remorse. Not because it wasn't exactly what I wanted, but because it was a huge investment. I suddenly thought of a dozen other things that same amount of money could have bought. I didn't want any of those other things as much as I wanted that bike, but I was worried that I *should* want those things more. So by the time the bike arrived, I had convinced myself—in an effort to justify the expense—that it was going to revolutionize my life. And I was almost disappointed in it for being the only thing it ever claimed to be, a bike, and that I still had to pedal it for it to work.

I realize it makes me seem ridiculously un-romantic (and somewhat vulgar) to compare my boyfriend to a bike, but that's the comparison I have to keep in mind when I find myself expecting him to be the answer to every challenge and disappointment in my life. He's still just a guy. A yummy, funny, smart guy. But a guy.

During the past month and a half, we've fallen into a comfortable pattern and routine. I usually spend one or two nights a week at his place, and we have dinner at Mom and Dad's every Wednesday, but for the nights when he needs to grade papers or wants to spend time with Johnny or his friends (or just alone), I've joined some classes at the gym (yoga and spinning) and have reacquainted myself with a former high school friend who also attends the spinning class.

Suddenly, life isn't so one-dimensional.

Now, watching him sleep with one bent arm flung behind his head, it's easy to think the best of him. He looks so peaceful and guileless and beautiful, like he's never had a bad thought about or for anyone. He looks like he doesn't have a care in the world, like he's not shouldering the responsibility of supporting himself and another grown person who doesn't have the capacity to do so. It's also hard to imagine simply by looking at his sleeping face that he may feel the strain associated with trying to make the right decisions not only for himself but as they pertain to a certain elementary school librarian's happiness.

Not that I would ever purposely put that onus on him. I'd like to think my happiness doesn't rest in the hands of someone else. But to say that would be lying. It's not possible to be in love with someone but claim their decisions have no bearing on your happiness. So I don't think that by admitting that, I'm confessing something pathetic or that I need to fork over my modern woman card.

Unable to resist touching him for another second, even though I know it's selfish to wake him up, I trace a finger up the inside of his milky-white bicep. He flinches wildly but doesn't open his eyes or say anything, so I cuddle up to his side and rest my head on his chest, near his armpit. He brings his hand out from behind his head and circles my shoulders with his arm.

"Are you trying to tell me you're ready to get up?" he mumbles sleepily.

Feeling like a child who hasn't mastered the art of hinting, I sheepishly reply, "Maybe."

Goosebumps rise on every square inch of my body as he rakes his fingers from my hairline to my neckline. "Well, don't let me stop you. Feel free to make some breakfast. You don't even have to get dressed; Johnny's already gone to work by now."

I place a kiss on his nipple. "I don't want breakfast."

"Fine, but I still have ten more minutes before the alarm goes off and reminds me that I have to spend seven hours around two dozen creatures with questionable hygiene, poor social skills, and wild mood swings. Then there's the students…"

Laughing at his joke, I burrow even closer to him by hooking one leg over his and pressing the length of my body to his side. Faux-innocently, I declare, "Ten minutes is plenty of time for what I have in mind."

He tenses. "Oh."

When I giggle, he defends himself. "I'm a little slow in the morning before my first cup of coffee."

"Well, you'll need to hurry up, because now we only have eight minutes until the alarm."

"Unfortunately, that's still plenty of time," he replies as I slide the rest of the way on top of him.

Much longer than eight minutes later, I've stepped from the shower, and I'm trying to put on pantyhose as quickly as possible without putting a finger through them while Jamie's calmly and swiftly tying his necktie with short, swishing motions.

As he folds his shirt collar over the ribbon of cloth, he says ultra-casually, "I have a job interview at lunch, so…"

I freeze with one leg three-quarters of the way into the

nylon tights. "Oh?" I inquire with hardly enough breath to manage that tiny word.

This is one subject we've managed to skirt. We've done a decent job of pretending like nothing's going to change on the last day of school, a little more than three months from now.

Somehow I manage to make myself move and finish dressing while he replies, "Yep. An associate professor position at UNC that your mom told me about." He straightens the knot at his throat.

How can one be relieved and dismayed at the same time? It's possible. And it feels horrible.

As if I'm worried that I'll be pointing something out that he hasn't already noticed, I hesitantly say, "But that's still teaching. I thought you didn't want to teach."

"I don't." He smiles curtly at me in the mirror. "But beggars can't be choosers. I'm just hoping that teaching archaeology to adults will be slightly less torturous than teaching phonics to kindergartners."

"Oh. I see."

Now he turns to face me and laughs at the look on my face. "I didn't mean to upset you."

"I'm not upset," I try to reassure him.

"Your mom already put in a good word for me with the department chair, and the money's decent. I'd be an idiot not to explore the option."

"You don't have to explain anything to me." I step into my dress and slip my arms in. After I zip it most of the way in the back, he steps over and finishes the job. "I don't want you to feel like you *have* to apply for—or take—a job because my mom's involved. Or limit yourself to jobs in this area, even if there aren't any here that interest you."

I give him a meaningful look and duck away to retrieve

my shoes from his closet floor, where I placed them last night.

"I'm not doing anything out of obligation, if that's what you're afraid of."

My smile's brittle enough to crack in two when I say while sliding my feet into my shoes, "I'm not afraid of anything."

He's too nice to call me on that lie. "Okay. Well… I was only telling you so you'd know where I was at lunchtime."

I kiss him on the cheek on my way past him to leave the bedroom. "Sure. Thanks," I say lightly. "Hey, do you have any of that cereal left? You know, the granola clusters kind? Love it!"

I'll be damned if I'm going to be the one to take what we've built during the past six weeks and kick it down with a bunch of histrionics and serious talk.

꿈

My cuticles look like someone stuck my hand in the paper shredder next to my desk. They're ragged, chewed, sore, and—in some of the worst cases—bloody. That doesn't mean I'm going to stop abusing them, though. I couldn't, even if I wanted to stop. I was hoping to get news from Jamie about his job interview (playing it cool and pretending like I don't care, of course) when he brought his class down for their library time, but Sam was escorting the kids. Before I could ask her what the deal was, she told me, "Thank God, I can go back to my desk for an hour! Thanks, Kendall!" and rushed out.

I'm pondering how bad it would look if I called her at her desk to ask her why she's watching Jamie's class and deciding that I care less about that than having to wait another minute to find out when Brody slaps his latest selection on the checkout counter.

Without even looking at it, I scan the bar code. That's when I notice the checkout record.

"Brody, you've already checked this out six times," I inform him dully. "Go pick a different book."

"Meow!" he objects. "I like this one. It has my favorite cat in it!"

"Broaden your horizons," I insist. "You can get this one next week, I guess. But this week, get a different book." I hug it to my chest.

He doesn't move. "You need a Band-Aid. You're bleeding on your fingers."

Quickly, I curl them under the book. "I'm fine."

"Okay. Hey. We have a substitute today. Only it's not a real substitute. It's Miss Sam from the office. She's boring. She makes us color forever and ever. Big boo!" He blows some wet raspberries and gives me a double thumbs-down to underscore his point before stepping away, thinking that the conversation is over now that he's said his piece.

I stop him, though. "Whoa! Where's Mr. Chase?" It's a long shot that one of the students will know, but Sam *does* have a big mouth. It would be just like her to come straight out and tell the kids.

He shrugs. "I dunno. Maybe he barfed and had to go home."

I'm about to reveal that's not the case before remembering I'm talking to a six-year-old. Lamely, I concede, "Maybe."

That's when it occurs to me that Sam may not know any more than Brody does. The chances of Jamie telling her the truth about why he had to be gone for the afternoon are slim. It's not that his looking for another job is any big secret, but I don't think he's willing to share anything that may get back to Renalda. I haven't asked him outright what's going on between him and our boss, because that would violate the terms of our unspoken agreement not to talk about work, but he's decidedly brusque with the school principal whenever they come in contact.

Renalda doesn't seem to be bothered by it. She's either good at ignoring rude behavior or blissfully oblivious that the behavior is even happening. Or a combination of both. I haven't figured out what her strategy is. But Jamie's goal is easy to spot: be as cutting and sarcastic as possible if Renalda refuses to be ignored, which is often the case.

It's only forty-five minutes until the end of the school day, so I decide to be strong and wait until the students are gone so I can go into my office, close the door, and call Jamie without worrying about being overheard or letting on to someone else that I may not know everything that's going on.

I have no idea what his prolonged absence means. I've thought of everything from an extended interview to a bad car accident. But I've consoled myself with the knowledge that Jamie obviously talked to Sam himself, so it's probably nothing as serious as a car accident.

I've settled on the extended interview idea, but what does that mean? That only happens when an employer really likes the candidate. Has Jamie resigned himself to being a teacher... again? If so, what's the point of all this? Why quit a job and sell your house only to take another job exactly like the one you quit? He can split hairs all he wants, but if he hates teaching as much as he says he does, then teaching at a university isn't going to be any more enjoyable for him than teaching at Whitehall.

He also forgets that I know what a UNC Associate

Professor makes, and it's not much more than he's already making. If the position is on the tenure track, that may be a bit more promising, but he's not going to get into the big bucks unless he's a tenured professor. Maybe that's his ultimate goal? He said selling the house will buy him some time to figure things out; perhaps that means he'll have a few years to climb the academic and salary-grade ladders at UNC.

But again…

He doesn't want to be in a classroom! Period.

On auto-pilot, I get through the rest of my time with Jamie's class, but as soon as the last student's rear end clears the doors, I dash into my office and dig my cell phone from my purse. With red-tipped, angry fingers I press the buttons to connect me to Jamie's cell phone. It goes straight to voicemail.

Now, what does *that* mean?

It means I'm going to have to stop by the pharmacy on my way home and buy a vat of antibiotic ointment and a case of bandages for my poor hands.

⚬

Thirty seconds after 4:30, I'm in my car, practically burning rubber as I leave the parking lot. Five minutes later, I'm at the nearest pharmacy for first aid supplies. Five minutes after that, I'm administering aid to my chewed-up digits. Ten minutes after that, I'm sitting on Jamie's front porch, trying to decide my next move, considering his car's in the driveway but nobody's answering the door, and he's still not answering his cell phone. It takes me about a minute to conclude that I'm going to wait here until he answers the door or the phone.

Fifteen minutes later, the cold wind has me reconsidering that idea.

Anyway, it's obvious he doesn't want to talk to or see me, so it's pathetic to force him to do either one. I decide to leave him a voicemail message, saying I'm wondering about his interview and telling him to call me when he feels up to talking about it.

When I dial his number, I'm surprised it doesn't go to voicemail right away, like all the other times. Even more interesting is the fact that I can actually hear the ringing phone coming toward me. I walk to the front door, but it's not as muffled as it would be if there were wood or glass separating me from the sound. That's when I see Jamie pedaling up the street on his bike.

He dismounts at the edge of the yard and nods toward the accessory pack mounted to his bike's stem. "That you?"

I hold up my phone and wiggle it before hitting the disconnect button. "Yep. Guilty."

Smiling, he takes off his helmet. "Uh-oh. Why are you guilty?"

"Because it's about the seventh time I've called you in the past two hours," I confess. No use denying it, since he has an electronic record of my mobile stalking.

He takes his cell phone from the pack and looks down at it. "It sure is. Huh. I must not get any reception out where I was riding." When he motions for me to follow him to the garage, I skip down the steps, burrowing further into my coat.

"Kind of cold for a bike ride, isn't it?"

"Nah! Not when you have the right clothes. I know you think they're funny, but..." He trails off as he lifts his bike onto the heavy-duty hooks mounted in the wooden ceiling beams. As he's unlatching his pack from the frame, he explains, "Anyway, I wanted to take a ride now that a professional has guaranteed that all the parts are where they should be. Plus, I needed to run out to Phoenix Ridge to fill out the last of the paperwork before Johnny's big move. Thought I'd do that and clear my head at the same time."

As if it was my misunderstanding, I say, "Oh. I didn't realize you were taking the whole afternoon off. I was sort of worried when Sam brought your class to the library. I figured your job interview ran a little long. Or something."

He gives me a cryptic smile as he leads me from the garage and pulls down the heavy door before locking it with a key that he pulls from an impossibly tiny pocket in his equally tiny pants. "Nope."

When we get into the house without him saying another word on the subject, I try not to show my annoyance at having to drag it from him. "Well? How'd it go, then?"

He unzips his jacket and peels the formfitting garment from his arms. He drapes it on the back of a dining chair, which he grips with both hands and squeezes until his knuckles turn white. "I dunno. Okay, I guess. I mean, they know it's not my dream job, but—"

"Did you tell them that?"

"No! But it's evident when I get excited talking about field work but don't have much to say about lecturing and researching and paper-writing. They're not idiots." Sighing, he adds, "We'll have to see how desperate they are to fill the position."

"But it's *good* that they know how you feel, right?" When he simply blinks back at me, I continue, "Because they should hire someone who really wants the job."

"You don't want me to get that job."

It's not a question, so I don't feel like I have to admit to anything so mean.

"Are you worried that I'll be working at the same place as your parents? It's a big campus, and they're both in completely separate departments."

His off-base conclusion confuses the heck out of me. "What? No! I *know* how big the school is; I went there, remember? Anyway, why would you think that?"

He kicks off his shoes, hooks them onto the first two fingers of his right hand, and carries them down the hallway to his bedroom. "I'm trying to figure out why you wouldn't want me to get the job," he answers quietly.

I trail him, my eyes glued to his straight back. "I don't want you to trade one miserable job for another one, that's all. I want you to be happy, and you've made it clear that academia isn't what's going to do it for you."

Precisely and with care, he sets the shoes on the empty spot in the rack with his four other pairs of cycling shoes. "There's more to life than what I do forty hours a week to pay the bills."

"That's what you've been telling yourself—unsuccessfully—for the past five years, Jamie. It's obviously not true for you."

More clingy clothing gets the peel treatment, but for once I'm not distracted by what he's revealing underneath. I can't take my eyes off the sad look on his face when he says, "Just let me worry about that, all right?"

With a sinking heart, I say, "No."

"What do you mean, 'no'? It's my life, my career, my—"

"Mistake?"

Dismissively, he goes into the bathroom and turns on the shower. "Please. Not everything in life is so dramatic. It's a job. It'll pay the bills. More or less."

"'More or less'?"

"I'll have to do some creative budgeting so that I can swing Johnny's rent at Phoenix Ridge, but—"

"Fuck Phoenix Ridge!"

Now he pokes his head and bare shoulders around the edge of the doorframe. "Calm down," he demands, demonstrating an infuriating control over his own emotions, betrayed only by the deep line between his eyes.

I take a quick, deep breath but plunge on. "I thought the point of Johnny going to… there… was so that you could take a less conventional job, one that allows you to travel again and get out in the field."

He ducks into the bathroom once more. I hear the shower curtain rings slide on the rod and the water slap against his body before he says, "That was a fantasy. The point was to give Johnny his own life back. Now I have to finance it. Period."

"You're so full of shit," I mutter.

"Huh?"

"YOU'RE SO FULL OF SHIT!" I yell more loudly so he can hear me above the shower noise.

"And you don't know what you're talking about."

I stand in the open bathroom doorway and speak to the silhouette behind the curtain. "I know a *lot* about being too afraid to do what I truly want to do and making safe choices, even if they're repeats of mistakes I've promised not to make again. I know what that looks like."

"Good for you. But that's not what's happening. And this argument is stupid. Because I probably won't even get that job."

"Good!"

"Thanks."

"It's not the right job for you."

"Well, if it doesn't work out, I may be serving you your

QUIET, PLEASE!

tall lattes in the morning and asking if you want to super-
size your fries at night. That's *much* better."

That shuts me up for a second. Just a second, though. I
gulp and address the shark in the bathroom: "What about
calling Marena? I thought you said that's what you were
going to do."

He's quiet for so long that I think he may not have heard
me. Before I repeat myself, though, he says, "It's not
worth it."

Even though it effectively kills my side of the debate, I'm
secretly glad he doesn't want to ask Marena for anything.

The taps squeak off. I hand him a towel around the
curtain. While he dries his hair and face, he muffles, "I've
thought of all the angles, all right?" More clearly, he elabo-
rates, "This job at UNC is actually close to ideal. It's tenure-
track, so the money will be good eventually. And I'll have
summers off to travel, when I can afford it. I may even get
some trips paid for by the university."

Unconvinced, but sick of arguing about it, I allow,
"That'll be nice."

He pulls the curtain back to reveal himself wearing
nothing but a grin. Hands on his hips, he asks, "So, where
do you want to go first?" He punctuates his question with a
wiggle of his eyebrows.

CHAPTER THIRTY-FIVE

The day of Todd's visit has arrived. I've been hiding in my office for most of the day, wearing mittens to keep myself from chewing my fingers, which have only recently healed from the day of Jamie's first interview at UNC. Renalda's been in here twice, once to ask if I had any hairspray and the other time to giddily announce that Todd would be "helicopterin' onto the playground at 2:15." During her second visit, I had to abruptly excuse myself to the ladies' room, where I stayed until I absolutely had to be in the library for my next group of kids.

I keep telling myself that everything will be fine. It's going to be a very short visit. He may not even see me. Except for that moment when he presents the award. But we'll be in front of a big group of people. And after the presentation, he'll probably be "helicopterin'" away as suddenly as he arrived. If not, I can always find some pressing business to attend to... in the bathroom.

At first I think I'm imagining it. Or that my nerves have finally frayed to a point that my eyeballs are vibrating in my skull. Then the pulsing gets stronger. The Japanese maple outside one of the long, narrow windows in the library bends nearly all the way to the ground. Jamie pokes his head through my office door.

"Uh... hey. I believe the peacock has landed," he informs me. Ridiculously happy to see his friendly face, I smile at his attempt at levity.

We haven't seen much of each other lately. When he hasn't been at Phoenix Ridge, getting Johnny settled, he's been extremely preoccupied with the UNC-Charlotte interview process, which is taking forever. I'm not sure the President of the United States is vetted this thoroughly. Jamie's been told the pool of applicants was enormous, so they've had to go through several rounds of interviews to narrow it down. They're doing another round next week. This time, Jamie will be meeting with the Provost for Academic Affairs, who he says is a real ballbreaker and is very anti-male. This gives me hope. Actually, I'd hoped he wouldn't get this far, but his field experience has carried a lot of weight with the selection committee. Damn it.

For the past hour, Freddie, Sam, and Renalda have been fluttering around the library, setting up the chairs, cake, and punch, but the two women have been bickering, so I've made no effort to help them. I'm stressed out enough as it is. I'd end up spilling something or dumping the enormous sheet cake on the floor. Plus, it's difficult to work in mittens.

I shed my winter hand-wear and join Jamie in the doorway. "What are you doing here? Where's your class?"

"Bonita's keeping an eye on my students for me so that I can be here for this. You look nice today," he says, tucking a piece of hair behind my ear. "Nice legs."

I know he's trying to make me feel better, but it's going to take more than looking "nice" or having "nice legs" to keep me from feeling like a complete and utter loser next to Todd. Still, I haven't forgotten my manners.

"Thanks."

I resist revealing that the crotch of my tights keeps sagging between my legs (if it goes any lower, he's not going to need me to tell him, anyway) or that I changed my clothes at least five times this morning before settling on this ensemble, which now seems dowdy and very school librarian-ish. The hem of the skirt hits my legs at an unflattering place, and the blouse is exactly that: a blouse. Ick. As inappropriate as it was, I should have stuck with the second outfit, a short black skirt, tight white silk shirt, and stilettos. Then again, in that getup, I looked like a cross between a hooker and a chain restaurant hostess who forgot her suspenders and assortment of fun pins and buttons. I also looked like I was trying out for a Robert Palmer music video remake.

The high-pitched whirring from outside stops. Jamie wiggles his finger in his ear. "Yikes. I could have done without that."

I could do without this whole thing. But it'll be over in twenty minutes, tops. Right? Then no more diarrhea, headaches, or cold sweats in the middle of the night… Just back to worrying about my boyfriend's career. It's so much easier worrying about other people's worries.

When there's a flurry of activity behind Jamie, I strain to see over his shoulder. He helpfully steps aside so that I can get a good look at Dr. Underhill striding through the library with Todd. They appear to be having a competition to see who can be the most jovial.

"Oh, fudge," I whisper.

"It's going to be fine," Jamie replies. "Unless you don't want it to be. Personally, I think you should call him out in front of everyone and make a scene."

"No!" I grip his arm. "You're not thinking of doing anything like that, are you?"

He laughs. "It's crossed my mind, especially since I don't have anything to lose."

"Jamie, that's not funny."

"Relax. It's not my place, not my battle." He glares in Todd's general direction. "I must say, it would be a total turn-on if *you* did it, though."

"You'll have to get off some other way, because that's not happening. I need this job, and I don't need him having yet another memory of me making an idiot of myself." I try to discreetly adjust my tights from the outside of my skirt. "I'm just going to accept the award and hope he doesn't recognize me."

Jamie returns his attention to my face and raises his eyebrow. "You guys slept together for two years."

"Don't remind me."

"I'm sure he doesn't need a reminder."

"I'm counting on the fact that he's had so many partners since then that he doesn't remember anything from Kansas City."

"A whole city wiped from his memory? That would have to be some piece of a—"

"Kendall Dickinson! Is that you over there?"

My stomach drops as Todd takes two steps to his right to get a better angle and see around Jamie.

"Nonononono," I mutter, panic-stricken.

Jamie lays a supportive hand on my shoulder. "Calm, cool, collected," he murmurs.

I beam as every head in the library, now full of School Board members, school administrators, and even a reporter from the tiny local paper, turns to see whom Todd Marshall could possibly be addressing.

"Yep. It's me!" I chirp, as if I'm as delighted by this run-in as he is.

He makes it over to me in three big steps, looks directly at Jamie's hand, then at Jamie, and envelopes me in a bear hug. Stunned, I do nothing to stop him. Eventually, he stops squeezing and holds me at arms' length.

"Look at you!" he cries. "I thought to myself when I saw your name listed as the school librarian on the order, *how many other Kendall Dickinsons in North Carolina can there be?* But I still couldn't believe it. It's really you, though!"

"The one and only," I return lamely as I study his tan face. He's so… plastic-looking. Most obviously, he's had his teeth capped. His eyebrows are perfectly shaped and trimmed, too. And is he wearing colored contacts? I don't remember his eyes ever being that blue.

I'm squinting into his left eye in an attempt to see a line from the lens when Renalda crashes our reunion.

"What's this? Y'all know each other? Kendall, you didn't mention that! I'da remembered that!" she gushes.

Todd ultra-casually answers, "Yeah. Kendall and I worked together in Kansas City. Seems like a lifetime ago." He looks around the library. "This suits you. You seem to fit in here better than you did in Kansas City. I gotta say, I never saw you as the type to be working with kids, though." His gaze rests once more on me. Or more accurately, on my chest. "Anyway… you look great. Being closer to home, in familiar surroundings, really suits you."

At this statement and its lecherous accompanying look, Jamie finally steps in. "Maybe we should get in place for the presentation," he suggests tightly.

Todd blinks up at him. "Oh. Hi." He offers his hand, which receives a stony stare from Jamie. "And you are?"

Finding my voice, I quickly supply, "This is Jamie Chase. He's one of the kindergarten teachers here at Whitehall."

When I stop there, Renalda giggles. "And your boyfriend, silly! You can't leave out the most interestin' information!"

Oh, gosh. This is a hundred times worse than I thought it was going to be. I completely disregarded the Renalda Factor in all my nightmares of this scenario. Freshman mistake. I'm still not used to working with such a boob.

Thankfully, Sam saves the day. "Okay, everybody! We're ready to go. Over here! At the podium. Dr. Underhill, you're up first... sir."

When everyone moves away, I hastily say to Jamie, "I'm sorry. I froze up. I just... I didn't mean to—"

He waves me off. "Whatever. It's not a big deal."

Even though his expression is neutral, I can tell it's a bigger deal than he's willing to admit. Unfortunately, I don't have time to make amends. Dr. Underhill's getting right to the point. I'm going to have to approach the podium any second now.

"...That's why we're proud to present this award to Renalda Twomey and Whitehall Elementary for submitting our first-ever Operation Educate winning idea. Renalda, come on up here and share a few words with us."

Everyone claps. Renalda smiles at the School Board members and the Operation Educate selection committee as she makes her way to the podium and receives the engraved wooden plaque from Todd, who's beaming like he knows these people and cares about more than the money in his pocket from scoring an entire school district, as opposed to the original plan of only one school receiving the E-Lend upgrade.

From behind me, Jamie leans close to my ear and whispers, "Get ready. She's going to call you up there. She's looking at you."

I force myself to breathe and nod. Yeah. He's right. She's looking right at me. And now she's deliberately looking away from me, at the plaque.

"Well, my lands! This is quite a thrill, everybody! When Dr. Underhill challenged each of the schools to come up with an idea for a program that could be implemented district-wide, well…" She laughs self-deprecatingly. "I was flat stumped!"

Butterflies jump in my tummy. *Okay. Here it comes.* I lick my lips so that I have enough moisture on them to smile when she says my name and asks me to join her.

"But then one day, it came to me! And I knew it was a winner right away."

I'm panting now with the effort to stay conscious as a sickly familiar feeling builds in the pit of my stomach. I stare down at my feet.

"I can't take all the credit, though," she continues.

My head snaps up. *Oh, thank God.* I preemptively grin in her direction, but she stubbornly keeps her eyes on the people seated near the podium in rows of folding chairs.

"I'm a God-fearin' woman, after all. Can't forget to thank God for His inspiration!"

The crowd murmurs and chuckles appreciatively. Dr. Underhill's smile widens. Todd's expression looks a little forced, but I think the mold they used to make his new face isn't giving him a choice about smiling.

Jamie places his hands on my upper arms, but I shrug him off.

Now Renalda looks to the back of the crowd, where we're standing. "And I'm so glad that my idea is goin' to be such a blessin' to the entire district, but especially to the

Whitehall school library and our cute-as-a-button librarian, Kendall Dickinson!" She gives me a finger wave. "I know she's chompin' at the bit to get these tablets for our students and use this amazin' software that Mr. Marshall here has invented. Oh, look! She's gettin' all choked up just thinkin' about it."

I will *not* cry in front of these people.

Without even thinking about how it looks or what the consequences may be, I spin on my heel and rush from the library. I find the nearest door that leads to the outdoors and push it, not caring that it's a fire exit and immediately sets off the ear-piercing alarms. Good. Let 'em wail!

I duck around the building and speed-walk to my car. I'm halfway across the parking lot when the students begin streaming from the building, their teachers barking instructions.

"Straight lines! Walk all the way to the edge of the playground. Do *not* touch that helicopter!" Bonita barks. "Oh, Jamie! There you are. Thank goodness. One class is hard enough to control in this situa—Wait! Where are you going?"

I glance over my shoulder and see that he's in hot pursuit. Shit. I don't even have my purse or car keys. Impulsively, I crash into the brush that lines the wooded area behind the parking lot. And hit a chain-link fence that I didn't realize was there. I stumble along the fence, still moving away from Jamie, until I come to the end of it and slip into the semi-cover of the budding trees.

It's a tangled mess of undergrowth and low-hanging branches in here, though, so it's not long before I find myself hung up on a tall sticker bush between two trees. While I work unsuccessfully to free myself without damaging my shirt, I hear Jamie cursing a few feet behind me. Then he's standing next to me.

"You do realize you walked through a huge patch of poison ivy back there, right? And that fence is covered in it," he informs me, sounding put-out about it.

"Nobody asked you to follow me."

"I don't have to be asked. Are you okay?" He wipes his sweaty forehead on his upper arm, holding his hands stiffly as if he's afraid to touch any part of himself with them.

"I'm fine," I lie. "Are you really allergic to poison ivy, or something?"

"Fairly."

"You should go back into the school and wash your hands with soap and hot water, then."

"Yeah, well someone pulled the fire alarm, so I'm stuck out here until they clear the building," he remarks pointedly.

"I didn't pull the alarm; I opened the door. Big difference." Finally free from the thorns, I look him directly in the eye for the first time. And dissolve.

"It's happening all over again!" I wail. "I… She… And everyone… They were staring at me like I was a piece of furniture. Or like when the tablets arrive, I'll look at them and say, 'Pretty!' but won't know the first thing to do with them." Vacuously, I coo, "'How do you turn them on? I should call Renalda and ask her!' When it was *my* idea. Mine! Not Renalda's. Renalda couldn't have come up with this idea if God had sent it to her in a dream, as she's apparently claiming. She came to *me*! She hounded *me* for weeks. *I* lost sleep over it. Not her! 'It just came to me.' Well, that's not a lie. I delivered it to her desk, and she couldn't even be bothered to read over it before sending it to Dr. Underhill. Why does this keep happening to me?"

Pushing his glasses higher on his nose with the very edge of his wrist, Jamie answers, "I don't know."

What I should be asking is, how do I keep *allowing* this to happen to me? Why didn't I have my name all over that thing? Why didn't I deliver it to Dr. Underhill myself? Why didn't I make him aware that I was the one in charge of Whitehall's idea? Why would someone who's been through such a traumatic intellectual property theft ever put herself in that position again? I must be the stupidest effing moron on the face of the earth."

"No. Now, come on."

"I'm not saying it so you'll disagree and make me feel better. I'm saying it because it has to be true. I'm even stupider than Renalda, because at least she's smart enough to figure out how to keep her job when it's obvious she does nothing but wander the halls, get her hair and nails done, sneak off for 'afternoon delights' with her geriatric boyfriend, steal people's ideas, and sexually harass her male staff members."

The snot, the tears, the mascara... they're all over my face. I can feel it, but there's nothing I can—or want to—do about it. This is happening. It's ugly. It's raw. It's what night-mares are made of. I can't happy-talk it away.

"Well, what are you going to do about it?" he finally asks when it seems I've cried myself out.

"What *can* I do? Everyone—but you and Sam—loves that ridiculous woman. If I accuse her of anything, I'll look like a villain."

"So? Who cares what everyone else thinks?" He holds his right hand close to his face and examines it before drop-ping it to his side. "If nothing else, you need to confront her privately. She needs to know that you know she's a fraud."

"What's the point?"

"Your self-respect? It seems like you're angrier at yourself than her. You'll never forgive yourself if you don't stand up to her."

I look down at my snagged tights and dirty shoes. "It's the one thing that I regret the most with Todd."

"I know."

"You're right; I have to talk to her."

I suddenly realize that the schoolyard in the distance is quiet and that everyone must have been allowed to go back inside. "Come on. You need to wash that poison ivy oil off your skin. I'm going to catch Renalda before she leaves… and before I lose my nerve."

We pick our way back to the closest clearing and across the parking lot. When we're nearly to the doors by his classroom, he pauses with his hand on the door handle, looking truly conflicted. "No offense, but you probably want to clean up a bit before going to talk to her."

"Oh. Yeah. Good thinking. Nobody else needs to know how upset I am by this, right?" I give him a shaky smile.

"Exactly," he agrees, visibly relieved that I didn't take offense to his suggestion. "Meet back at my room later?"

Hoping I don't look too deranged, I smile broadly. "Sure!"

He opens the door and holds it for me so I can pass by and slip to the bathroom, ideally before anyone sees me.

Too bad Todd's on the other side of the door, on his way to his makeshift helipad.

CHAPTER THIRTY-SIX

"Kendall! Hey! Oh!" Todd reaches out, pulls a leaf from my hair, and tosses it to the ground. "What happened? You're... wow. A little disheveled."

Ignoring him, I say to Jamie, "It's fine. Go wash your hands before you have a major problem."

Reluctantly, he heeds my advice but says, "I'm right inside these doors if you need me."

"I think she'll be all right, pal," Todd replies.

Jamie's the second person to ignore him.

If Todd notices we're treating him like the Invisible Man, he doesn't let on that he cares. He watches Jamie leave and turns back to me with a grin. "Huh. Did the hunky kindergarten teacher teach you a few things in the woods during the fire drill? You always were adventurous like that. Remember that time at the——"

I proudly lift my chin and interrupt him before he can make me relive any of the times I had sex with him. "So, this is ironic, huh?"

He grins. "How do you mean?"

I'm not sure if he doesn't know what irony is or if he

doesn't understand how this situation is ironic. Either way, it proves that he's not smart enough to have come up with a program like E-Lend. I should have taken him to court and had my lawyer run him through a series of IQ tests. I would have won.

Knowing I'm running out of time before Renalda leaves for the day, I say, "Never mind. I don't have time to explain it to you. Anyway, it was *fabulous* seeing you again. You have a real knack for being part of my worst nightmares."

He laughs. "Oh, Kendall. You were always so funny. I wish I didn't have to leave so soon, or we could go out for a few drinks, catch up, you know?"

I nod toward his helicopter. "I think I know all I need to know about the life you stole from me, but thanks."

He looks genuinely confused. "Is that what this"—he motions to my wrecked face—"is all about? I gotta say, I'd hoped you'd gotten over that. It's not healthy to harbor grudges and envy others their good fortunes."

"Your good fortune was meeting me and stealing my hard work. You bet your ass I hold that against you."

Behind me, the first parents are arriving for the after-school pick-up routine. With the exception of Jamie's students' parents, most of them usually stay in their cars until they hear the dismissal bell and even then, they only bother themselves to walk as far as the sidewalk so that their kids don't have to cross the parking lot alone. Today, however, the helicopter in the middle of the playground is a major topic of discussion. They're convening on the edge of the schoolyard as they point and try to get information from each other. None of them knows the story behind it, but they're coming up with some interesting theories, according to the snatches I can hear.

Todd shakes his head at me. "So sad. I'm sorry for you,

Kendall. I've been worried about you, and now I know my worst fears are true."

Renalda can wait. This is a once-in-a-lifetime opportunity that I'm not going to pass up. I don't even care that some of the parents have edged closer to us as my voice has grown louder with each thing I say to him.

"Yeah, I'm sure it's hard for you to sleep at night. Good! It should be," I spat. "How do you even justify it? *That's* what I want to know. What do you tell yourself?"

"I don't have to tell myself anything. You can play the victim all you want, but you and I both know that without me, E-Borrow wouldn't exist. I wrote the code, I charmed the Library Board into adopting the system, and I've marketed the shit out of it." He smugly inspects his shiny fingernails. (Is he wearing clear nail polish?!)

"You cut me off at the knees! You *stole* my thumb drive with *my* presentation on it and got to work before me on the day I was going to show it to Brad! And it's called E-Lend, Todd. Just because you changed a tiny part of the name doesn't make it yours."

"You were going to take credit for everything. And for something that was *yours*, I sure spent a lot of time on it. Not to mention that's all you knew how to talk about, so I had to suffer through endless evenings of 'E-Lend' this and 'E-Lend' that." He rolls his eyes. "I'd say I paid my dues, sweetheart."

"Don't call me 'sweetheart!' And you were my *boyfriend*. I didn't realize being with me was such a hardship. Of course, I was under the false impression that you cared about me and would be excited about something that *I* worked so hard on."

He snorts. "Oh, since you brought up hard-ons, let me tell you how difficult it is to get one when you're in a relationship with a girl who thinks she's so smart but goes out of her way to make sure that no one knows it but bitches when nobody gives her credit for anything. Major woody killer."

The whispering and murmuring around us increases in volume.

"I never heard you complain. As a matter of fact, you *always* got off, even though I had to be a self-service orgasm machine after you and Tiny Todd passed out every night. So don't even…"

"Ooh, that one hurt," a dad mutters nearby.

Todd retorts, "Well, it's just as well you did it yourself, since no one could ever do anything as well as you could."

"It would have been refreshing if you had tried—just once. But then again, you were always take, take, take. I don't know why it came as such a shock that you'd take my idea and make yourself into a bazillionaire with it."

"God! I hope your new life will teach you a few things about humility. God knows your parents didn't do you any favors by letting you believe that the sun rose and set on you. 'You're the prettiest; you're the smartest; you're the funniest.' Pretty safe thing to say when you're the *only* child. Talk about seeing and hearing what you want to believe."

"Ain't that the truth! I wanted to believe that you were a decent human being, so I wasn't prepared for that stunt you pulled on me. You are such a… a… butthole!"

"Oooh, big words!"

I point a finger at him and pay no attention to his taunt. "Well, you failed, Todd! Just so you know. Because you didn't ruin my life, after all."

"Kind of looks like I did," he counters. "You're a school librarian at a dinky elementary school out in the sticks. You're still screwing your co-workers (although I'm sure it's a lot easier to convince a kindergarten teacher how great you are than it was to convince me). And you look like a train wreck."

A mother near me gasps. Then she whispers to a fellow parent, "I had no idea she and Mr. Chase were... *you know*."

Close to tears, I say, "That's not true. I mean, I *do* look like a train wreck right now, but being this school's librarian isn't a bad thing. As a matter of fact, I'm really good at it. *I* was the one who came up with the idea for the Operation Educate program."

"Really, Kendall? Don't embarrass yourself even more."

"I *did*!"

"No you didn't; that fat hick, old lady principal did." He imitates Renalda's accent. "Praise the Lawrd!"

"Hey!" one of the dads protests. "Buddy, you got a problem with the way people around here talk? Because I don't think I like your Hollywood face."

Todd suddenly seems to notice what I've been painfully aware of the whole time: we have an audience. A big audience.

The bell rings as Todd kisses up to the offended father. Jamie leads his class through the doors next to us and freezes when he sees we haven't moved. Brody runs into his backside.

"Hey! Ow!" he cries, looking around his teacher to see what's caused the quick stop. "Oh hey, Miss Dickinson! Wow. You look diff'rent! All goff, like this high school girl who lives next door to me."

"Hi, Brody." I rub in vain at the smudges under my eyes.

Now that the kids are present, this is an even bigger scene, and I realize it's time to make my exit. Todd's still trying to make amends with the angry dad, so I don't even bother saying another word to him. Let him think he got the last word. It doesn't matter, anyway.

When Jamie asks, "What's going on?" I edge past him and say, "Nothing. I need to go find Renalda."

Inside the school, the hallways are packed with kids making their ways to the exits. As I walk against the flow of traffic, a couple of female students ask, "What's wrong, Miss Dickinson?" or "Are you okay, Miss Dickinson?" but for the most part, they're all too focused on lugging their backpacks and lunchboxes toward the doors, where their parents are waiting to ask them about their days and take them home to after-school snacks. I finally reach the familiar confines of the bathroom and am relieved that I have it to myself.

I pull some toilet paper off the roll in one of the stalls and hold it under a trickling faucet to dampen it. Blotting, then scrubbing the black makeup under my eyes, I curse my allergy to waterproof mascara and my inability to control my emotions. After several swipes with the one-ply, sandpapery tissue, I now have angry-looking red blotches under my eyes, instead of black marks. Much better.

I know I should be thinking about what I'm going to say to Renalda, but I can't stop replaying the conversation with Todd. I was particularly careful not to use profanity once the parents showed up, but I remember with chagrin that I said some explicit things about our lame sex life.

Oh, gosh. If one parent complains, I'll probably be fired. And of course, someone will complain. I mean, a parent called the office to gripe after overhearing Jamie say, "Crap," one day in response to a parent pointing out to him that he had a pen mark on his pants. So it's not even a matter of "if" someone calls to report my argument with Todd, but more a matter of "when." And how many.

All the more reason to hold nothing back when I talk to Renalda.

CHAPTER THIRTY-SEVEN

When I get to the main office, I still don't look like my usual self, but there's no time to fully recover. As a matter of fact, I'm half-expecting Renalda to be gone already. She's been at work six hours, after all. I think that's a personal record for her. But both she and Sam are still here. Sam's at her desk, looking particularly diligent, and Renalda's in her own office, chatting with Dr. Underhill.

Sam looks up from what appears to be a contact list and cocks her head at me. "Hey. Where'd you go? The firefighters searched the whole building for you, because we didn't see you out in the parking lot with the other staff members."

Sheepishly, I answer, "Oh. I was the first one out, probably. I, uh, needed some fresh air."

She sympathetically replies, "I don't blame you. I'm so sick of her nonsense. If I had a dollar for every time she took credit for one of my ideas, I'd have a tidy sum to add to my 401K. But I've never come up with anything as important as your tablet idea. I can only imagine how much you want to kill her."

Keeping my voice as low as possible, I say, "Yeah. Well, I'd like to talk to her in private about it. How long do you think Dr. Underhill will be here?"

She shrugs. "Who knows? He's been on her case all year, but suddenly, they're best buddies, thanks to this Operation Educate thing. It's probably saved her job, to be honest."

"Great. I—" The sound of Todd's helicopter starting and its rotors chopping drowns out the rest of my sentence. As the loud beating fades into the distance, I open my mouth to finish.

"There she is! Miss Dickinson, you left so suddenly. Are you feeling okay?" Dr. Underhill's booming voice startles me.

I whirl around to see him standing in Renalda's office door. I smile shakily.

"I'm fine," I finally manage to articulate. "I was, uh, hoping to talk to Ms. Twomey about the library makeover."

He nods easily. "Ah. Yes. Exciting stuff. Well, if you don't need my input on anything, I'll leave you two to it."

Do I need his input? Do I want to confront Renalda in front of him? Ultimately, I want him to know. Maybe this is the most efficient way to go about it. And I'll definitely have the element of surprise on my side. This way, Renalda won't have a chance to formulate a defense for herself. She'll have to answer my accusations on the fly, in front of the Superintendent.

But Sam's revelation that this whole idea may be the only thing keeping Renalda from being fired makes me hesitate. I don't know if I'm ruthless enough to call her out if it could mean she'd lose her job.

"All right then," he says when Renalda quickly insists that we have it covered and will call him if we have questions. She knows exactly why I'm here, but playing dumb is her specialty—hell, she's turned it into a lifestyle. "Congratulations again, ladies."

"Wait!" Comes from behind me.

We all fix our eyes on Sam.

She raises her chin. "Dr. Underhill. Sir," she begins but then doesn't say anything else.

He lifts his eyebrows. "Ye-es?"

She stands but remains behind her desk. "Uh, I think there's something you should know about the Operation Educate idea."

"Sam!" Renalda scolds with a nervous half-smile. "Let's not waste the Superintendent's time. He's a very busy man, and I'm sure he's heard everything he needs to know about the idea."

Renalda's determination to keep him in the dark seems to strengthen Sam's resolve. I can actually see her make the decision to tell him the truth. Before she can say anything else, though, I turn to Dr. Underhill and blurt, "It was my idea."

He looks back and forth between Sam and me. She says, "That's what I was just gonna say. So…"

Shaking his head, he asks her, "You're claiming it was your idea, too?"

Her hands in front of her, she quickly clarifies, "No! I mean, I was going to tell you it was Kendall's idea."

Before he can address the intel he's just been given, Jamie pokes his head into the office. When he sees the people gathered, he straightens and puts his hands in his pockets. "Oh. Uh… Dr. Underhill. Good to see you." He gives him a terse nod and glances at me with wide eyes.

I wince back at him to let him know the moment of truth has arrived. He smiles broadly.

Distractedly, Dr. Underhill says, "Likewise, Jamie," before returning his attention to Renalda and me.

To my disbelief and horror, Renalda starts crying.

I quickly look at Sam, who's sucking on her teeth and looks bored. She's staring directly at our boss, so I know she's seeing what I'm seeing, but she may as well be watching a public access show about painting with watercolors. Jamie looks equally nonplussed.

I try to take my cues from them and remain calm, but Dr. Underhill intones, "Inside. Both of you. Ms. Kingsley… no interruptions, please."

"But—" I try to interject.

"Inside the office," he insists.

I trail a sniffling Renalda, who turns petulant as soon as we're in her territory. She plops into her desk chair and crosses her arms over her chest.

I take one of the chairs in front of her desk, while Dr. Underhill takes a chair close to the door, as if he's guarding it to prevent either of us—mostly me—from leaving.

"We're going to get to the bottom of this, right here, right now. Ms. Dickinson, is it true you were actually the originator of the winning Operation Educate idea?"

I refuse to look at Renalda when I quietly answer, "Yes."

He sighs.

Renalda's voice quivers when she says, "Oh, Dr. Underhill! I musta misunderstood! You know I gave Kendall credit when I accepted the award *on behalf of Whitehall Elementary*. It's not about one person. It's for the good of the whole school!"

I can't stop myself from nearly shouting, "And that would have been fine. But you said 'the idea just came to me,' implying that it was *your* idea. Then you thanked God and your parents and the rest of the world before saying how thankful you were that *I* would be benefiting from *your* great idea."

"You're twistin' my words!"

"Ladies, ladies! This isn't productive." He rises and paces in front of Renalda's door.

I stare down at my lap.

"I'm just sayin'!" Renalda insists. "If I made it sound like I came up with the idea from start to finish, I'm sorry. I didn't mean to. It was easier than explainin' the whole cotton-pickin' story."

"Well, you've put me in an embarrassing position," Dr. Underhill tells her.

"I didn't mean it!"

He rubs the back of his neck and mutters, "Unfortunately, it's not the worst mess you've ever gotten me into."

She has nothing to say to that.

Now *I'm* starting to feel guilty, though. Am I being petty? Is all this worth it? I mean, she's an idiot; that goes without saying. But it's not a Nobel Peace Prize. The award went to the school, and the school will get to reap the benefits of it. That's all that matters, right? Who cares if Renalda got to make the stupid acceptance speech? Who cares if everyone thinks she's smart, when she's really not? Do I need constant recognition from other people to know that I'm intelligent? No. I know I am. And the people who matter in my life know I am.

I raise an index finger and clear my throat. "Dr. Underhill?"

"Hmm?" He stops pacing and gives me his full attention.

"Listen. I think this may be getting blown out of proportion."

He cocks an eyebrow. "Well, we like to give credit where

credit is due, Ms. Dickinson. And the last thing we want is for one of our bright staff members to feel taken advantage of." He looks pointedly at Renalda, who slides lower in her chair. "But I appreciate your willingness to be fair-minded about it and put the best construction on things."

I smile wanly.

"However…" He strokes his beard. "I don't like being deceived. Plus, since there was money involved—" The shocked look on my face gives him the answer to his question before he even asks, "You don't know about the prize money?"

He whirls on Renalda, who stutters some nonsense about surprising me during the last school assembly of the year.

Finally, she shuts up long enough for him to interject, "Ms. Dickinson, would you mind leaving Ms. Twomey and me alone for now? I'll be in touch with you soon to tie up any loose ends regarding this matter."

Neither of them is looking at me, but I still mutter an acknowledgement to his statement and a goodbye while I rush toward the door.

As I'm turning the doorknob to let myself out, I hear Dr. Underhill say to Renalda, "When's that retirement party?"

She giggles weakly. "Oh, I'm not retirin' this year!"

To which he replies, "Yeah. I think you are."

CHAPTER THIRTY-EIGHT

I can't even remember the last time I went to work with a hangover. But that's happening today, thanks to my night out with Sam and Jamie at the martini bar, where we celebrated Renalda's impending retirement and my Operation Educate redemption. I hit the snooze on my alarm so many times that I barely had time to shower, swallow four aspirin, and drink an entire bottle of water before rushing to work.

When I've been in the completely silent library for a few minutes, I actually trick myself into believing that everything's going to be okay. Then Jamie bursts into the room, coming backwards through the doors, the tinkling of the two cups of coffee together in his one hand sounding like the ringing bells at Notre Dame. I close my eyes against the nausea the noise provokes.

He bangs the cups on the checkout counter and yells, "GOOD MORNING!"

"Oh, geez. Please stop shouting," I whisper as I squeeze my eyes shut even more tightly.

Laughing, he says only slightly more quietly, "I should have known you were ten times worse off than Sam, since you have the alcohol tolerance of a tsetse fly. Here. Drink this coffee."

The ceramic cup sliding toward me on the Formica sounds exactly how I imagine it does when tectonic plates grind against each other before causing the magnitude of earthquake that triggers a tsunami large enough to take out an island in the Pacific. When I feel the hot mug nudge against my fingers, I open my eyes and look down into it. Its caramel color indicates that Jamie's made it precisely how I like it.

Shamefaced, I gaze up at him through my eyelashes and smile/wince. And do a double-take.

"Oh, your face!" I say on a sharp intake of breath and quick jerk upwards of my head that makes stars dance in front of my eyes.

He half-smiles. "I told you that poison ivy and I don't get along."

Not only is his face blistered and swollen, but it's also covered in an oily ointment that makes it look shiny and even more oozy than it already is. Which is really oozy.

"How'd you get it all over your face?" I ask, forcing myself to take a big, scalding gulp of coffee.

On a shrug, he answers, "I must've touched my face and gotten the plant's oils on it."

I tilt my head and slump my shoulders. "You look like you motorboated a poison ivy patch."

He chuckles at my colorful description, obviously not as concerned about it as I am. "Well, the kids'll dig it. The grosser the better, right?" He wraps his red, welted hands around his cup and drinks. "It'll be better in a few days. I still have plenty of prescription-strength medication from the last time this happened."

"This has happened *before*?"

He tells me about a cross-country bike race he partici-
pated in, during which he wrecked on a trail and landed in
a huge bed of the poisonous plant. He wound up in the
hospital, because his reaction was so severe that time. "So,
this is nothing," he concludes. "Unsightly, but not
dangerous."

"I'm sorry I led you through it."

After another sip of coffee, he replies, "You're worth it,"
before inspecting an open sore on the knuckles of his right
hand.

My eyes well up. "Awww… if I didn't feel like ralphing
and your face didn't look like *that*, I'd give you a big kiss
right now."

That makes him laugh. "Okay, then. I'll take a rain
check on that one."

"And it's not helping my stomach that you're picking at
your bloody hand. Stop scratching!"

He shoves his hand in his pocket as if he's ashamed of it.
"Oh. Uh. Sorry."

Before I can accept his apology, the first bell rings,
almost bringing me to my knees. Jamie adds to the pain by
slapping at the counter. "Well, hang in there. In eight hours,
you can go home."

It's pretty sad that someone who looks like he does today
is giving *me* a pep talk.

&.

It would figure that I'd have a hangover on a recess duty day.
Noises that nearly trigger a panic attack on a normal day
are magnified at least a hundred times. But I'm cool. I can
handle this. I have no one to blame but myself, anyway.

The first thing I say to Jamie when we take up our post

at the edge of the playground is, "If you blow that whistle by me, I will cry. Then I will throw up all over you."

He laughs. "Okay. I'll try to give you ample warning."

"No! No whistle-blowing. Promise me."

Shaking his head, he says, "No can do. There are times when the whistle is absolutely necessary, a matter of safety."

"I will break up with you," I state unemotionally.

"Maybe you should go stand somewhere else," he suggests. "Over there, for example." He points to a spot relatively far away from the action but with a vantage point that will still allow me to supervise most of the kids.

"Fine," I grumble, gingerly high-stepping on my heels through the clumpy grass of the makeshift soccer field. When I reach my destination, he waves cheekily at me. I barely resist the urge to flip him the bird while grinning.

I've just figured out a comfortable stance that allows me to stand without my heels sinking into the earth when Brody runs up to me. "Hey, Miss Dickinson!" he greets me.

"Inside voices, Brody, all right?"

"But we're outside. I CAN SHOUT AS LOUD AS I WANT TO!"

Oh, God. Please help me to not wring this child's neck.

"Okay, but let's not. I have a headache." When all else fails, confide in the child and pray for mercy.

He scrunches his shoulders up around his ears and winces. "Ouch. My mom gets those a lot. She had one yesterday. That's why she almost forgot to come get me."

This information is slightly interesting. "Your mom was late picking you up yesterday? Why didn't you come up to the office and wait with Miss Sam?"

Wrinkling his nose, he intones, "Bo-ring!" Then he points to the playground equipment. "I went over there and waited. She wasn't too late. We got to see the helicopter take off! Mom made us watch from the car, though."

"Cool. She was right to put you in the car."

"I guess. It was real loud. And windy. But awesome." He imitates the sound it made.

I brush his spittle from my arms. "Okay, okay. Good sound effects, but you're getting me all wet."

He giggles. "Oops. Sorry. Who was that guy in the helicopter, anyway?"

"Just some rich guy who thinks he's important," I answer, unable to censor myself in time.

Brody wipes his mouth with the back of his arm. "Yeah, well, Mr. Chase doesn't like him."

I can't help but be curious about what may have alerted the six-year-old to that, but I merely say, "He's a difficult guy to like. Not a nice person."

"Good. Cuz Mr. Chase punched him real hard in the face."

"What?" My eyeballs pulse and ache in my skull with the force with which I say that one word.

"Yeah! Ka-tow! Over by the helicopter." He points as if the aircraft is still there.

Ironically enough, it's close to where Jamie's standing now. When he sees Brody pointing and both of us looking his way, he waves at us with his now-bandaged hand. Brody waves back enthusiastically, but I don't. I'm too busy trying to picture what happened yesterday between Todd and Jamie.

I'm disgusted with myself that I feel somewhat satisfied at the idea of Todd getting punched in the face. But I don't want the punch to have been from Jamie. That's so Neanderthal-ish. Plus, I think I did a good enough job of dealing with Todd. I didn't need a cleanup man.

Weakly, I tell Brody, "He shouldn't have done that in front of you."

"I was hiding." He sounds so proud of it that I almost laugh. "Everybody was gone. And that blond-headed guy was talkin' to Mr. Chase. And Mr. Chase wasn't really sayin' anything. Then they went over to the helicopter, and it was funny, because one second, Mr. Chase had his hands in his pockets, and he was lookin' down at the ground while that rich guy was talkin' and laughing'—it was like he was telling a joke—but the next second, Mr. Chase was punchin' the rich guy in the face. And the guy who was in the helicopter to fly it—"

"The pilot?"

"Yeah. The pilot had to jump down and pull Mr. Chase away from the rich guy."

I cover my mouth. "He punched him more than once?"

"Yeah! Lots of times! Like in the movies, when a person holds another person's head like this"—he simulates a head-lock—"and keeps punchin' him over and over. It was hilarious!"

I glance over at Jamie, but he's looking the other way, watching a group of students crowded around a toad and daring each other to touch it.

"That's not funny," I say. My head hurts too much for me to think of a diplomatic way to ask what I want to know next, so I simply come out with it. "Did you tell your mom about all this when she got here?"

My stomach drops when he reveals, "Oh, she saw it. She got here right when Mr. Chase started punchin' that guy. But the pilot was already holding Mr. Chase before she could help. Mr. Chase talked to her for a while. He just kep' sayin', 'Sorry. I'm sorry.' But Mom thought it was funny. That's when I stopped hidin'. When I ran to them, she was tellin' Mr. Chase that she wouldn't tell anyone about him beatin' up that guy if he didn't make a fuss about her bein' late to get me."

"Oh, gosh!" I mutter, closing my eyes and rocking back on my heels, which immediately sink into the ground. I windmill my arms to keep my balance. Brody runs behind me and pushes against my back.

"Whoa, Miss Dickinson! Don't fall over!"

Stepping completely out of my shoes, I grit my teeth through the pain as I bend over to pull the pumps from the soft dirt.

As I straighten, I see my knight in shining armor jogging our way.

"I'm fine!" I toss up a hand in an effort to get him to go back to his spot. "I don't need your help."

Grinning, he stops in front of me and says, "Actually, I was thinking Brody needed my help more than you did."

"I had it, Mr. Chase," the boy claims, coming back around to my side. "She's pretty heavy, but I'm real strong, like you. I was just tellin' her about yesterday, when you punched out that one guy."

It's hard to read Jamie's expression through the swelling and blistering on his face, but the set of his jaw is unmistakable. He purses his lips. "Thanks, Brode. I'm sure you told it quite colorfully, too."

"I did! I told her how you held the guy's head and kept punchin' and punchin' his face. But I forgot to tell her how he was cryin' when the pilot made you stop."

I gasp.

Jamie nods as he looks down at his shoes. "Well, you've told her now, so… good job. Why don't you go make sure your classmates don't hurt that toad over there with all their poking?"

As soon as the kindergartner's gone, I say, "Unacceptable."

"You're right," he readily agrees. "I snapped. But I apologized to everyone involved."

The dampness from the grass under my feet is starting to soak into my pantyhose, so I put my shoes back on and stand on my toes to prevent a repeat performance from a few minutes ago. "He's still going to sue your ass. And justifiably so."

"Nah. He's not going to sue me."

"You're an idiot."

"Yeah, but you weren't supposed to know about that." He puts an arm around my shoulders, a rare instance of physical contact when students are present.

"Ah, but I do now. I know you're no better than any other stupid guy who feels like he has to prove how manly he is by asserting his authority through physical violence. It's disgusting." For some reason, though, I can't stop smiling.

"I agree. I totally thought I was above that. Plus, you always described this guy like he was some kind of bodybuilder, so it was stupid of me to even put myself in that position; I could have gotten pummeled."

"Your face looks like you did, anyway. And I take it that's why your hand's all bloody? *Not* from the poison ivy, but from slamming your knuckles into Todd's grille?"

He flexes his fingers. "Both, but yeah. Those capped teeth were hard as diamonds. I guess that's my punishment for giving into my biological instincts."

"Do *not* blame biology for what you did. What did he say, anyway, to provoke that?"

He removes his arm from my shoulders and takes a step to the left, putting some daylight between us. "Uh… Hmm… I don't even remember."

"You're a liar."

"Maybe."

"Fine. I probably don't want to know, anyway."

"You probably don't."

"At least not today. My head already hurts too much."

"You're really milking this hangover, but in this case, it benefits me, so I approve."

"I'm not seeking your approval."

"Fine."

After taking a huge breath, he pops the whistle in his mouth and blows. The veins stick out in his neck. Dropping the instrument of torture and letting it dangle around his neck, he bellows, "Line up!" while trotting away from me and toward the students.

I totter after him with ringing ears and a throbbing head. What a bastard.

When I get back to the library, I'm still fuming and plotting what I'm going to make him do for me tonight. A foot massage in a hot bath sounds like heaven right now, and the promise of it may be the only thing that gets me through the rest of the day. But first I need drugs. I head toward my office so I can dig in my desk drawer for some ibuprofen.

Renalda spins around in my chair, startling me enough that I gasp and flinch back toward the door.

She smirks, her hands steepled under her chin as she declares, "You little bitch."

CHAPTER THIRTY-NINE

Her tone is so wondering that it sounds nearly complimentary, so I catch myself right before saying, "Thank you."

Instead, I say nothing, staring at her while all the blood rushes from my face to my toes, which—oddly enough—actually relieves some of the pressure and pain in my head. Who knew that the ultimate cure for a hangover was abject terror? Who knew that Renalda had it in her to inspire such fear?

Standing, she advances and points her thick, manicured finger at me. "Let me tell you somethin', Missy. I am onto you. You're a troublemaker. You *and* your boyfriend."

"Jamie had nothing to do with this!" The fierce protectiveness her accusation triggers in me takes me by surprise.

"I don't have any proof of it this time, but he's been a pain in my hind end all year. I find it hard to believe that he didn't put you up to this." Her hands rest on her ample hips.

I jut out my chin. "Excuse me, but nobody had to put me up to anything. What you did was wrong."

She rolls her eyes. "Well, I know he's ticked off at me, so he's probably thrilled at the latest turn of events. You know, tit for tat."

The smug look on her face is pushing the button in my brain that overrides all sense. "None of us had to do anything to get you fired; you did that all by yourself."

"You better watch it, Missy! Anyway, I'm retirin'; I wasn't fired."

"I'm sorry, but—" I glance at the clock, dismayed that we're about to have a big audience of fifth graders. "I have a class arriving in about two minutes," I decide to inform her, hoping that it grants me a reprieve.

With an icy smile, she says, "What I have to say won't take long." When I merely cross my arms over my chest, she continues, "I think it's sweet that you're protectin' your boyfriend, but we both know that *he's* the one who thought up that Operation Educate idea. I don't know why he let you take credit for it—probably to make you feel good about yourself or to make people like you more or to get you in the sack—but he woulda been better off savin' his own hide with the idea. He mighta kept his job if he'd just signed *his* name to it."

I shake my head at her. "I don't... I mean... what are you talking about? *I* came up with the idea."

"Just like I did? It just *came* to you?"

"Yes!" I blush, remembering how it did come to me. "That is, it really did just come to me." I stop myself right before adding, *"In the shower."* She probably doesn't need to know that.

"Likely story. Well, I think it's pretty ironic that you got up on your high horse and accused me of takin' credit for someone else's idea. And Jamie may not be here next year, but that's not good enough for me. I've got friends, Sweetie. I've been principal at this school for fifteen years. If you decide to come back next year—which I'd highly advise against—you won't have your smart, hunky boyfriend to protect you."

I blink rapidly. "Are you threatening me?"

My next class files through the doors behind their teacher.

Renalda shoots a huge smile at them. "Well, hello there, kids! Are you ready to have some fun with Miss Dickinson?" After she gets several eye rolls from the students who are too old to be talked to that way, she turns back to me and says cheerfully, "I'm jealous! Toodles!" and exits the library.

After a few seconds of staring at the swinging doors, a clearing throat catches my attention. I turn to Mrs. Kull-mann and give her a shaky smile. "Um... Oh! Right. Yes. I'm ready."

She narrows her eyes at me. "Is everything okay?"

More confidently, I nod. "Yes. Absolutely. We'll see you in thirty minutes." To the kids, I say, "Follow me, guys! We're doing a research scavenger hunt today... no Google or Wikipedia allowed!" This announcement elicits the moans and groans I expected, but they're a little less satisfying with Renalda's threat still echoing in my head.

The pressure on the arch of my foot teeters on the apex between pleasure and pain. I clench my teeth but otherwise try to relax into it by closing my eyes and concentrating on the feel of Jamie's thumb pressing into the spot on the sole of my foot just below the base of my toes. It doesn't take long, however, before the feeling stops resembling anything close to pleasure and remains firmly on the "pain" side of things.

"Owww," I murmur, resolved to keep my eyes closed.

The response to my utterance is deeper probing.

My eyes fly open as I pull my foot away from his grasp. "Gaaa!"

He looks sharply at me and blinks.

"Dude!"

"Too hard?" he asks innocently, reaching for my foot again.

I let him take it and try to relax against the couch cushions. "Uh, yeah. Hence, the 'ow.'"

He smiles sheepishly. "Sorry. I didn't hear you. I was distracted." He pats my foot and squeezes it gently. "Didn't mean to hurt you."

When he goes back to staring off into space, I wiggle my foot at him.

Distractedly, he gives my toes a half-hearted squeeze. His preoccupation is perplexing... and somewhat worrisome.

"Hey, why the long face? Or does the poison ivy make you look pouty?"

Pinning his eyes to my feet, he answers casually, "I didn't get that job at the university."

I've never had such conflicting emotions about one piece of news before. While I try to process what I'm feeling, I say, "I thought you had another interview next week."

"They called me this afternoon to cancel. Informed me that the search committee didn't need another round of interviews to help them decide." Now he looks up at me and smiles. "Why are you looking at me like that? I thought this is what you wanted."

"I didn't *want* you to be rejected by a bunch of stuffed-shirt, pompous assholes who don't know how smart and talented you are." I sit up and put my feet on the floor. "I mean, who do they think they are? What does this person they hired have that you don't?"

"A vagina," he quips.

My mouth falls open. "That's illegal!"

He shrugs. "Well, obviously, that's not the reason they told me they hired her. I believe the exact words were, 'Ms. Stansfield has extensive field and classroom experience—'"

"So do you!"

"'—at the *university* level.'"

"Oh. Well, screw them."

He runs a hand through his hair. "No. Screw me. Because I'm running out of options. And time." Chuckling at himself, he adds in a terrible English accent, "I'm beginning to think I acted a bit rashly, Miss Dickinson."

Although I never thought the post at UNC was right for him, I began to realize how scarce the jobs were and became more thankful my mother had brought his attention to it. If nothing else, I figured it would tide him over until he could find a better fit.

I grab his hand. "Then tell Dr. Underhill you've changed your mind and want to keep your job. It's better than no job."

Neither rejecting nor accepting my suggestion, he states, "It was stupid of me to get cocky and stop looking when I made it through the first round of interviews at UNC."

I feel and sound hopeless when I ask quietly, "What are you going to do?"

His answer is to screw his mouth sideways and chew on his lip. Just when I think he's going to give me a serious answer, he looks up at me with a twinkle in his eyes. "Food service is my fallback. Your mom and I are going to open a restaurant together."

Despite being annoyed that he won't give me a straight answer, I laugh. I'd actually prefer that fallback plan to what I know is the real one. At least I know my mom—no matter how cute she thinks his butt is—won't try to steal my boyfriend.

CHAPTER FORTY

I found out yesterday that Jamie's backup plan—which is now his primary plan—really is Iceland. Thanks to Marena, they're excited to have him on the team. And since he has no other prospects here in the States, he's going to go.

He told me in a most nonchalant manner while we were making dinner, although he waited until I had put down the knife after chopping the salad ingredients. I managed not to throw up, but I didn't eat much dinner.

I have to be okay with this—around him. When I'm alone, I'm a complete basket case. You don't even want to know what my pillow looks like. I figure I'll wash the pillowcase when this is all over. Until then, what's the point? As long as I hold it together when I'm with him, that's all that matters.

"This is going to be great. Right?" he asks me for what feels like the billionth time.

I smile over my book at him. He's packing a box of tools he's planning to pre-ship so they're waiting for him when he arrives in Iceland. Tightly, I reply, "Really great. Just what you wanted, right?"

He grins but then appears more thoughtful. "Well, not *exactly*. But you know. Close enough, I guess. It would be petty to complain."

And the last thing he'd want to do is admit he was wrong, I barely resist the urge to point out. Instead, I say, "Not really. Sometimes reality doesn't live up to the dream."

Inspecting a sieve at close range, one eye squinted shut, he reveals a little too casually, "Yeah, well, I still have one job interview left, tomorrow."

This is news to me. I set my book aside and sit up straighter. "You do? Where?" I try not to let the pathetic hope escape from my chest and creep into my voice. The effort makes my words wobble.

He continues meticulously packing the box. "Here in town. It's not in archaeology, but I'm qualified, I think. And it pays plenty." When I'm silent, waiting for him to be more specific, he looks over at me. With a defiant lift of his chin, he says, "That's all I'm going to say, though. Because you're not going to approve, and I don't want you to make me feel bad about applying for it."

That statement stings on several levels, but I grit my teeth and reply, "Okay. Fine. Is this a job you'd enjoy? Something you'd actually like to get?"

After thinking about it for a second, he nods. "Yes, I would. It's crazy, but the more I think about it, the more I want it."

My curiosity is killing me. I squirm on the sofa, scooting to the edge of the cushion so I can be closer to him. He chuckles at the wind-up to my wheedling, "C'mon! Tell me what it is."

"No!" he says around a nervous laugh. His hand shoots

up to his glasses. "You'll make fun of me. Then you'll tell me all the reasons I shouldn't want it. Then I'll be unsure of myself in my interview, and I'll screw it up."

"Jamie!"

He firmly shakes his head. "Uh-uh. You'll find out eventually, one way or another." The box taped, he slides it toward the front door and tosses the roll of tape onto the coffee table.

"In the most likely event that I *don't* get the job here—"

"The mystery job," I tease.

Smirking, he concedes, "Yes, the mystery job... Are you really okay with taking care of some things while I'm gone? I don't want you to feel like you have to do all this stuff for me."

"If, by 'all this stuff,' you mean living rent-free in your house and hanging out with Johnny a couple of times a week and making sure your utility bill gets paid on time and keeping this place clean so the realtor can show it to prospective buyers at a moment's notice, then yes. I'm really okay with that." I pick up my book to hide behind it again.

He comes over and takes it from my hands, tossing it next to the tape on the coffee table. Pulling me to my feet, he murmurs down at me, "You really are the best girlfriend in the world."

"More like the universe," I joke, "but I know." After a slow, lazy kiss, I add, "Just keep that in mind when you're huddled around a fire with *her*."

With wide-eyed innocence, he queries, "Who?"

"Nice try. You know who."

"Well, since I'll be wearing my locking underwear, there's no need to worry."

"It's not funny." I smile to keep things from getting too tense, but I mean every word.

"Oh, yes it is." But he gives me another very serious kiss. Then, pulling back, he says, "Close your eyes."

At first, I'm wary, but I eventually do what he says. "Iceland is a means to an end," he begins. "I don't want to go there. I don't want to go anywhere where you aren't."

Is he trying to make me cry? I smile and coo, "Awww. I know."

"Just let me finish."

Chastened, I mutter, "Sorry."

He pulls me closer and rests his chin on top of my head. I press my ear against his chest and let his voice rumble through my skull. "It's okay. I just want you to know, though, that my idea of a perfect life is a lot different than it used to be. I... I don't need to travel all over the world, looking for things to make me feel like I'm doing something worthwhile. I'd be happy living in a cozy house in a sweet North Carolina town that's frozen in the sixties, making love to you every night—"

"Every night. Wow, this is quite the fantasy," I manage without letting on that the tears are as close to the surface as they can be without spilling over.

He laughs, but there's a self-conscious twinge to it. "Yeah. Well... I think I blew it."

I want to pull back and look at his face to try to figure out what he's talking about, but I don't want him to see me cry.

Anyway, he's squeezing me even more tightly now as he says, "I have to tell you something."

I tense. Immediately, I think the worst. He's done something bad. Really bad. He's broken my trust. He's betrayed me somehow. Oh, gosh. I can't handle this. Again.

If he can tell I'm on the verge of passing out from panic,

he doesn't let on. Calmly, slowly, he states, "I never really quit my job."

It takes a while for me to process this seemingly simple sentence, but when I finally do, I ask, "You were fired?"

"No! Not really. I mean, sort of." When I push away from his chest and stare at him, he explains himself in a rush, "Renalda came into my classroom right after Christmas Break to harass me about our breakup, and I wasn't in the mood to talk about it to anyone, but especially not her, so I got into it with her, and one thing led to another, and somehow we got on the topic of Jane, and she told me that Jane was considering filing a formal complaint against me with the union, so I blew up and told her I'd had it, and if Jane was going to continue to be allowed to push everyone around, then I was going to have to find a different place to work, and when Renalda asked me if I was giving her an ultimatum, I told her, 'I guess I am,' so… she chose Jane. Over me."

I gape open-mouthed at him.

"I lost my temper, okay? And she called my bluff." He shakes his head as if he still can't believe it.

Having recently had my own scary encounter with our boss, I can easily picture how this went down. For some reason, though, I don't tell Jamie that. I don't want him to know about her threats. I *really* don't want him to know how afraid I am of her threats.

When I continue to keep mum, he continues, "You know, the closer to the end of the school year we get, the more I realize how much I'm going to miss Whitehall, but it's not my decision to stay or go."

Last week, we met Jamie's replacement, some fresh-out-of college Mensa member with a minor in child psychology.

I already hate her. I bet she doesn't even wear funny cycling clothes.

"Well, shit. That sucks," I understate. "Why didn't you tell me any of this?"

He shrugs. "At the time, we were broken up. Then, by the time we got back together, it just didn't seem that important… and I was sort of embarrassed about it. But I also saw it as a gift-wrapped opportunity to do something different. I mean, I saw it that way after I stopped shitting my pants at the thought of not having a job to pay for Johnny's housing at Phoenix Ridge."

I plop onto the couch like I have no bones.

He sits next to me and pulls me against his side. "It'll all work out, though." The forced cheeriness returns to his voice. "I'll be in Iceland six months, tops. And if the house sells, I'll come home for a little break before that time's up, to take care of all that. And while I'm in Iceland, I'll keep my ears open for jobs in places that I know you'd love. Westernized places with indoor bathrooms and safe, running water. Then next summer, you can come visit *me*. It'll be fun."

I give him a smile that comes off weaker than I'd intended. "Yeah. I know. This is just a blip, right?"

"Just a blip. And we still have about a month before I leave, so… let's not waste time being all sad and sulky when we can be… naked." He pushes me down on my back and kisses my laughing mouth.

The cafegymatorium is buzzing with last-day-of-school energy. The kids are wired, the teachers are euphoric, and the handful of parents who have trickled in towards the end of this final assembly of the year seem to all be wearing the same expressions, a strange mixture of relief and dread. The only person who's visibly unhappy is Renalda. She's been emceeing the proceedings as if they were part of a mass funeral rather than an Honor Roll recognition ceremony and end-of-year celebration. Fortunately, Dr. Underhill has been on hand to liven things up on the many occasions she's been overcome with emotion.

Jamie and I are standing against the wall with all the other teachers, keeping our eyes on the students in their rows of chairs in the middle of the gym floor. I'm feeling pretty maudlin, but unlike Renalda, I've managed to keep my smile firmly in place for the kids. Jamie's acting like there's nothing out of the ordinary. As a matter of fact, he's particularly cheerful. I'd say it's just an act, the product of not allowing himself to think too much beyond today, but he seems genuinely happy. Maybe he's in denial about leaving for Iceland in five days. Or maybe…

Maybe he really *is* glad to be going. Maybe he changed his mind and can't wait to get some time away from me. I've tried not to be clingy in the lead-up to his departure, but… it's hard. I'm going to miss him more than I'm even willing to admit to myself. Maybe it's a good thing I'll be busy this summer, getting the e-tablet program up and running and overseeing the library makeover. Still, it's going to suck.

Big smiles!

Brody comes bounding over to us on his way back to his seat after receiving his Honor Roll ribbon. He holds the maroon strip of material out towards Jamie. "Here, Mr. Chase. I want you to take this with you when you go to Timbucktooth."

"What?" Jamie sputters, taking the ribbon from Brody.

He nods confidently. "Yeah. That's where my mom said you were going."

Jamie clears his throat and tries to compose himself. "Oh. Yeah. Well… I mean, I'm not really… It's not…"

Brody pats his hand. "It's okay, Mr. Chase. We know you're gonna miss us, but maybe it'll be more funner out there. You can send us a postcard."

Before Jamie can respond to that, the six-year-old returns to his seat, where he proudly tells his other classmates what he did with his ribbon. Soon, Jamie has his hands full of two dozen more.

He's quietly imploring his students to go back to their chairs, and I'm barely holding my emotions in check when I notice that it's gotten strangely quiet and still around us. Renalda is standing at the podium, shooting daggers in our direction. Jamie gently shoos the last student to her seat. His grin instantly morphs into an equally stony glare back at our soon-to-be-former boss. She blinks first.

After a dramatic throat-clearing, she beams at the rest of the people gathered in front of her. "Students, parents, faculty… thank you for bein' here today to celebrate these wonderful students and their academic achievements. Let's give one last big round of applause to everyone." She steps back from the microphone and claps.

When the applause dies down, she resumes, "For those of you who weren't here at the beginnin' of the assembly to see me receive my service award from Dr. Underhill, this is, indeed, my last year as Principal of Whitehall Elementary." She pauses and swallows a few times.

Next to me, Jamie rocks back and forth on his heels. "Here we go," he mutters. I thread my arm through his in a show of sympathy and solidarity.

Fake cheerfully, she continues, "Ahem. Yes. And while it's

been an honor to serve here the past fifteen years, it's time to hand over the reins to someone new. I don't even know who it is, kids! Isn't that a hoot? But I know Dr. Underhill's been workin' hard to find someone real special for y'all. So, now I hand it over to Dr. Underhill to introduce Whitehall's brand new principal!"

The squirmy kids offer their lukewarm applause as Dr. Underhill steps up to the podium and Renalda remains standing just off to his side. "Thank you! All right! I bet you had no idea your new principal's been here with you this whole time, watching you, getting an idea of what's in store for him next year, did you? Well, he is."

At that tidbit, everyone, including the teachers, including me, frantically searches the large room for an unfamiliar male face. I zoom in on one, a tall, balding guy in a suit and tie. When he sees me staring at him, he waves his hands in front of his chest and shakes his head, mouthing, "It's not me!" Then I see he's standing next to a third grader who's practically his clone.

Before I have a chance to do much more looking around, Dr. Underhill's chuckling and urging everyone to settle down. "Okay, okay. That was fun, but I guess it's time to stop teasing you. Would Whitehall Elementary's new principal please join me up here on the stage?"

At first, no one moves. It's silent in the cafeteria for probably the first time all year. Then Jamie's laughing. Startled, I look up at him as he pulls his arm away from mine and heads toward the stage. My eyes widen and my heart stops as I wonder what kind of joke he's playing.

That's when Dr. Underhill spots him and says, "Ah, yes. Mr. Jamie Chase! Hop on up here and say hello to your new —or maybe not-so-new—student body."

There are two seconds of silence, punctuated only by

the soft clicking of Jamie's dress shoes on the gym floor; then the place erupts. He laughs and shields his newly poison-ivy-free face with the hand holding all his students' Honor Roll ribbons. I cover my mouth and lean back against the cinderblock wall, needing its support. Renalda looks like she's about to pass out, too. Jamie turns to her to shake her hand when he's finished shaking Dr. Underhill's, but she flatly refuses him. Instead, she turns on her heel and disappears behind the heavy, maroon, velvet stage curtain. He watches after her for a few seconds but eventually shrugs and turns back toward the clapping students, teachers, and parents.

He catches my eye and gives me a sheepish wince. I blink back tears and return a wobbly smile. I'm surprised to realize I'm not mad at him for keeping this from me; I'm too relieved he's staying to care about anything else. Maybe the anger will come later. But right now, all I feel is joy. I'm afraid I'm not conveying that very well at the moment, though. The longer he looks at me, the more worried he seems.

Finally, the cheering tapers off enough that he can say something other than "Thank you" and be understood. After a deep breath, he grins and says, "Wow. When Dr. Underhill gave me the news just this morning that I would be Whitehall's new principal, I felt like doing that, too. But, you know… the first bell rang, and I knew my class would make fun of me for acting like that."

Everyone laughs. Mine comes out like a heartsick goose's honk.

"I know you guys are focused on summer right now, and that's the way it should be, because I want you to have plenty of fun and go on lots of adventures between now and August so that you come back to school, ready to go. Big

349

things are coming to Whitehall. You'll have a brand new library, for one thing. Miss Dickinson will be working on that all summer, just for you. And for another thing, we're going to be the best elementary school in the district!"

This elicits screams and cheers that distort my hearing and would normally make me want to run away, but for the first time ever, I'm right there with them. I cup my hands around my mouth and yell, "Yeah!" I'm laughing at myself and the unbridled elation I'm feeling when Jamie looks my way again. His shoulders relax.

"Anyway, I know you want to get out of here and get your summer started, but before everyone goes, I have just one more thing I need to say. Well… ask, really. I guess." Suddenly, he sounds like he's out of breath. He chuckles at something while he looks down at the ribbons in his hands. His free hand pops up to finger his glasses. Pushing his hair off his forehead, he looks out over the heads of the students and locks eyes with me.

"No, no, no," I mutter, suddenly knowing exactly what's about to happen. It's not that I don't want it to happen; I just don't want it to happen here, now.

Evidently reading my lips, he laughs nervously. "I see you're already saying no, because you don't like to be the center of attention, but too bad."

I pinch the bridge of my nose and purse my lips, which makes him laugh harder.

"Kendall, I want to know: Will you marry me?"

The girls gasp and giggle; the boys make barfing noises. But nobody says a word. That is, until Brody pipes up, "C'mon, Miss Dickinson, you know you want to say yes."

I probably couldn't speak if the library renovation depended on it, but I do manage a vigorous nod.

Jamie trots down from the stage but then backtracks to

the podium. "School's dismissed! Have a great summer!" he booms into the microphone before rushing to me and sweeping me into a crushing hug. "Do you really mean yes?" he asks next to my ear. When I nod again, this time into his neck, he says, "I just couldn't wait another second to ask you. This has been the longest day of my life."

I finally feel composed enough to pull away and let him look down at my face. He smiles affectionately. "I didn't mean to make you cry."

"Yes, you did," I accuse. "But this is the best crying I've done in weeks." It's the first time I've admitted to the despair I've been feeling at the prospect of his leaving.

"Dr. Underhill's suggestion that I apply for Renalda's job was an answer to a prayer. I thought it was a long shot, but..." He shrugs. "...I was shocked when the interview went as well as it did. Still didn't think I'd get it, though. When Dr. Underhill told me the news this morning and said he wanted to announce it during the assembly, I was shocked. But there was no chance to tell you. I'm sorry."

Before I can tell him it's okay, someone taps me on the hip. I'm surprised when I around that we're nearly alone in the gym. There are just a few teachers milling around, helping Freddie put away folding chairs. The tapping on my hip is coming from Brody's index finger.

"Uh... 'scuse me, Miss Dickinson, but I need to ask Mr. Chase a question."

I step away from Jamie to give Brody a better view of his teacher... er, principal (that's going to take some getting used to).

One hand on his hip and one eye squinted shut, he asks, "Mr. Chase, are you still goin' to Timbucktooth this summer?"

My laugh dies in my throat as I realize I don't know, and I'm afraid of the answer.

Jamie's quick head shake resuscitates my heart, and I'm still recovering when Brody holds his hand, palm up, toward Jamie. "I think I want my ribbon back, then."

Jamie regards his fistful of Honor Roll ribbons. "Oh. Uh… Hmm… Not sure which one is yours, so…" He plucks one from the fray and hands it over to Brody. "Will this do?"

The soon-to-be-first-grader snatches it and grins. "Thanks!" he tosses casually on his way out the doors with the other stragglers.

Jamie returns his full attention to me. "Finally. Complete silence."

"You're telling me. These have been the noisiest months of my life."

"So, how does that quiet house in Hartford sound?" he asks, his twinkling eyes belying the seriousness in his tone.

"It sounds like absolute Heaven," I answer.

ALSO BY BREA BROWN

The *Underdog* series (chick lit/sports romance):

- *Out of My League* (Book 1)
- *Rookie of the Year* (Book 2)
- *Opportunity Knox* (Book 3)
- *Ready or Knox* (Book 4)

The *Secret Keeper* series (chick lit/Christian romance):

- *The Secret Keeper* (Book 1)
- *The Secret Keeper Confined* (Book 2)
- *The Secret Keeper Up All Night* (Book 3)
- *The Secret Keeper Holds On* (Book 4)
- *The Secret Keeper Lets Go* (Book 5)
- *The Secret Keeper Fulfilled* (Book 6)

The *Nurse Nate* series (chick lit/romantic comedy):

- *Let's Be Frank* (Book 1)
- *Let's Be Real* (Book 2)
- *Let's Be Friends* (Book 3)

Stand-alone novels:

- *Daydreamer*
- *The Family Plot*
- *Plain Jayne*
- *Quiet, Please!*

Made in the USA
Coppell, TX
09 June 2020

27108743R00208